KONDOR

KONDOR

by Gregory Ward

McArthur & Company

Toronto

First Paperback Printing 1998

Canadian Cataloguing in Publication Data

Ward, Gregory
Kondor

Canadian ed. ISBN 1-55278-009-0

I. Title.

PS8595.A73K66 1997   C813'.54   C97–930374–5
PR9199.3.W37K66 1997

Jacket Design by TANIA CRAAN

Interior Design and Page Composition by JOSEPH GISINI
OF ANDREW SMITH GRAPHICS, INC.

Printed and bound in Canada by BEST BOOK MANUFACTURERS

McArthur & Company Publishing Limited
322 King Street West, Suite 402
Toronto, Ontario Canada M5V 1J2

10 9 8 7 6 5 4 3 2 1

*I am deeply grateful to the people who
helped me find this story. Thanks to my beloved wife,
Sally, who makes everything grow.
To Kim McArthur for listening so long and
wringing her hands under the table.
To Arleen Hartman and John Ranally, to Ken McDonald,
Wesley Wark, Bernice Holman, Helmut May,
Monika Steiner, Jerome Hoog, Kerry Wilson,
Hagen Mayer, Andrea Dods and Hans-Jürgen Ellger.
Special thanks to Jennifer Glossop and
Pam Erlichman for their splendid eyes and ears.
Above all, thank you Jan Whitford for your wisdom
and your faith in me, above and beyond.*

— GREGORY WARD

And drawn by my ardent desire,
impatient to see the great abundance of strange forms
created by that artificer, Nature, I wandered for some time
among the shadowed rocks.
I came to the mouth of a huge cave before which I stopped
for a moment stupefied
by such an unknown thing. I arched my back,
rested my left hand on my knee, and with my right shaded
my lowered eyes;
several times I leaned to one side, then the other,
to see if I could distinguish anything,
but the great darkness within made this impossible.
After a time there arose in me both fear and desire —
fear of the dark and menacing cave;
desire to see whether it contained
some marvelous thing.

LEONARDO DA VINCI
FROM *CODEX ARUNDEL* 155 R

CHAPTER 1

On a bright morning in early May, a Gulfstream V leased to the Dorner Automobile company touched down at Frankfurt Airport. The only passenger was the ex-president of Dorner's American subsidiary, a tall, vigorous man in his late seventies who had traveled overnight from Cleveland. The corporate jet was equipped with a berth, but Hansjorg Peiper had been sleepless throughout the flight, though he did not appear tired to the young man who met him at Frankfurt.

Hansjorg embraced his son, chatted amiably as they passed through the terminal and out to a chauffeured luxury car, a Dorner 920 in metallic dark burgundy. The car transported them downtown, southeast to the Untermainkai by the river, where the young woman driver turned left past the Jewish Museum, then signaled right for the Untermain Bridge.

"I need to walk across the river," Hansjorg said to his son. "I've been cooped up since yesterday afternoon. You look like you could use some fresh air."

Kristian Peiper asked the driver to stop. "You know Herr Dorner's building, Sophie?"

"30 Schaumainkai. When will I pick you up?"

Kristian looked at his father for an answer.

"He won't be expecting you," Hansjorg said. "He requested only to see me but this might be your last opportunity to say good-bye. We'll both go in."

"I called earlier in the week," Kristian said. "His doctors put me off."

"Just look in then leave him to me," Hansjorg said. "He can't have much strength left. Imagine saying that about Erich Dorner, of all people."

The car drew up beside the cobbled quay. Hansjorg got out while his son spoke to the driver again in accented though fluent German. "I forgot to check the opera program. Would you mind calling while you're waiting for me."

"*Die Gezeichneten* by Franz Schreker," the young woman said, smiling. "It starts at eight o'clock. There are still good tickets. Shall I reserve two?"

Kristian matched her smile, for just long enough that Hansjorg noticed the moment. Kristian thanked her and joined his father on the sidewalk.

It would not have been immediately apparent to passersby that the two men walking across the bridge were father and son; Hansjorg was tall and lean, his silver hair brushed flat to a narrow, aristocratic head. If the father looked youthful, Kristian Peiper appeared older than thirty-five, his hair slightly greying, shadows under the eyes bearing witness to the long days and weekends he had been working. He was never without his briefcase, balanced always on the left side by a laptop computer.

But for now he didn't feel the weight of his work, even the sober prospect of their sickroom visit lightened by the pleasure of being together. They maintained an easy cheerfulness as they mounted the Untermain Bridge.

"Do you know Schreker?" Kristian asked.

"You'll enjoy it," Hansjorg replied. "The Nazis labeled him a degenerate."

"Sounds like a fairly solid recommendation."

"There's an orgy in the last act."

They smiled and linked arms, connecting snugly through the summerweight suiting as they crossed the Main, looking down at the painted barges steaming southwest to the mother Rhine. Cleveland, their home, was a city on a big river, a city of bridges.

"That young woman seems very organized."

Kristian caught the suggestive tone, resisted it. "There's nothing she doesn't know about Frankfurt. She's been an incredible help all week."

"We should be getting three tickets. It would be a nice way to thank her." Hansjorg felt his son stiffen slightly and his smile grew. "She's very pretty, don't you think so?" When Kristian didn't respond, his father's smile faded." Come on, you're working too hard these days. When did you last touch a piano?"

"I can't remember."

"You've forgotten how to relax. Everything except this Kondor."

He referred to the business that had brought Kristian to Frankfurt a week ago, the imminent launch of Dorner's new Kondor minivan, on which he had been a driving force in Cleveland. Largely Kristian's brainchild, the launch was seen by every industry analyst in the world as the last hope for the ailing automotive giant.

"You worked harder than me," Kristian said. "You shouldn't talk. Dorner's been your whole life."

"No, Kit, I tried to maintain a balance. Your mother would have backed me up on that. You've already lost your marriage to this car, don't jeopardize your health as well."

They reached the Sachsenhausen side and took Schaumainkai west, past the handsome public buildings that fronted the river, museums of Art, German Cinematography, Architecture, Ethnology. To live on the

Schaumainkai, to keep company with these institutions and command a riverfront view, one needed to be rich. For Erich Dorner, attended around the clock by private medical staff, it was costing a small fortune to die here.

The apartment consisted of the upper two floors of an elegant eight-story building with a mansard roof inset with gable windows. They passed through security, and took an ornate, antique elevator to the eighth floor where they were admitted to Erich Dorner's apartment by his steward, Manfred.

"We've converted the linen closet into a nurses' station," Manfred informed them as they took wide stairs to the upper floor. The day nurse would like to see you before you go in."

The closet, though purpose-built, would have made an adequate bedroom. Oak shelves lined the walls, partially given over to the medical supplies and medication needed to relieve Erich Dorner's suffering in his last days. In front of a rear facing window, a modern workstation was equipped with a phone/fax and a monitor, the kind of one-way receiver that parents sometimes connect with an infant's room. They waited while Manfred went to find the nurse, Kristian experiencing a thrill of apprehension when the monitor on the desk emitted the muffled sound of shallow coughing, subsiding into a groan. Transfixed by the sound, father and son were surprised by the nurse's arrival.

"He's sinking, Herr Peiper. But he's making a Herculean effort for your last visit. He's been refusing his morphine since yesterday afternoon, strictly against the doctor's recommendation. If you understood the pain associated with certain types of cancer, you would know what that's meant for him."

"I have some idea," Hansjorg said quietly. Kristian's mother had died of leukemia five years ago.

"Is he expecting your son, Herr Peiper? I wasn't aware..."

"He won't stay long," Hansjorg assured her. "A few minutes. Herr Dorner is his godfather."

Kristian left his briefcase in the linen room and followed the nurse and his father down the long corridor to his godfather's bedroom. He had visited this townhouse many times in years past, always impressed by its opulence. Aubusson underfoot, Empire furniture, prime examples of Orientalist oil painting in massive frames.

The nurse stopped outside a walnut-paneled double door with ornately gilded handles. "I can't allow either of you to stay long. There's a bell beside the bed if you need me for anything."

Hansjorg stood close to Kristian outside the door when the nurse left, spoke in a low voice. "We must be prepared for a shock, Kit. This will not be the Erich Dorner you remember."

Kristian met his father's grey eyes. "It's the end of an era, isn't it? Our history."

Hansjorg smiled faintly, with approval, then opened the door.

The bedroom, too, celebrated nineteenth-century abundance. In such a setting of palms and gilt and sumptuous fabrics, the enamel and stainless steel equipment necessary to keep Erich Dorner alive took on a brutal sterility.

The pervasive cancer had already consumed his flesh, his skull shrink-wrapped in mottled skin, his cheeks and temples and eye sockets sucked in as though the disease had caused an internal vacuum. Yet here he was smiling, exposing his yellowed teeth, reminding Kristian that a lifetime of heavy cigarette smoking had helped carry him here at last, at eighty-six.

"Kristian, what a wonderful surprise," the old man whispered, though still with the pruned, staccato quality that had characterized his voice in years of health.

"Hello, Uncle Erich." Not a real uncle, but Kristian had always called him that.

"He insisted on coming," Hansjorg said proudly from the other side of the bed.

"He has respect for the past. A good thing...to know your past. And I am the past. Almost...almost."

Skeletal, tremoring hands fumbled for Kristian's, drawing him down to the edge of the bed. "You look like your mother but you're Jorgi's son all through. I hear all about you. You should be running the show in Cleveland, not that swine Tevlin. I'm going to speak to Junia about it. You think she'll listen?" Erich let go of his hands. "Look out of the window." Kristian twisted towards one of three large gable windows immediately opposite the bed. "No. Get up. Go over. Look at the view."

Kristian did so.

Dorner found his voice, hoarse and ragged but still audible. "What do you see?"

Kristian could see why Erich Dorner had chosen this place to end his days, rather than any of his other properties, the Bad Homberg estate, the schloss at Rudesheim: it was this view of the skyline.

Kristian saw the towers around Taunusanlage, monuments to the glory of Germany's industrial giants which have earned Frankfurt the nickname "Mainhatten." He saw the bank buildings, in the only city where every bank in the world has representation. But the Dornerturm to the north stood above them all, taller even than the famous pencil tower by the showground.

"I had the bed moved, so it's right in the middle of the window. It will be the last thing I see."

The skyscraper had been designed to suggest a piston from an internal combustion engine, a shaft supporting a cylindrical upper section. The Dornerturm's glass skin, impregnated with silver, gave it the appearance of being clad in seamless steel. Completed ten years ago at a cost of one-quarter billion deutsche marks, it had been Erich Dorner's final triumphant act as president of Dorner AG Frankfurt, before his daughter Junia succeeded him. Erected as a landmark for the new North Plant off Autobahn 66, the Dornerturm had been his way of telling the world that the tiny concern he had founded in 1937, and then rebuilt from the ashes of the Reich, had by now eclipsed Mercedes, BMW, even Volkswagen as Germany's biggest auto maker.

"We were dreamers, your father and I. Look, Kristian...look at our dream now."

Was he up to date, Kristian wondered? Surely, even on his deathbed, Erich Dorner knew about the company's own agonies. Perhaps the medication was affecting his thinking.

The voice relapsed to a whisper and Dorner crooked a twig finger, summoning Kristian back to the bedside.

"In 1945 we had nothing *but* dreams. We made six cars a week."

Hansjorg smiled tightly at his son. "In a good week. The plant was rubble."

"Frankfurt was rubble," Dorner whispered. "*Germany* was rubble! We were up to our knees in water, falling bricks, live wires."

"Unexploded bombs."

"You would have been proud of your father."

"I'm proud of him now, Uncle Erich."

The yellow smile, tightening as he tried not to cough, his eyes tearing from effort and sentiment. "Good boy. He's a good boy, Jorgi."

Erich Dorner's cold fingers lay on top of Kristian's hand, tapping out the rhythm of his words: "Potatoes and acorn coffee. That's how we lived. Barter to keep the line running — we got a dozen fan belts for a bar of chocolate, a set of tires for a carton of American cigarettes. We bartered finished cars for parts, for food, clothing for the workers. Your father and I...we sweated blood on three hours sleep a night."

It was the story Kristian had grown up with, the vital, central myth of his life. Erich Dorner and his *wunderkind* design engineer, Hansjorg Peiper, heroic midwives attending Dorner's rebirth from the wreckage of Hitler's insanity. How they pioneered features that had revolutionized an industry, a bright enough prospect that the occupying Americans had rushed to claim a 40 percent stake.

"They wanted the whole thing," Erich Dorner said. "They wanted control, but they never got it." The cold fingers closed affectionately upon Kristian's. "Damned Yankees!" he said in English, with a reckless chuckle that precipitated a fit of desperate coughing, which brought the nurse. Kristian and his father both rose from the bed as she entered, but Erich Dorner clawed for Hansjorg's sleeve. For some moments he held on, unable to speak, eyes bulging from their hollowed sockets as the spasms racked him.

"Please," the nurse implored them. "You must go now."

"No!" Dorner hissed between clenched teeth. "Hansjorg stays."

"Herr Dorner, really..."

"I need...Hansjorg...alone."

"Perhaps in a little..."

"*Hansjorg!*"

A shocking urgency in the command, a burning intensity in Dorner's gaze. Hansjorg Peiper shrugged helplessly at the nurse, then followed her and Kristian to the door. This was not a hospital, it was Erich Dorner's home and the nurse was privately hired, his to dismiss whether it killed him or not.

"You're going to the plant?" Hansjorg asked Kristian in the corridor.

"For eleven. Junia's previewing the Kondor for the area dealers. She wants to see me afterwards. She wants my continuity report."

"You mustn't be late. Take the car. I'll get a taxi."

"I'll send Sophie back for you."

"Whatever."

Kristian glanced back into the room with a brave smile. "Good-bye Uncle Erich. I'll see you at the show."

The Frankfurt Auto Show was not until September, two months away. Dorner did not have two weeks. It would have been an emotional moment had he been listening, or perhaps the old man might have returned a gallant scrap of wit. But he was turned away, his fingers scrabbling on the wall beside the bed until they found the bell push. Why, Kristian wondered, when he had only just sent the anxious nurse out of the room?

She had not returned to her station, the linen closet empty when Kristian returned to collect his briefcase. He was on his way out of the room when he turned back, startled. The monitor was still on, his father's voice unmistakable despite the tinny speaker:

"*In the name of god Erich...*"

"*Listen Jorgi, just listen!*"

Erich Dorner coughing, then a hoarse whisper, only intermittent words and phrases intelligible to Kristian.

"*No one else to stop her...everything...fifty years...only way...krokus... stop her...*"

Kristian heard the nurse, turned to see her emerge from a service staircase beyond the door to Dorner's bedroom, at the end of the corridor. Instinctively, he went to the desk by the window and switched off the monitor.

He glanced right as he crossed to the main stairs with his briefcase, saw the nurse at the end of the corridor with Manfred behind her. The steward was carrying a parcel, a shallow box wrapped in brown paper and tied with string. He stopped at his employer's door and knocked.

Was it Manfred that the summons had been for?

Kristian nodded to the nurse, was on the stairs when he heard his father's voice again, faintly, thanking Manfred before the bedroom door closed again. He looked around, smiling uncertainly as Manfred trotted down the main stairs after him, no longer carrying the package.

"I apologize, Herr Peiper. I was detained. Allow me to see you to the elevator."

Breathless solicitude as Manfred overtook him and prodded the call button with a pink, well-manicured finger. No longer young, about to see the end of his employment here, but after many years of service, he would be well remembered in Erich Dorner's will.

Kristian tried to sound casual. "You had something for my father just now?"

"It was for Herr Dorner, sir."

"I see."

Manfred smiled very slightly as the elevator door opened. "I don't know what it was, sir. Perhaps you could ask your father."

Kristian stepped inside the elevator, embarrassed.

"Whatever it was was quite old."

"Old?"

"I would say so. The paper was brittle. I hope we'll have the opportunity to meet again, sir."

Sophie Kempf was listening to rock music. She turned it off as soon as Kristian got in the car.

"Is your father coming?"

"He'll be a while. If you wouldn't mind dropping me at the plant and going back for him."

She glanced in the rearview mirror. A heart-shaped face, her deep-set violet eyes and dark brows contrasting with her pale, fine-grained complexion, "Herr Dorner's dying?"

"Yes he is."

"You were close?"

"All my life."

Sophie Kempf executed a flawless U-turn and headed back to the Untermain Brücke. After six days, Kristian had decided she was almost as good a driver as his father's chauffeur back in Cleveland. But driving was Wendel Storey's vocation, which was not the case with Sophie. Her employment with Dorner, ferrying its executives and clients around Frankfurt, was bankrolling her plans for a teacher's certificate. Unlike Wendel, who hadn't made grade eight, Sophie Kempf had majored in psychology at Heidelberg. He had enjoyed her company this week. Even her sensitive, intelligent silence was a comfort now, filtering through the dark cloud gathering around him, the fog of questions.

Stop her...

Who? Had Erich meant Junia, his daughter?

And *krokus*? Like "*Kondor*," the word sounded identical and bore the same meaning in German or English, but surely he wouldn't have meant the flower.

Kristian wouldn't have to wonder for long, his father would tell him. Better to put it from his mind, focus on the meeting with Junia after the preview. As director of marketing for Dorner America, Kristian was responsible for the entire U.S. product line, including the

Kondor. The purpose of his week in Frankfurt had been to establish continuity with his counterparts in the rest of the world, to stake out the common ground amongst a dozen different national strategies for the minivan.

They were diverted by tram line repairs at Mainzer and Kaiserstrasse, into the web of streets radiating from the Hauptbahnhoff, Frankfurt's great central railway station. The Dornerturm was north of the city core, but Kristian didn't want to take the Bundesstrasse.

"Take Mosel," he said. "I want to see something. We've got time."

She glanced right to change lanes. He'd seen her every day for the last six days, her chin-length dark hair brushing her jaw when she turned her head. She was small, slender and athletic. It must have been her shampoo that gave off the faint scent of strawberries because she wasn't the perfume type.

Kristian's wife had been tall and elegantly beautiful. Never energetic or robust, Melanie had operated in a kind of perpetual, self-conscious slow motion with her long, decorous limbs.

Kristian dismissed the guilty comparison and addressed himself to the numbers on Mosel. On the edge of the red-light district, most of the addresses were small, seedy-looking businesses.

"There. Pull over for a minute."

Sophie did so, raising her dark eyebrows when she saw where Kristian was looking. Across the street, on the corner of Mosel and Nidda, a plain but shabby, two-story emporium featured mannequins in bondage gear against displays of sex toys and pornographic videos.

"That's where my father grew up, on that corner," Kristian said. "There was an apartment building there, quite gracious, all kinds of stonework."

He had told her earlier in the week that Hansjorg had been raised in Frankfurt, his own father the chief curator at the Stadelsches Kunstinstitut, his mother a professor of violin at the University of Mainz.

Sophie followed Kristian's gaze, pleased by his confidence. "Didn't you say they had a house in Steinau an der Strasse."

"That was just a cottage, a holiday house. This was home. Dad's bedroom faced the street on the fourth floor. He told me he used to sit in the window for hours watching the cars go by, drawing cars, dreaming of the day his parents would take him to watch Herr Dorner's racing team. Hardly their thing, but Erich Dorner was Dad's hero. He'd sent him a dozen job applications by the time he was sixteen." He leaned back in the seat, smiling. "I'm sorry, I shouldn't be boring you with this."

She turned to face him, her hair caressing the delicate line of her jaw. "It must be hard for your father right now."

"Yes, Erich Dorner's been a lifelong friend."

"When did your father start working for him?"

"In '45, right after the war when he came out of the army. Seven years later he was running the Cleveland operation. Quick learner."

"You must take after him; U.S. director of marketing at thirty-five." She smiled at his surprise. "Good guess?"

"And you?"

"Thirty." She glanced at the dash clock. "You said eleven at the plant? We'd better go, the Bundesstrasse starts jamming near lunchtime."

She put the car in gear and pulled out into the traffic.

Kristian said, "Did you happen to call the opera yet?"

"Two tickets for this evening. Sixth row center. You obviously like music."

"Dad's passionate. He plays the violin. Collects them."

"And you?"

"A little piano. I haven't really kept it up. Too busy."

"Too bad. Are you any good?"

"I used to be all right." He caught her eye in the rearview mirror. "If you're not busy tonight, Dad and I were wondering if you'd care to join us." He saw her look of surprise. "I'm sorry it's last minute. You've probably got other plans."

She turned. "No. I don't have plans. Thank you. I'd love to come."

"And have dinner with us afterwards?"

"I know a place near the opera. Pavarotti eats there. You like Italian?"

"Very much. Maybe we could meet at the hotel bar for a drink first. Could you make it by 7:00 p.m.?"

"Easily. My apartment's less than fifteen minutes from the Excelsior. Thank you, Herr Peiper."

"Kristian. You've been a fantastic help this week. I don't know what I would have done without you. I'll miss you in Cleveland."

Kristian had often imagined the scene Erich Dorner had described: an infernal, romantic darkness lit by high voltage strobes and gushing sparks, a symphony of shrieking metal and the pealing of giant tools. A kind of jungle where men toiled, stripped to the waist, muscles sheened, their welding hoses looping pythonlike.

By comparison, the body facility at Dorner Frankfurt's North Plant was a serene haven, a lofty, spongelike vastness that drank up the sounds of the widely dispersed jobs. Kristian walked down wide aisles, his shoes hushed on rubber-clad floors, vigilant not for sparks or bounding white hot nuggets, but only for those workers whispering to and from their jobs on complimentary bicycles. Along the welding line, scorched and sweating bodies had been replaced by robots painted in primary colors, unfazed by heat and bouncing sparks as they performed their precision dance.

The dealers are our infantry. And the automobile showroom is our front line.

Erich Dorner's favorite maxim still applied; even now that Total Customer Satisfaction were the industry watchwords, you still had to treat your dealers right, which was why Junia Dorner had invited the Hessen sales network, the home team, to preview the Kondor prototype four months before its official unveiling at the Frankfurt Auto Show.

The sleek, silver-grey vehicle rested on a platform near the entrance to the plant canteen, while Junia Dorner extolled its virtues to a small army of sales representatives: the lowest maintenance engine in production car history, thermoplastic body panels to defy rust and sustain a full 15 kmh impact without a scratch; a revolutionary aluminum frame, lightweight and easily recyclable without compromising structural integrity or the legendary Dorner commitment to safety. Side airbags, of course, not just in the driver and front passenger doors, but protecting the rear passengers as well.

The body design spoke for itself: simple, understated...the obviousness which has always been a designer's elusive grail. Dorner's "New World Car" (one of the slogans Kristian was developing for the Kondor's U.S. introduction) had the attributes of a car and a van in one aerodynamic package. As rarely happened, the production model closely resembled the vehicle Kristian had nurtured with the Cleveland design team when he had first pinpointed the need for Dorner to build a popular vehicle.

Junia left the platform to hearty applause, her audience warmed by the prospect of lunch and liquid refreshment in the canteen. Like his father, Kristian had always maintained a high respect for sales people. He greeted those he knew, offered Hansjorg's warmest regards, listened to the sales stories traded like currency, the I'll-be-backs and the wankers, the guy who came in with a fat roll of hundreds, if the salesman got greedy and let him peel off too many bills for the car, no sale. Stories about each other, like the night Wolf Stengel got shitfaced on an incentive trip to Paris and the guys paid a middle-aged transvestite to be in his bed when he woke up in the morning.

No more enlightened than their American counterparts, but in many cases preferable to the executives who surrounded Junia near the exit, like an attendant shoal of fish, who disdained salesmen the way they disdained factory hands, twitching like puppets in their need to correctly interpret and react to their boss's signals, the agony of deciding whether to clasp their hands in front or behind, to laugh or merely smile.

Her departure, surrounded by this entourage, was Kristian's cue to return to the office tower for his appointment. Security was rigorous in the Dornerturm as it was in the plant. A second fingerprint scan admitted him to a soaring marble lobby where six emplaced automobiles, their chrome and paintwork polished to a mirror finish, represented six decades of Dorner production. He took a glass elevator up to the presidential suite, its shaft channeled into the south face of the building. Kristian watched the city fall dizzyingly away then flood out around him, the Renaissance churches and half-timbered guildhalls around cobbled squares, pockets of ancient history between the skyscrapers. He could see the river, even the Untermain Bridge, though a billboard on the Frankfurt side hid Erich Dorner's riverfront house. The government was waging a crime war; all week Kristian had been seeing the burly image of the interior minister, Julius Beck, appearing in national television commercials and outdoor displays like this one, talking and looking tough. "Iron Fist." The slogan was the current buzz all over the country. Juvenile crime, drugs, Asian gangs and now the Russian Mafia moving in: it was time for a Beck, many Germans seemed to be saying.

Kristian felt a tingle of apprehension in his extremities as he stepped out onto the hundred and second floor, part vertigo, partly the certainty that Junia Dorner was going to rub his nose in the last quarter's losses. He graduated from a second security point and crossed to the meeting room, his shoes whispering over luxurious grey carpeting, until he reached double doors with a mirrored grain, deep orange and black, spread-eagled like a Rorschach butterfly.

Not the main executive boardroom, which was on the floor below. This room was attached to Junia's personal quarters, intimately scaled for private meetings, windowless and luxuriously paneled, blushed with subtle recessed lighting, now filled with the fragrance of coffee from a silver service on the rosewood table. The effect should have been one of welcome and warmth, but Kristian's hands remained stubbornly cold and damp with apprehension.

An employee in a white steward's jacket appeared from a door at the back of the room. He poured coffee for Kristian, told him Fräulein

Dorner would be in immediately, retired through the same door to Junia's quarters. Kristian had never actually seen it, the luxurious suite from which she commanded her automotive empire via fibre optics and satellite. Insomniac and workaholic, she seldom visited her mansion in the Taunus Hills or the schloss at Rudesheim.

The door opened.

"Kurt found you some coffee? I saw you at the plant. Did you hear the applause? My God, Kristian, I hope the public are as easy to please. No, no, I'll do it."

She poured for herself with her small, unadorned hands. For some reason she always made him think of the Spanish pianist, Alicia de la Rocha, a favorite of his father's. The tiny hands, perhaps, and Junia had always looked more Spanish than German with her black hair drawn back in its customary *mono*, her eyebrows like dramatic circumflexes above her liquid brown eyes. Three hours' sleep a night had never affected her in the past, but this morning her eyes were pouched with grey.

"Your report?"

Kristian hefted his briefcase onto the table but she stayed his hand from opening it. "Did you see the *Wall Street Journal* this morning? We made the front page." She sipped coffee and carried the cup and saucer towards him. "The editorial generously concedes that we *might* be able to hold our own in Europe — apart from the Aerospace division, naturally — but the U.S. is 'a nightmare we seem incapable of waking from.' I thought that was particularly trenchant."

"What else did it say?"

"Nothing you don't already know: the high deutsche mark exchange is killing us in the showroom, labor problems, and of course Detroit is finally building good cars." She smiled tightly. "Not as good as ours — nice of them to notice — but not nearly as expensive. Things have changed rather drastically from your father's day."

"Did they talk up the image problem?"

Junia stirred her black coffee. Kristian didn't recall her having put sugar in it. "Your father arrived this morning, I understand."

"Uncle Erich wanted him to come."

"How is he?"

"Very well. He was going to come anyway, next week."

"Which would probably have been too late." She sipped coffee and switched the subject back. "It's not your fault, Kristian; we had it too good in the eighties, we could do no wrong. America wanted German product, German engineering, so we played down the fact that we're 40 percent U.S.-owned. We played too well: now we're the Krauts and it's time to buy domestic. Screw the Krauts now we've learned how they do it. Buy a Chevrolet!"

"We've got another chance with the Kondor. I know we do. It's an exciting car, Junia."

"It'll be our *last* chance!" She drained her cup, cast it down on the rosewood table. She sat on the edge, gripping it with both hands. "We have to handle this very carefully. Yes, it's a good car. It's not electric, it's not maintenance free, it can't fly...but it's a good car. It's what people want, but they won't take it unless we lower our tone. You understand what I'm saying?"

"Market down market." Kristian had been saying it for years, long before Frankfurt had decided to listen: market good cars, not status symbols for professionals.

"I'm seriously thinking of rebadging the Kondor," Junia said. "Get some distance from the Dorner marque."

Kristian started. "Rebadge? Sacrifice our reputation for quality and safety? Orphan it?"

Junia Dorner stood rigid. "I'm prepared to do anything...anything to make sure the Kondor is a success. And so must you be. Your advertising people in Cleveland, that overweight man, what's his name?"

"Phil Baylor?"

"Meet with Baylor as soon as you get back. See what he thinks of rebadging. I want campaign concepts that will make us accessible. More American. I'll worry about Europe."

"Aerospace?"

Junia made a noise in her throat. She took his elbow and steered him towards the main door. "I do not even want to talk about it. You think we're hurting in the showroom, you should come to Osnabruck."

Dorner Aerospace, always a euphemistic thorn in Kristian's conscience, was located at Osnabruck, surrounded by a moat of razor wire and electronic surveillance. Since the collapse of the Soviet Union and the official end of the cold war, since reunification and the American withdrawal, orders for premium quality military hardware had all but dried up. Once the company's most profitable division, Dorner Aerospace was now a millstone, dragging Junia ever deeper into debt to both the German and U.S. governments.

She opened the door and held it for him. "So you were over the river this morning. How is my father today?"

"He's very brave."

"Really? I don't think he's ready to die. I think he's terrified of death, when he's not heavily sedated. I didn't see Hansjorg down in the plant. I thought he would come, he knows so many of the sales people."

"Your father asked him to stay when I left."

A shadow crossed Junia's face. "Anything in particular?"

"I don't know. He just seemed anxious to talk to him."

"Talk? He can't even think on that much morphine."

"He refused it since last night. I guess he knew it would be their last visit."

Junia puzzled at the grey broadloom. "He must be in agony." She looked up. "What did he talk about?"

Kristian shrugged. "The past. Reminiscences. The old days at Dorner."

"You have no idea if there was anything specific? Your father didn't say anything to you?"

"No. But..."

Her gaze intensified, searching him. Kristian shook his head, surprised by the level of her interest. "It was nothing."

"Tell me please."

"When I was leaving, I saw Manfred take something to your father's room. A parcel."

"Parcel?"

"A brown paper parcel." Kristian shrugged. "I have no idea."

Junia was still for another moment. Then suddenly she was transformed, smiling again as she shook her head, her hand placed affectionately in the small of Kristian's back as she shepherded him towards the security point by the elevator.

"Old men's business. We must leave them to it. They've been like father and son since time immemorial. We mustn't be too curious, but you have my private number. If there's ever any reason to call me...anything you'd consider personal." She waved aside the security guard, pressed the call button for him. "I'll see you at the show if not long before. Get onto Baylor right away. Make sure he understands what's at stake. We've got to make history with this launch, Kristian. We must do anything and everything to ensure it."

CHAPTER 2

Kristian's laptop had been running all afternoon. The low battery indicator was flashing as he worked on in a tapestry-upholstered booth in the Excelsior's lounge bar at 7:00 p.m., composing an e-mail for Phil Baylor.

More American. Junia had finally conceded it. Maybe what they needed was an American spokesperson, he wrote to Phil, but nothing like Chrysler back when they still made livingrooms on wheels, with Ricardo Montelban into his lounge act.

Kristian looked up from the screen from time to time as he worked, but he missed Sophie's entrance. He heard his name, found her standing uncertainly in front of the booth.

"Still at it?" She was carrying her short evening jacket, wearing a simple black dress with wide shoulder straps that accentuated the relative square of her shoulders, the definition in her slender arms.

Kristian shut the screen and stood to welcome her. "Done. Sorry."

"Don't apologize for hard work." She took the chair opposite him, smiling. "Not to a German woman. Where's your father?"

"He sends his apologies. He's not feeling well."

"Nothing serious I hope."

"It was his visit with Erich Dorner this morning; it must have affected him even more than I thought. I'm afraid he's not moving from his room tonight."

The waiter came and they both ordered Riesling.

"I think it's hit him close to home," Kristian said. "There's only ten years difference, they're essentially the same generation."

"Your mother died quite recently, didn't she?"

"Five years ago. Leukemia. Dad and I have always been close, but that drew us even closer. Same thing when my marriage ended, we started spending a lot of time together."

"That's good. Usually you just hear about generation gaps."

The wine arrived. Kristian raised his glass to her. "Here's to closing gaps."

The bar was intimately proportioned except for its high ceiling, dominated by a single great chandelier dimmed to a gentle radiance. Sophie Kempf's eyes gleamed with its light as she raised her glass. The green-stemmed crystal chimed. "Does that mean we're going to e-mail each other?"

Kristian laughed. "Come on, I'm in Frankfurt all the time. I'll be here for at least a couple of weeks in September, for the auto show."

"I'll have started school by then."

"You'll have to cut class."

She smiled slowly, the light glowing warmly in her eyes as she sipped her wine.

"Do you always stay at this hotel?"

"Either here or at the Schlosshotel Kronberg."

"Very grand. Don't you ever stay with family?"

"We have no family here."

"Not on your father's side?"

"Nobody."

"Did they all go to America?"

"The apartment I showed you this morning...it was bombed, Christmas eve 1942. Dad was away in the army, but his whole extended family was in the apartment — his parents, his three sisters, uncles, aunts. Everyone."

"My God."

"The building took a direct hit. Not even a real raid, they figured it was a single crippled bomber trying to limp home, unloading."

"That's terrible."

"It was another reason Erich Dorner became such a father figure for Dad. But tell me more about you, your family."

A middle-class family from Mainz, father a sales manager for Henkell Trocken, mother a housewife, a younger sister just out of high school, working at a resort in Mexico. Living in Frankfurt since university had taught Sophie a lesson, she said: the ostentatious presence of money — the system — had reinforced her need to do something worthwhile.

"Teaching?"

Kristian leaned back against the banquette as she told him her plans, his fingers splayed on the tapestry, caressing its coarse texture. It felt good to relax for the first time this week. Good to be with Sophie Kempf. Not at all good, the prospect of leaving tomorrow.

At 7:15 Sophie looked at her watch.

"How are we for time?" Kristian asked.

"Fine, it's no more than ten minutes to the opera from here."

"See how I depend on you? What am I going to do without you?"

Once again her eyes filled with light. "I know what I'd like you to do right now."

Behind his steady smile, Kristian's heart beat faster.

"I'd like you to play the piano for me."

He started in surprise. "Now?"

"I'll look after your computer. One song." There was a baby grand in the corner of the bar. A cocktail pianist had been playing when Kristian arrived, between sets now. "You told me you could play."

31

"I think I said I used to."

"No, you said 'I play a little piano.'"

"That's a grand."

"It's a little grand."

"I'm rusty."

"I'll order oil."

"There's a house pianist. That guy over at the bar. It's his gig. He might not like it."

"I'll ask him."

Kristian played Gershwin, "Someone to Watch Over Me." Maybe she knew the tune, but probably not the tender words. He focused on the meaning of the song — "play the ideas, not the piano" a teacher had once told him — allowed that to steady his fingers over the chords. He saw her smiling across the room, then he shut his eyes and began growing the changes, his right hand tumbling into the sweet melody. He was unaware of the attentive quiet in the bar, or of Sophie, until the last chord was decaying and he felt the lightest touch on his shoulder, then the back of her hand against his cheek in a soft, fleeting caress.

"That was beautiful."

The people in the bar applauded, led by the cocktail player. Kristian turned on the bench and smiled up into her eyes. "They're beautiful words."

"Tell me."

"The truth? *Oh how I need...someone to watch over me.*"

For a moment he was aware of nothing but her gaze, excitement tinged slightly with regret as the moment fell softly around them. Kristian's voice was husky when he finally spoke.

"How are we doing for time?"

"We should think about going." She handed him his laptop.

"I'll run upstairs with it. Dad would appreciate me checking in. Five minutes?"

"Kristian?"

"Yes."

"I think I'm going to miss you too."

They occupied one of three suites on the eighteenth floor permanently reserved for highly placed Dorner executives. There were four other guests in the elevator, but he had no sense of them.

She wasn't at all like Mel: tiny in comparison, without Mel's patrician, untouchable beauty because Sophie was intensely touchable. She had a freshness, a resilience, her body strong and supple. He reached his floor and lengthened his stride down the corridor, seeing her face, her violet eyes full of intelligent light and good humor, her slightly parted lips that would taste like sweet fruit. He would kiss those lips tonight. At least that.

I want her.

Distracted by business all week, he had not openly acknowledged the power of Sophie Kempf's attraction, aching with it as he used his key card and opened the door to the suite.

Hansjorg was in the bathroom with the door closed and the bath taps running. Kristian was about to knock and call out when he stopped, turned, walked towards the partially open door to his father's bedroom.

Kristian had seen him only briefly on his return from the plant, but twenty minutes had been enough to show that his father was profoundly troubled. Never a man to show weakness (Kristian remembered his stoicism during his wife's illness), it was too easy to say merely that Hansjorg had glimpsed his own fate on Erich Dorner's deathbed.

And there again was Uncle Erich's steward, Manfred, with a package under his arm. An old parcel wrapped in brittle brown paper.

No one else to stop her...everything...fifty years...

Krokus?

He remembered Junia Dorner's unexpected interest in the morning's events in the house by the river, the package that Hansjorg had received at Erich Dorner's door. Kristian hadn't yet broached the subject with his father, had no idea whether or not he had carried the parcel away from Sachsenhausen.

Was it here?

Kristian felt an equal pang of curiosity and guilt as he lifted the lid of his father's suitcase, on a stand behind the door. It was empty.

So were dresser drawers, except for the few items of clothing Hansjorg had packed for his brief stay.

So was the closet, and the space under the bed.

Cheeks burning, Kristian went out, retrieving his laptop which he had left standing by the door. He carried it into the sitting room, to the credenza where his recharger was plugged into the baseboard outlet. There would be a lot to do on the plane tomorrow, even a few loose ends to tie up tonight before he went to bed, recharge it now while he remembered. Or was he merely drawing out the delicious anticipation of returning to Sophie Kempf?

He plugged in the recharger, then the modem jack, flipped open the screen in order to send the e-mail to Baylor; they were six hours behind in Cleveland, lunchtime, it would give Phil a half day in order to get inspiration for the Kondor spokesperson. He turned the computer on and went to the mirror in the vestibule while he waited for Windows to boot up.

"Is that you Kit?"

"Hi. You're socked in?"

"Go and enjoy yourself. We'll see an opera together at home."

Trying his best to sound cheerful, but Kristian could hear the tiredness in his voice, and something beyond that, a deeper strain. "Sure you're okay, Dad? Is there anything I can get you?"

"I'll be fine. What have you done with Fräulein Kempf?"

"Downstairs in the bar."

"Convey my regrets. Go on now, she's far too pretty to keep waiting in a public bar."

Kristian stood closer to the three-quarter length mirror — reproduction chinoiserie — stuck out his tongue, held his palm flat to his face to test his breath, smoothed his hair back from his forehead then lifted his arm like a wing and sniffed under the lapel.

Although he may not be the man some
Girls think of as handsome

Gershwin might have been describing Kristian tonight: he was looking and feeling far from his best, pale and tired from months of late nights on the Kondor, little time or inclination to exercise, too many order-in lunches and dinners. There was no luster in his complexion, even his hair lay flat and dull. He had to wonder what Sophie Kempf saw in him, physically.

He straightened and turned to the door, suddenly, overwhelmingly nervous, closing it behind him when he remembered Phil's e-mail. He went back into the livingroom, sat at the credenza, reached for the pointer-ball then froze.

A Windows 95 desktop but the background was unfamiliar. And there was no e-mail icon in the array. With growing alarm he wondered if he had somehow picked up someone else's machine, the same model Compaq, but no...here was the long scuff mark on the case, sustained on an escalator in a Cleveland mall. Anyway, he had been using it right up until Sophie arrived at the bar; it hadn't been out of his sight except for those few minutes at the piano, during which time it had remained with her.

Where were the spreadsheet and word processing programs containing his work, most of which he had neglected to back up?

A week's work!

His fingers trembled over the keyboard as he went into file manager, gripped with terror as the program presented him with total absence of user files.

This was not his computer. He had logged countless hours on it, knew it intimately, had been using it less than half an hour ago.

He switched on the desk light and peered more closely at the keys. Now he could see that the Compaq was in pristine condition, unlike his own which was begrimed with use. He lowered the lid and reinspected the scuff mark, his face growing dark with the realization that the shallow scar in the plastic case had been recently inflicted: there were tiny curls of plastic along the outer edges of the marks where they had been gouged. A licked finger left a clean trail in a layer of dirt too uniformly applied, revealing a new surface.

This Compaq was new. A brand new laptop, the identical make and model to his own, which had been deliberately distressed, doctored to resemble his own as closely as possible.

Kristian stood slowly, unsteadily, unaware of the seconds ticking by.

It had to have been someone in close proximity to it, close enough to make careful note of its condition. Someone who had had only one chance to exchange it for this counterfeit model, through one tiny window of opportunity.

He had gone to the piano at Sophie Kempf's insistence.

She was standing in the crowded hotel lobby outside the bar, wearing her short jacket, smiling beautifully.

"Everything okay?"

Kristian smiled back and offered his arm and together they walked towards the revolving doors onto Mainzer Landstrasse. He used this hotel a lot for business. The staff knew him. There might even be an industry acquaintance in the throng. The lobby was no place for a confrontation.

He waited until they were outside, in a warm evening tainted by the fumes of the homebound traffic on Mainzer, assaulted by its roar.

He released her arm and stopped on the sidewalk, not speaking until he had seen the transformation in her face, watching her sweet smile fade and harden, the lovely dark brows drawing together, the thrusting intelligence behind her deep-set violet eyes losing purchase, spinning...

"Where's my computer, Sophie?"

She took a slow step back.

Kristian followed. "You exchanged my laptop for another one when

I was playing the piano. You went to a lot of trouble to deceive me. Why?"

Her breathing quickened. Her face darkened with fear.

"You switched them, didn't you? You got me to the piano so you could make the switch. *Right?*"

She flinched from the rising anger in his voice.

"Who are you working for, Sophie? Is that your name? Who are you doing this for? Why?" He looked around wildly along the sidewalk then out at the streaming traffic. "Are they watching us now?"

She looked down at the pavement, stonefaced herself.

"Where's my computer? It's full of work I need. Answer me, God damn it!"

She had backed across the full width of the sidewalk, pressed against the coined limestone wall of the hotel, Kristian hard on her.

"Why, Sophie? Another car company? Does someone think they're going to find..."

She was shaking her head.

"For Christ's sake who then?"

"I'm so sorry, Kristian. I know you won't believe me but I just wanted to be with you tonight. I was trying to pretend it wasn't happening. They made me do it, I swear I didn't want to. They said I'd be fired if I refused."

"Who?"

"Someone from the company."

Kristian started back. "From Dorner?"

"Yes."

"Why?"

"It was all arranged on the telephone. This man said they were checking senior executives, there were questions about you. He didn't tell me anything else."

"Who?"

"I swear I don't know."

"How do you know he was from Dorner?"

"He knew all the details of your schedule, and my employment."

"But you didn't meet him."

"I never met anyone until tonight, just an ordinary middle-aged man in the bar. He took your computer and left another one at the table. A few seconds. We didn't speak."

"Where's mine?"

"The man on the phone said they only needed to keep it for a short time, a few minutes. It would be returned to your room. They said you'd never know it had gone. Where are you going?"

Kristian was several meters along the street before he turned back. "Don't go back into the hotel, I don't want anyone seeing you there. The restaurant on the Opernplatz, what's it called?"

"The Charlot."

"Go there. Wait for me. You owe me some more answers."

He ran back to the Excelsior's main entrance, slowing his pace across the lobby so as not to draw attention to himself, cursing the elevator's slowness, running again when it released him on the eighteenth floor.

Whoever brought it back, he would be ready.

His heart was pounding by the time he reached his door, his fingers trembling with the access card. He heard a noise behind him, a uniformed maid letting herself out of a room and knocking on the neighboring door. Would that be how they would return it, under the guise of turning down the beds and distributing chocolate mints on their pillows?

But he was too late to find out.

His Compaq laptop was exactly where he had left the substitute.

His father was still in the bath. He hadn't heard anyone come into the suite, what was Kristian doing back here, weren't they going to the opera? They'd be late if he didn't hurry.

He was hurrying, he called through the door. It wasn't a good time to burden his father with this, he decided. Wait until he had some answers from Sophie Kempf.

Kristian made a quick check of the most important files before he left. If it was true what Sophie had told him, whoever had wanted to check the hard drive's contents would only have had to do a bulk download — a fast enough process with today's equipment — then examine it at leisure. Nothing seemed amiss, but it was hard to concentrate given the storm of questions raging in his head.

Espionage, in which Sophie too had been duped? Or was it true that his own company had seen fit to violate his privacy in such an underhanded fashion? Either way, he would find out.

Anger, disappointment, burning curiosity — all these emotions whirled around him on his cab ride to the Charlot, an intimate Italian restaurant within sight of the Alte Opera, almost empty now that the performance had started.

Kristian didn't feel real betrayal until he had explained his way past the maitre d' and checked the restaurant, both the main floor and the small upper gallery, and found that Sophie Kempf wasn't there.

He called her apartment from the restaurant and several times from his hotel room.

There was no reply, and no listing in the Frankfurt book to provide him with a street address.

CHAPTER 3

KRIMINALDIREKTOR GRENTZ'S OFFICE WAS ON THE SECOND FLOOR of the Federal Criminal Police Office headquarters in Wiesbaden. He kept his wife and five children in a photo cube on his desk, which meant that at any given time one member of the family was relegated to the bottom of the cube. Greta had a private bet that Grentz didn't notice or care who it was, that it was the office cleaner who periodically turned the cube either by accident or compassionate design. The Bundeskriminalamt was Grentz's family.

"Kriminaloberrat Tors tells me you intend to leave us, agent Schoeller."

"Yes, sir. I've applied and been accepted for teacher's college, starting in September."

He scratched the dry skin on the back of his hand, leaving visible grains of epidermis on the black desktop, triggering the memory of his half-hearted, never repeated proposition — a drink sometime? — which still made her flesh crawl.

"I wish there was something we could do to tempt you to remain in the BKA, agent Schoeller. We don't like to lose someone with credentials." He gazed into the computer screen on his desk. "Psychology major, seven years with the Schutzpolizei, three here. A year of forensics, fully upgraded in electronic surveillance, markswoman first class..."

Not an official term in a community that defined itself in official terms. Even Grentz realized that he sounded unctuous, looked sternly at her to compensate.

"For instance, if you were to request a transfer to the Sicherungsgruppe, I would possibly be able to endorse you at this point."

Even six months ago, Greta would have leapt at the opportunity: the Security Group, located near Bonn, had a heightened executive function in the BKA, including paramilitary operations, tactical surveillance and crisis response. The SG was where the action was. Even now the offer caught her off guard. Grentz saw it and pressed his advantage.

"It would be unfortunate for you to leave thinking that your last field assignment was in any way indicative of things to come, Schoeller. Naturally it is always your prerogative to refuse assignments that require any level of...intimacy. Your section chief tells me you were unhappy with your term at Dorner."

"Kriminaloberrat Tors misread the problem, sir. It wasn't the assignment, it was having to function without a briefing. I would appreciate knowing why the BKA is investigating Dorner executives."

Grentz gave his pale smile. "And you expect me to tell you."

"I did some research of my own on the company. It rather clarified the problem for me." She paused just long enough to underscore his discomfort. "I learned that Dorner revolutionized production a few years ago by adopting the Japanese team system. The workers don't merely stand at the line screwing in rearview mirrors or tail-light lenses; each worker gets to work on the whole car, all over it. They get to see the bigger picture Herr Kriminaldirektor. They develop pride in what they're doing, a feeling of worth. They don't feel like grunts."

He smiled. "And what happened when Dorner adopted this system?"

"Production and quality improved, sir."

"Not enough, it would seem, since Dorner are on their knees as we speak." He pursed his chalky lips to repress a smile. "However, you needn't concern yourself with Dorner any longer. The company is no longer our business. Which permits me to be more openhanded than Tors when he gave you the assignment: I can tell you now that the investigation in which you played a part was extremely low priority, a favor to the Federal Corporate Tax Office."

Greta frowned. "Tax violation?"

"Hideously complex. We are relieved to have it off the desk." Grentz looked at his watch. "Tors will grant you access to the Dorner file if you insist on seeing it, but I warn you it makes dull reading..." Peering again at the screen, jokingly. "Unless of course we see accountancy among your impressive qualifications. Good luck with it." He rose from his desk and went to the door. "Let me reiterate what I said just now about the SG: based on your résumé and your excellent record, I would be prepared..."

"Thank you for your confidence, sir, but I've made up my mind."

"Don't be too hasty. Ask Ulrich Mayer how he likes it in Bonn."

Greta managed to hide her surprise, although it made sense that the spymaster would be intimate with the comings and goings of his office.

"I'll do that. We booked the pistol range for 5:00 p.m." He probably knew that too.

"Good for you. Mayer is also a fine shot as far as I remember. He'll be better now. The facilities in Bonn — all the facilities — make us look like a shabby storefront operation. Think about it Schoeller."

The handgun range at Wiesbaden was a case in point. Measured in yards not meters, the facility had been bequeathed to the Bundeskriminalamt by the departing American air force. The concrete was returning to sand in places, the retrieval winch for the paper targets squeaked and jerked like a dilapidated washing line.

Appropriately, Ulrich Mayer was using an American revolver, Greta's stainless steel 357 magnum, a Smith and Wesson with a bobbed hammer and custom grips by Cole of Van Nuys, California — a weapon in every way different from the 9 mm Sig Sauer automatic, standard BKA issue, that had grown warm in Greta's hands.

Grentz was right, Uli had improved. They had been friends for too long for competition to be anything but friendly: Greta would have been pleased to see the level of his marksmanship had it not been for the uncharacteristically grim way Uli went to work with the magnum.

She watched him reload and fire six rapid rounds from a Weaver stance, the paper silhouette flinching a rhythmic jig until the tight grouping had blown out a ragged chest hole.

"Hole in the heart."

Greta screwed up her face. "That's an ugly thing to say."

"I refuse to apologize, he called me a faggot."

"Uli stop it. You're not funny."

"Pretty shooting though, huh?"

"That's hardly the word. You're shooting accurately. What's eating you?"

"I like this gun, you know. Don't put a muzzle vent on it, you get some kick like this, you know you're projecting something."

What, Greta wondered? Anxiety, anger, something else...? Thinner than the last time she saw him, a month ago, though still heavenly looking: like a Symbolist version of a Nordic angel except that he was Jewish on his mother's side, with a platinum brush cut for his halo. Over the years, Greta had noticed how people tended to smile around Ulrich, apart from other gays.

He led her down the firing line, from the twenty- towards the fifty-yard range.

"Let's stop now, go get some dinner," she said. "I don't think I'm in the spirit of this."

"Couple more groups."

"Go ahead. I know when I'm beat."

Ricochet wasn't a concern on the longer range, and Ulrich graduated from wadcutters to hardball, lead in copper. Six in quick succession, the magnum bucking harder with the higher load. Six more from the speedloader, another six then another, thrashing the gun, his sensitive mouth set hard between the yellow ear protectors.

He collected up the ejected cases in his Red Sox baseball cap while Greta reeled in the last target, looking with disapproval at the close group in the silhouette's forehead. Ulrich balled up his cap and held out her cordite-reeking gun, grip first.

"No."

"What? You always insist on cleaning it. I'll do the Sig."

"You don't have to give it back to me. It's yours. A present."

"What are you talking about?"

Greta smiled. "I won't need it. Discipline problems, I'll call their parents."

It took a few seconds for it to dawn. He smiled slowly. "My god. You did it. Finally."

"As good as. Grentz is trying to talk me out of it. I'll let him drool for a couple more days but I'm going. Come on, I'm starving."

She put her arm around his waist and led him towards the armory door where the cleaning equipment was stored. "You're way too thin. They're not feeding you in Bonn. Pasta's what you need. The Charlot."

"I'm buying then."

"Sorry."

"Don't argue, I'm packing a magnum. It's good news Grets, worth celebrating."

"Grentz reckons you're going to try and talk me out of it. Aren't you?"

He stopped at the empties box, let the shell cases trickle out of his cap, put it back on and tugged the peak down over his grey eyes, serious again.

"No," he said. "You're doing the right thing."

They had met at university, roomed for two years as Schutzpolizei recruits, Greta staying two longer in the Frankfurt city police then following Uli into the federal office before his transfer to Bonn. As a treat, on those rare occasions they felt flush, the Charlot on Frankfurt's Opernplatz had been a fixture in their relationship from the earliest days in the Schutz, raw recruits as green as their uniforms. Greta, Ulrich and Otto Volk, a Hauptkommissar now, still at the old station on Keplerstrasse.

"Seen him lately?"

"Getting comfortable. Paunchy."

"The beer."

"Cock of the walk since his promotion. Mister fixit. He's got a whole network of villains, Otto's machine, lot of little wheels to grease."

"It's a wonder he's still honest."

"Where it counts he is. Leona keeps him in line."

"She must be nearly due."

"Six weeks."

"I'll call. Have you told them you're quitting?"

"You're the first to know."

Ulrich smiled and saluted with a glass of mineral water. He hadn't touched alcohol for five years. "Thank you for the Smith."

"Someone had to get a present. I don't think Grentz is going to spring for the gold watch. All I'm going to get is deprogrammed."

Uli's expression tightened. Watching him, she could see fine new lines at the corners of his eyes and mouth. And there was a new place behind his eyes, behind the genuine warmth of his feelings, that was out of reach.

"So how *is* Bonn?"

"Interesting work, good pay, flexible hours. Of course, we don't get the summers off like you teachers. Soft touch. You know Regine and Jean Pierre are going back to Corsica." Uli's sister had married a Swiss, both of them high school teachers. They'd bought a thirteenth-century tower near Calvi, renovating it for a vacation home. "You should go stay with them," Uli said. "You know you've got an open invitation."

"I know you just changed the subject."

"I can't talk about the SG."

"Sorry. Minor league mindset here. Tell me about the weather in Bonn then, or is there some strict SG protocol on that?"

"The weather's bad."

He said it almost under his breath, and for a second Greta glimpsed an open window in the blind wall behind his eyes. Then Ulrich blinked and it was gone.

"I'm sorry," she said. She grabbed the half-liter carafe and poured, then picked a slice of Italian bread from the basket between them, peeled off a length of crust and popped it into her mouth. "On the other hand I'd be more than happy to divulge the details of my sensational farewell performance."

"You don't have to."

"Oh I'd love to. I'm so proud of it. Grentz needed someone under thirty with tits and a driving license and guess who qualified?" Ulrich cast an anxious glance around the restaurant. They were alone on the Charlot's small upper gallery, only one couple visible on the main floor, and the waiters in their mustaches and long white aprons, sauntering like gunslingers.

"I don't want to hear details of field assignments."

She took a gulp of wine. "Don't worry, I don't know any. That's what made it all so worthwhile, like so much that we do. My contribution to federal law enforcement last week? Playing Grentz's head games with a perfectly decent, hard-working, openhearted American auto executive."

Uli sat up, interested in spite of himself.

"Meet Sophie Kempf, company chauffeur," Greta went on. "Driving this poor guy around for a week." She chuckled without mirth. "Actually the first man since Andreas who could have talked me into bed. Didn't though. Nice guy. Really nice guy. Smart. Key exec. Looked like he needed some fun, though."

"An American company?"

Her speech slowed a little. "An American subsidiary of a German company."

"Dorner?"

"Good guess." Greta watched him for several seconds. "What do you know about Dorner?"

"What everyone else knows, they're in bad shape. All you did was drive this guy around?"

"I was supposed to monitor where he went. The car was wired, I was recording our conversation, whatever he said on the cell phone, which was nothing remarkable."

Uli looked at her intensely. "How thorough was your briefing?"

"Why should that matter?"

He waited.

"There was nothing to suggest why we should be showing interest — not enough for me to get his laptop for an hour so they could suck on the hard drive. He cottoned on, by the way. Nothing I did, he just realized we'd made a switch. I didn't enjoy deceiving him."

"It's never wise to get involved."

"We were together for a week, in a car. He was an honest man."

"How do you know?"

"I have good instincts."

"No you don't: Andreas was a pig."

Greta fingered her glass but didn't drink. "How do you know about Dorner? They weren't under investigation for corporate tax violation were they Ulrich?"

"Who said that?"

"Grentz. A tax case which was now closed. Tors showed me a file on Dorner to support this tax angle. It was too handy."

Ulrich inclined forward, his whole body tense, no attempt to hide his concern. He opened his mouth to speak, stopped, looked towards the gallery stairs where the waiter was carrying up their gelato and coffee. They sat silently as he laid out the dishes with wafers and long spoons, poured expresso, then descended.

Ulrich spoke in a near whisper: "Did Tors know you were skeptical, that you thought the file was a placebo?"

"They trained us better than that."

"You're sure?"

"Why?"

"Keep your voice down."

"What is it, Ulrich? The SG are on this, aren't they? My God. You're after Dorner in Bonn."

"Listen! You're out, you're getting out. Stay out. You're doing the smartest thing. Leave this behind, all of it. Smile and eat your ice cream. Don't ask any more questions. Dorner is not a good subject for you."

After that he was unassailable. They finished the meal in silence, settled the bill then walked across the Opernplatz, their path crossed by latecomers running to make the performance which must have already begun: above the murmur of traffic out on Taunusanlage and the whisper of the Lucae fountain, they could hear faint strains of music from behind the Alte Opera's floodlit, reconstructed facade. For years it had been a bombed-out shell, the haunt of vermin and the ghosts of pre-war divas.

"I think we were happier in the Schutz, directing traffic."

"You've forgotten the paperwork."

"That hasn't changed. Maybe for you."

She glanced sideways as they entered Leerbachstrasse, trying to meet his eyes across what felt like a sudden chasm between them. They reached the car, a grey Opel Vektra from the BKA pool, Uli's key in the lock when he withdrew it, turned and leaned back against the door, facing away from her. Directly overhead, the street lamp made platinum fire of his brushcut.

"Ulrich?"

He glanced along the street, then turned to her. "Dorner is dangerous, Greta. You can't imagine. For me, for you too if you don't walk away right now. Leave it. Promise me. Swear to me you'll..."

"Where from, Uli? If this investigation didn't come down from Tax Fraud, who generated it? Which section? Just tell me that and I'll forget it. I swear. I liked Kristian Peiper, he's a good memory. Just that much Uli. For old time's sake."

Ulrich got in the car, unlocked the passenger door, turned on the engine then the radio, tuned it to a rock station and cranked the volume up until it hurt her ears. It was an unnecessary, angry gesture because he didn't speak, rather he inscribed the single letter and the following two numbers with his finger on the dashboard. It didn't matter that the car's interior was spotlessly clean, with no dust in which to leave a mark: the pattern was simple, instantly recognizable to Greta.

K44.

Rechtsextremismus.

Located in Bonn, under SG command, Section K44 was exclusively for the investigation and control of the extreme right.

CHAPTER 4

PHIL BAYLOR HAD BOUGHT HIS 920 S ON A SPECIAL DISCOUNT FROM Kristian, for two-thirds the $60,000 suggested list. Precision power, a whisper-quiet interstate ride. Kristian was in the passenger seat, addressing his senior vice-president of marketing, Perry Salkield, who was riding in the back.

"We've got to do it, Sally. I know you don't like it, but we've got to bite the bullet and kill this Eurostyle thing. Americans are getting more patriotic by the minute." He glanced sideways to include Baylor. "You fine demographers have any idea how many people in America buy Country and Western albums? I assume you know how ungodly *rich* Garth Brooks is."

Baylor chuckled, a rumble that started in his massive gut. "Stand by your *man*, Sally." He looked around and winked at Salkield. "Look out, we're gonna haul that gold-plated dipstick out of your corporate butt."

"We're not talking about fifteen-dollar CDs here," Salkield returned. "Dorners are expensive because we build them properly.

Even the 3-Series is a clear seven grand more than a Chevy pickup, if that's where you imagine the market."

"I'm with Kris," Baylor said. "You want to talk expensive? Talk about bass boats, talk about his 'n her snowmobiles with the trailer and winter covers. How about a fucking motor home? Figure how many of your grunts working the line out there in Oakwood sail Winnebagos down to Saint Pete's every Christmas. How many full-dress Harleys in your employee parking lot this summer? That's on *top* of two family cars, three if they've got a teenager."

"He's right," Kristian said. "Americans love vehicles, it's an obsession right up there with food and sex. I've been saying it for three years: we have to convince these people that Dorners are *good* cars, not lawyers' and stockbrokers' cars, then maybe we'll start getting some Garth Brooks numbers here. We may have to eat a price cut till we're on track."

They exited 90 in Lorain County, took a road between the interstate and the Erie south shore until it dwindled to two quiet lanes cutting through a long valley. Two miles in, there was a dairy farm on one side, the pristine buildings and grazing Holsteins like dabs of fresh paint against the land. Fifty years ago there had been a farm on the opposite side too, until the property was bought by an Ohio-Italian salvage merchant named Dominic Porrera.

At a casual glance, a thousand cars parked in orderly rows on the valley side looked like some kind of convocation, a rock festival or a religious jamboree. From the road, it took a harder look to see that they were wrecks, along with battered trucks and rusting army vehicles and even a wingless DC3. The toy box jumble that had so delighted a six-year-old on Saturday mornings, beginning in the mid-1960s.

Except for the size of the operation, and the model years of the wrecks, Kristian saw that the changes had been subtle. The long uphill approach was still an obstacle course of potholes although Baylor's car took them in graceful stride. They parked with a dozen others in the mud below the yard, looking up at the razor wire and a red-painted sign warning customers of dire consequences for attempting to smuggle out undeclared small parts. To underscore the message, a tan Doberman whirled insanely around a pen just inside the gate, looping drool. Dom used to have a friendly German shepherd called Axel, Kristian remembered, chained to a big maple in front of the office. He and his father used to bring him treats. Axel's chain must have eventually ringed the tree and killed it — it was a stump now, some kids playing King Of The Castle there, whipping each other with red Twizzlers.

"Sonny Hacker," Phil howled. "You want a spokesman and you don't want Ricardo. Sonny's your ticket."

"To the breadline," Salkield groaned. "This is going to be the ruin of us."

Baylor ignored him, addressed Kristian exclusively. "Who knows how big this could get. We make a few spots with this creep, get him in *People* magazine, on Letterman, cut a country CD." Baylor framed his plump hands into a screen. "*A SALVAGE YARD, SOMEWHERE IN AMERICA, 2010.*"

"Why are you drawling?" Salkield interrupted, dialing his cellular. "You're from Akron."

"I'm getting into character."

"Which one, the burned-out hack or the rapacious ad baron?"

"I don't have to take this crap from you, Salkield."

"Dorner decorates your lobby, Philip."

Kristian shifted impatiently in his seat. "Leave each other alone and get the hell on with this."

"This junkyard bandit," Baylor went on. "He's strictly Altamont, right? 10w30 and rancid beer stains, vandyke beard, long greasy hair."

"Helter Skelter," muttered Salkield. "I'll call Charlie Manson's agent right away."

"Something of a collector, pissed as hell because of course he doesn't ever get any Kondors. Not a one. He's got Ford vans, he's got GM, he's got fuckin' Toyota, but do you think he'll ever...EVER...get a Kondor?"

Kristian smiled with a touch of pride. "Thermoplastic panels, aluminum frame — he might be in for a long wait. This is Maytag, Phil."

"Tried and true. Save ourselves a fortune on market research."

The junkyard was one idea for a series of thirty-second television spots to accompany the Kondor launch. Since the Kondor was not going to be rebadged after all, they needed commercials that would introduce the American public not only to the Kondor, but to a more accessible Dorner.

"Now the tow truck comes in," Baylor hurried on. "And wouldn't you know, it's just another old broken down Dodge Caravan..."

"We can't do that," Salkield said.

"Whatever, but it ain't a Dorner, so of course old Sonny gives it one vicious kick with his cycle boot." Baylor massaged his treble chin. "He needs a good line, something to snarl at the camera." His small eyes lit up. "'*This is discrimination*!' How about that? A little sardonic humor for the tag line: '*Dorner. For discriminating drivers.*'"

"I would be extremely careful about the use of a word like that," Salkield scolded.

"Don't get your knickers in a twist, Sally."

"Why not? We're a Kraut outfit with history in the Third Reich. The last thing we want to be is discriminating."

Baylor chuckled. "Okay, but we're not going back to *Our Car Is Your Castle*. We'd better fucking not be."

"No," Kristian said flatly. "Frankfurt's already agreed it won't fit the new image."

Salkield arched an eyebrow. "'Our car is your apartment'?"

Kristian sighed and reached for the door handle. "Let's look around."

He got out, inhaling the scent of timothy from the farm across the valley. It brought a jolt of memory, the clear sensation of his father's hand warm around his own small hand, letting go as they begin to run, their legs unwinding from the car as they race each other to the perimeter fence.

He waited while Baylor extricated himself from the car, grunting with the effort. Although Kristian's height, around five nine, he was anchored by his three-hundred–pound mass. "Coming Sally?"

"I'm expecting a call."

"So bring your little telephone."

"I'm in the automobile business. It upsets me to look at salvage. And it's muddy."

Kristian felt relieved as they headed towards the gate. Perry Salkield was one of the best marketing executives in the eastern United States, but his Odd Couple routine with Phil Baylor had been getting on Kristian's nerves since Cleveland.

"Lot of cars," Baylor said, panting slightly as they passed through the gate. "Don't see any Dorners yet."

There were ten acres of cars. Dom's had always been primarily a parts and salvage operation, and it contained cannibalized examples of most makes and models built in the United States in recent memory, and most of the imports. That included Dorners, though not in anything like the numbers contributed by other manufacturers. The overwhelming majority of wrecks were American cars from the seventies and early eighties, a low point in Detroit's history both in build-quality and design. The Lead Sleds, the Big Boats, beached here in a kind of tragic stasis: Galaxies and Strato Chiefs dropped from orbit; Malibus and Granadas and Parisiennes rooted here forever with plain Ohio milkweed jutting through plundered engine compartments. Impalas and Mustangs with atrophied muscles, Cougars and Wildcats long delivered of their teeth and claws, sinking into the pasture, sedentary hulks on squashed tires.

"Perry's wrong," Kristian said. "This is the best education in the world for a car guy. Dad knew it, that's why he used to bring me up here."

"When did you start coming?"

"I must have been around six."

Baylor made speed to catch up, puffing, his wide hips rolling. "How's he doing? Guess it must be on your mind, huh?"

"Still not great."

"But there's nothing physically wrong with him?"

"Not that he's telling me or his doctor. I don't know; ever since we came back from Frankfurt, he's been depressed. Spends most of the time in his room, doesn't see people, watches TV. Never used to glance at it."

"You think it was Erich Dorner's death? They were the same era, must be sobering."

"I don't know, Phil. I've tried to make him see someone."

"He can't be thrilled about the way Tevlin's running things. You hear that with heavy hitters when they retire. I mean, the guy spends fifty years making major decisions for Dorner, always in the public eye, making a difference. Now all he can do is cringe every time Tevlin fucks up, which I understand is not infrequently. He must feel impotent."

"I appreciate your concern, but it isn't that. He's been retired three years, perfectly fine till that day in Frankfurt."

"You ever get any further with that laptop thing? Did you call Junia?"

"She denied any knowledge."

"You believe it?"

"She sounded pretty surprised. Scared."

"She's a great actress."

"I think it was genuine. She called me back next day, said she'd had people try and trace the driver, no luck. She was worried about industrial espionage, naturally. Not that there was anything really sensitive in the laptop, nothing that would set the Kondor back."

"You really think it was your competition?"

"Who else?"

"No connection to that business with your dad, at Erich Dorner's place?"

Kristian had told Phil about that, too, frustrated by the sudden, unprecedented breakdown of communication with his father. "Mechanical drawings" had been Hansjorg's explanation for the package. Suspension designs from the old days, one of Hansjorg's first projects, nothing that would interest anyone but an engineer. He'd actually forgotten them at Erich's house.

"You never asked him about the conversation you heard on the intercom? 'Krokus,' whatever that was?"

"The flower I guess. It's the same word in German, except with *k*s."

"Did you ask him?"

"No."

"Why not?"

"I don't want to interrogate him, the way he is right now. I shouldn't have been eavesdropping anyway, it wasn't my conversation."

Phil knew when to ease off. "What about that autobiography he was working on?"

"Lost interest. The notes and photographs are sitting in a box at home."

"Get him back into it. Sounds like he needs something to keep him busy."

Kristian shrugged. "I don't know if he'd even find a publisher now. They like DeLoreans and Iacoccas. Dad's always been too ascetic, too decent to make interesting reading. They want rascals."

"Come on, there's got to be a market. A lot of eyes on Dorner with the Kondor launch coming up. How many guys make *Time*'s Man of the Year?"

"That was 1965. The world forgets."

"Cleveland doesn't forget, buddy. Hansjorg Peiper still means cars around here boy."

They continued up the valley, through this dead city of cars. Both men fell silent, under its spell, oblivious to the other parts-vultures picking over the wrecks. Kristian wondered if they sensed the cars' vulgar eloquence, the way he had always done: a forgotten toy wedged down behind a seat, a candy wrapper, a stir stick. Eloquent, too, the faded vacation bumper-stickers that chronicled the lives of American families, along with their unpaid parking tickets and ketchup sachets and ball pens in map pockets and rusted glove compartments, keeping company now with dead leaves and field mouse droppings.

The crash wrecks cried loudest, their haunted energy fixed by the traumas of statistical people — the reckless drunks and boy racers, the squabbling, distracted families and sleepy truckers and couples in heat; and of their victims, those hapless drivers who merely forgot to kiss the dice one day as they backed out of the garage.

Suddenly Kristian stopped.

"Holy..."

"What?"

"Up there. Jesus, it's still here!"

Kristian led him up through the streets of the city, past the landmarks of conked-out cranes, construction machinery, gutted buses...to the top of the valley side where an old Dodge army truck — of course it hadn't moved — lay camouflaged in sun-faded khaki and undergrowth.

"My God...I used to drive him for hours up in that high cab, raking the shift, stomping the brake, pounding that old dome horn." Kristian went closer, climbed onto the running board, peered inside the cab. The steering wheel was gone, and the bench seat. A broken beer bottle with a bleached label lay under the brake pedal.

"We did it all, man! Crossed deserts and mountain passes in this thing. Running supplies past the banditos. Thick with bandits. Catch you, they cut off your eyelids and stake you out in the sun. Had to drive real fast."

Kristian climbed onto the bed where his father used to lift him up to grip the canopy hoops to do pull ups, counting aloud in German while Kristian tried to beat the last count, from their last visit. Only one hoop left, level with his chin now, a few rags of faded canvas fluttering as the day's warmth began to rise from the valley floor.

"When would this be from?" Baylor said, trying to catch his breath after the climb. "Korea?"

"Older. World War II."

It was a moment before Baylor said: "I don't think I ever asked you this. Tell me to mind my own business if you want."

Kristian smiled. "Don't be so coy. You want to know what he did in the war, right?"

"Mind me asking?"

"I reckon you qualify." Phil had served as a combat pilot in Vietnam; he still flew, a Cessna Centurion hangared at Burke Lakefront. "First half he was in the Wehrmacht. Captain. Sixth Army under General Paulus." He looked at Baylor for a reaction. "The Sixth were on the Eastern Front. At Stalingrad." Baylor nodded, soberly, the customary response to that name. "He spent the second half in Siberia, as a guest of Joe Stalin. Almost all his friends froze or starved to death. I think it's not out of the question that he had to eat one or two of them. He never talks about it."

Kristian jumped down with a bright, determined smile. "He sure told me a lot about cars. Taught me all about internal combustion up here, from these wrecks, showed me how it all works. We installed a pit in the garage at home, put in hydraulics, everything. We restored three cars together from the ground up."

"That Spyder you drive? The '58?"

"The other two were Detroit muscle, a Javelin and a Hemi-Cuda. Lethal. Didn't I tell you that?"

"So you came here for parts."

"Sure. Then later on, when I had a career at Dorner, we just used to come here out of habit. I don't know. To think. Be together. Talk." Kristian gave a short laugh. "We're car guys. Look around you, the place is littered with eight-, nine-year-old models rusting to shit. There's instruction here."

It was hard for Kristian to articulate the lesson that had carried him, at thirty-five and without any of his father's direct influence, to the top marketing job at Dorner Cleveland. He couldn't have learned it as well anywhere but in this valley, surrounded by the ultimate, inescapable end to his day's work, all his bright dreams-for-sale stripped of paint and power and hype, of prestige and pedigree and sex appeal — all the complex symbolism and psychology of his game.

A lesson in objectivity, creativity, a sense of humor. A way to avoid the blinkered conformity that marked the cookie-cutter suits who had brought the American car industry to its knees by the early eighties.

"I think he used to bring me up here so that I'd learn to keep a part of me free from Dorner. From career and ambition. The same part of him that always belonged to philosophy, books, music."

"Yeah, I knew he was heavily into music."

"I'm supposed to be driving him to Severance Hall tonight. The Cleveland Orchestra's honoring him for forty years of patronage." Kristian looked at his watch. "We'd better get going. I've got to work the phones for a couple of hours before I strap on the tux."

"Think he'll go?"

"If I have to drag him there."

Friday afternoon, with the Indians playing at home: I 90 was slow heading back into Cleveland, stalled for construction near Hopkins International. Kristian made half his calls from the car, decided to finish them at home rather than crawl back to the Oakwood office in rush hour.

Baylor dropped Perry Salkield first, then took Kristian home along Merwin Road, following the Cuyahoga's intestinal triple-S through the Flats. An almost square mile in area, Cleveland's Flats are quite literally the city's underworld — under the Main Avenue Bridge, under the Detroit Superior Bridge, the Hope Memorial Bridge and the Old Superior Viaduct. Shadowed and partially concealed by Cleveland's world of bridges, the undeveloped part of the Flats is an abandoned jungle where the ghosts of vanished industries live in the ruins of factories and their jettisoned hardware, all of it succumbing to the resilient flora. In stark contrast with the gentrified warehouse section nearer the Erie lakeshore where his apartment was situated, this jungle had always made Kristian think of post-doomsday science fiction.

Beyond the restored warehouse facade, the building's developers had taken pains to extinguish all traces of its history. Kristian understood that his own apartment had once been a coffinmaker's workshop, that workers had sanded a quarter-inch off the wide pine floorboards to excise a hundred years of spilled carpenter's glue. They had put in high ceilings that made the modest rooms seem much bigger, a small but efficient kitchen, and a gas-log fireplace which Kristian hated in spite of its clean, instant heat.

He had bought it with Melanie as a *pied à terre*, two years ago at Christmas, five months before he moved out of their Kirtland Hills house. At the time, Kristian had not dreamed that it would ever become his full-time bachelor residence.

Or had he? Had they both?

It wasn't his home, which made him careless about it. Between the cleaner's weekly visits, the dishes went undone and the bed unmade, newspapers and magazines and work papers littered the sofa and the kitchen table and the toilet tank — any horizontal surface. He had been an equal partner in the domestic affairs of the house they had shared, so what was this? A gesture of bravado after the pain of separation, a cry of appeal to his wife to say *look, I don't manage well without you*?

Was the Kondor alone responsible for his neglected health these days, or was that another gesture?

Whatever the message, it hadn't reached her; she had not been here since the split, they had not communicated in months other than through their attorneys.

He took a beer to the livingroom windows, looking northwest through the Main Avenue Bridge, to the dull grey blade of Lake Erie out beyond Whiskey Island. The Flats were gearing up for the weekend.

Weekends felt different now. Saturdays had been their best days, time to read the paper, walk to brunch, work on the house and garden together. One day out of the whirlpool of separate career engagements, scribbled notes on the fridge, carphone calls to cancel plans. They made love on Saturday mornings, with growing infrequency and never with the result that Melanie most desired. Her fault, the doctors were certain, and he would have been happy to adopt. But Mel didn't believe the doctors. She wanted her own child, as she let him know in subtle, relentless ways. She never felt hungry anymore, she was "empty"; she was getting older, she reminded him, all the time.

Sometimes Kristian believed he had been deliberately careless about his one brief, unsatisfying affair in nine years of marriage. A way to free them both from a fruitless commitment. Other times he missed her and loathed himself for his weakness. Of course Mel's divorce lawyer would have howled at any such whimpering: given the Peiper family's financial position and Kristian's own substantial salary, Mel's counsel wanted six figures a year for her client.

He made his remaining calls, a necessary distraction from the building anger that would inevitably climax with a mental replay of his last night in Frankfurt — Sophie Kempf, Junia Dorner — perhaps angriest with Junia because of his own reluctance to confront her. He suspected more than she was telling him, but he'd allowed the incident to go unresolved, buried like everything else under the mountain of work before the Frankfurt show, now only weeks away.

It was 6:00 p.m. by the time he had showered and laid out his evening clothes, enjoying the ritual of brushing the tuxedo and adding studs and cufflinks to the dry-cleaned shirt. A uniform he had been required to wear often over the years, for industry and society functions, at first always as an addendum to his father. There was a period of rebellion during college, naturally, of pretending to disown his status as Hansjorg Peiper's son, though the small, safe fires he had set, like movie effects, had served more to illuminate his bridges than to burn them.

Because at heart he had always welcomed the elegant stiffness of a wing collar, the festive restraint of the tux, bespeaking self-control, power and dignity — all the qualities that he had, until recently, attributed to his father.

The house where Kristian grew up, where his father now lived alone with his housekeeper, Ingrid Koch, was in Cleveland Heights, on Canterbury Road. Most of the roads in the Heights bore such names: Clarendon, Fairfax, Monmouth...privileged addresses where the large sequestered homes conspired in the fantasy of old English nobility with their oak timbers and leaded windows and clusters of tall chimneys. It had always given Kristian much satisfaction that the corner house at the end of Canterbury — his house — offered stark simplicity under the same lush mantle of oak and ash.

A white, cubic house in the International Modern style, built in the twenties with flat roofs and large, wraparound windows. Hansjorg had never wanted to live anywhere but here, loved the house as his wife had done. Its Modern purity had been tempered and softened under her influence, her warmth and good taste reflected everywhere in quirky and eclectic furniture and art. Years ago Hansjorg had bought a farm in Virginia because she liked to ride, but had sold it as soon as she died. There had been no yachts, no Manhattan penthouse, no occasional domiciles in Europe or the Caribbean, although he could easily have indulged in any of those things. There would have been no point: Dorner and music and books had always been his consuming passions, all of them abundant in Cleveland. His only real extravagance were the violins.

"He hasn't been near the instruments," Ingrid whispered. "He had the television moved up to his room on Tuesday. I take his meals up but he won't let me in to clean."

She was wearing a smart green linen outfit, for a date with her regular gentleman caller, also Austrian and in his sixties.

"You need a break," Kristian soothed. "Go out and have fun." He glanced at his watch. "Is he dressed?"

The housekeeper twisted her hands. "I haven't been out of the house all week, I can't bear to leave him when he's like this."

"Stop beating yourself up, Ingrid. He's my problem tonight. Don't worry about getting back."

She smiled and picked a piece of lint from his lapel. "It's nice to see you at home, Kristian."

He looked around the hallway. "I was thinking about moving back for a while. What do you think?" He saw how her face lit up, put his arm around her shoulders as he walked her across the hallway, towards the passage leading to the kitchen. "Maybe I could borrow Wendel a couple of days a week, get some work done on the way to the office. Did he take Dad out for a drive this morning?"

"Of course. Maybe he actually *talks* to Wendel, I don't know. He sure isn't talking to me. All I hear is that *verdamt* TV." Her voice grew hushed again. "All these years, his music, and now..."

She pulled away, marching him back along the kitchen corridor into the hall and through the livingroom door. "I daren't ask him, so I don't even know if the dials are right."

Hansjorg's collection of violins were kept in several display cases in the livingroom. Over a dozen instruments, kept at optimum temperature and humidity in special cases.

Their appeal for Hansjorg was threefold: he played them, practicing one sacrosanct hour a day when he was home, as therapy after the rigors of his work; he loaned them to gifted local performers, often students for whom such fine instruments would otherwise have been far out of reach. And he loved them for their physical beauty as well as their sound.

Dark ebony fingerboards, dramatically flamed maple glowing under old, deep varnish, the elegant trajectories of the pernambuco bows — Kristian had always felt the spell of his father's collection. Place of honor went to a 1720 Stradivarius, but there were two Amatis, a century older than the Strad, worth half a million apiece, also a late nineteenth-century Vuillaume that supposedly sounded better than any of them.

Though he had never played violin, happy to accompany his father on the piano, Kristian was intimate with the collection, which made it easy for him to spot the empty space.

"Where's the little one?" He went nearer the case. "The three-quarter. He would never have loaned that out."

The housekeeper's silence made him turn.

"Did he take it out?"

She nodded timidly.

"That's good, isn't it? Maybe he'll turn off the TV and play it. Why that one though?"

Ingrid's hands covered her mouth, her eyes wide in appeal. Her small bosom rose and fell under the green linen. She had wanted him to see the empty space, it was why she had brought him in here.

"Ingrid what is it?"

"Come. I'll show you."

"Did something happen to it? Look, don't worry. If you had an accident, you mustn't feel..."

"No accident."

He followed her into the hall, once more past the broad staircase towards the kitchen that had been her uncontested preserve since his parents bought the house in 1955. It had remained essentially unchanged since Kristian's childhood, the same oversized appliances bearing some of the same design elements as American cars of the period. The enamel was spotless, the chrome lovingly polished; like everything in the house, it was a testament to Ingrid's scrupulous propriety, which was why the broken violin, hidden in a pot drawer, caused her genuine agony.

"You mustn't breathe to him that I found it. He tried to hide it. I found it last week, in the garbage outside the back door, right down in the bottom. I was taking the bag out to the curb when the bow poked through."

Unlike most other instruments in the collection, the three-quarter size violin held mostly sentimental value, but that was great: it had belonged to his youngest sister, Silka, who gave it to him to be a comfort on the Russian front.

Kristian reached down into the drawer and lifted it out by its broken neck, the body dangling, twisting at the end of the strings.

"I noticed it missing the day before I found it. I asked him, he said he'd lent it out. He lied to me. Never before. Never."

Other than the break between neck and body, the instrument looked unharmed except for the bow which had also been snapped in two. The damage to the little German violin would have required considerable force, impossible to do by accident. There was no question that his father had broken it deliberately.

"Why?" Ingrid whispered.

Kristian tried to smile. "Maybe he fluffed a difficult passage, got mad."

Ingrid snorted at what they both knew was a ridiculous explanation. Beyond the fact that Hansjorg hadn't practiced or played since his return from Frankfurt, it was unimaginable that this most self-controlled of men should lose his temper to such a degree, and then lie about it.

She looked down at the drawer. "I don't like this. It gives me a bad feeling."

Ingrid crossed herself as she pushed the drawer shut. She had come to work for Hansjorg in Frankfurt as a fifteen-year-old DP, from an Austrian village in the remote northeast, near the foothills of the Carpathians. Despite her natural intelligence and the fact that she had never returned to Europe since the war, her superstition always seemed centuries old. Ingrid's war had been hard, she had never overcome an almost desperate frugality: she unraveled worn-out sweaters to reuse the wool and refused to peel vegetables, saved string and supermarket bags and wrapping paper, which burst from kitchen cupboards and drawers.

But she was relieved at the prospect of having Kristian in the house again. They discussed domestic plans until they heard a polite knock at the back door, her gentleman caller. She retrieved her coat and purse, then Kristian escorted her to the door. "Promise me you won't spoil your evening over this."

"And you...not a word to him about it!"

Kristian delivered her to a deferential elderly man called Schumacher, clutching a green Tyrolean hat, then went upstairs, slowly. It was unsettling, the idea of living here again. After Melanie, the thought of coming back to Canterbury Road seemed like a defeat, a retreat from normal life which he'd always seen as comprising a wife and children in a home of his own. He saw the sudden specter of himself as a bachelor grown old here, living with the past. He remembered, with the inevitable flush of shame, that for a few ridiculous minutes, one night in Frankfurt, he had been fatuous enough to imagine Sophie Kempf in this house.

Kristian reached the wide landing, listening to the muffled, bullying din of the television from his parents' room. He would always think of it as that. He paused, looking at his mother's photograph at the top of the stairs, clowning for the camera on Copacabana Beach in the early fifties, where Hansjorg was establishing Dorner Brazil before they came to Cleveland. His alter ego, complementing his ascetic side, she was wearing toreador pants and a big red sun hat and matching sunglasses, Latin-looking with her dark curls worn unfashionably, beautifully long.

He looked at the other, older family photograph, the only surviving picture of Hansjorg's German family. He was not in it, having taken it himself just before his departure for the Eastern Front. The family was playing chamber music, for piano and strings, Hansjorg's parents and his three sisters, graceful, animated, with a radiant intelligence. Silka had been nineteen, Johanna and Barbara in their early twenties when the apartment was bombed.

Such an event had, over the years, made Kristian feel protected in one sense, by the likelihood that such terrible luck could not be visited twice upon one family — which did nothing to diminish his sense of loss, of his three aunts in particular.

He knocked at his father's door, got no reply, turned the knob with a reluctant hand.

The TV was playing to an empty room. It was dark, the atmosphere closed and stale-smelling. The curtains were drawn across the steel-mullioned windows. Had they been closed all day? Kristian heard running water through the slightly open door to the ensuite bathroom.

"Dad?"

No reply. Kristian went in.

He was standing, staring down into the wide pedestal basin with his back to his son, wearing pajamas. Between the TV and the rushing tap he had not heard Kristian come in, remained unaware of him now.

Kristian stood there, fascinated and alarmed by his father's repetitive, automaton movements as he washed his hands, rubbing and rubbing, so engrossed in the procedure, it seemed to Kristian, that any word would come as an unpleasant shock. He even grew afraid that his father would look up and see him reflected in the mirror.

Slowly, as inconspicuously as possible, he backed out through the doorway. He turned off the television to signal his presence. He drew back the curtains to admit a soft evening light, then opened a window.

"Ingrid? What are you doing?"

"It's Kristian, Dad."

The scrape of slippers on the bathroom tiles. His father appeared in the doorway, impassive, his hands dripping at his sides.

"How long have you been here?"

"I just came up." He smiled cheerfully. "Your big night. Got the notes for your speech?"

Hansjorg grunted and wiped his hands on his pajamas. His slippers swished across the carpet towards his walk-in closet.

"Dad, come on. They're honoring you. And you deserve it."

His father chuckled, a dry and hollow sound as he disappeared inside the closet. "Yes, I have more than kept the Cleveland Orchestra in rosin and oboe reeds over the years. How was the office?" The rattle of clothes hangers. "Did we manage to sell anyone an automobile today?"

Kristian sat on the edge of the bed in dismay. He had never before heard a whisper of complaint from a man whose presence had been required at countless functions during his long reign as CEO at Dorner America. And through all the years of flesh-pressing and speech-making, he had seen his commitment to the orchestra as a holiday from duty, a treat. An honor.

"I took the afternoon off."

"That'll help."

"Phil Baylor and I went up to Dom's. First time in years. I missed you up there."

"What do you need to go there for? You want to see a car grave-yard, look behind Plant Two."

Kristian bit down, because the sting contained the venom of truth: he'd meant the Dorner sales bank, an untended empty lot behind the chassis plant, where unsold inventory awaited dealer orders. A car maker's limbo, up to a thousand "pieces" can end up in the bank at the close of a model year, deteriorating in the mud and weeds. Right now it was almost full.

He came out of the closet carrying his evening clothes like a burden. "That man's weight will kill him one of these days. You'd better start looking around for another agency." He threw the pile of clothes down on the bed.

Kristian tried unsuccessfully to keep the hurt and anger out of his voice. "*Wirklichkeitsfremd.*"

Hansjorg looked up sharply.

"The inner life," Kristian persisted. "*Vita contemplativa.* The private realm. You used to sell me so damn hard on that, remember? You used to talk that up all the time at Dom's. Your humanist thinking. Synthesizing your business life with a kind of...what was it you used to say? Devout solitude?"

"Did I? How pretentious of me."

"I could never talk to anyone but you about things like that, not even Mum."

He watched his father, shocked by the absence of any reaction to her mention.

"That's not what's happening now, is it? What kind of solitude is this, Dad? Where are you?"

Hansjorg stood by the bed, staring down at his clothing.

"Where's my bow tie?"

Kristian watched his father return to the closet, his flat leather slippers slapping his heels.

Like an old man.

Still conditioned by a lifetime of wonder at his father's agelessness, the realization shocked Kristian. But there was something else here, more sudden than advancing age, that was eating him like a parasite, devouring everything that Kristian had loved and respected: his warmth and wisdom and dignity. Something that had overtaken him with terrible speed since Frankfurt.

His blue-white skin still looked flawless when he removed his pajamas, his long limbs were still sinuous, the muscle well defined. He still had a full head of hair. But his posture was altered, tested by whatever invisible weight was bearing down on him.

Hansjorg turned his back and walked, naked, to the burled maple dresser where he kept his underwear and socks. He had small white buttocks. Boyish.

Kristian made a last effort to sound cheerful. "Phil and I are working on the image problem, Dad. Loosen things up a bit. He says we've got a gold-plated dipstick up our corporate butt."

Hansjorg smiled, but not at the vulgarity. He had one eyebrow raised, his eyes glowing darkly, tauntingly.

"An image problem? My goodness Kristian, I've been coping with that for years. Take it from an old soldier! And you know how I dealt with it? Not with silly commercials. Oh no, I made lots of fine speeches about Dorner's romantic past, those glorious victories at Monza and the Nurburg Ring in '37, Erich Dorner coming from nowhere with two home-built cars against the great silver Mercedes and Auto Unions, David and Goliath. Never a word about who was in the stands, of course. Nor about how he steered 300 million Nazi investment Reichmarks away from Porsche, in such favor that You-Know-Who laid the cornerstone of the new, subsidized Frankfurt factory. I understand

Hitler was flanked by Ley and Himmler that day, with an SS Honor Guard, the massed standards of the National Socialist Motorists Corps snapping in the breeze off the Main river! I used to leave all that stuff out, naturally."

Kristian stood, appalled by the malevolent light in his father's eyes, the cruel, sarcastic voice he had never dreamed of hearing.

"Instead I would tell the good American people a lot of reassuring anecdotes about dear Doktor Erich Dorner and how he only wanted to be left alone at his drawing board, reluctant...oh yes...reluctant master of a servile labor force and an unlimited advertising budget courtesy of the Ministry of Propaganda. 'A German car in every garage'...that was Goebbles' rallying cry, you know." He chuckled. "Until the war removed Erich Dorner's serfs to the Russian Front in exchange for cattle trucks of absolute slaves, the Russian prisoners of war, the Jews and gypsies, as production switched from cars to land-mines, armored vehicles, cockpit assemblies for dive bombers. Of course I never made too many speeches about *that*, although dear Erich Dorner couldn't help any of it, could he? He had to do what the SS told him. But I would skip it anyway, to get on to the romantic stuff again, tell them how the Royal Air Force had bombed our little factory to a gutted ruin, how we labored like heroes to rebuild. You remember the live wires and falling bricks, don't you Kit? The famous acorn coffee, performing our own *Wirtschaftswunde*r...our little economic miracle! The little company that could!"

Hansjorg had been dressing all this time, quite casual in the preparation of dickey and cummerbund and braces, matching mother-of-pearl studs and cufflinks, detached wing-collar and black bow tie, handkerchief point and evening shoes.

"So. Let us be heroes again tonight, for the American people at Severance Hall. Let us honor the memory of Doktor Erich Dorner, your godfather, whose name you bear. The man who bargained with Himmler and SS Obergruppenführer Oswald Pohl, at great personal risk, for better working conditions at the plant. Who deceived them

— another Schindler! — to save his sick and exhausted slaves from the Auschwitz shuttle. Shall we?"

Hansjorg Peiper straightened, fully attired, using a pair of boar-bristle brushes to sweep the silver hair flat to his head. He put the brushes down and stood stiff and straight for his son's inspection, smiling slightly.

"So what do you think? A hero for one more night? The dashing young captain from the valiant, doomed Sixth Army, back like a ghost from the frozen mists of Siberia? The *wunderkind* engineer? Shall we go?"

Kristian remained standing by the bed, speechless, looking into his father's grey eyes, clearer now than they had been in many weeks. A cold clarity.

What was in the package?

Not design drawings.

Erich Dorner gave you something else that morning.

Something that has changed you.

But Kristian didn't ask, knowing there would be no answer from his father tonight, perhaps never. It was as though a veil had lifted, only to show Kristian something impassive, immutable, terrible. A warning not to proceed any further, and a sign that Hansjorg Peiper was fully conscious of the transformation in himself.

He was willing his own descent.

CHAPTER 5

THE CLEVELAND ORCHESTRA, WHICH CALLS SEVERANCE HALL ITS home, is one of the world's most respected musical institutions. Hansjorg Peiper had served on its board for forty years, had helped establish its Youth Orchestra, had created scholarships for, and endowed, the music departments of a dozen schools and colleges in the state of Ohio. As CEO of Dorner America, Hansjorg had made his company the single biggest corporate sponsor of classical music in the United States.

Father and son had not spoken during the short car journey from Cleveland Heights to the hall. By now, drinking whiskey in the Members' Lounge before the concert, a growing anger was added to Kristian's shock. He could see his father across the noisy and crowded lounge, amongst his peers and admirers, transformed again, every inch the old Hansjorg Peiper that Cleveland's elite had always venerated: handsome, dignified, wise and accessible, every inch the elder statesman.

He was still a celebrity in the city, still courted by the business press for ideas and comments, by those who desired endorsements or keynote speeches, and by those who knew of his patronage of the arts and approached him on that score. But this was a special night, the suppliants postponed their demands so that Hansjorg was besieged only by well-wishers, including the Senator for Ohio.

"It takes an old friend to see through the mask," Nathan Hutchence said in Kristian's ear while he waited for his change from a round of scotch. "I was hoping tonight would pull him out of himself. Looks convincing, doesn't he?"

Nathan was fifteen years junior to Hansjorg, but they had been neighbors long before the relationship had turned to their mutual advantage. Hansjorg had usually tolerated Nathan's Republican zeal, had gnawed innumerable bones of contention with him. As an only child, Kristian had always been bemused by the Hutchence family of seven, had been to college with Nathan's oldest daughter, where romance had bloomed for one short summer, encouraged by both families. It wasn't the first time, since the Frankfurt trip, that Nathan had voiced his concern.

"I wonder if there isn't something more than Erich Dorner's death here," Nathan said. He took a careful sip of whiskey. "Your father hasn't said anything to you, anything specific?"

Kristian drained his glass. "I couldn't believe it tonight. He was even putting Uncle Erich down."

The senator leaned closer. "In what way?"

"Sarcastic. The way he talked about Erich's achievements, all the things Dad used to venerate. Like he…"

"Yes?"

Kristian shook his head, drained his third scotch in fifteen minutes. "I don't know. It's probably nothing."

"What is?"

"The word *krokus* mean anything to you? I don't mean the flower. At least I don't think I do. The German word *krokus*?"

Nathan was gazing hard at Kristian, his tumbler stalled halfway to his mouth. "I don't believe so. What's the context?"

Kristian shook his head slowly. "Don't worry."

"Come on, something's making you uneasy here. What?"

Kristian fingered his glass.

"Listen," Nathan said. "If you want a disinterested response, you've got the wrong guy. I'm on that spook panel, you know. You have my attention here." He meant the Senate Intelligence Subcommittee. Kristian understood vaguely that he had dealings with the CIA these days.

Briefly, Kristian described the snatches of conversation he had heard through the monitor at Erich Dorner's house, the parcel Manfred had delivered to Erich's room.

"Did you ask your father what was in the parcel?"

"He said mechanical drawings. Suspension designs."

"You have a problem with that?"

Kristian drained his glass as the five-minute bell sounded. "Probably not."

Nathan watched him judiciously for several seconds. "Okay. But keep me posted. You've made me curious here. In the meantime, I think your dad should see someone. Depression...you shouldn't ignore that. Let me know if you want a name. Keep in touch all right?"

"I will. Thanks Nate."

"Call me."

Kristian was on his way to the washroom when he heard his name, turned to see a skinny black girl, no more than fourteen or fifteen, in a party dress, peering at him through large, unfashionable glasses. She was carrying a violin case.

"Excuse me. You're Hansjorg Peiper's son aren't you?"

"That's right. Can I help you?"

"My name's Jenifa Alsop." She spelled it for him. "I wanted to see your father, but he's got so many people talking to him, I didn't...I wanted..." She reached out a hand for Kristian to shake, then proceeded to rush the lines she had obviously rehearsed.

"Your father leant me a violin in the spring and I don't know when he wants it back. I have his number but I keep getting the answering machine or this lady who says she'll give him a message but he never calls back."

Jenifa Alsop faltered, looking for deliverance to where three other teenagers hovered near the door.

"I wrote something for him, some music. It's here in the case."

She was so ingenuous, Kristian made an effort to be pleasant. "That's wonderful. I'm sure he'll be delighted. Go get your friends and we'll buttonhole him."

Jenifa Alsop glanced hesitantly towards the exit, then thrust the violin case into Kristian's arms. "I'll find you at intermission."

"You don't have to give this back now."

"I do, it's a Spidlen, it's worth thousands."

The orchestra had programmed Bach in Hansjorg's honor because he loved Bach above all other composers, as well as new music "*commissioned by a grateful orchestra, dedicated to its greatest friend.*"

Kristian closed his program as the concert master came on to warm applause from the capacity audience. The only empty seat was beside Kristian in the front row, with a silver plaque on the back bearing his father's name. Hansjorg was backstage, waiting in the wings to make his entrance with the conductor.

Always, as an adult, even during the years when his mother was alive and he lived with Melanie, Kristian had taken an annual subscription to the Cleveland Orchestra with his father. Like those Saturday trips to Dom's in his childhood, and the restored cars in his youth, it had been something shared.

However terrifying that specter in the bedroom, Kristian did not feel afraid at this moment. After the presentation, his father would be back to listen as he had always listened...intensely, his eyes gently closed, the translucent lids showing their delicate tracery of capillaries, his long fingers splayed on his knees, his fingertips stirring in sympathy with the players on-stage as they performed the timeless, healing music. Bach would mend his spirit. And at some point, at the least expected moment when the music had taken Kristian also, he would feel the warm cap of his father's hand on his knee.

And afterwards they would talk.

There was an eruption of applause as the Cleveland's general manager, Bert Luciani, appeared from stage right. Kristian looked around, fielding benevolent smiles from the packed rows behind and around him. Most of these people were subscribers, many were friends. A handsome company, and because Kristian knew them, knew how hard most of them had worked for their places here tonight, he did not suffer the illusion that expensive evening dress and premium concert tickets tend to create, of innate privilege and habitual leisure. These people were doers like his father. That was why they grinned and whooped for Bert.

"As you can see from the program," Bert announced, "we've got one of those Dead White German Males for you."

Relaxing laughter. Bert working the room as usual.

"Which makes it something of a change, as well as a great honor, to welcome a very much *alive* White German Male with us this evening — albeit an *American* German." Simmering laughter and a spatter of applause. He waited for silence, until his new expression of sobriety and sincerity had permeated the hall.

"Many of you know Hansjorg Peiper because you are in business. Whether or not you are in *his* business, you are no doubt aware of the many wonderful ways in which he has transformed the lives of thousands of people in this town. We have also felt Hansjorg Peiper's magic touch. Hansjorg and Dorner have been very special friends to us for forty years."

He stopped for applause.

"Our music educators at every level are Cleveland workers, too, and they too have felt his generosity again and again. So have the gifted young players, the virtuosi of tomorrow, whose hard work and glorious talents would never have had the chance to flower without Hansjorg's generosity. Ladies and gentlemen, please welcome Hansjorg Peiper."

Severance Hall was on it feet, thundering its appreciation as

Hansjorg entered stage left beside the conductor. Kristian felt pats on his shoulders, looking to stage right as two children, a boy and girl of nine or ten, marched forward to meet the man of the hour, bearing the Cleveland Orchestra's gift to Hansjorg Peiper — a collection of personalized autographs in a gold frame — Perlman, Stern, Kramer, Mutter, every violin star that had played with the Cleveland during the last five years, a long-term project that Bert Luciani and Kristian had kept secret from Hansjorg.

Luciani, beaming and applauding, stepped once more to the microphone to make the presentation, reading the big names. "On behalf of us all, stars and yet-to-be stars, it is my great privilege to present Hansjorg Peiper with this token of our gratitude. May he remain, an inspiration to us, for many years to come!"

The orchestra struck up "For He's a Jolly Good Fellow" at a bright tempo, which the audience joined in, full throated.

Kristian moved his mouth, but he failed to produce more than a murmur. He was watching his father, who was not smiling, not even at the children handing him the gift. He was perspiring heavily, a sheen on his tall brow.

Other than Kristian, only the children so far seemed to have noticed the expression on Hansjorg's face. They drew back, confused by the lack of acknowledgment, alarmed by what they saw.

The song ended and Bert signaled the audience to be seated. Kristian remained standing at the center of the front row, galvanized by the intense gaze directed towards him. It was an expression Kristian had never before seen or imagined, a look of mortal terror. It made no difference that his father was standing several feet above him on-stage — he seemed to be diminishing, his aristocratic features shedding definition in a kind of instant atrophy. He mumbled something at Kristian, lost under the anxious murmuring of those in the forward rows who were now beginning to register the developments on-stage.

Hansjorg Peiper stiffened suddenly, seemed to be experiencing a spasm of pain although his eyes never left Kristian, not even as Bert

Luciani rushed to his side, managing to take his upper left arm and catch the toppling picture at the same moment.

At last Kristian broke through the spell of his father's gaze. He ran to the stage, taking the narrow steps at stage left three at a time, past the startled bass desk and the cellos until he reached his father.

There was noise and movement all around them, from the orchestra, from Bert and the conductor, both supporting Hansjorg by now, wanting to know if he needed a doctor. Bert went to the microphone to summon one, the conductor turned back to attend the confused orchestra, leaving Hansjorg to his son for a moment.

Only Kristian heard the urgent whisper as Hansjorg clutched him, pinning his son's arms with a painful, trembling grip. He spoke two words of German:

"*Verzeihe mir.*"

Hansjorg tore his hands away from Kristian's arms then turned and pushed past Bert and the conductor.

For several seconds Kristian was rooted to the stage, conscious of nothing but the words his father had spoken.

Hansjorg had gone around the violin section, was now disappearing into the wings stage right. Kristian plunged after him, the musicians recoiling as he blundered through their midst, terrified for their instruments. He caught his foot in a cable of one of the stand lamps, grabbed for the stand as he fell, bringing several others down on top of him then an avalanche of Bach. By the time he had reached the warren that is Severance Hall's backstage area, there was no sign of his father.

By now Kristian had been joined by Luciani and Sheldon Bond, the stage manager, the three of them flinging doors open on dressing and rehearsal and storage rooms, disregarding one door from behind which they could hear scales on a violin as the scheduled soloist — a young local performer — warmed up in virtuosic oblivion.

"You drove him?" demanded Luciani, still holding the framed autographs. "Where did you park? In the reserved section? Maybe he went to the car already. Go check. You'll have to go through the main foyer from here. If you find him, don't leave. We've got half a dozen physicians from the audience, a goddam medical team. Jesus Christ, what a mess. Did he say something to you out there?"

"How do I get to the foyer?"

He went quickly as Bond directed him, crossing the foyer towards the down elevator when a voice from the ticket office window hailed him.

"Are you looking for Mr. Peiper?"

"Where is he?"

"Mr. Bond just called through," the young woman said. "I told him I saw a tall elderly gentleman leave the building in a big hurry a few minutes ago. He looked rather distressed, so I went after him as far as the exit. He got into a cab. Mr. Bond said for me to tell you to wait here if I saw you."

"What kind of cab, you remember?"

"Yellow?"

Kristian rode the elevator down to the underground parking area where he had left the Spyder. Hansjorg and thus Kristian were among the few patrons with parking privileges otherwise reserved for staff and performers. He started the sports car, swung it in a slalom of hard turns, the high compression engine howling in first gear, the performance tires whinnying in the cavernous gallery as he accelerated up the exit ramp and out onto Euclid Avenue.

He changed up, through all the gears and at the red line by the time Deering branched into Cedar Road, east towards Cleveland Heights. The rush hour was over. Up against a full-sized cab, Kristian believed the Dorner Spyder could whittle their seven- or eight-minute lead to the point where he arrived home more or less with his father. Perhaps Bert would have thought of dispatching medical help to the house, in case Hansjorg had anything desperate in mind.

Kristian's dress shirt was sticking to him with a cold glue of sweat as he saw again the look on his father's face and heard the two words.

Could he have misheard against the din?

Misunderstood?

But the image of his father's stricken face, his terrified eyes pinpointing Kristian in the crowd, had dashed any hope of misunderstanding.

Verzeihe mir. Forgive me.

In God's name, for what?

Drive now. Not think.

He drove due south on Lee Road, only a few blocks from home now but he hadn't seen any yellow cab. It wasn't on Canterbury either.

Kristian almost collided with the taxi as he flew into the main driveway, wishing for ABS as the Spyder drifted sideways on the loose gravel. By the time he had corrected it and braked to a stop, the two vehicles where inches apart, bumper to bumper. He saw the cab driver getting out. He rolled down his window and shouted his apology as he backed up, out onto Canterbury Road so that the cab could pass. This was no time for a confrontation.

"Come on asshole," Kristian muttered under his breath. The driver was standing by his vehicle, scowling, denied an exchange of unpleasantness. He drove out at a deliberate crawl, and at last Kristian accelerated towards the house. There was no other vehicle in the driveway, and Kristian found himself hoping now that Bert had neglected to contact any authority. Kristian needed a little time with him, to talk. For Hansjorg to talk. To make it clear what those two words had meant. Time would be limited. There would be press here any minute. TV news. Kristian had seen the local network cameras at the hall.

Kristian tried the front door. It was locked. He had brought his key ring from the ignition, but realized now that the keys for this house were on the ring with his company car keys, in his business suit at the apartment. Going out with his father, he had seen no reason to bring them.

He rang the bell, waited. Knocked. Waited.

He stepped back and looked up. The exterior of the house was floodlit, triggered automatically by sensors at the property line, making it hard to see if there were lights on inside the house.

He went to the side door in the slender hope that he had forgotten to secure it after he had seen Ingrid out with her date. But of course it was locked, because Kristian himself had encoded the burglar alarm in the front hall before they left; the sophisticated system monitored fastenings, including door locks, would have alerted him immediately if the side door deadbolt had not been engaged.

He trotted around to the back of the house. Yes, there was a glow upstairs, it looked like the landing light. He glanced towards the detached garage, reassured at least that all three doors were lowered, and that the gate was closed at the end of the narrow secondary driveway where it ran out of the big corner lot onto Northcliffe Road — what used to be called the tradesmen's entrance. His father was undoubtedly in the house.

The back doors were also locked. He rang anyway, then stood back and called his father's name at the top of his voice.

Kristian now looked about for something with which to break a window, but the immaculate yard offered no suitable instrument, nothing to throw but fine gravel. Only the top sections of the windows tilted open for ventilation, and the flat steel mullions were as good as bars at preventing ingress. Only the livingroom windows at the front of the house opened far enough for him to climb through, and there was a jack handle in the Spyder's trunk to break the glass.

Kristian ran back around the house, almost to the Spyder when he froze.

The front door was wide open.

He could see a running figure at the far end of the driveway, nearly at the road, disappearing into the darkness.

"Dad?"

Kristian was bellowing a second time when he heard a car engine start up on Canterbury. A squeal of tires, then the sound faded into the night.

His hands were trembling as he removed the steel jack handle from his car and walked to the front door, where he called his father again, and now his voice sounded thick with fear. He crossed the hall to the livingroom, hefted the steel bar and threw the door open. He waited a second, then switched on the light and reeled.

Both violin cases were open, half a dozen violins, with their bows, laid out on the floor on a thick canvas sheet, partially rolled up in preparation for being carried away.

Someone — the figure on the driveway? — had been about to steal them.

Kristian ran back into the hall and shouted again, desperately loud: "Dad? Where are you?"

He called again from mid-stairs, again from the landing in front of his mother's photograph. Again, much more quietly as he reached the door of his parents' room.

Kristian saw his father's dress shoes first, protruding from behind the bed.

He was lying on the carpet, slumped back against the night stand. His hair was in his eyes, his mouth hung open. In his rumpled tuxedo, slack-mouthed, he gave Kristian the momentary, ludicrous impression of a society drunk. The telephone receiver was slipping from his fingers, its cord wrapped once around his torso.

The wound that had killed him was to the back of his head, the bloodstain crawling around his white wing collar.

Kristian fumbled for the telephone base that Hansjorg had dragged off the night stand. The LCD printout had recorded a number that he had started to dial before he was interrupted. He had begun a long distance call, the number 1 and then an area code, 416.

Kristian didn't move from his side even as the ambulance team banged into the hallway below. He had been trying with all his might to give some thought as to how it might have happened, how the man he had seen at the end of the driveway could have gained entrance without tripping the alarm. But his father's blood was a powerful, irresistible distraction, the way it had crept around his snow white collar, like a blush, until now just one tiny point of white was left, at the tip of one wing.

Plip.

All red. A red collar.

One of the paramedics had red hair. Permed-looking. He too seemed interested in the blood, and especially in Kristian's jack handle.

CHAPTER 6

GRETA OCCUPIED THE GROUND FLOOR OF A TWO-HUNDRED-YEAR-old house at 15 Löwengasse, a one-way street off Berger Strasse, the ancient road that had bisected Bornheim since it was a separate village. Even now it was a reluctant part of Frankfurt, the city jealous of its concentration of cobbled streets and rowdy half-timbered inns, monopolized by students now that Sachsenhausen was on the tourist track.

It was tranquil on summer evenings with the universities out; with the kitchen window open, Greta could hear the parting gossip of twilight birds in the linden trees on Löwengasse; inside there was the scrape of a chair from upstairs in Herr Kraus's, the Hausmeister's, apartment; close at hand, the complaining hum of the stove clock struggling towards 8:30 p.m., the babble of chamomile tea, Greta pouring while Regine dealt photographs onto the small table.

"This year you're going to say yes. Next summer you'll be lining up teaching jobs and you won't have time."

Tall and fair like her brother, but slightly stooped. Greta wondered whether it was from dealing with children all day.

She passed a photograph of a square tower on a hill overlooking the Mediterranean, ancient and unadorned except for three small unglazed windows in the upper levels, revealing the walls' massive thickness. "The people from the village used to take refuge in the tower when pirates attacked."

"So you'll be safe from Corsican separatists."

"No sweat. They like Germans if only because the French don't. Distinct change of attitude in the village when they found out Jean Pierre was German Swiss."

"What's it like inside?"

"A lot of work: two of the floors are rotten, there's no electricity, but it's livable while we chip away at it." She took a sip of chamomile tea. "We would appreciate your company and your labor."

Greta laughed. "At least you're honest."

"Mornings. Afternoons and evenings you can do what you like. And I promise you won't have to deal with the kids unless you want to. Plus free authentic teacher wisdom, as much as you can stomach."

Greta warmed her hands around her mug. "I need some now. I'm terrified I'm doing the wrong thing."

"You probably are. They'll break your heart, if you can find a job."

"Thanks a lot."

"And you have no real control. Unless you teach in a boarding school, you do what little you can but then they go home. Ninety percent of mine are immigrants, drifting between two cultures, belonging to neither. I'm damage control, that's all."

"I don't want to teach rich kids."

"Then start getting some calluses. You look for college potential, you get dope and concealed weapons and a rage to be ignorant. And they're disgusting to look at — ritually mutilated flesh, cheap jewelry, bad posture."

Greta had been to the inner city school where Regine was vice-principal. She knew Regine's unconditional devotion to her students. It must run in the family, she thought — Ulrich had the same high-minded, unswerving dedication to his police work.

"Will Uli come to Corsica?"

"He said no. I was disappointed. He's got a month's vacation time he's never used."

"When did you speak to him?"

"Earlier this evening. He certainly looks like he could use a holiday. I'm worried about him, Grets. He's lost weight, he looks... preoccupied. You have to ask him things twice, he's not listening."

"You saw him this evening?"

"He's staying with us till Sunday night."

"I didn't know he was in town."

Regine frowned slightly. "When did you last see him?"

Greta felt a prickle of indignation. "Not since I had dinner with him at the Charlot a few weeks ago. Is he here for the SG?"

"I assume so. If it's something else, he hasn't told us. He hasn't been very communicative lately."

Regine's hand moved a few inches across the table towards Greta's before she withdrew it, folded her arms. "Tonight after dinner he just announced that he was going out, walked out of the front door. I got mad, demanded to know where he was going, told him he was abusing our hospitality. I shouldn't have said that."

"Where was he going?"

"A club. He seemed depressed. I've never known him like this." Her long white fingers gripped her arms, her stoop increasing. "I know the kind of places he goes to. I've always tried to be broadminded about it, but that doesn't stop the worry. I know what they do. It's pretty much a free for all, isn't it."

"Is that what you're worried about?"

Neither of them had to spell it out. Ulrich's sister lowered her gaze.

"Regine, for Christ's sake Uli would tell you if he was sick. He would tell *me*. He's not stupid, or suicidal. Half the time he spends in clubs he's networking, he uses the scene, keeps his ear to the street."

"I wish he'd get into a relationship."

"He's in one, with the SG. His work hardly allows much opportunity for domestic bliss."

"Maybe it's getting to him," Regine said dejectedly. "Having to be two people all the time. Leading two lives."

"I disagree. He's always been accepted on the force for what he is — a committed cop, far more than I ever was. It's some achievement to feel that way after this long. I don't think Ulrich will ever burn out."

Regine gave her a tight smile of thanks, reached over and squeezed her hand before she stood and gathered the photographs. "Why don't you come over tonight, watch a movie? Jean Pierre's got a guy over from his office, doing something on the computer. He's cute. Seems smart. Earns a paycheck."

Greta tilted her head impatiently. "Thank you Regine, I'll tell you when I need a dating service. I'm enjoying being on my own."

"Bullshit. You know, that's the only real regret I have about Ulrich being gay — you two would have been great together."

Greta smiled. "We are great together."

"I mean great great. Haven't you met *anyone* since Andreas?" Regine's instincts were well honed: she immediately read Greta's hesitation, and the gloomy look that followed. "Well?"

"I met a guy."

"And?"

"It didn't work out. That's all."

"Come on."

"I blew it."

"That's hard to believe; a gorgeous, smart, kind-hearted woman like you."

"Yeah."

"I want the lowdown."

"Sometime. Not tonight."

Regine shrugged. "Okay." She stood. "You know where I live." She went ahead towards the front door, paused by the coffee table in the livingroom where a stack of library books threatened to topple onto the floor. She tilted her head to scan the spines.

"Been doing some reading?"

"I'm taking them back for Herr Kraus." Greta fought to stem the tide of colour to her face. "He's not very mobile these days. He's seventy-something."

Regine read aloud: "*The Rise of the Right, Fascism in the Nineties, The New Nazis.* God, is he pro or con?"

"Con, of course. You think I'd do his fetching and carrying otherwise? He's a sweetheart."

"That's what Himmler's family said. What did Herr Kraus do in the war?"

"Give me a break. He's always reading politics. Last month it was China."

Regine straightened and looked around the small livingroom. Greta had kept the budget Scandinavian furniture she had bought with Ulrich when they first moved in, the apartment almost unchanged in the intervening years, reflecting Andreas's disinterest, her own busy career with little free time.

"It's probably time to move, Grets. New career, new place. How long have you been here, ten years?"

"Eight. Five with Uli, three with Andreas."

Regine sniffed. "Those three alone justify a clean slate. Get rid of those bloody cats for a start."

Andreas's only legacy, apart from the crack in Greta's self-confidence — how could she have been so *wrong*? — were six gaudy plaster cats, four feet tall with bright wire whiskers, mutely articulate.

They had been the prototypes, done when he still lived here (rent-free) as a revenge against what he perceived as an art scene conspiracy, that far more than any serious attempt to make money. Greta had come to loathe their cocked insolence but she kept them for a hair shirt, a reminder to beware of handsome strays with silver tongues and a little talent. And her growing antipathy towards the cats was a chart of her recovery rate, the daily lessening of guilt for ditching their creator, tired of propping Andreas up when he couldn't get a show, or when the critics ignored his sculpture. Tired of playing hunt-the-bottle using the rules she had learned from her parents.

Greta was wise to herself, knew pretty much why she had been attracted to Andreas: for all that she loved Ulrich, she had worried that he was a substitute for a man of her own, a life partner, a prospective father for her future children. Dark, hirsute, and in the beginning at least, a passionate lover, Andreas had been a reaction to that worry. He was the antithesis of Ulrich in every way — slovenly, disorganized, creative, self-destructive, without conscience. Uli had always reminded Greta too much of herself, their shared need for control, the reason they had chosen police work. But in the end Andreas had inflamed her controlling instinct as his true, dark colors emerged, the downward, spiraling pattern of his life's design. She had tried to pull him up, pull him back, but he had snapped the line.

Greta fished the chamomile teabags out of the pot and dumped them in the compost bucket. The composter in the tiny backyard had been pre-Andreas, Uli's innovation along with a vegetarian diet (short-lived in Greta's case) and an end to the *Zeitung* hard copies that thumped through the letterbox every morning in favor of environmentally friendly and non-littering Internet news. Andreas sober could barely turn a computer on, but Greta had maintained the Internet habit, using it both as a handy refuge from Andreas and a quick way to catch up with the day's events when she came home from Wiesbaden.

She logged on, cursing the old 486's slowness, knowing she would have to abandon plans for a new computer with tuition to pay and no salary for at least a year. The use of a BKA car and her Pentium laptop were the only things she missed about Wiesbaden, where Tors had proved himself a fastidious quartermaster: the computer, the spare magazine for her Sig, everything down to the last staple in her desk drawer had to be accounted for and returned. Even her memory had been inventoried in an exhausting period of debriefing, conducted with chilly efficiency, as though leaving the BKA under any circumstances was a disloyal, if not treasonable, act.

The PC's hard drive at last plowed its way through to the *Zeitung*'s home page, the evening edition. Greta began to browse through the day's top stories, although her attention was not fully focused, knowing that her confidence with Regine had been a front. Regine had echoed Greta's own fear for Uli, held in abeyance since that night at the Charlot by the argument that his state of mind — and health — were the result of job stress, notoriously high in the SG.

She clicked from domestic to world news on the *Zeitung*'s home page: a priest murdered in Rwanda, UNICEF was requesting a consumer boycott to fight child labor, a new scandal was brewing in the British royal family.

Greta clicked *BACK* to her browser, the *Zeitung* gone before the name registered, like the afterimage of light.

She went forward two pages and there it was.

Peiper.

A prominent American businessman with strong ties to Germany had been killed in his home in Cleveland, Ohio.

Hansjorg Peiper, the former CEO of Dorner America, had been murdered last night, Friday night, at approximately 8:30 p.m. Eastern Standard Time.

Greta strained towards the screen, her hand growing slippery around the mouse.

He had returned home unexpectedly early from a concert. He had surprised an intruder in his house, had been fatally injured in the ensuing struggle. The authorities had been summoned moments after his death by his son, Kristian Peiper, who was assisting police.

Kristian's father.

Kristian.

Even now, weeks later, the sight of his name caused a release of adrenaline, an upheaval. There was a letter to him one click away on the word processor, unsent owing to the dictates of BKA security.

His pain. Kristian had been so close to his father.

"Assisting police?" She recognized that phrase from her own years on the force, with all its loaded ambiguity.

Uli had told her nothing more about the Dorner investigation, beyond the fact that it was a K44 matter, but that spark had ignited a blaze of curiosity such that by now, after several weeks of intense reading (including the books on the livingroom table), Greta had her own theory about Bonn's interest in the Dorner company. She was eager to test it on Ulrich.

Was Hansjorg Peiper's death connected to that investigation?

And what, as she had asked herself countless times, had been their interest in his son?

Ulrich knew.

Frankfurt's red-light district runs out from the Hauptbahnhof, streets like Nidda, Kaiser, Elbe and Mosel forming the warp and weft of a spider's web. The city is too cosmopolitan, too much in flux to ever become mired in civic guilt, wears indecency on its sleeve although it has never, like Cologne or Berlin, become an international center for the gay subculture, for the fetish bars with active backrooms and a golden shower night once a week. Such places exist, but the Mineshaft, despite the hard-core tone of its name, was more typically Frankfurt in that it catered to the businessman on a flying visit, no time to cruise but crisp airport deutsche marks for an escort.

It was the fifth club Greta tried, a dark shaft descending three levels below the street with a circular dance floor at the bottom. Raw steel balconies and stairways and banks of video monitors, Industrial Post Modern from the early eighties and showing its age. The Mineshaft had long been abandoned by the straight club scene to which it had originally catered, a gay fixture for as long as Greta could remember.

Vice was not in the BKA's jurisdiction, but Ulrich and Otto Volk had both plied these waters in the Schutz just as Greta had patrolled the train station, trawling in plainclothes for underage "Natashas" with fake ID. Two Arab boys in suits and ties dancing tonight with a middle-aged Arab might have been borderline, but the Eurasian rubbing shoulders with Ulrich at a second level balcony table was probably twenty.

The club was quiet at this early hour, which made it easy to spot them. Greta paused on the stairs above, in shadow, long enough to see the Eurasian reach into an ice bucket and pour into both glasses on the table — Uli drinking champagne? — filling his own glass first, tipping the bottle to empty it then looking around the mezzanine for a waiter.

No, perhaps not a waiter, because now the boy produced a fold of paper from his jacket pocket, opened it, took another furtive look around before dipping his head to the wrap and licking. He tipped the remaining contents into his right palm, was offering it to Ulrich when he became aware of Greta behind him.

"Mind if I join you?"

The Eurasian's hand slipped under the table. If Uli was surprised, he didn't show it. He looked numb.

"What are you doing here?"

"Shouldn't I be asking you that?" Greta smiled icily at the boy. "Something in a wrap? Let's see...KitKat?"

Ketamine was a reasonable assumption: a powerful anesthetic used by vets on farm animals, it was a current fad in Frankfurt clubs, usually licked from the wrap rather than snorted or injected into muscle. Ketamine was a potential heart-stopper, dissociative, dangerous. She reached down and took hold of the boy's lapel, heard a seam stutter as she pulled him smoothly out of his chair.

"Let him go Greta."

There was no protest or resistance from the Eurasian. He had a handsome physique beneath the dandy suit but he was passive under the Ketamine.

"Franz is all right," Ulrich said. "We go back."

"She a cop?" the boy slurred.

"That's right, Franz," Greta lied. "And I go back too, far enough to know that our friend here doesn't drink nor is he interested in your fucking cow powder. Disappear, Franz. Before I arrest you."

He looked at Ulrich, who nodded. Franz shrugged, bent down and kissed Uli lightly on both cheeks, whispered something in his ear then glided to the stairs with no apparent loss of dignity. Greta thought of a snake that had shed, revealing an identically smooth, pretty skin underneath.

"He's a whore, isn't he."

"You're telling me. Bisexual, makes twice as much that way. You mustn't underestimate him, he's almost as smart as you."

"But a lot prettier."

"I wouldn't say so. Just more my type."

She took a seat opposite her friend. "I bet he left you with the bill."

Uli gave her a hollow, red-eyed stare. "Did you just come here to ruin my evening?"

"I need you to talk to me."

"I'm drinking champagne."

"I noticed."

"Want some?"

"The bottle's empty."

"I'll order another."

"I saw Regine tonight."

"She'd love you to go to Corsica."

"She's worried about you. So am I. You and I had a conversation over dinner a few weeks ago. Dorner...K44. Since then you've been avoiding me, you look like shit and you're drinking for the first time in years. What's going on?"

He looked away, down towards the dance floor where a semi-circular wall of monitors ran the videos that went with the dance music, the usual flickering, mechanical formulae.

"You can't talk to anyone else, can you Ulrich?"

He looked at her defiantly. "There's nothing to talk about. The investigation's been terminated. A non-investigation, and it's still dangerous. Worst of both worlds. I meant what I said in the Charlot: stick with ice cream."

"Or KitKat? That's dangerous too."

"I didn't do any."

"Good, so you're coherent." She leaned closer. "A little background, Uli. Anything. Just tell me why Dorner was a K44 matter?"

"I have to go to the washroom." Ulrich made to stand up but she caught his arm. "Why? Was Dorner funding the DNV?"

Ulrich couldn't hide his surprise this time. After the weeks of puzzling it out, Greta couldn't resist a tiny smile of gratification.

"The Deutsche Nazional Volkspartei. Unconstitutional, illegal since 1982. Terrorist attacks on six guest-worker hostels this year, two government installations, several private citizens. A dozen deaths including the chief executive of the Commerzbank, assassinated in an armored Mercedes last March. So far so good?"

Uli waited and watched.

"A neo-Nazi party with an insatiable appetite for hatred, top of K44's list, committed to rebuilding a militarized, fully re-armed fascist state. Expanding its ideology, cultivating fascist elements anywhere it can find them: in the former Soviet Union, in the Balkans, on the Net. I've been into the DNV website. Camouflaged, a little hard to find, like you're going down into the Internet sub-basement. Like putting your head into a toilet."

Ulrich reclined, clasped his fingers behind his blond head. "I'm supposed to be impressed? You could read the tabloids and know any of that. You've said nothing that would warrant K44's interest in Dorner."

"Dorner's aerospace division."

Greta stared at him until his hard stubbornness had dissolved into grudging approbation. He smiled without humor. "You, me, Otto: I always said you were the smart one."

"I'm a worker. Grentz and Tors gave me nothing, you tossed me half a wishbone, so I researched on my own. Dorner's aerospace division has been collapsing since Unification, over empty order books.

Junia Dorner's bankrolling the DNV because she sees them as agents for potential weapons markets."

"Seems obvious for the first time in months. You should be in charge of the BKA, not leaving us."

"But you're saying the investigation's been shut down."

"Why do you think I'm celebrating?"

"You don't look happy. Why was it shut down?"

"That's obvious too, isn't it?"

"Junia Dorner has friends. Who?"

"You're not eating your ice cream."

"Ice cream's for kids."

"This is poison."

"Who are Junia's friend's? K44?"

No reaction.

"Higher?"

"Out of sight, out of mind: that should perfectly describe your profile with your former employers at this point." He reached across for Franz's champagne glass and drained it. "I hope for their sake there aren't any secretive kids in your classroom."

"Who shut down the Dorner investigation, Ulrich? Who's protecting them? The SG? BKA command?"

"If all this is such fun for you, why did you quit?"

There was only one more level to go in the hierarchy of the Federal Police, which was cabinet level.

"*Beck?*"

Julius Beck was Germany's interior minister. Greta's voice dropped to an appropriate whisper. "Iron Fist is covering up her funding of the DNV?"

Ulrich shut his eyes for a long moment. When he opened them, all prevarication was gone. She saw fear and relief, and a glimmer of excitement. "Three hundred thousand auto sector jobs, Greta. Guaranteed government loans to Dorner, 4 billion marks. The Kondor launch is Junia's last chance to pay them back. Think about it."

"A government cover-up."

He thrust angrily towards her. "It's not even *about* the DNV any more! There's something in Bonn, in the forensic lab. It came to light by accident, in the original investigation."

"What?"

His voice grew hushed. "Far older than the DNV. Unimaginable..."

Greta coaxed him with stubborn silence but she felt him slipping.

"Uli? What's in your lab?"

"This is insanity." He got up from the table.

"What about Hansjorg Peiper?"

His eyes flashed. "What about him?"

"Is that why he died?"

Ulrich blinked once. "I'm going now."

"Talk to me. Was he killed because of something in your lab?"

He collided with the ice bucket as he turned, both of them watched it rock back and forth on its elegant silver stand, his arm a long blur as he smashed it aside, ice cubes like a meteor shower glittering through the Mineshaft's dark space, cascading across the floor. He slipped on a cube as he made for the stairs, jerking to regain his balance, an awkward, ugly spasm.

"Uli!"

Ultraviolet went on all over the club signaling that night time, prime time, had begun. The light blackened Ulrich's face as he turned at the foot of the stairs.

"Go to Corsica. I'll pay your airfare. The tower's got thick walls. You should learn to appreciate thick walls."

CHAPTER 7

Like Frankfurt on the Main, Cleveland Ohio is a city divided by a river, another city of bridges — a museum of bridges. Sleek, functioning marvels of engineering or rusting anachronisms, they are an ever present symbol of a society dependent on transportation, over its bridges and under them, by rail and road and the Cuyahoga, to and from the terminal, eutrophic waters of Lake Erie.

The lake was a complex, striated grey this afternoon, under a fine rain nine days after Hansjorg Peiper's death. Still Kristian walked the three blocks to the Justice Center in the Mall, which is what Clevelanders call the heart of their city.

Cleveland Police Headquarters occupies nine floors of a building that appears to have little to do with heart. A tough, granite-clad twenty-three–story tower, its combative stance is emphasized rather than moderated by the sinuous Noguchi sculpture in the forecourt. Kristian had been summoned to the sixth floor where the aseptic atmosphere contrasted dispiritingly with the homely clutter of the Cuyahoga Sheriff's Department, where a Lieutenant Deems had conducted the first two interviews.

Deems had been a rumpled, middle-aged chain-smoker wearing a friendship bracelet woven by his granddaughter and an expression of permanent discomfort. Kristian had liked him, pitying him his foot-sloggers Wallabies and his hemorrhoids, or whatever affliction caused him to hover so lightly in his chair that it gave an impression of shyness.

Kristian had been expecting a change in the investigation — the publicity surrounding his father's death had reminded him of his father's stature in Cleveland. He had been waiting for matters to move to the corner office, but not like the one he found himself in this afternoon, having declined coffee from a clerk who had shown him in and then left him alone.

The office was empty, unassigned or in transition between occupants, devoid of any personal touch except for a National Rifle Association membership certificate framed on the wall, and an expensive-looking, large-scale model of a Gatling gun on the floor beside the desk, pointing at the visitor chair.

Kristian moved the chair and waited for twenty-five minutes in the big empty room. The more his resentment grew, the more he missed Deems and his bowling trophies and his rubber overshoes collapsing where he'd left them in March, on a snowmelt-stain by a hat rack.

He was about to go and complain when the door opened. Kristian saw a man similar to Deems in age and weight but much fitter, in a good suit that draped nicely over a carefully maintained physique. His voice, like the proffered hand, was big and assured.

"Sorry you had to sit around, Mr. Peiper. Did they get you a coffee?"

"It's all right."

He went to the desk. "My name is Callaghan. I'm on loan here for a day or two, from the Bureau, not worth bringing a lot of clutter." He saw Kristian glance at the Gatling gun. "Drove up from Quantico this time, bought it on the way. Special ordered it six months ago. Calibrated for .22, performs exactly like the real thing. You have to keep reloading, but that's the fun of a Gatling, right?"

His smile grew a shade broader. "I can see you're not a shooting man, Mr. Peiper." He had pale grey eyes that drifted like smoke. "You wouldn't hurt a fly and I would. I confess, I got fairly excited, fella I bought the Gatling off told me he's developing a miniature weapon for nailing houseflies on the wall. Imagine. Money's mainly in the scope of course...blow up a bluebottle big as a prime buck, big enough you could quarter it. CO_2 behind a projectile like the end of a pin but accurate as a Remington 700-40XB. Whole new way to hunt!"

For a brief second his drifting eyes lingered, long enough to reveal a formidable reserve of energy and intelligence.

"I won't attempt to be solemn, Mr. Peiper, or to console you. I didn't know your father but I assure you that I intend to leave no avenue unexplored in this investigation."

Kristian felt no assurance, only a prolonged chill from the drifting grey eyes. Callaghan landed in the desk chair. He swung his feet up onto the desk and crossed his solid ankles. He was wearing expensive Italian shoes with stitched leather soles. He had brought no notes, no files.

"To that end I would first like to ask about your father's security system. Trips on the doors and windows of course, motion detectors, every activity within the system monitored by Guardian Security here in Cleveland. That right?"

"Yes."

"Guardian records everything on their mainframe, including keypad activity." Callaghan saw Kristian frown. He smiled faintly. "I realize you've already covered this with Lieutenant Deems, but us law enforcement types, we're pack animals, Mr. Peiper: all that training, all our prescribed rules of behavior. It's a dog's life, so you'll have to let me stake out my territory a little bit here. Dominant male, that kind of thing?"

Kristian thought he could feel his nape hair stir. His joints contracted, compressing him.

"Guardian's computer tells us that the alarm system at Canterbury Road was armed at 7:13 p.m."

"Yes. We armed the system before we left for the concert hall."

"Who entered the keypad code, you or your father?"

"I did."

"So you knew the code."

"Of course. It's my home."

"The printout from Guardian shows that the code was entered again at exactly 8:05 to disarm the system, while you and your father were still at Severance Hall. In other words, whoever entered the house at 8:05, whoever it was that your father discovered in the act of violating his home...this individual knew the security code. Which means he learned it. Our question has to be from whom? Who else knew it besides you, Mr. Peiper? Your father's housekeeper, Ingrid Koch knew it."

Kristian tried to keep his voice neutral. "She's been with the family since before I was born."

"But her personal life has changed in the last while. I understand she's planning to get married."

Kristian didn't try to hide his surprise.

"You didn't know?" Callaghan smiled. "Fancy that. And I've only been in town a couple of days!"

"I knew she was dating someone."

"You met him?"

"Couple of times."

"But you're surprised to hear of their plans."

"I can understand. Ingrid must have felt it inappropriate to share her good news right now. I've spent considerable time with her since that night. She is hardly less affected than I am. My parents were her life for nearly fifty years."

"But life *is* surprising, isn't it Mr. Peiper?" The eyes lingered. "After twenty-five years with the Bureau I still find it unwise to presume anything about anybody."

"Why don't you focus on the security company if you want to know whether someone leaked the code?"

Callaghan shook his head. "We already have. Guardian is a blue chip outfit, their monitors and clerical staff are bonded and screened...rigorously enough that they actually have the Cleveland Police Department contract." A pale smile. "They are the guardians of this very building, Mr. Peiper. What about Wendel Storey?"

It was impossible now for Kristian to hide his antipathy towards Callaghan. "What I said about Ingrid goes double for Wendel. He would have laid down his life to protect my father."

"Bit simple is he?"

Kristian forced himself to remain calm. "He's dyslexic. If you don't know the difference between simple and dyslexic, I suggest you read up."

"Okay let's talk about your father. Born in Mainz, State of Hesse, in 1918, grew up in Frankfurt. Engineering degree from Heidelberg, hired by Erich Dorner in 1945. As an engineer?"

Whatever Callaghan was trying to achieve, psychologically, Kristian resolved not to help him. He answered calmly: "Yes, but Dorner was strategically bombed in the war. For the first two years they spent more time clearing rubble than engineering cars. The few units they did turn out were mostly bartered on the black market for machine parts. And food."

"You make them sound almost heroic."

"Do I? I'm proud of my father."

"Proud of the fact that two-thirds of Erich Dorner's work force during the war consisted of slave labor?"

Kristian's voice grew quiet with controlled anger. "This had better be leading somewhere."

"As long as the possibility of conspiracy exists in your father's death, we have to ask ourselves who his enemies were, don't you think?"

"My father had no enemies."

"Really? No blots on his record, none at all?"

"What do you mean?"

"No unpleasantness that might have made him an enemy or enemies?"

"Enemies? My father was the best friend this town ever had. He knew his workers, he knew their kids' names and their brand of smokes. He abolished the time clock, put them on the honor system, gave them pride."

Kristian looked with cold, smiling hatred at Callaghan's impassive face. "I think I see what you're after, Agent Callaghan. By the way, is that what you are?"

"That'll do."

"Then at least get your facts straight. First of all, Erich Dorner was forced by the SS to use slaves. He treated them no differently than his paid workers in spite of SS interference. He risked his own neck to keep them from the trains."

"Aah."

"Secondly, as you've already mentioned, my father did not join the company until 1945...*after* the war. If this is supposed to be the 'unpleasantness' you referred to, you'd better speculate elsewhere."

"What *did* he do during the war?"

"Deems knows. Didn't his file tell you or are you still pissing on his lamp post?"

Callaghan smiled appreciatively. "He was in the *Wehrmacht*?"

Kristian leaned back in his chair. "Good accent. Very good. Know a bit about World War II do you?"

"I've done a little reading."

"Really. What have you read? The whole *Time Life* set, all however many volumes? Watched "The World at War," did you, with Walter Cronkite? I guess you know all about Stalingrad, then."

Callaghan folded his big arms. "Say whatever you want to say."

"I don't want to say anything to you, but I obviously need to. The Sixth Army had twenty-nine thousand wounded without any dressings or drugs when their defense collapsed. They were starving and frost-bitten. For two days they still could have broken through the Russian cordon and joined up with the rescue force, but Hitler wouldn't give the order. Two hundred and eighty-five thousand men in the Sixth, five thousand of them made it back from Siberian POW camps after the war. Do the arithmetic, Agent Callaghan. That was the only 'unpleasantness' of my father's war."

Callaghan smiled at his expensive shoes. "The Russians lost 20 million Mr. Peiper. Up against soldiers of your father's army and equipment manufactured by companies like Dorner. But all right, let's change the subject. What about the Brazilian period? In 1952 he went to Rio de Janeiro to organize Dorner Brazil?"

Kristian sat straight up. "That's right, Agent Callaghan: reunited at last with all those German 'businessmen' spirited out through *Die Spinne* or was it *Odessa*, with SS tattoos in their armpits." Kristian stood, turned silently and walked to the door.

"Are you really this sensitive?"

Kristian kept going across the big empty office. "I listened to enough of this shit in grade school. My uncle was Heinrich Himmler, didn't you know that?"

"Be sure and let me know when you're feeling cooperative. I understand you're moving back to Canterbury Road?"

"Temporarily. For Ingrid's sake more than anything."

"How considerate. I would ask you to please inform this office if you're planning any other movement, for instance if you intend to leave the country."

The innuendo brought Kristian up short. He turned in the doorway. "Why?"

"We may need to reach you for any number of reasons. Surely you wish to be of maximum assistance in the investigation. Your father was murdered nine days ago."

But there was more. Callaghan's tone of voice made it perfectly clear. Kristian's smile was bemused. "Are you telling me I'm a suspect here?"

Callaghan said nothing. His eyes meandered to a standstill, trained unblinkingly on Kristian's face.

Kristian leaned against the door frame in astonishment. "Because I knew the security code for my father's house?"

"I have been given information gathered by Lieutenant Deems. I am obliged to consider it."

"What information?"

"Statements from a number of patrons in the Members' Lounge at Severance Hall before the concert that night, people who knew you and your father well."

Kristian narrowed his eyes. "Statements?"

"That there was an unusually cold and strained atmosphere between the two of you. That you seemed angry with your father, that you were drinking heavily, again unusual for you. The barman reported that you consumed three whiskeys in a space of fifteen minutes. Though you had driven to the concert hall together, I understand your father left without you. The driver who took him home stated that his cab almost collided with your sports car in the driveway at Canterbury Road, you were in such furious pursuit…"

"*Pursuit*? Kristian shouted. "I wanted to see my father! I was worried, god damn you!"

"Twenty minutes elapsed between the time the cab driver left his house and the time you called the authorities. You reported having seen a man running from the house, but the police found no footprints."

"What are you talking about? You already *know* why: the ambulance, police cars, media…they churned up the gravel…"

"Another fact is that you are in the midst of an expensive divorce."

"I'm sorry?"

"Your father was never particularly openhanded towards you, was he?"

"I don't believe this. What's happening?"

"I'm simply stating facts."

"You bastard! I never *asked* my father for money. He knew I didn't want his support like that. I make a good salary, Callaghan, four times yours."

"That may well be, Mr. Peiper, but you will not actually become a millionaire until your father's will is executed at which time, as you know, you will be one more than fifty times over."

For a moment Kristian stood motionless in the doorway, his dis-belief so profound he could only smile.

Then it faded.

"You want something fifty times over, Agent Callaghan? Fuck you. FUCK you!"

Kristian went back to Old River Road, to Lake Erie.

He had spent his whole life beside the lake, the earth's curve visible in its span. How come the water didn't roll off the earth, he had wondered as a child, pouring across the city to carry everything away? The same curve hid Ontario on the far shore, which allowed him to imagine distant places where sun-baked cities thrust minarets and jeweled palaces into cloudless skies, where cannibals jigged on hot sand beaches and trade winds stirred the palms.

As he grew older, Kristian never quite let go of the fantasy, realizing that it held a grain of truth since Cleveland was connected to the Atlantic and the rest of the world, albeit artificially, via the Welland Canal and the St. Lawrence Seaway. As an adolescent, that knowledge was a comfort, the idea that the door of his gilded cage was always open.

Kristian arranged his passage up the Welland on a Greek tanker the summer before college, across Lake Ontario and along the St. Lawrence to the ocean. In Europe he had used a Eurail pass or hitch-hiked when he could have picked up a car free of charge from any Dorner dealership on the continent.

For a while it had been necessary for him to deny Hansjorg's high culture along with his career, a time to fall out of taverns with beer and rock and roll running through him, pissing Miller into the snow to rewrite his future against all expectation of conformity. But he never stopped loving his father, or respecting him, knowing it was reciprocated. He had never felt like those of his friends with exiled fathers — diminished men, their emotions stunted by their work, whether powerless in it or addicted to it, violent or overindulgent in their need to keep control at home.

He respected the man who had known Stalingrad and the sudden, complete loss of his family in Frankfurt. Events that might have broken or poisoned other men had lit a flame in Hansjorg, a pure fire to cleanse the past and light a new life. It had lit and warmed Kristian's life, too, and the lives of ten thousand workers at Dorner Cleveland.

In their hearts, father and son had never stopped going up to Dom's.

The tears had been easy in the last ten days, though he kept them private, resolute in his duties: the difficult communications with family and friends and a greedy press, the funeral arrangements complicated by security considerations since the Unitarian ceremony was attended by all three Tri-State senators including Hansjorg's old friend Nathan Hutchence. Dietrich Kamp had come from Germany, the computer software billionaire and media celebrity whose processor formed a vital part of the Kondor, who had been Hansjorg's lifelong friend. Amidst so much public grief, Kristian had concealed his anger, even from himself, until this afternoon.

He turned away from the apartment window and the futile frustration of watching a steel freighter on the horizon, slow as a minutehand as it plied east from Toledo. The steel industry had vanished from Cleveland, a dying city when Hansjorg had stepped into the breech. Cleveland would remember Hansjorg Peiper with the honor due him, and it would be extended to his son. Cleveland would run a cretin like Callaghan out of town on a rail.

He got a beer from the fridge and drank half of it at a single tilt, his teeth clamped on the neck of the bottle. He paused for breath, his head hanging, blind with sudden rage until he heard the bottle explode and saw the mess on his kitchen wall and floor.

There was a message on the answering machine from Nathan Hutchence. How was he? Would he call tonight after 9:30?

He had just got off a plane from Washington when Kristian called back, was sitting down to a late supper with his wife.

"I'm sorry Nathan. I'll call back."

"I hear you were down at the Justice Center this afternoon. How did it go?"

"I saw an FBI agent called Callaghan. I didn't like what he was inferring."

"What was that?"

As briefly as he could, Kristian outlined the course of Callaghan's interview, his own parting outburst.

"I'd probably have punched his face for him," Hutchence said. "I'm shocked beyond words, Kris. Don't you worry, I'm going to make it my personal business to see that the Cuyahoga Sheriff's Department or the FBI hangs, draws and quarters this redneck asshole. Are you all right? Why don't you come on over. I'll get Sarah to throw a plate in the oven."

"Thanks, but there's a bunch of stuff I need to look at here, been piling up the last few days."

"Sure?"

"Yeah, thanks. I'm fine. Better for talking."

"Oh, one thing: at Severance Hall, that terrible night...you told me about a conversation you'd accidentally overheard between your father and Erich Dorner, that a parcel changed hands. You asked me about the German word *krokus*."

Kristian was picking up an almost studied casualness in the senator's tone, or else he was imagining it.

"I'm making inquiries but nothing's turned up yet...I'm afraid the intelligence community is awash in mysteries, if indeed *krokus* falls within this sphere."

"Thank you Nate."

"Nothing new from your end?"

"So far, no."

"And one other thing: did your father say anything to you on the stage that night? Bert Luciani thought he saw...well he wasn't sure."

Kristian hesitated only a moment. "No. He didn't say anything to me. The last words between us were in the car on the way to the concert. Nothing important, Nathan."

Kristian's hand remained on the phone for several seconds after he had replaced it on the cradle. For all his good will, there was something about Nathan Hutchence that Kristian had never warmed to, none of the feeling of closeness he shared with, for instance, Jay Steele-Perkins, the family attorney.

Was that the only reason he had held back?

He cleared the question from his mind as he cleaned up the beer and broken glass and moved on, tidying and trashing months of disorder and neglect in his apartment.

From the beginning, he had been lonely here. All the plans he had entertained for his life after Mel, as a single man, had been abandoned almost as soon as he moved in here. The classics never got read or listened to, he had never learned to cook those healthful meals, sipping good wine as he seasoned and stirred. He had hardly turned on the stove except to boil water for instant coffee. Dinner out, anything quick because eating dinner alone was the loneliest business in the world. Chinese or Indian or McDonald's, he hardly noticed any difference. He'd rented a Yamaha electronic keyboard, a decent one with a convincing piano touch, but he had barely touched it. He was glad to be going back to Canterbury Road for a while, to Ingrid's cooking and his mother's Bechstein grand.

He paid overdue bills and balanced his checkbook, something he had made a habit of doing at the Kirtland Hills house, to remind himself that he worked for what he had, to fortify himself against accusations of patronage and privilege.

He did these things and drank beer until it was night and the Flats came awake, the familiar neon crying boogie and booze and chocolate cheesecake. A swathe of lights ending abruptly at the border of the lake, as though Erie was a vast invisible country, a mysterious neighbor, sober and remote, the lights of the sliding freighter-cities like signals from an alien galaxy.

He turned to the last item of unfinished business in the apartment, the cardboard box of biographical material he had brought over from Canterbury Road. It had been Phil Baylor's suggestion, at the funeral, that he make a start where Hansjorg had left off.

The book had been Kristian's idea in the first place and he had created the momentum, contacting Dorner archivists in half a dozen countries, gathering print and photographic material and film footage to do with his father.

Kristian took the box with its familiar contents to the kitchen table where he removed six differently labeled packets of photographs. "Dorner Cleveland" was by far the largest, then "Dorner Brazil" then "Dorner Frankfurt," which represented the immediate post-war period. There was a large packet concerning Hansjorg's private life, and a very small one covering his life in Germany outside of Dorner. It contained the only two known photographs of him in uniform, and a reprint of the snap from Canterbury Road, of his lost family playing chamber music. All other evidence of that time had been destroyed when the Frankfurt house was bombed.

Kristian tipped them out onto the table. It had always struck him how much clearer the army pictures were than those of the German family, obviously taken with a good camera, probably a Leica or a Rollei. Hansjorg looked so young; his complexion, clear even as an old man, was lucent between the high collar of his captain's tunic and his crop of thick, dark brown hair. A studio portrait, bright-eyed, half-smiling, full of pride in the uniform of General Paulus's Sixth Army.

The second photograph was candid, Hansjorg in shirtsleeves, sprawled on the hood of a Dorner half-track, laughing with two other tanned, cigarette-smoking boys. August 1942 on the Volga, Army Group Center still intact and well supplied, flushed with victory at the Maikop oil fields. As a child, Kristian had poured over the picture with a guilty fascination, almost able to think their thoughts and smell the tang of their Russian tobacco, searching for some harbinger in the knowledge that by Christmas, both Hansjorg's companions had bled or frozen to death at Stalingrad.

He picked up the third, familiar, photograph, of the grandparents and aunts he had never known except in his imagination and from this one snapshot taken by Hansjorg on his last leave home, that had survived the war with him.

It was always a source of deep pride for Kristian that his grandfather had refused to espouse National Socialism. Prior to 1933, Professor Peiper had been chief curator of the Frankfurt Stadelsches Kunsinstitut and a leading expert on Renaissance drawings. Stripped of his position and forbidden to lecture for failing to take a public vow in support of Hitler, only his wife's tenure at Mainz University had kept the family solvent. They had made many sacrifices in order to keep their vacation home in Steinau an der Strasse, an hour north of Frankfurt where the brothers Grimm spent their boyhood. Kristian had been there to visit the Peiper house, in a fairy-tale town of cobbled streets and half-timbered buildings. He hadn't needed photographs to imagine his family making music or hiking in the Vogelsberg hills or swimming in the Kinzig river under its ancient oaks. The bathing scene had been particularly vivid in Kristian's adolescent imagination, his heart aching with more than a familial sense of loss for his three eternally youthful, beautiful aunts.

Kristian picked up the envelope to refill it, surprised when another small photograph dropped out onto the table.

It was another picture of his father, one he had never seen before.

Hansjorg was even younger here than in the army portrait, no more than sixteen or seventeen, standing somewhat apart from a young blond woman outside a small, two-story wooden house with a tin chimney. The woman looked about twenty-five, not any one of his sisters.

There was little depth of field, but Kristian could see it was neither Frankfurt nor the Steinau house. A picket fence surrounded it, running off into the unfocused background that contained the faint silhouette of an automobile. The pair were bundled in scarves and overcoats as though they had just stepped out into the snow which lay thickly on the ground and on the roof of the house. The photograph bore a stain at the top, left by a rusted paperclip.

Kristian turned the small photograph over, hoping to find some annotation, but there were only fox marks on the old card, from the same damp conditions that had rusted the paperclip, its image clearer on the back. His father must have added the snapshot recently, since the book project foundered. It was a worthwhile find given the critical scarcity of material from the pre-war period, but where had it come from, and who was the woman? She looked forlorn, even more so than Hansjorg. The photograph seemed full of sadness and tension.

Kristian squinted at the indistinct car. With Hansjorg in his mid-teens, it would have to be around 1935. An Audi or a DKW? A Wanderer? Kristian's knowledge of automobiles was encyclopedic, but this one was so out of focus he could only guess. It certainly looked big at a time when any kind of car was a rare luxury in Germany, in distinct contrast to the modest house.

Kristian put the material back in the box and moved on to office work, preparation for the Frankfurt Auto Show less than two weeks away. He worked until hunger and an empty refrigerator — and his loneliness — drove him down to the Flats. The night had turned as warm as July, washed clean by the day's rain. A clement Friday night down here meant action and noise, fastest and loudest at the Power House, shaking the foundations of the Main Avenue Bridge as the boogie thundered out of the Howl at the Moon Saloon.

This hadn't been Kristian's scene for many years, not even as a single man, but he made it tonight and drank tequila-Miller boiler-makers. He knew that nothing else, nowhere else, could drown the words that had whispered in his brain like a possession for nine days. That he had been afraid to divulge to Deems or even to Nathan Hutchence tonight, knowing it would give them currency. Two words in German, that he was terrified even to think.

Desperate for distraction, for the first time since moving down here from Kirtland Hills, Kristian thought about getting laid. Mister Libido!

It had been so long, he had almost forgotten the joke. Mel never found it funny, complained that it had enough personality already without Kristian inventing this persona, a gangster in a silk suit and a rakish purple hat. He had once inserted a tiny feather from his pillow into the opening...cock of the walk, a Latin lover with an attitude, but his wife had told him to grow up and turn out the light.

Tonight Kristian didn't need her to constrain him; the bar was full of attractive women, but none of them was muscular and petite at the same time, with dark, chin-length hair and violet eyes.

CHAPTER 8

CORSICA COULD HAVE BEEN WONDERFUL: BREEZES FROM THE OCEAN and the thick, cool walls of the tower moderating the September heat, one car an hour on the coast road, no ringing phones, beach walks and long reading afternoons earned with mornings of honest labor on the tower. Ten days on the island should have left her refreshed and relaxed, and while Greta felt outwardly toned from sun and salt water, she was tight inside, wound up like a spring.

Regine wasn't like her brother in looks, had missed their mother's blond beauty, but in every other way — patterns of speech, a way of tucking in her chin when she laughed, the movement of her hands sometimes — too many things reminded Greta of Ulrich. There had been no release in talking to Regine or Jean Pierre about Uli, no way of sharing her deepest concern for him, whatever it was in Bonn that was undermining him, whatever the secret in the SG lab towards which, having cleared German customs at Frankfurt, Greta was about to take an alarming step.

She had collected her single bag — shorts, T-shirts, pedagogical paperbacks — was heading for the U-bahn terminal for the ride down-town when she heard herself paged. Otto Volk, was her first thought. He'd brought her out to the airport in a Schutzpolizei prowler, late for her flight, had run several lights to get her here in time. Bless him, had he come to pick her up as well?

But it wasn't Otto on the terminal house phone. She didn't recognize the young man's voice, or his name until he reminded her where they'd met.

"In the Mineshaft. With Ulrich Mayer."

Franz Truong was the Eurasian, the hooker with the KitKat. Greta struggled to think coherently as her inner spring clenched tighter.

"Where's Ulrich?"

"I'm here alone. I'm in the north parking complex, level D, section seven. White BMW 320I. Come up quickly."

"How did you know I was here?"

"He told me."

Greta felt a slight lessening of tension, although Truong sounded jittery. "Did he send you?"

"No. This is about Ulrich. I have to talk to you. Please hurry. I'll explain."

Greta found a plan of the parking garage near the toll booth, rode the elevator that would bring her out one level below D, and furthest from section seven. She took the last level on foot, cautiously, watching in every direction for occupied cars, loiterers, anything suspicious. She kept low when she finally emerged onto D, using vans for cover, sighting through tinted side windows until she had identified him. He seemed to be alone, the surrounding cars empty as far as she could see. She watched him for five more minutes through a Toyota Previa, then walked to the car.

Truong's compact BMW had been extensively modified, everything white — white ground effects, whitewall tires, white alloy wheels. The interior was also customized, Recaro buckets in fragrant white leather.

"Business must be good Franz. Are you dealing as well?" She pulled the door closed, only now registering the degree of fear ingrained in his handsome features. His soft, almond eyes flicked constantly between the mirrors, narrowing further as a couple carrying suitcases came out of the nearest elevator.

"I checked this level," Greta said. "Who might be interested in us, Franz? The SG?"

Truong swallowed hard. "I'm a contract agent. Uli recruited me a year ago. He ran me in the Dorner investigation. I know you talked about it at the Mineshaft. He regretted that conversation." He paused for a second. "Especially the part about the forensic lab in Bonn."

She watched him narrowly. "Go on."

"It's a film. The SG have a film."

"Of what?"

Truong's voice rose in a gradual crescendo. "I don't know what the subject is. I know it's old, needs reconstruction. They shipped in equipment and reconstruction specialists from Agfa. Uli said the security round this thing is unbelievable. He said it was like they've got the Holy Ghost in there."

"Does he know what it is?"

Truong nodded. "At first he was sharing what he had. I had a right to know, it was me that lifted the film from Junia Dorner's townhouse, part of the original investigation. The SG thought it would be evidence of Junia's involvement with the DNV, but it turned out to be something else. Something much bigger."

"Bigger how?"

"Terminal."

"Make sense."

"For Junia Dorner. A death sentence for her company, three hundred thousand employees worldwide. No more Kondor, 4 billion lost in guaranteed government loans."

She remembered Ulrich's brief allusion to the film that night. He had used the word *unimaginable*. Frustrated, she twisted in the seat to face Truong squarely. "Why am I here Franz?"

"The film in Bonn is one of two copies. Erich Dorner had the other one which he gave to Hansjorg Peiper before he died. Uli thought Hansjorg's death was a result of Beck's people trying to get it back."

"Minister Beck?"

"He's always had a tame element in the SG. Now he's using it to protect Junia. Uli reckons they didn't get Peiper's copy in Cleveland, it's still out there somewhere and they're scared shitless. It's Beck who set up the security round the lab while they reconstruct Junia's copy." He paused, watching her, setting her up. "Except Uli said he'd found a hole. An opportunity."

Greta held his gaze for several seconds then sagged into the leather bucket, the inference overlaying her like a cold shroud. "Tell me this isn't happening."

"The last time I spoke to him, four days ago..." Truong's voice tremored, he was coming unraveled. "He didn't say it but I know him. I know what he's planning to do. He's going to take the film from SG headquarters. He had this crazy look. He called them dogs, Junia and Beck. The bitch and her dog, rolling in shit. He said animals need controlling."

"*Controlling*?"

"It isn't just the company Beck's protecting. He's linked with Junia in another way. Their connection to the DNV goes deeper than the bottom line. It's more than money. Beck's political agenda isn't what the public sees. He's further right than anyone dreams and Junia Dorner's promised him financial backing. They've got plans; he helps her now, she'll scratch his back when he announces his campaign for the chancellory. She'll bring him any blue-collar votes he won't already have, she'll give him big business, a massive campaign donation. Beck's already popular for his crime war."

"'Iron Fist,'" Greta murmured. It had been Beck's battle cry throughout his ruthless but underfunded campaign. He was popular for qualities that would have disqualified him from any other office, but even voters in the political center apparently found it acceptable to have a thug in the Interior Ministry. They complained about Kurds and Turks gunning each other down on German streets, about ethnics getting the jobs, too many refugees from the Balkans. A lot of Germans didn't want to be New Europeans, felt angry and threatened by assimilation, just wanted to be Germans. The same sentiment that was gaining ground in France.

Greta gave Truong a slight, grim smile. "So Uli wants to save us from the Fourth Reich? With a slingshot?"

"With a film. Whatever it is, it's got the power to bring down Junia Dorner and Beck along with her. That's Uli's thinking."

"What thinking!" Greta's eyes flashed with sudden rage. "Her lawyers' fees are more than the BKA's annual budget! He wants to go against Beck? A cabinet minister?"

"I told him."

"And now you're telling me. Why?"

"You've got to talk to him. I know he trusts you. Respects you. You were in the BKA, you've got history together. He'll listen to you. He promised me he'd talk to you before he did anything stupid. I made him swear."

Greta looked mercilessly at him. "Scared for that pretty skin, aren't you Franz."

"For him."

"Really. Your relationship: would that be strictly professional? I mean his profession, not yours."

"We're friends."

"Just friends?"

Truong's face tightened across his delicate cheek bones, his eyes glittering with the beginnings of tears.

"I see," Greta said. "By the way, is prostitution a cover or a career? Both?"

"I'm stopping that."

"Really. You'd better not be HIV positive. You hear me, rent boy? You won't need AIDS or the SG if you've infected him; *I'll* kill you."

Truong swallowed hard. "He agreed to call you today at 1:00 p.m. That's an hour from now. It has to be a public phone."

"Where?"

With no laundry facilities in her apartment house, Greta had long been in the habit of using the Happy Wash on Berger Strasse. Not inconvenient, it was a way to keep up with the neighborhood gossip or just to relax, lulled by the tumbling clothes behind the dryer port.

There could be no relaxation this time. She saw a desperate alarm in the flinging arms and legs of the clothes behind the dryer ports, like passengers trapped in the hold of a sinking ship, waving frantically.

At seven and a half minutes past one, the payphone rang by the janitor's cupboard at the back of the laundromat. One of the older, two-way phones that German Telecom had not yet replaced with the newer "out only" models, it was a favorite exchange for many of the laundromat's regulars to make and take calls. Greta was waiting by the notice board, snatched it up on the first ring, her knuckles blanched around the receiver. "Uli?"

"Greta, listen carefully. Are you listening?"

There was a flat, dark tone to his voice.

"Yes," she said.

"Was the parking garage clear when you met Franz?"

"As far as I could tell."

"Any sense you were followed since the airport?"

"I don't think so."

"Have you used your phone?"

"Not yet."

"Who's in the laundromat?"

"Regulars."

"Just regulars?"

"There's only two other customers. I recognize both of them."

Silence.

"Uli?"

"No."

"What?"

"Forget it. This is too risky. Hang up, Greta. Don't try to contact me. This isn't going to work. I can't involve you in this."

"You won't involve me. You're going to talk to me, that's all. That's what friends do, they talk. Listen to me: the Palmengarten, in the Palm House by the carp pool, where we used to go for lunch in the Schutz with Otto. I'll take the U-bahn, choose an empty car. I know how to do this. *Counter Surveillance in the Field*...we had the same instructor. Remember the guy with those wild tufts in his ears? I got A-minus. Uli?"

No answer.

"I've thought this out," she insisted. "I'll use the public phone in the Iris House. Give me a number. I'll call you exactly one hour from now, only if I'm certain I haven't been followed, then we can meet. Give me a number, Uli."

"Friends don't..."

"Give me a number."

The Palmengarten lies at the heart of the city, a haven for Frankfurters who wish to forget, for the space of a lunch hour, that they live at the crossroads of Europe. Above the trees, they can still see the tops of the steel and glass towers, but the garden is a wide and beautiful distraction.

By September, Germany's most spectacular show of flowers has waned, but the pristine gravel walkways also wind between displays of rare shrubs and succulents, and the garden's main attraction, its collection of palms, remains protected from the seasons in a zeppelin-sized greenhouse.

It was a clear day with no trace of the humidity that often creeps down the Main Valley as the summer ages, a fresh breeze conspiring to keep the industrial smog south of the Stadtwald.

The garden was filled with tourists. Greta had to pass the bandshell on her way to the Iris House. A concert was about to begin, West African drummers in bright caftans mustering on stage while a clown kept the audience entertained, their laughter ringing in Greta's ears as she passed, harsh and unreal, increasing her anxiety.

The Iris House lies on the west side of the garden, nineteenth-century *Jugendstil* elegance preserved in white wrought iron and stained glass. The modern age encroaches no further than the outer lobby, with the toilets and public phones. Greta dialed and the line was picked up instantly.

"You're certain you weren't followed?"

Choose a location with multiple exits where people are in transition: hotel lobby, bus, subway station. Remain in place. Observe.

"No company. I'm clear."

"Is anyone else using the phones?"

There was a boy three phones away in a turned-around baseball cap and oversized clothes with soul patches. He had spilled half a dozen cigarettes from a soft pack onto the floor. The last one lay just beyond his reach as he tried to pick it up, tethered by the phone cord.

"It's okay. Just a kid."

"How old?"

"Thirteen, fourteen. He was here when I came in. Christ, how much heat is on you?"

"I'll see you by the carp pool. Give me thirty minutes. If I'm not there in thirty, don't wait."

Now the silence was Greta's.

"Margaret?"

"You took the film, didn't you? You already did this. You took their film."

"You don't understand."

"Sweet Jesus. You did this. You've got it."

Ulrich's voice rose on a sudden tide of emotion. "I had to act. They were moving it out next week. The SG facilities couldn't handle the reconstruction..."

"You swore to Franz. You *swore* to Franz you'd talk to me first!"

"God damn it, it was going to Agfa! There would have been no chance then. This is a cataclysm. You have no idea. *Krokus* material like this..."

"What?"

"Beck has to be stopped. He's getting middle-class support, it's not the *lumpen* fringe anymore. Junia Dorner's vital to him. This is the only way."

"What's '*krokus*' Uli?"

"Oh God."

"You mean the flower?"

"Walk away Greta. Now."

"Spell it."

"Please. Right now."

"Okay I'm walking. I'm walking over to the Palm House. I'm going to the carp pool and I'm going to wait for you and you're going to be there in thirty. Don't be late."

The African drummers were performing as she recrossed the garden, a throbbing pulse overlaid with virtuosic counter rhythms. The sound followed her to the Palm House, distance giving it a secretive, ominous quality. Talking drums, cryptic, encoded.

She looked around furtively before she entered the greenhouse, saw a man reading a newspaper on a bench, another man twenty yards away with his back to her, stooping to read the plaque on a cactus display. Either one of them could have been talking into a lapel microphone, handing her to a relay. But she'd been careful, had taken a lot of extra time in the U-bahn off Zeppelinallee. At least an A-minus.

The Palm House lay on the eastern perimeter of the garden, a vast, antique, iron-framed greenhouse containing every known species of palm. Inside it was a sultry jungle where the shrieks of exotic birds cut the thick air.

They used to come here for lunch, the three of them, from the quiet Schutzpolizeirevier on Keplerstrasse, just a few blocks east of the garden. Greta and Uli and Otto Volk, regular lunchtime visitors to the Palm House, its tropical atmosphere a welcome counterweight to the dull regimen of paperwork or the noxious monotony of traffic duty. Otto still came here occasionally, Hauptkommissar now.

Years since her last visit, but the hyacinth macaw was still in its cage by the entrance, shelling a peanut with its scimitar beak and weirdly prehensile claw, blinking at Greta as she passed. She took the familiar winding path to an ornamental rock formation at the far end of the greenhouse, climbed narrow steps cut into the rock, up to a lookout level with the top of the tallest palm.

She went to the edge and looked out across a little Amazon, down into the carp pool at the base of the rocks. The fish were easier to see from up here, patrolling specters in red-gold mail in the black reflecting water.

She stepped back, the sudden unwelcome feeling of being exposed while unable to see anything or anybody beneath the palm canopy below.

By 2:30, Greta was beginning to perspire from the humidity. She descended to ground level and made a circuit of the greenhouse. She arrived back at the entrance without any sign of him.

At 2:45, she went outside to breathe. The drums were still playing, building to a climax. Even at this distance, the rhythm was palpable, physical, as though the drummers' hands and fingers were actually touching her, kneading, prodding, pounding...

At 3:00, by which time Ulrich was half an hour late, she was sweating heavily. She scanned the interior one last time, dizzied by the kaleidoscope of palms that had suddenly lost all romantic associations. She saw the leaf-forms as blades, curved and razor-sharp.

She spoke Uli's name at last, tentatively. She called again, louder, without discretion, a gaping second before the answering shriek ripped like an explosion through the greenhouse. The shock spun Greta around, her heart in her throat as the hyacinth macaw hurled itself at her, thrashing and thrashing the cage bars with its hooked beak.

"*Uli! Uli! Uli! Uli! Uli!*"

Greta was still shaking when she got home, still listening to the shrieking in her head. She could hear her own voice clearly in the bird's mimicry, on an endless loop, screaming.

There were no messages from Uli on the answering machine. Of course not. She felt dizzy, with a building headache. She hadn't eaten since breakfast on the plane, but eating was out of the question.

She stared helplessly around the apartment, unable to anchor herself with the familiar. There was an unfinished chess game on the kitchen table, that she had begun with Herr Kraus before she left for Corsica. If only life had stood still, undeveloped, in stasis like the chess pieces, instead of moving towards this.

She had never heard raw fear in Ulrich's voice before.

Greta hadn't stopped sweating since the Palm House, exacerbated it now as she ran down Löwengasse to Berger, to the Happy Wash. She dialed and redialed the number she had called from the Iris House but there was no reply. She waited in a red plastic bucket chair, willing the phone to ring.

It rang six times between 4:00 and 5:00 p.m., never for Greta. She had no effective plan. Out of the question now, for her own and Uli's safety, to make even the most casual inquiries through BKA channels, but she couldn't leave Uli out there alone, wherever he was. He wasn't rational. Something had happened to him, changed him. Whatever the danger he had courted from the SG, he was in worse danger from himself.

He needed his friends.

She had called the scribbled number every ten minutes during her hour of vigil in the laundromat. She had called Franz Truong's number repeatedly, without success. She somehow doubted that Uli would be in touch with him now, and as an occasional, low-level contract agent, Truong would have no special vantage point.

Right now there was only one place to turn for help, and that was Otto Volk. Otto was in the Schutzpolizei, the Frankfurt city police, independent from the federal office in Wiesbaden. He commanded an extensive network of informants, a shadow army of Frankfurt villains eager to do the Hauptkommissar a favor. A people person.

He also had a wife, Leona, a legal secretary, seven months pregnant.

Greta agonized for several minutes before she decided that the risk was acceptable. Otto was professionally discreet, a reputation that allowed him to maximize his contacts. Little risk in calling his station; there were at least twenty separate lines at Keplerstrasse, a hundred calls an hour — Greta had spent whole days with a flattened ear, answering them.

"IPA convention," the duty Obermeister complained. "He hasn't been here all afternoon. That Greta?"

"How's it going Stefan?"

"They're probably down at the Inter-Continental," Stefan observed glumly. "Pouring beer down each other's throats."

Greta vaguely remembered Otto mentioning the International Police Association convention. He was secretary of the Hessen chapter, played bass drum in the marching band.

She called the hotel, asked reception to page Hauptkommissar Volk, with the convention.

"He's with the Frankfurt Schutzpolizei?"

Greta frowned. "How do you know?"

"Hauptkommissar Volk was just at this desk, madam. Five minutes ago. He seemed quite distraught."

Greta felt her stomach roll. "Why?"

"He used the fax service, received a message. I gave it to him myself. He seemed upset by it. He asked me to call him a taxi."

"Can you remember where he was going?"

"I believe he ordered the taxi for Holzhausenstrasse."

He'd gone home.

She ran back to Löwengasse. She put a clip round her jeans cuff and hauled her bicycle down the hall to the back door, it's tires chirruping on the ceramic tiles like a puppy nagging for a walk. With access to the BKA pool, she hadn't needed a car of her own, feeling the loss now. But Otto's apartment was close enough and she needed physical activity. Keeping still was the only impossibility.

She ran the bike across the small patch of lawn behind the building, through a gate leading onto the narrow lane behind the house. Parked cars on both sides. Two of them occupied, a grey Audi and a blue Renault, a couple in the Renault. She mounted and rode around the corner towards Berger. Neither car followed.

She fast-pedaled through Gunthersburg Park, along a narrow cycle track, no one behind her. A straight run west on Hallgarten until it became Nordend, and now she was on Holzhausenstrasse, a quiet, middle-to-upper-income street with well-kept verges and linden trees planted at precise intervals.

Otto and Leona occupied the second floor of a whitewashed Weimar-era house at the east end of Holzhausen, a convenient five minutes from his station. Greta rang twice before Leona appeared at an upstairs window.

"Bring your bike into the hall. You're just in time for some sake."

"You're drinking?"

"See it from the kid's point of view: floating around in the pitch dark for months, you'd appreciate a slug once in a while."

Greta carried her bike inside. The house had high ceilings and handsome plaster detailing, the entranceway wide enough to house a dozen bicycles. A hundred-square-meter apartment at such an address should have been beyond a Kriminalhauptkommissar's salary, in a city where downtown accommodation was at the highest premium in Europe. It was the kind of deal at which Otto excelled, hard to blame him when he so often used his position for good, to kickstart neighborhood crimewatch programs, cleanup campaigns, anti-drug education in local schools.

"Otto's still out with his IPA buddies," Leona called down the stairs.

"Their last night, thank God. He was so excited yesterday, did a swap with a highway patrolman from Oklahoma, brought home the dearest little cap badge for his collection, from Tonga!"

Her mahogany laughter boomed down the stairs. She was Brazilian mulatto with gold flecks in her eyes, aggressive and big-hearted, bigger than ever now that she was pregnant, but her good humor dissolved as soon as Greta reached the top of the stairs. Leona cupped her chin, lifted her face.

"Whoa...this isn't a casual call."

"I think I'd better have that sake."

She followed Leona into a spacious, white-tiled kitchen decorated with travel posters of cobalt oceans and white sand, all the places they had traveled on two salaries, free of children. Leona took the sake bottle from a saucepan on the stove, poured into earthenware cups, scrutinizing Greta as she handed one to her.

"You okay? You want to talk about this?"

"You don't like police business."

"I thought you were done with that."

"A few loose ends."

Greta took the warm cup in both hands, inhaled the savory steam, sipped. Leona usually avoided the subject of her husband's work unless he volunteered information. They shared enough, she had always maintained, without the details of his beat. There were enough cop shows on the TV. Leona went to the table, sank down in a chair and raised her cup. "You look like you need a laugh. What's the definition of heaven? Heaven is where the police are British, the cooks French, the mechanics German, the lovers Italian and it's all organized by the Swiss."

"What's the definition of hell?" Greta said.

"Shit, you've heard it."

"I've forgotten."

"Hell is where the cooks are British, the mechanics French, the lovers Swiss, the police German — I like that part — and it's all organized..."

Greta heard the front door open. Footsteps in the hallway below, a familiar smoker's cough on the stairs.

"Talk of the devil," Leona said.

Otto was in uniform. Paunchy, not tall enough for it. His thinning hair was plastered to his forehead, dark crescents of sweat spread through the green twill under each arm. He blinked at them from the doorway, started towards the kitchen table then swayed, hanging onto the door-frame for support like a man experiencing an earth tremor.

"You pig," Leona sang out. "You're drunk."

But it was more than that. Greta felt herself growing cold at the sight of him.

He came to the table, lowered himself, fumbling behind him to position the chair. Greta could smell his breath, beer and French tobacco, from his Gitanes. He reached into his breast pocket. He took out a folded sheet of paper with shaking hands and spread it out on the table.

Greta read it over his shoulder, the cover sheet first, at her own speed, oblivious to Leona reading aloud:

April 4th, 16:45 hrs.
Polizeiprasidium Frankfurt am Main, State of Hesse
From: Obermeister Amon Kirschner
Response to request from -3. Polizeirevier (Keplerstrasse)
re: Schutzpolizei Traffic Accident Report.

Greta beat ahead, in terror, through the bureaucratic thicket.

Schutzpolizei Obermeister Frülich, badge # 48, Report # 6001
Subject: Mayer, Ulrich, Telemannstrasse 14, Bonn. Single car accident.
Time: 14:10. Location: Burgentandweg, near Waldfriedhof Oberrad.
Subject DOA at 14:30, Rotkreuzkrankenhaus, Königswarterstrasse,
Frankfurt/Main. Attending physician, E. Langsdorff.

The words and numbers swarmed, a dense cloud over the essential message. Otto's voice filtered through it only gradually.

"After the parade. We were in the bar at the Inter-Continental. Some of the Frankfurt people…there was this rumor…you know how fast the word gets around. Lot of people remember Uli. Who wouldn't?"

He almost looked at her.

"I didn't believe it. I called the Prasidium. I made them fax the accident report to the hotel."

Leona was watching Greta, alarmed by the bright, false light in her eyes. Greta's mouth formed a kind of smile as the sake rose like acid in her throat, pitching her voice sharp and rough.

"They've got it wrong," she said. "Someone at the Prasidium was in a hurry to get off for the weekend. They got it wrong."

She rocked on her feet.

Leona reached for her but she twitched away.

"I'm driving."

"What?" Otto said.

"I'll have to, you're drunk. Down to the Prasidium. We're going down and we're going to sort this out. Right now."

Otto stared at her. "You knew, didn't you."

"Get up."

"Not until you tell me why you're here."

Greta opened her mouth.

She saw his wife through a scalding mist, reaching for her again. She struggled only for a moment against the great, hard swell of Leona's belly.

CHAPTER 9

THE GLOOMY WARRENS OF THE FRANKFURT POLIZEIPRASIDIUM occupy half a city block on Friedrich-Ebert-Anlage, off the Platz der Republik. Dark and forbidding, its balconied entrance guarded by a cruel imperial eagle, tourists usually assume it was Gestapo headquarters in the city, which was never the case. Since 1917, the Prasidium has been the center for civil police administration for Frankfurt Main.

Otto showed his green ID card to a guard in a booth inside the entrance, then started towards the sweeping double staircase with Greta close behind.

"*Bitte*?"

She turned at the bottom step as the guard came up behind her. He held out his hand.

"You have identification?"

"Lieutenant Schoeller is with the Bundeskriminalamt," Otto explained.

"Identification please."

"I don't have it."

"You must have identification or an appointment."

"Christ!"

The guard grew an inch as Otto's utterance crashed through the vast granite hall. They heard doors opening on the mezzanine level, looked up at two uniformed officers peering interestedly over the rail at the top of the stairs.

"Wait for me in the car," Otto said gently. He went up the stairs, addressing the men at the top. "Is Roland Hopf around?"

"Off duty at six."

"Bernd Resow?"

One of the cops turned, called behind him: "Berni still here?"

The guard followed Greta to the main exit. His manner softened as though he sensed a crisis, her fragility. "There's a waiting room if you want." She shook her head and put her shoulder to the ornate steel door. She glanced behind her, back towards the grand staircase, trying to picture Otto in five minutes time, back to normal, his gut jiggling as he trotted back down with the good news:

They had the wrong Uli Mayer.

Or:

The car's a mess but he's fine. Wait till I find the careless bastard that filed the report.

But he did not descend, and the staircase remained empty with its extravagant wrought-iron banister and stained glass backdrop, grotesque ornamentation in such a place as this. A place of accusation and lies and confinement.

Of heartbreak.

A low moan escaped Greta's lips as she crushed her shoulder against the heavy street door and started along Friedrich-Ebert-Anlage towards the car. With every step the wound tore wider, unbearable agony by the time she reached Otto's old Mercedes and pulled on the door handle — pulled and pulled with mounting anger though it was clear that the car was locked.

Greta sagged against the door, her hands in fists against the roof.

She paid no heed to the pedestrians giving her a wide berth as they hurried east across the Platz der Republik towards the Opera, or west for their evening classes at the university. Nobody stopped. They were too close to the Hauptbahnhof with its legions of obsessed and dispossessed, the drunks and junkies staggering through the vale of despair. Around here, even in the shadow of the Prasidium, Frankfurters remembered to keep moving and not make eye contact.

At some point her agony changed its shape, became the anticipation of Otto's slack face when he returned, and with that Greta walked away from the car. Without any conscious plan, she turned up Mainzer Landstrasse, wide and empty now that the business day was done, its normal six lanes of traffic down to a series of light spurts. She headed northeast into respectable territory, synchronizing her breathing with the movement of her legs as if to conjure a mantra from the rhythm, with which to numb her pain.

She made no conscious decision to leave Mainzer Landstrasse where it merges grandly with Taunusanlage; it was as if something washed her off the main thoroughfare onto the green wooded margin and finally the cobbled pathway that is the formal approach to the opera house.

She didn't stop until she had circumvented the cascading Lucae fountain in front of the Alte Opera, at last reaching a row of elegant shops and restaurants flanking the Opernplatz on its east side.

She stood in the doorway of the Charlot, her forehead resting against the glass panel, her breath misting it although she could see Uli perfectly clearly at their usual table up there on the gallery. Charlot never filled up until the Opera let out, empty now except for the dark, swaggering waiters and Uli...

Still. Golden.

He had ordered wine, waiting for Greta to come. He glanced at his watch then towards the door. He saw Greta and came to his feet, smiling and waving through a gauntlet of waiters. The door was thrown open.

"Fräulein? Can I help you?"

Signor Mancini eyed her with disdain — her hair damp with per-spiration, the stains of her tears on her cheeks. "You understand, we are..." He stopped, eyes narrowing while his mouth dropped. He leaned out from the doorway, peering into the half-light. "Signora Schoeller? My God! What has happened?"

Greta turned and ran. She didn't look back until she had almost reached the fountain, by which time there were four white aprons outside the Charlot. Italian voices drifted out across the Opernplatz, raised in speculation and argument above the sibilant whispering of the fountain.

She turned away, towards the Alte Opera's floodlit grandeur, a bronze Pegasus crowning the reconstructed facade. Greta shut her salt-dry eyes, waiting to hear the beat of its wings, for it to sail down to carry her away into another night where there were no fax machines.

Otto's Mercedes came in from Taunusanlage, cruised slowly past the Charlot before he spotted her, his tires squelching over the cob-blestones. He spoke through the open window.

"Come on Grets, get in." When she didn't respond, he got out, took off his stained uniform jacket and draped it around her shoulders. "Come on, we can talk in the car."

"Is he still at the hospital?"

The Rotkreuzkrankenhaus, the Red Cross Hospital near the zoo. Otto saw her into the car, lit a Gitane and sat staring out through the windshield.

"I wouldn't have got any of this if Resow hadn't been there. Seems the computer's a little confused down at the Prasidium. Who was this officer attending at Burgentandweg? Bit of a muddle: this guy Frülich's name on the log, from Revier 5. But that's impossible unless he can be in two places at once, in which case he's wasted in the Schutzpolizei."

"Just tell me please."

"Frülich was on duty at the Hauptbahnhof. We checked. So who attended the accident? They don't know. They'll try and sort it out. I called the Red Cross Hospital. According to the report, a Doctor E. Langsdorff was the attending physician. He's supposed to have pronounced an Ulrich Mayer DOA of massive head injuries at 2:30 this afternoon. He also signed the release for his body. I asked to speak with Doctor Langsdorff. They paged him. They looked on the duty roster. No one in administration at the Rotkreuzkrankenhaus had ever heard of him. I spoke directly to emergency. A doctor and three nurses were still there from the afternoon shift. Yes, an Ulrich Mayer had been admitted at 2:30."

"Did they see him?"

"One of the nurses, briefly. He can't have been killed instantly, his head had been bandaged. The doctor told me his admission didn't follow the usual procedure. A BKA pathologist and two plainclothes were waiting at the hospital."

"*Sicherungsgruppe.*"

Otto nodded. "The pathologist was Langsdorff. He signed for the body and they took it away."

Greta was regaining her ability to think. She was frowning. "What kind of car?"

"A white Dorner 600. Front end collision, no other vehicle involved."

"What...he hit a tree? *What?*"

"A bridge abutment."

"Ulrich Mayer hit a *bridge* on the Burgentandweg? Don't be stupid. He was an expert driver. Anyway, where would he have got up enough speed?" The Burgentandweg was little more than a forest path to access the Waldfriedhof Oberrad, a small cemetery south of the river. It was barely a kilometer long.

"And why the Red Cross Hospital?" Otto said. "In the city center, north of the river? The Städtisches Krankenhaus in Offenbach is fifty times nearer the cemetery."

Otto always smoked down to the filter. He flicked the butt out of the window, turned back to her.

"Did the SG kill him? Is that why we've got this fucking paperwork in place, to make it look like a regular traffic accident?"

She shook her head slowly, as though exhausted by its weight. But of course she knew. They both knew. She had told Otto everything before going down to the Prasidium — everything Franz Truong had confided at the airport this morning.

"The SG killed him to save Junia Dorner's ass?" Otto demanded. "To save the fucking Kondor?"

"Without the Kondor, Junia's finished. Without Junia, Beck can kiss good-bye any shot at the chancellory. That's what Truong said."

He lit another Gitane, blew a contemptuous stream of smoke towards the open window where the night blew it back. "A fucking bum boy? Since when is this little shit such an authority?"

"I underestimated him too. When I saw him in the Mineshaft that night with Uli, I just figured shallow, cut out of a fashion magazine. He isn't. He's smart and tough. Scared though, and he'll be a lot worse now. He'll go to ground when he hears about Ulrich."

"I don't like wild cards. He's the only person who knows how much you know because he came whining to you. If the SG get hold of him, I don't care how tough he is, he's going to fold. Your name's going to come up. I want to see him. Where does he live?"

"I only have a number."

"Give me an hour. I'll find him."

"He tried to help, Otto. Remember that."

"Yeah? Well what the fuck am I trying to do here? Rent boy wants to lie low, I think that's a great idea. I've got friends can help him disappear so the SG don't know from fucking square one where to start looking."

He O'd his mouth and blew a perfect smoke ring. Greta opened her door, swung her legs out.

"Where are you going?"

"I can't breathe that garbage any more."

He flipped his butt out the window. "Wait up! I need Truong's number."

Greta stopped five meters from the car. For a few moments she stood very still with her back to him, then she turned and came back. She ducked her head inside the smoke-filled Mercedes, her voice low and even, suddenly sure.

"I was fully qualified for the SG. You know that don't you? Grentz offered me Bonn when I told him I was quitting."

"Hey. You're a winner."

"You're not the only one with qualifications here. I know these streets too. I'm going to find out what that film is, Otto. I'm going to find out what '*krokus*' means. I'm going to find out what Uli died for and then they're going to wish like hell they'd never trained me."

CHAPTER 10

IT TOOK GRETA THREE-QUARTERS OF AN HOUR TO WALK HOME through the tired summer streets, through a callous city ignorant of her loss.

In spite of the exercise, her restlessness grew like a fever. She bathed, but the hot water failed to sedate her.

She stood in her bathrobe in the bedroom doorway, testing the fit of an idea that had occurred to her on the way home, trying to measure its risk potential against her need to know.

For sure.

She went through the telephone directory until she found the number of the police auto pound in Fechenheim, which she copied down. She dressed and went along the street to the Happy Wash. She wondered, as she rang through, whether Jerzy Jawolski was still the night-superintendent at the pound, knowing she would have to disconnect if anyone else picked up.

She recognized his reedy voice immediately. "It's Greta Schoeller, Jerzy. Remember me?"

"Dear lady. I could forget? I think of you each time I brew a pot of tea or move a chess piece. Our last unfinished game stands forever undisturbed in my heart. Still one sugar? How is my dear young friend?"

"Not good Jerzy. You remember Uli Mayer, used to be in Schutz with me."

"Of course. He looked like an angel."

"He was killed today."

Jerzy fell silent.

"The report says he was in a traffic accident on the Burgentandweg, near the cemetery. You might have got the car. A Dorner 600. It sustained a frontal collision."

"What color of car?"

"White."

"I'll look in the yard. Can I call you back in five minutes?"

"I'll call you."

It was twenty before he picked up on Greta's fourth try. "I'm very sorry, I had to go into the lockup."

He meant the garage at the back of the compound, a secure area for vehicles awaiting forensic or insurance investigation.

"There's a most interesting car here. Perhaps, Greta, you should come down."

The main police auto pound in Frankfurt is situated in an industrial section between the Güterbahnhof rail yard and the Fechenheim Oberhafen, two of the numerous dead-end canals on the Main's north bank linking river and railway, for the freight exchange that has been going on for more than a hundred years. Even close to midnight, the docks area is one of feverish activity, underscored by the intermittent racket of trains and the constant, oppressive umbrella of traffic noise from the Autobahn 661 overpass.

The auto pound was enclosed by a high fence topped with razor wire, a grey concrete place at once dreary and menacing. Greta had been here a hundred times for the Schutzpolizei Traffic Division, visits relieved only by the regular renewal of her acquaintance with Jerzy Jawolski.

Greta let the taxi go and walked up to the access gate, looking through the wire at the array of damaged cars and the scores of vehicles towed here every day for parking violations, awaiting their incensed owners. Jerzy had been watching for her, limped from his hut to open the gate. He hadn't changed, except that his ageless gnome's face was unsmiling tonight. But he remained courtly as ever, kissed her hand in the usual way.

"What can one say or do? Except to offer a hot cup of tea with one spoon of sugar. I remember, I remember. Perhaps tonight a little stronger something since the Hauptmeister isn't here to sniff us out. Then I'll show you the car. How long has it been? Two years?"

"At least. It's good to see you Jerzy."

They took tea with schnapps in the portable that served as guardhouse and office for the receipt and release of vehicles and the payment of fines. Nothing had changed in the hut: the same humble cooking ring and brown English teapot, same chess board on the table with a game in progress, a Polish journal of mathematics open beside it, a pad of frantically scribbled calculations. The enigma of Jerzy Jawolski, the reasons for him having ended up in this desolate night-world as obscure as his actual age.

"Perhaps we should not linger too long. Soon the bars are emptying and we will get business. People ask why I never drive, I tell them they should have my job on a Friday night. Bring your cup. I'll show you our interesting car."

The garage was a restricted brick building, set jealously apart from the main yard. Some of the vehicles it contained represented important evidence in criminal cases, others had been seized by customs or narcotics, yet others were undergoing insurance investigation. An electronic prompt whined as Jerzy slipped his identification card into a slot at the entrance, and the heavy door nudged inwards.

They entered a square foyer. The Hauptmeister's office was on the right, behind a window of glass bricks, an oddly flamboyant touch in an otherwise utilitarian building. To their left was the clerical office. Jerzy led her to an open door immediately ahead, flicked a gang of switches that made strip lights jump on inside the garage. It was about the same size and layout as the service department of any large auto dealership, except that there was only one bay door at the rear of the building, probably reinforced. There were about a dozen cars inside, different makes, some of them up on hydraulic lifts, about half of them damaged, two severely. One of these cars was a white Dorner 600 sedan.

The Dorner's windshield was smashed on the driver's side. It had sustained a hard front-end impact, although there had been no invasion by the engine into the passenger compartment, thanks to the Dorner's much-touted crumple zone. Greta couldn't help but think of their recent TV commercial, focusing on safety like all Dorner advertising: a battering ram hurled by an unseen dark force against an impregnable castle gate, along with the message that hadn't changed since the thirties: *Our Car Is Your Castle*.

"Why is the windshield smashed out?"

"He wasn't wearing a belt."

"But the airbag activated." She could see it hanging, deflated, from the steering-wheel housing.

He watched her carefully, spoke in the same way: "It's only supplementary. They always tell you that. You need a belt."

The drooping white bag was spotted with blood stains. Blood also on the head restraint. Greta clenched her teeth, reminding herself, even as she flinched from the car, that she had seen such sights a thousand times at a thousand accident scenes, and many worse.

She took a long, steadying breath. "You said the car was interesting. What's interesting about it?"

"There's no paperwork."

"What does that mean?"

"Dear lady, the Hauptmeister, apart from being corrupt to the bottom of his dried well of a soul, is obsessed with paperwork. Duplicate, triplicate, on and on. How else could he skim off so many thousands of deutsche marks a year? The clerks are terrified. It's more than their jobs are worth to omit an umlaut. He keeps a copy of everything, personally, locked away in his office. I looked. There's nothing on this car. Come, we'll check once more."

"You have a key?"

Jerzy smiled as he limped back towards the foyer. "The Hauptmeister-without-a-soul thinks that because I am a lame and ugly polack, that I am also an imbecile."

He opened the glass-bricked office with his contraband key and switched on the light. It was large and surprisingly well appointed given the Spartan grimness of everything else in the pound. An olive-green leather chair behind a scrupulously tidy rosewood desk, a tooled desk blotter, gold pen set. Several large prints adorned the walls, expensively framed, all taken from oil paintings of World War II Luftwaffe aircraft. The exception, larger and hanging apart from the others, depicted a Panzer Mark IV rearing against a burning sky with ruins in its wake.

Jerzy had a second key with which he unlocked one of four steel cabinets loaded with color-coded hanging files. He glanced up, noticed her attention on the tank.

"His father served with an SS Panzer Division in France. Roasted alive in the Falaise pocket. Something to be proud of, no? Another year or two of graft and our dear Hauptmeister will be able to buy the original oil. Perhaps he already has it at home."

He continued fingering the files with nimble intimacy while Greta walked around the office. The Hauptmeister had had a visitor since the cleaning crew was here: an occasional chair in front of his desk, an ashtray on the corner of it containing a single cigarette butt.

"Does he smoke?"

"Tobacco is not amongst his many vices. I saw that ashtray too."

"You don't know who the visitor was?"

"Everyone had gone when I arrived at work."

In an otherwise empty metal waste bin by the matching rosewood credenza was a crumpled soft cigarette pack. Winstons, a domestic pack, not for export; she could see the broken U.S. Customs and Excise seal across the top.

"He gets American visitors?"

"Not that I know of." Jerzy stood. "There is nothing here."

"Could it have been misfiled?"

He chuckled. "That possibility is so infinitesimal as not to be worth our consideration. Which means, dear lady, that the white Dorner 600 in there does not exist here in our little world. As of tomorrow, when the truck from the wrecking yard comes to take our lambs to slaughter and that Dorner goes into the crusher, it will never have been here. The Hauptmeister thinks, therefore we are."

Greta turned to the door. She crossed the reception area and paused in the still-open doorway to the lit garage. Seeing the white Dorner 600 from a distance and a different perspective, she knew now what had been puzzling her for the last five minutes.

"There's something wrong with the pattern of the windshield damage," she told Jerzy, limping behind her towards the car. "I saw dozens of head injury accidents in the Schutz, there's too much breakage for an airbag-equipped car. I think the glass was knocked out deliberately. Do the front doors still function?"

The driver's door was stiff but it opened.

"So they didn't need to break the glass to access the victim."

"Why then?"

"I think whoever attended the accident was trying to hide something."

She ducked inside, resting one knee on the seat while she inspected the head restraint, cloth-covered like the seats, with a once blue herringbone pattern under the dark, still-damp stain of Uli's blood.

"What are you looking at?"

"There's too much blood on the headrest. Even if he hit the window, why blood on the back of his head?"

The answer was in the headrest behind the back seat, also on the driver's side. When it became clear that the bullet was lodged too far inside the restraint to reach with her fingers, Greta took needle-nose pliers from the mechanic's tool chest in the nearest bay and pulled it out very carefully, using as little pressure as she could with the pliers so as not to damage the rifling pattern.

"A bullet? My God. Show me Greta."

She remained for some moments kneeling silently in the back of the car. Her whole body felt suddenly, painfully stiff as she climbed out, a petrifaction.

He didn't touch it, content to look with distaste at the almost pristine round lying in her palm.

"Without paperwork on the Dorner," Greta said, "does this exist?"

"Probably not," he mumbled. "You used to know about these things as I remember. Why isn't it squashed?"

"Steel jacket. Only a top marksman would use it, if he was certain of a kill and wanted to minimize..." She hesitated. "Trauma. It makes a small entry and exit wound. It looks like a .308."

"The caliber is significant?"

She nodded slowly. The current regulation issue for *Sicherungs-gruppe* marksmen was the Steyr SSG2, a heavy, phenomenally accurate .308. "Take it. Go on, feel the mass."

She dropped it into his thin white hand, watched him turn the round in his fingers.

Greta looked into Jerzy's sad, wise eyes as he returned the bullet to her. She closed her fist around it.

"It feels hard, doesn't it," she said quietly. "For something that doesn't exist."

CHAPTER 11

JASON STEELE-PERKINS WAS BORN LONG BEFORE HIS CHRISTIAN NAME became widely fashionable, so called because his father had been a classics professor at Oxford in the twenties. Relishing an Eton-and-Oxford accent unalloyed from having spent forty of his sixty-three years lawyering in Cleveland, Jason liked to point out that an argonaut was also a predaceous, ocean-dwelling cephalopod mollusk, related to the octopus, the male of the species having a specialized tentacle to hold his sperm. This tentacle, Jason liked to remind mixed company, could detach itself and independently crawl into the female's mantle. He would then display Spock-like surprise at the ensuing laughter, which made them laugh much harder.

Kristian wondered if he would ever again see that side of Jason. All Kristian's life, the Englishman had been much more than the family attorney, a regular dose of hilarity at Canterbury Road, but he had been dealt a heavy blow by his friend's death. He looked changed, older. Even the clipped yew of his Oxford accent had wilted this morning, once his calling card for many of Cleveland's most powerful families, along with his peerless legal ability. But he had arrived at the house at 11:00 a.m. on Monday morning with the usual fastidious punctuality, as the legal author and executor of Hansjorg Peiper's will.

"I've got a bit of a conflict which I've decided to resolve in your favor, Kit." Only family, and Jason, had ever called him that. "We've run into a slight irregularity in your father's financial affairs."

The attorney perched on the edge of the sofa with his elbows on his knees, where normally he would have settled back amongst the cushions with his long legs elegantly crossed. He looked uncomfortable in every way. Kristian had been standing in the curve of his mother's grand piano, relaxing against it. Jason's expression brought him, frowning, to an armchair facing the older man.

"As you know," Jason continued when Kristian was settled, "your father imposed certain conditions on me as his executor. One of these expressed his desire that in fulfilling my authority and responsibility as such, I should seek instruction, where necessary, from Blake."

"I know you saw him yesterday." Blake Cockerham had been Hansjorg's accountant almost as long as Jay had been his solicitor; they were both trustees of the family's affairs.

"Blake told me something rather surprising. I wasn't sure what to do about it until this morning, whether or not I could tell you with a clear professional conscience. My conflict, you see, being that I must observe solicitor-client privilege but at the same time also fulfill my obligation, as executor, to the beneficiary. That is, to you."

Kristian tried not to sound impatient. "What did Blake say?"

"I decided I'm off the hook since your father's estate was not created, legally speaking, until the moment he died, so that in a way I am no longer, strictly speaking, his solicitor in this matter of his will since he is not, legally or in any other way...actually...alive. If you see what I mean."

Under other circumstances, Jason would have solicited amusement in such a ramble. Perhaps the uncharacteristic hesitation as he navigated his legal maze reflected how unused he was to *not* being funny.

"At the same time, Kit, my obligation as executor also began at the moment of your father's death, and that stands very clearly."

"I appreciate your sense of propriety, Jason. You're stalling. Am I not going to like this?"

"Actually it's none of your business." Kristian saw an embryonic, painful smile. "Nor is it mine or Blake Cockerham's, strictly speaking. On the other hand..."

"*What?*"

"As you know, your father's estate, including his stock in Dorner and other investments, his real estate holdings, including this house and its contents, has been valued at $57 million U.S. A good deal of money but not quite as much as Blake was expecting at the final tally. According to Blake, your father had been liquidating some of his Dorner shares, in relatively small increments but over quite a long period of time, certainly the last five years, possibly much longer. I don't have to tell you, your father was a good businessman and an astute investor, very much ran his own portfolio, free of money managers. Blake had been aware of these Dorner liquidations over the years, had always simply assumed that Hansjorg was topping up his cash accounts — as you know, he was in favor of staying liquid with interest rates fluctuating and currencies the same. Thing of it is, when Blake started to call in these bank accounts last week, he was surprised at how little cash they contained, especially since your father had made some of his heaviest stock sales to date just a month previously. The sale amounts showed up in the accounts, yes, but never for more than a few hours, after which they were withdrawn. In every case, the bank records show a transfer of funds to a branch of the Canadian Imperial Bank of Commerce in Toronto, Ontario, where the money was converted to Canadian dollars."

"I didn't know Dad had a Canadian account."

"He didn't."

"What do you mean?"

"It wasn't his account."

"Whose was it?"

"We don't know. The CIBC isn't playing ball. They don't have
The account holder doesn't wish to be identified and we have no m
date to make the bank disclose that identity."

"Is it an individual?"

"Again, we have no way of knowing."

Kristian's frown deepened. "Offshore? A service account fo
Canadian offshore fund?"

"Blake would have known about it from the tax end. I've kno
him as long as your father. There is no more vigilant or thoro
accountant in this state."

"A new investment. Maybe Dad just got into it."

Jason shook his head emphatically. "No Kit: Blake used
authority as trustee to call up past cash account statements going b
five years. He found exactly the same pattern: sales of stock, usu
Dorner, a matching deposit in a cash account, a same-day transfe
the CIBC in Toronto."

For a few seconds he held Kristian's gaze.

"How much?" Kristian said quietly. "Altogether."

"Over the last five years, slightly under two million dollars. Th
U.S. dollars. Canadian, add roughly 40 percent. That would mak
nearly three."

"Three million? And we don't know why?"

"So far not a clue."

"Do the police know?"

"Not from Blake or myself. We thought we'd leave that decisio
you. Certainly police intervention would loosen tongues at the CIB

A moment passed.

"Dad was calling a Canadian phone number that night."

"Yes, there is that."

"Jay, we've got to know."

"I agree. But my advice would be to keep it in the family u
Blake's done a bit more spadework. We think we may yet be able to

power of attorney to get details of the account. When are you going to Frankfurt?"

"On Saturday. The show starts Monday."

"How long are you there?"

"About four days."

"Then what say we give it till you get back. If Blake and I haven't had any joy by then, we'll see if Cleveland homicide can loosen tongues at the CIBC. Hansjorg had plenty of business associates across the lake. These accounts may have nothing at all to do with that phone call. I strongly recommend we don't involve the police until we've exhausted all other options. I've seen this sort of thing before, Kit; hard on the heels of the police comes Inland Revenue, licking its pencil."

Kristian looked taken aback. "We don't have anything to hide do we?"

"No, no...of course not. Blake assures me everything is in order. But it'll complicate matters vastly, believe me. Of course it's up to you. If you feel the police should know sooner, we'll make the call."

"Let me think about it."

"Don't think I'm underestimating this, though. Apart from Wendel's and Ingrid's nest eggs, you are the sole heir to your father's estate and the fact remains that it has been unaccountably eroded over the last five years." Jason leaned forward, closer to him. He smiled sadly. "I know that money's never meant all that much to you. I never said it before, Kit, but I've always respected you enormously for that."

Jason was his old self again, confident, warm, protective. He got up from the sofa, came to Kristian's chair, reached down and squeezed his shoulder just as he used to do when Kristian was a boy.

"I want you to know that if you need me for anything — anything at all to do with this discrepancy — there'll be no question of a fee."

"Jay..."

"Absolutely. I've considered myself part of this family for forty years. It's the least I can do. Right then." Jay straightened, glanced towards the hall then at his watch. He was aware that Ingrid and Wendel Storey were in the kitchen waiting to have their rightful expectations confirmed.

Kristian had known the terms of his father's will for years, that Hansjorg's lifelong chauffeur and housekeeper had not been overlooked.

Jason started for the door. "At least there's *some* good news to impart this morning."

Kristian stood. "It's all right, I'll go get them."

"Let me. I'm going to prevail upon Ingrid for a cup of tea and a ginger biscuit before we go any further. I ought to mention Toronto, see if it rings any bells, perhaps your father mentioned something to her or Wendel. Or would you rather I left that to you?"

"Go ahead."

"Oh, before I forget." Jason came back, reaching into the breast pocket of his chalkstripe suit. "I'd better let you have this back."

It was the photograph Kristian had brought to their last meeting, disappointed but hardly surprised that Jason had no idea where it had come from, or the identity of the sad blond woman with Hansjorg in front of the little house. "I asked Blake when he was in, not a clue. Don't look very happy, do they? Did you show Ingrid and Wendel?"

"They didn't know."

Kristian stared at the open doorway to the hall after Jason had passed through it. He wasn't thinking about the photograph, or even about the transferred millions. He was still feeling that avuncular squeeze of his shoulder and missing his father with terrible, shocking suddenness.

He looked around the room, regretted having had the violins transferred to a bank vault after the break-in. Despite the elegant presence of his mother's Bechstein, the livingroom was transformed without Hansjorg's collection. The scene of so much music-making over the years; Kristian could picture his mother listening with her feet up on the sofa, Hansjorg silhouetted against the French window, tall and straight with the violin at his chin, Kristian at the piano.

Music.

The part of his father that had been far removed from his achievements and celebrity and success.

Wirklichkeitsfremd.

The private realm. The realm of the heart, of wisdom and compassion, the art of wonder. An apolitical world, to which Hansjorg's courageous parents had opened wide the door with art, literature and music, ignoring the insane dictates of *Gleichschaltung* with its brutal suppression of intellectual life. The Peipers would have revered Rembrandt and the "degenerate" Kokoschka equally, Goethe alongside Thomas Mann, Wagner together with Mendelssohn. They would have remembered the way the music sounded before the madness, when there had still been Jewish players in German orchestras.

Kristian stood and lifted the lid of the piano bench. There was a volume of Mendelssohn's *Songs Without Words* somewhere — Hansjorg had loved them for their lyric beauty, not so technically demanding that Kristian couldn't indulge his father without hard practice.

He was pulling the collection out from the pile when he noticed a slightly crumpled brown manila envelope sandwiched between two pieces of music, his father's full name handwritten on it. Kristian had opened the unsealed envelope before he realized why it was familiar: it contained the music Jenifa Alsop had handed him that night at Severance Hall, in gratitude for the loan of a violin. Kristian had given it to his father before taking his seat in the auditorium, the last words they had spoken together.

Jenifa had written a short *Largo* for piano and violin. Kristian put the piano part on the stand, was setting the envelope aside when he saw handwriting on the back, in faint pencil, almost illegible against the manila.

He had to hold it to the window for the morning light to reflect in the pencil marks. Three words, the writing so unsteady it took a moment to recognize it as his father's normally firm hand. A short list:

Toronto
Dieter
Crowcass

Jason had joined Ingrid and Wendel at the kitchen table for tea and ginger snaps. Unlike the chauffeur, who was sitting awkwardly at the table with downcast eyes, Ingrid was in a lively mood. She explained immediately how the envelope had got into the piano bench.

"It was on the hall table, with the bills and such. You know I wouldn't have let it all pile up except the police told me not to touch anything till they were done with the house. Then I saw it was music in the envelope so I put it in the bench." She smiled wistfully at Jason and Wendel. "The two of them were always leaving their music lying around."

Jason matched her smile, but he had noticed the peculiar urgency of Kristian's inquiry. "Is it significant, Kit?"

"I'm not sure. The word *crowcass* mean anything to you?"

"The flower?"

Kristian showed him the peculiar spelling. "Your father's writing," Jason said, "but it's not German is it?"

"No it's not, that would be *krokus*."

"Not like your father to misspell any word. His hand looks shaky."

"I think he wrote it in the taxi that night, on the way home from Severance Hall. Like Ingrid says, the envelope had music in it, from a young woman called Jenifa Alsop. She gave it to me just before the concert to give to Dad."

"Could 'Dieter' be Dietrich Kamp?" Jason wondered.

"I thought about that. They were good friends."

"And there's Toronto again."

Ingrid, puzzling at the list over Jason's shoulder, looked at Kristian and shook her head. "We were just telling Mr. Steele-Perkins, your father never talked about any Canadians, no one I can remember. Right Wendel?"

The chauffeur's eyes remained averted as he got up from the table. It seemed to cost him an extra effort, as though his already heavy physique was somehow weighted. "I'd like to drive you to the office, Mr. Kristian. In the 920. In your father's car. If that's all right."

Kristian exchanged a concerned glance with the other two still seated at the table. "Sure. Thank you, Wendel. I guess I can leave the Spyder here."

"I'll pick you up after work, bring you back here for it. I'll be out in the car whenever you're ready."

Jason got up. "I should be going too. I've got a 2:00 p.m. flight to Cincinnati." He said good-bye to Ingrid, and Kristian saw him to the front door.

"I wonder what's wrong with Wendel," Jason said as he snapped his briefcase. "This is a man who just found out he can retire in comfort in Florida and put five grandchildren through college."

"Don't expect him to be overjoyed," Kristian replied. "Dad's death hit him hard. He didn't just lose his employer, he lost a daily companion. In many respects, I think he lost his whole concept of himself. Wendel worked for Dad most of his adult life." He opened the front door and walked Jason out to his Jaguar. "What's happening in Cincinnati? Client?"

"A New Age guru! Made 30 million last year preaching self-actualization on late night TV, building himself into a corporation. You may have seen his execrable infomercials."

"Haven't looked at the tube in months."

"All the accumulated wisdom of his twenty-eight years." Jason got into his car while Kristian held the door. "I'll think about Dietrich Kamp, and this crowcass thing." He reached for the grab handle but Kristian held on to the door frame.

"I've heard the word before, Jay. Or something that sounded like it. I didn't want to get into it in front of Ingrid and Wendel, but it was at Erich Dorner's house, the last time Dad and I were there just before he died."

Briefly he recounted the fragments of overheard conversation, the package delivered to Erich's room.

"Have you told anyone else about this?" Jason asked.

"I mentioned it to Nathan Hutchence."

Jason frowned. "When?"

"I was sitting with him at the bar at Severance Hall the night Dad died. Had a couple of drinks together. I knew he was on that intelligence subcommittee. I'd probably had one whiskey too many, I guess

I imagined it might be some kind of code word, something up his alley."

"What did he say?"

"He'd never heard of it."

Jason squinted through the Jag's raked windshield as if at an obstacle in the road.

"What's the matter?" Kristian said. "You have a problem with me telling him?"

Jason started his car. "We'll talk," he said over the smooth rush of the V12. "As soon as I'm back from Cincinnati. I'll call you. Go make Wendel's day. You should let him drive you every morning if he needs to."

"We don't want to make him indispensable."

"True. I guess we have a duty to let the Florida concept sink in, for his wife's sake."

CHAPTER 12

"I CHANGED THE OIL, GAVE HER A WAX. RUNNIN' LIKE A TOP. YOU JUST tell me when you want me to pick you up at the office." Inconvenient to have to come back to Canterbury Road for the Spyder, but it was important for Wendel. "I appreciate this Mr. Kristian."

"No, Wendel. Thank *you*."

It had always been "Mr. Kristian," like *Mutiny on the Bounty*. Kristian wondered what he was going to do with his father's car: he had no use for a big luxury sedan, but he would not sell the 920 until Wendel felt ready to let it go. Never a specified part of his job, he'd always done the maintenance, using the pit Kristian and his father had installed years ago for their restorations, in the garage behind the house. Till the Florida concept sunk in, as Jay put it, the chauffeur would continue to come back to Canterbury Road every day just as he had done most of his working life, to wash and polish and tinker, and drink tea with Ingrid in the kitchen as though waiting on his employer.

What surprised Kristian this morning was Wendel's driving. For forty years he had been one of the few people to come close to Kristian's idea of a perfect driver. A heavyset black man, becoming corpulent in his mid-sixties, Wendel's movements were usually entirely quiet in a car: he never crossed his hands on the wheel but let the rim whisper through them; he never moved his big shoulders, only his head and that often, never relying on mirrors to change lanes or make turns; he accelerated with silky smoothness to exactly the posted speed limit, having developed a private system in order to understand road signs, to overcome a profound dyslexia.

But this afternoon he seemed agitated, hunching his shoulders continually as though, for the first time in his life, his chauffeur's uniform was a discomfort to him. At the first traffic light heading west out of Cleveland Heights, Wendel's moist brown eyes shuttled constantly between the mirrors, always avoiding Kristian's eye in the back.

He stopped at a red light on Fairmount Boulevard. It changed to green.

"You okay Wendel?"

"Yes sir. I'm fine, thank you."

"The light's green."

Wendel's upper body became wood. About to turn south onto Lee Road, Kristian noticed that he fumbled for the indicator.

"Wendel?"

"Yes sir?"

"Is there something you'd like to talk about?"

The chauffeur stared straight ahead, the muscles knotting in his heavy jaws as he sped up slightly, ten miles per hour over the posted limit, to thirty on a straight open stretch of Lee.

Kristian had to smile. "Going for the land speed record?"

Wendel looked at the speedometer in shock, braked so suddenly they both tilted forward. He whispered something almost inaudible, but Kristian could not remember an occasion when he had ever heard him come even this close to a curse word.

"I'm going to be honest," Kristian said. "I think there's something here you're not telling me, but you would like to. Am I right about this?"

His silence grew stubborn.

"In that case," Kristian said, "I'm going to confide in *you*. I am led to understand that my father cashed in 2 million dollars worth of stock in the last five years. I'm told he sent the money to Canada for reasons I can't even guess at. That's why Mr. Steele-Perkins asked you and Ingrid about Toronto." He watched Wendel closely in the rearview mirror. The chauffeur had begun to perspire.

"The police know?"

Kristian narrowed his eyes. "Not yet. Why should you care?"

Wendel's shoulders rose and fell with his deep, unsteady breathing.

"You ever drive my father to Canada, Wendel? You ever drive him onto the ferry at Sandusky? You don't even have to go around the lake, do you, you can drive right on at Sandusky and go all the way across to Leamington, Ontario. You're now about twenty over the speed limit, by the way."

Wendel slowed.

"The way I figure it, someone like Dad doesn't send 2 million bucks anywhere they don't have some significant interest."

Wendel was driving better now, through the light, early afternoon traffic. "Over there," Kristian said. "There's a whole bunch of meters, take your pick."

"Here?"

"Just do it. Park the damn car."

He waited till Wendel had parked, then unbuckled and leaned forward until his arms were folded around the front passenger seat headrest.

"We've known each other all our lives, right?"

"Yes sir."

"This is a private conversation, right?"

"Okay."

"So talk to me."

Wendel looked away towards the street as he began in a voice of quiet misery.

"I wasn't going to tell no one. He asked me not to. He trusted me!"

"I know that. You're not betraying him, Wendel. You could never betray him to me."

He was still for a moment. Then he nodded. "Remember some times I used to take him up to that spa?"

"The Swiss Cottage?"

"That's right." Hardly a cottage, it was a rambling health spa on fifty acres in Bay Village, bordering Cahoon Memorial Park. Run on Spartan Swiss lines, the emphasis was on health rather than luxury, though steep membership fees kept it exclusive.

"You know that little garden they've got there in the grounds, that oriental place?"

He meant the Ryo-kaku Tei, a Japanese tea garden in a grove of poplars, a secluded place where guests could come for spiritual restoration after the physical rigors of the spa. Kristian had been there once with Melanie in early fall, a few weeks before they had acknowledged it was over. The wind had come up while they sat in silence by the little tea house, whispering their unspoken truth through the condemned leaves.

"He was meeting someone?'

"Yes sir, I believe he was."

"A woman?"

"I never saw who he was meeting."

"How often was this?"

"Every couple of months. And always the same thing: he'd get me to drop him off there and come back at the end of the day to pick him up. My brother lives out in Avon Lake, I'd go over there. Since your father retired, it would always be on a weekday, so..."

"You mean to say you were taking him out before he retired?"

"Couple of years while he was CEO. Ever since he stopped driving himself for his pleasure. He could have been taking himself out there for who knows how long before that. I was doing it for sure about seven years altogether. After I dropped him off, I used to drive up to the parking lot by the main building to make my turnaround. Not too many cars there in the week. People like you and me, you know...if you like cars, you notice them. I noticed this particular car mostly cause it was there every time we were, for the last couple of years anyway. And because it was a Dorner 920 just like this one, except it was an S." A car like Phil Baylor's, more stiffly sprung, with another forty horsepower and high performance tires.

"How many times did you notice this particular car in the lot?"

"Like I said, every visit for about the last two years. I'd say eight, maybe ten times. Couldn't have been the manager's car or nothing like that because the staff got a separate lot around back. Also, it had Canadian plates."

Kristian caught his breath.

"Ontario," Wendel said. "They got a blue crown on. Blue on white. It was an Ontario car." He looked round. "What is it Mister Kristian?"

Kristian squeezed his lower lip between his thumb and forefinger, rolled it into a thoughtful spout. Maybe Jay and Blake Cockerham wouldn't need power of attorney after all.

"Did you notice anything else about it, other than the plates, anything to say who it might have belonged to?"

"No sir. I didn't think much of it at all at the time, just that it was a top-of-the-range Dorner and it was always there. Then that Lieutenant Deems, he asked me if Mr. Peiper knew any Canadians. I told him sure, he knew lots of people up there from business. But then he says did he have any personal friends from Toronto and I thought about that and told him not that I know of. Then I ask him why he wants to know and he tells me about the phone call your daddy tried to make that night. That's when I remembered about the spa, and the plates on that 920 S."

"But you didn't tell Deems."

Wendel looked around suddenly, impassioned, his voice rising. "In the forty years I worked for him, your daddy never asked me to keep a secret. I talk to plenty other chauffeurs working for rich men. You know how many of them sit in the car every week outside some fancy apartment until the boss comes back reeking of you-know-what? Then it's an extra Christmas bonus or a bottle of Chivas to help them remember it was the golf club or the Masons they was at."

"Was my father meeting a woman, Wendel?"

"Maybe it was a woman's car; there was always a pretty box of Kleenex, ladies gloves sometimes, the driver's seat pushed forward a ways. Even if it was a woman, there wouldn't have been no hanky panky. He wasn't like that. Nothing he ever had to feel ashamed about in front of your mother nor anyone else. Nothing he ever asked me to keep quiet for him except this one thing. That's why I never told Deems."

"I understand. I'm sorry this is upsetting for you." Kristian was silent for a time. "I guess you weren't able to get the plate number."

"No sir. I was not able to read the number." Wendel was adjusted to his disability, and he knew Kristian too well to show any embarrassment over it. Yet the reluctance was creeping back into his voice. He was hunching his shoulders again, hooked a finger into his stiff collar. Kristian heard the button pop.

"What is it Wendel? Please, I need to know this. The last thing my father did before he died was try to call a number in Toronto. In five years he transferred 2 million dollars to a Toronto bank account. I need to know."

Wendel gave a great sigh. "What I saw...it wasn't at the spa."

"What do you mean?"

"Last time I ever took him out there, must've been right after you got back from Frankfurt. Your daddy had his big briefcase with him as usual. Except he wouldn't let me carry it down from his room or put it in the car, like I always did for him. I noticed he kept his hand on it all the time we was driving. He wasn't looking well. I thought it was his bladder trouble, something."

Hansjorg had developed a chronic urethritis in the last year, unresponsive to antibiotics, the only weakness in an iron constitution.

"He tells me we're going out to Bay Village and then I knew I'd be spending most of the afternoon at my brother's. So we're on our way out there on Lake Road, by Freeze Vale Cove, and your daddy gets caught short, like he sometimes did when his waterworks was troublin' him. He asked me to find him a gas station. 'When you gotta go,' that's what I told him. So I found a Texaco on Lake, and I stopped and opened the door for him.

"He wouldn't leave that briefcase. Oh no. He kept on hugging it like it was going to jump out of his arms if he let it go. I went ahead of him to the office, got the john key for him, gave it to him. Guess he wasn't looking where he was going. He caught his foot in the air hose some careless so and so left lyin' out."

"He fell?"

"Oh I caught him okay, but he let go of that briefcase. I guess it wasn't shut right cause the snap popped and this can rolls out along with a bunch of his papers. Rolls right across the forecourt till it hits the curb around the pumps. When it bumped the curb, that's when the top of the can came off and I saw the film."

"Film?"

"Big old metal reel with a film on it. It was starting to unravel. I got there first, I was going to help him pick it all up..."

Wendel stopped, swallowed.

"What happened?"

"He barked at me."

"Barked at you?"

"In forty years he never spoke sharp to me. Not once. 'Leave it! Get back in the car!' Just like that. Then he grabbed it, stuffing the film back in, looking over his shoulder like he was afraid someone'd see him. I went runnin' after the papers before they blew away, but it was like he didn't even see them. He wasn't thinking about nothing but that film."

"Did he say anything when he got back in the car."

"No sir. That was strange too. He'd always talk to me. My hands were shakin' so bad I couldn't hardly steer the car, but I got him to the spa, and sure 'nough when I came back from my brother's to pick him up, he wasn't hangin' onto his case no more."

"You don't think he had the film any more?"

"That's right. I reckon he gave it to whoever it was he'd been meeting out by the spa all those years."

A pickup truck went by with a broken muffler, flushing pigeons from the forecourt of the Maple Heights Town Hall, wheeling through the flat afternoon sky, lost against the grey. Kristian hadn't realized how far south they had come, to the point where Lee angles into Broadway Avenue, which would take them southeast almost to Dorner, in Oakwood.

"He never said anything else about it?"

"No sir he did not. The subject never came up again. Not a word."

"Could you tell the year of the 920?"

"Hard to say with the 9-Series. It hasn't changed much in a while."

"We rounded the front end a bit since '93, tail lights got freshened. Was it roundy at the front?" Wendel bit his lip. "It doesn't matter," Kristian said. "If I remember right, the S has only been available in Canada since '92. It shouldn't be hard to get a list of owners. It's high end, there won't be that many. We'll just go down the list."

"Then what?"

"Everything will be very discreet."

"You'll tell the cops?"

"I don't know yet. But there's nothing for you to worry about; loyalty is a rare quality, no one's going to blame you for being a good guy. Anyway, you could always volunteer the information before I say anything."

Kristian spent the rest of the journey in deep silence, for which Wendel seemed grateful, driving smoothly again.

Hansjorg had lied. Kristian felt it with the instinctive certainty of shared blood and a lifetime of knowing his father. The package that had changed hands that morning had not been engineering drawings, suspension designs, it had been a film.

But who had his father passed it to? Had the Dorner 920 owner been a Canadian with a bank account at the CIBC? Had he been trying to call her at the moment of his death?

At least Kristian knew how to narrow down the car.

CHAPTER 13

Ellen Mayer had bought a new outfit for the family gathering, dark navy, not quite black. Her blond beauty was as composed and preserved as her pristine home. It had always seemed unfair to Greta that her looks had passed to Ulrich and not Regine. In contrast to her mother, Uli's sister had come unraveled since she received the news in Corsica, her tan undermined by a gaunt pallor. She was on her fourth sherry as she took Greta upstairs, away from the ritual condolences, a short pilgrimage to Ulrich's room.

He had been a fastidious house mate, but the antiseptic orderliness of his boyhood bedroom was his mother work. It took away from Greta's sense of him, it was like looking at a museum reconstruction.

"Always in control. We couldn't have friends in the house unless they took their shoes off and washed their hands every five seconds and didn't touch the walls. They learned to stay away. We hated her for it. No, I did. I think Uli understood, even as a little kid. They say mothers and sons, right? Don't they?"

"Did she have friends?"

"Her hairdresser, her manicurist, dress shop assistants. Her perfect little world."

"She was in the Sachsenhausen camp, your grandparents died there, right? How old was she?"

"Five, six."

"So she's controlling. Things start to disappear on you, you learn to hold tight. My Dad was alcoholic, you never knew where the next slap was coming from. Laughing one minute, hugging you, you look around and he's coming at you. Chaos. The police wasn't such a hard choice; I needed to make order out of the chaos. Pretend to."

"Why did Uli join? He already had order."

"Maybe he wanted to prove you could wear a German uniform and be just."

"And kind. He was...always...kind."

Regine's voice broke and Greta held her as she wept, seated on the side of Uli's narrow boy's bed. Not for the first time she felt an overwhelming temptation to tell Regine the truth about his "accident," but it was need-to-know, and Regine had no need of dangerous knowledge or further devastation.

Otto arrived late, without Leona. He drank a glass of wine, refilled it and took a loaded plateful of Ellen Mayer's delicate canapés out onto the terrace.

"I got the round back from ballistics," he said between mouthfuls. "You were right, it came from a Steyr SSG2. The rifling and compression patterns both match." He took a gulp of wine, narrowing his small, quick eyes as he scanned the terrace. "I found Truong."

"Where?"

"In a leather bar on Kaiser, in the active room. Talk about Iron Fist."

"He knew who you were?"

"Sure. Uli had filled him in. You were wondering how Franz fingered Junia's film. It wasn't just her film."

"What do you mean?"

"You heard of Alpha Linen Supply?"

Greta frowned. "Green and white vans?" One saw them all over Frankfurt.

"Alpha's expanded," Otto said. "A Dutchman called Emil Meert bought them out. Moved into catering, landscaping, pool installation, the whole leisure thing. He also runs an employment agency that specializes in domestic staff. This is exclusive, services the top one percent income bracket. Stable hands, greenskeepers, butlers. You want a maid or a Lear pilot, Meert's got them trained, groomed, bonded, clean and discreet, with references."

Greta took an impatient sip of wine.

"There's an inner sanctum, a group of very select, super rich clients. Meert gets them 'companions.' He's a pander: either sex, any race, a reprehensibly broad age range. They call it Meert's Lonely Hearts Club. Junia Dorner's a member."

Greta drew a sharp breath. "Jesus. That's how Truong got into her townhouse."

"She was screwing him for a couple of months. I guess she doesn't have time or inclination for a real relationship. She can buy anything else in the world she wants, why not a new toy boy every season?"

The terrace door opened and a group of Uli's relatives came out. Greta drew Otto away, across the small, retentive garden. Ellen Mayer gardened with gloves on, imposing order without creativity beyond the placement of lawn ornaments. They stopped beside a wishing well, not even the illusion of depth, merely short dead grass at the bottom, an arm's length away.

"What else did he say? Did he know what 'krokus' meant?"

Otto shook his head as he lit a Gitane, tumbled a pillow of smoke back into his lungs, exhaled with a hiss. "He must have dropped something just before I got to the club. I could see I was losing him from the get-go, twenty minutes he was stupid wasted. One way to hide I guess, except the SG can still fucking see you. Between you and me, it wouldn't be a bad idea if our friend Franz overdosed before someone finds out we've had the pleasure of his acquaintance."

"I'm sorry Otto. I should have thought harder before I told you any of this. I was scared. I'm as bad as Truong."

"Fuck that. We're friends. Isn't that's what friends are for, to bury each other in warm shit?" He watched her with his eyebrows raised until she produced a ghost of a smile, immediately fading.

"Did he say anything about Ulrich?"

"Yeah, he said one interesting thing while he was still coherent. Shows you how obsessed Uli got over Beck and Junia Dorner. I mean, he was always intense, mister fucking moral conscience...you know, I always reckoned he was compensating for being a faggot."

"If you're not a pig, why do you talk like one?"

"Sorry teacher."

"Ellen's Jewish, her whole family died at Sachsenhausen. If he had his sights on Beck..."

"Thank you for the obvious, I don't need a fucking lecture."

"What did Truong say?"

"Uli must have been crazy, right? He found out about this meeting coming up at Junia's schloss in Rudesheim. Beck and an American called Vaughan."

"When?"

"7:30 Friday night, day after tomorrow. Uli figured — this is when he was still telling his boyfriend stuff — he figured he was going to get a listening device into the schloss, get some surveillance on them. He found out the exact location for this dinner meeting, a room called the Jagdzimmer." Otto drained his wineglass. He sucked his teeth for a moment. "Truong worries me big-time. Loose fucking cannon on deck. We don't need it."

"I think we should go see him again, together. Catch him when he's straight. We need to know what else he knows. Maybe there's other stuff he hasn't told us like this Rudesheim thing."

"I understand he's a regular at the Mineshaft on Wednesday nights."

"That's tonight."

"So it is. I'm not on duty either."

"Bring your dancing shoes."

The Mineshaft was busier than the night she had seen Uli here, but the same vapid music, the same mildly resentful looks from the line of men at the bar, available like a row of vacant parking meters. Greta wondered if their promiscuity said anything about male drive in general; was it a genetic desire, to run through sexual encounters in rapid, faceless succession? Was it only the anchor of female censure and the specter of disease that kept the majority of men from drifting like these opportunists at the bar?

Greta had mineral water while Otto ordered scotch, steadily, from a powerfully built barman with a heavy corn-colored mustache, dyed like his razorcut. By 11:35, with Truong still absent, Otto was bored and getting drunk. He confided to Greta that he had a rapsheet at Keplerstrasse on the barman who was also the Mineshaft's owner. Martin Schubert was a former mercenary, a corporal in the Serbian army in the Balkan conflict. Schubert didn't know Otto but he knew their visit wasn't recreational. He served them with watchful care, a doggedness to his glass-polishing until Otto told him to relax, they were just looking for Franz Truong.

The barman said he didn't know any such person.

"Well that's funny, corporal."

The club owner grew still, his toweled hand inside a beer glass.

"You see Martin, we understand that Franz is bisexual, which is interesting as it happens because my wife here and I were home watching the TV as usual, eating nachos, and I thought why don't we try something a little bit different tonight, you know, spice up the salsa?"

"Otto," warned Greta, averting her eyes as the barman looked at her. Otto usually bullied in proportion to his state of nervousness, high tonight in spite of the scotch.

Martin put the towel down and folded powerful, tattooed arms across his leather vest.

"Hard to believe right, cause cops aren't generally as degenerate as you fucking people." Otto sighed and emphatically squashed out his cigarette. "There's a middle-aged guy on the dance floor snogging with a chick in a blue shirt and black leather pants. If that kid's even seventeen I'm the virgin of the fucking chrysanthemums."

"He's twenty-two," Schubert muttered. "I checked his ID."

Otto drew an equivocal breath through his teeth. "Jeez, I don't know. Of course you and I could always have a little bet, then I could call my station, we get vice down here find out who's right. One warning already this month?"

Schubert chewed his top lip under its thatch of mustache, saved the agony of his decision as Greta took Otto's arm and drew him firmly towards the exit, hissing in his ear.

"What the hell's the matter with you? You know where Truong lives. You want to make a scene, don't do it on my time. The last thing we need is to draw attention to ourselves."

Otto was still glaring towards the bar. "People like that make me fucking sick."

Greta kept pulling him towards the exit. "Like what? Uli was gay for Christ's sake. You're really pissing me off now."

"Uli was Uli."

"And Martin's Martin and Franz is Franz except he's not here so shut up and let's go find him."

Franz Truong lived in a desolate, windswept apartment tower off Berliner Strasse that dwarfed the spire of the Paulskirche. Otto discovered the unlocked door as Greta rang, his hand drifting to the Sig Sauer under his windbreaker as he pushed it open.

The graffiti in the elevator, the threadbare carpet in the lobby and corridor, the faded aural patchwork of rock music and domestic squabbling elsewhere on Franz's floor had not prepared them for his apartment. Beyond the door lay a sleek exercise in chrome and white leather similar to the decor of his car, reflected in spotless mirrored walls and ceiling that expanded the livingroom to an infinity far beyond its modest bounds. White china and silk flowers, a plush white carpet, pristine issues of German *Vogue* fanned out on the chrome and glass coffee table to complete what seemed to be a deliberately retro flavor. Greta could see no reference to his Vietnamese culture. The sterile sophistication was both a testament to Truong's worldly success and a touching insight: these fresh, easy-clean surfaces would have helped him forget he was in a dirty business, although he needed no such diversion now.

He was sprawled naked on the floor of his small, all-white bathroom, propped against the wall between a pedestal basin and a shower tub with Marilyn Monroe's face repeated on the curtain, distorted by its folds.

A not-quite-empty syringe rested on the tiles beside him, its barrel between the first two fingers of his right hand like a cigarette. For Truong it should be chrome and glass instead of utilitarian plastic, an errant thought which shamed Greta. So did then the realization of how beautiful he was, the handsome penis lolling sleepily, like his head. His skin was a golden cream, flawless except for the small, slightly livid puncture in his thigh muscle.

"He was doing Ketamine in the Mineshaft," Greta said quietly. "That would fit with a muscle injection."

"KitKat's a party drug. Doing it here, on his own?"

"You think he really OD'd?" She went back through the livingroom, pausing a moment to look at the plush carpet, then continued into Franz's white bedroom. A basket of condoms lay on the night table, either for recreational sex or incalls. There was a small-screen television on a trolley at the end of the bed, along with a neat stack of videos, Hollywood blockbusters, musicals, gay and straight mainstream pornography. A walk-in closet contained a rack of fashionable suits, pants and jackets, and a white wicker laundry hamper. Like the rest of the apartment, the bedroom was immaculately tidy except for a pair of shoes tumbled carelessly into a corner, the only clothing visible. The shoes were incongruous since he must have put the rest of his things carefully away, on the rack or in the hamper. She walked back to the closet and raised the hamper lid, instantly recoiling from the odor of excrement.

Otto called quietly from the bathroom. She found him still kneeling beside Truong's body. "Can KitKat give you a nosebleed?"

"It makes you numb and dumb — you bump into something, sure it could."

"There's no swelling."

She squatted on the tiles beside him, inclined her head to look into Truong's nostrils which were rimmed with dark, dried blood. "There are tracks on the carpet out there," she said. "They don't show clearly on white, but it looks like heel marks, like someone dragged him in here."

"You're saying the overdose was inflicted?"

"Overcome somewhere outside this apartment, anesthetized. Someone trying to get a chloroform mask over his face would have had to clamp down."

"Nosebleed."

"There's a laundry hamper in his bedroom, you don't want to smell it. At some point he soiled himself — fear or the anesthetic or both. Whoever brought him here undressed him, cleaned him off then shot him up."

"Like Uli."

"With the same half-hearted attempt to make it look accidental. Any traffic cop would smell the rat in here, but these people don't have to be careful. They're immune, they've got Beck."

Otto stood with a grunt, still feeling the whiskey. He sat on the edge of the tub, fumbled out his pack of Gitanes before he remembered where they were. The unlit cigarette wagged in his mouth. "How much did he tell them?"

"We don't know that he talked."

"Jesus...how long were they watching him?" He stared at Truong's corpse. "We're next. We're fucked."

Greta shook her head as she walked away from him, into the doorway. "You can assume that if you want. It may be what it seems, an overdose, maybe even deliberate. I think he loved Ulrich. As long as there's a chance we're clear, I'm going to think about the next step."

Otto stood slowly, tipping his head back to scrutinize her so that for a moment he didn't have a double chin under the scrub of beard. "Next step? What are you talking about?"

"I might remind you that the BKA trained me in electronic surveillance."

For a long moment Otto simply stared.

"I did an upgrade in February. I can do pretty much anything Ulrich could."

He took the Gitane carefully out of his mouth, which left his bottom lip slightly hanging. "Something wrong with my hearing, Greta. Are you out of your freaking *mind*?"

She stared at him unwaveringly. "The DNV cover-up, Uli's death, this film whatever it is...it's all going to get buried forever. Is that what you want? Beck's going to start taking the glove off that iron fist one day soon, with Junia's help. You want to see them turn the clock back sixty years? And there's nothing we can do without hard evidence. We'll get buried like Uli and this kid. Taking on a Beck or a Junia Dorner isn't an option without a really big stick."

Otto continued to stare, slack-featured in amazement, deaf to her tirade. "You're talking about Rudesheim, aren't you," he murmured. "That's what you're doing here. You're talking about bugging Junia Dorner's fucking schloss."

"Not by myself. I'll need some Schutz ID. Maybe my old papers are lying around Keplerstrasse somewhere. I'm sure you've got a tame forger who could update them. You can do something by Friday. I know you can."

CHAPTER 14

Marketing was on the tenth floor, announced by a bright lobby appointed with sleek chrome and leather chairs and glass cabinets displaying promotional items — Dorner keyrings, sunglasses, glovebox-flashlights and scale-model cars — expensive trinkets with the stamp of quality and European style. Kristian reached his office down a corridor lined with framed stills from Dorner TV commercials.

A corner office, in a perpetual state of barely controlled chaos: bursting shelves and in/out baskets, books and papers and videocassettes toppling from his desk and the windowsills. One wall was entirely covered with framed marketing awards, askew.

He began the work he needed to complete before he left for Frankfurt on Saturday, budget approval for the latest in a series of TV commercials for the 6-Series family sedan. But he couldn't concentrate, glancing continually from his watch to the fax machine beside his desk, willing it to life. He had called Dorner Canada's head office in Toronto yesterday, after his drive with Wendel Storey. The Ontario Sales Manager had been out but his secretary had promised to fax Kristian a list of 920 S owners today, all those registered in Ontario going back to 1992, the first year for the model.

Kristian was familiar enough with Canadian demographics to know pretty much what it would contain — a couple of hundred names, almost exclusively male and professional, with expensive addresses mostly in or around the major urban centers — Toronto, Ottawa, London, Hamilton, Windsor. The name of his father's liaison would almost certainly be on the list, but there would be no fast or simple way of identifying it. Even if he phoned every number, what could he expect anyone to reveal on a cold call? He thought of the endless, awkward pre-ambles he would need to make, the frustration of answering machines.

But the name would be there.

He went back to the scripts, more of Phil Baylor's concepts to create a more accessible image for Dorner. One involved a "virtuosi-cally dull" presenter, an egghead in a lab coat delivering thirty seconds of unfathomable technical jargon to describe the Six's safety features while, in a small picture-in-picture, a Great White shark launched unsuccessful attacks on a diver's cage. Phil was offering several alter-native tag lines for his boffin to say at the end of the spot, including *We Put You in the Diver's Seat* and *Quality You Can't Get Your Teeth Into*, nei-ther of which made the least impression on Kristian this afternoon.

He looked at the storyboards without enthusiasm or censure, unable to connect with the concept in any critical way, let alone put a price on it. Two words echoed and re-echoed in his head, amplified to a deafening level by Wendel's revelation.

Forgive me.

For what? Did this regular rendezvous at the Swiss Cottage con-stitute some kind of betrayal? Personal or professional? Was this Cana-dian a long-time lover, or was Hansjorg passing company secrets?

The last idea was preposterous. Wendel Storey had seen a film: no one stored data on film, unless Wendel had seen a can of computer tape, but even that was wildly improbable in the era of CDs and massive hard drives. There were no competitors in Ontario, no auto manufacturers that weren't subsidiaries of foreign companies. Nor could industrial espionage explain the money to Toronto; purveyors of secrets got paid for their betrayal, not the other way round.

Kristian looked out of the window, watched the smoke straining away from the South Plant stacks, intensely, magically white against the sky. Down in the plant yard, an aspiring sheet of newspaper danced in the wind, rising suddenly on a gust, riding clean over the chainlink fence along the railway track.

No. It was obscene even to contemplate the idea of Hansjorg Peiper selling out his company. His life's work.

Kristian started as the fax on his desk jumped to life, his pulse quickening as he watched it discharge a cover sheet from Dorner Canada. The fax itself emerged as an alphabetical list of names with corresponding addresses and telephone numbers as well as the dealership from which they had purchased, or leased, their 920 S.

Abel
Angus
Alcock
Almeida
Anderson
Anlauf
Annis
Apicella
Assmann
Atkins
Baines
Buelow-Schwante
Byles

Growing dismay as the names crawled relentlessly out of the machine, the list growing to three pages. He removed them and counted. Two hundred and twenty-three entries, probably a good half of them would be from the metropolitan Toronto area since rural customers tended to favor domestic product. About thirty of the names looked German.

Was that a place to start? But how to begin in a way that would immediately put his father's liaison on the defensive, even if they we here?

At 6:00 p.m. Kristian was getting ready to leave the office w take-home work; Ingrid had made him promise for once to be hor for dinner at 7:30. He was packing his briefcase when Nath Hutchence called.

"Sorry it's taken so long to get this together, Kris, but after t fiasco with Callaghan I wanted to be sure and get this investigation track. You won't have to deal with the Bureau any more, or Clevela homicide. We've switched to a higher gear. You're going to have p fessionals in your corner."

Kristian remembered that Nate Hutchence served on the Sen Intelligence Subcommittee. "You mean the CIA?"

The senator's voice smiled. "Let's call it the Directorate of Bu ness Intelligence. But yes, it's a sub-section of the Agency."

"Doing what?"

"I must ask you to bear with us for a couple more days, but I w to set up a meeting right now. I want you to get together with a c league of mine. His name is Andrew Vaughan. He should have be dealing with this from the start."

"Can't you tell me anything?"

"I'm sorry to be evasive, Kris. As usual there's protocol to observed, and security considerations. They haven't actually told much. I have to leave this to Andrew. Don't worry, he'll give you straight goods. You can be assured he's eminently sane. Would you available to meet with him after your father's commemoration Thursday?"

Two days from now, in the main auditorium — a memorial ga ering to coincide with a pre-show booster for the Kondor launch. Ju Dorner was coming from Frankfurt to kindle the flame.

"I think so. Will you be there?"

"I'll try, although Washington's a jealous mistress I'm afraid.

you and Junia Dorner have plenty of history together, right? Work and family?"

"Junia's in on this meeting?"

"Andrew insisted on it. I believe she's using Bryce Tevlin's office during her visit?"

"Yes."

"Why don't you meet there then. I'll let you know the exact time." A pause. "You sound tired, Kris. How are you managing these days? All right? Can I help with anything?"

"Thanks. I'm okay."

"I'm still making inquiries about '*krokus*.' I must confess, you've peaked my curiosity here. I don't suppose there's any new light on it, from your end? The word, or the parcel?"

The fax from Dorner Canada was still on Kristian's desk about to go into the briefcase, inches from his hand.

"Kris? Are you there?"

"Sorry, Nate, there's someone at my door. I've got to go. Call me back when you have the meeting time."

He filled his briefcase and stood, confronting his reflection in the window glass, reaching for whatever was in the distant, unfocused corner of his mind, hearing the same studiedly casual manner of Nathan's asking — the second time of asking — that Kristian had caught on the phone at his apartment.

He wanted Jay's help first. That was his instinct, logical or not. There was still a little time before this meeting with Vaughan. If they hadn't made any progress by then, he would open up to Nate Hutchence.

But he had lied just now to get off the phone.

Why?

The question was still with him when he reached Canterbury Road at 7:00 p.m. Ingrid had lit a fire in the livingroom, laid a single place in the diningroom. While he would have preferred to eat with her at the kitchen table, he knew that maintaining convention and ritual meant a lot to her right now.

He insisted they drink a glass of wine together in the kitchen before dinner, amidst the fragrance of simmering goulash, to toast the news that a late October date had been set for her marriage to the man in the green Tyrolean hat.

"Do you still have Dad's violin here?"

She opened the drawer and handed it to Kristian.

"I thought I'd take it in to be repaired before I leave for Germany," he said.

"And I will pay."

"Don't be ridiculous."

"I will pay." There were sudden tears in her eyes. "He had it ever since I started with him, since 1945. It should be properly mended."

Kristian put his arm around her shoulders. "I think you should take it with you to your new home." He saw her about to protest. "Your fiancé has grandchildren doesn't he?"

Ingrid smiled through her tears. "Four of each. The youngest is five years. Melissa. She's a darling."

"Perfect age to start playing. And when Melissa comes to visit you, she'll have an instrument to play. Dad would have liked that idea. Is there a case for it? I don't remember ever seeing one, it was always in the display cabinet."

"I'll find a box."

Kristian followed her through a door at the back of the kitchen, into a tile-floored room with porcelain tubs and a washer/dryer combination of the same robust vintage as the kitchen appliances. Ingrid stored boxes in a low built-in closet next to the dryer, loathe to throw anything away. She pulled out the box for a Sony VCR that Kristian had given his parents almost ten years ago. "How about this?"

"Fine. That'll do as far as the repair shop. I'll get a case when it's fixed."

Ingrid was continuing to rummage, depositing boxes and paper in the doorway behind her. "We need something to pack around it. There's some soft tissue paper in here somewhere."

Kristian grinned at her back. "The things you squirrel away! Couldn't we give the recycling program a little business? Some of this stuff must have been here since the Creation." An example lay at his feet, a piece of brown paper, yellowed with great age, trained to the shape of the parcel it had wrapped.

Kristian leaned closer. The parcel had been shallow, about a foot square. The paper was faded to pale khaki, crossed with two darker lines where it had been bound with string.

He squatted and picked it up, moving aside as Ingrid emerged from the closet with the tissue. She began to say something, then saw what he was looking at. Her expression grew serious.

"That was in your father's room, in the wastepaper basket. I remember because it was the first time in all the years I worked for him that he wouldn't let me in to clean."

"When was this?"

"Just after you got back from Germany. It was two days before he let me go in. He was acting so strangely. He'd put the pictures back but none of them were straight." She saw Kristian's intense, puzzled expression, and nodded. "Sure. He took them down to use the projector."

"The movie projector?"

"He got it down from the attic, had it in his room. I thought he was playing the home movies. Seeing your dear mother, I thought *that* was affecting him."

"The home movies aren't here, Ingrid. I had them transferred to video years ago and I never brought them back. They're all at Kirtland Hills somewhere. What was he watching?"

"I have no idea. I just saw the projector in his room."

"Did you hear anything?"

She stiffened slightly. "I wasn't listening at the door if that's what you mean." She snatched the paper from him. "I kept this because it's good thick paper. The string I had to throw away."

But it wasn't good paper: the sheet crackled dryly in his fingers as he unfolded it. "Was there a box? Any cardboard inside?"

Ingrid went back into the closet, came out with a shallow box. "I think this was it. Yes, this was with the paper in his basket."

Approximately a foot-square and two inches deep with a lid, the sort of box that would package a small pizza. The cardboard was corrugated, as old and dehydrated as the paper wrapping. Somewhat flattened, whatever it had contained had left a circular imprint that could easily have been made by a film canister.

Kristian realized he was looking at the bottom of the box, only saw the stamp when he turned it over, faded to grey but legible:

C.R.O.W.C.A.S.S.

ALLIED HIGH COMMAND — PARIS

Case file No. 667356 Dorner AG Frankfurt

He went upstairs after dinner, stood in his father's room while the twilight deepened. He opened the window, just as he had done that night before the concert, and listened to the wind breathing through the great oaks along the property line.

He turned into the room, towards the open bathroom door, willing away the sound of running water, then the sight of his father in the doorway, his hands dripping at his sides.

Another, more immediate image overlaid it: the screen of his laptop in the diningroom a few minutes ago, its modem connected to the wall jack for an Internet search. Of course the word had nothing to do with the crocus flower, misleading for Kristian and, obviously, for Nathan Hutchence. An acronym, one he could have found in any good encyclopedia or comprehensive dictionary. He had learned that the Central Registry of War Criminals and Security Suspects had been a vital, high profile agency in the majority of cases prosecuted at Nuremberg.

Informed by the instant hits on C.R.O.W.C.A.S.S., he had tried to search deeper, stringing Nazi, Nuremberg, war criminals, atrocities...

hard to type these keywords with fingers weakened by fear, their implications searing his imagination.

The police had still not returned the telephone from his father's night table, so he made the call from the library.

Jason Steele-Perkins was on his way out the door, bound for the airport, back to Cincinnati returning tomorrow evening. The New Age guru was turning out to be a petulant client. "I don't care what he says on those infomercials, this young man is karmically challenged. He needs a bad lawyer not a good one, he needs to fall on his ass a few times. What can I do for you?"

There was no need to give him the background, he already knew everything to this point, including Wendel's tale and Kristian's resulting plan to contact Dorner Canada. When he had finished recounting this evening's events, there was a brief but profound silence on the line.

"I think I'd better come over, Kit. Screw the Cincinnati Kid."

"No Jay, don't mess up your schedule. When are you back tomorrow?"

"Flight gets into Burke Lakefront at 6:00 p.m. I could meet you downtown by 6:30."

"There's a restaurant in the Flats, Two Rooms, we had lunch there once. In the wine bar."

"Kit?"

"Yes, Jay."

"I won't have you jumping to any unnecessary conclusions over a piece of wrapping paper. You hear me?"

CHAPTER 15

THE RUDESHEIM WINE FESTIVAL WAS GOING TO BE THE BEST EVER. Fireworks on the Rhine, from several vessels in midstream, neon animation in the terraced vineyards behind the village, strolling medieval minstrels and roaming wine sellers. The Drosselgasse, Rudesheim's famous historic street, would be transformed for the week-long event, the T-shirts and cameras, cuckoo clocks and beer steins removed to temporary retail booths while the ancient shops were returned to authentic period functions with certain necessary concessions: an apothecary where tourists might buy aspirin and film, a money-changer who accepted Visa, a medieval infirmary where the inevitable Riesling casualties could experience modern medical miracles. But the festival's most spectacular attraction came courtesy of its patron, Junia Dorner, involving free tours of the schloss.

At 8:30 a.m., at eighteen years of age, the tourist information officer was brimming with energy and enthusiasm. It was hard to stop her even with a question.

"What time does the schloss tour begin?"

"Usually the tour operates from 10:00 a.m. to 6 p.m. It *is* still a private residence so only selected rooms are on the tour. That *does* include the Great Hall, the garrison and the torture chamber. Rudesheim *was* an important center at the height of the witch hunting craze. The interrogations took place up at the schloss. There's a secret staircase connecting the torture chamber to one of the bedrooms. A sixteenth-century archbishop had it installed. The court records are on display: they show that a record number of witches *were* condemned during the archbishop's tenure."

"You double as a tour guide, right?"

Genuine surprise. "How did you know?"

Greta smiled. "Where do we get tickets?"

"Unfortunately the tour is not available today."

Otto stiffened. "What?"

"There's a mechanical problem with the chairlift. A crew is working on it now. We're confident of having it running in time for the weekend."

He was growing pale. "The *weekend*?"

Behind the counter, Greta pressed her fingers into Otto's side to restrain him. "There's a road isn't there?" she said.

"It's too narrow and winding for tour buses."

"What about regular cars?" Otto demanded.

"There are no parking facilities."

"I guess we'll have to come back tomorrow," Greta said, smiling broadly at the young woman. "You have a plan of the castle? At least we can decide what we want to see."

The guide reached under the counter, produced a three-fold brochure. "The tour follows a prescribed route. Visitors are not permitted to deviate from it."

Greta opened the brochure and spread it on the counter. It showed a limited plan view of the castle, but only those areas on the tour route were indicated.

"Do you have anything more detailed?" Otto said.

"Sorry, that's it."

"It's so big," Greta said. "Imagine just one family living there. Have you ever been in the private section?"

The girl's manner relaxed a little. "Quite a few times when I was a kid. I was in my church choir. Herr Dorner used to invite a lot of the town people up to the Great Hall at Christmas. The choir used to sing. My sister had a job in the kitchen one summer, so I'd go up sometimes."

"The kitchen? Where would that be?"

"In here." She indicated one end of the Great Hall. "There's a bunch of rooms around it but they're not open to the public."

"There'd be a family diningroom, wouldn't there." Greta said. "Surely they didn't always eat in the Great Hall." She pretended to grow wistful. "Imagine sipping champagne and looking down at those fireworks on the river. I'd like to be rich."

"You wouldn't like the diningroom I saw." The information officer wrinkled her still-freckled nose. "It had animal heads all over the walls. Dozens of them. You wouldn't believe it, everything was made of antlers, even the chairs. Gundi showed me it when she was working there. I had dreams after. Those poor deer, they've got such big soft eyes. They looked so sad."

Greta exchanged a look with Otto. Truong had said the *Jagdzimmer*. The Hunting Room.

"Whereabouts was this diningroom?"

They walked down to the quay, where a Rhine cruiser was loading for the trip to the Loreley Rock. Loudspeakers near the gangplank were already issuing the Loreley Song with sentimental lust.

But the Rhinegau's claim as one of the world's great tourist attractions was valid: better-than-brochure scenery between Mainz and St. Goarshausen, of which the wine village of Rudesheim was typical: ancient, half-timbered houses spilling gently up towards terraced vineyards, the delicate spires of Bingen across the river, home of the mystic Abbess Hildegaard. Only Schloss Dorner, high above Rudesheim, linked to it by a double cable, failed to match the atmosphere of quaint charm.

Purchased and restored by Erich Dorner before the war, it was far from the ideal of a romantic German castle, the type of turreted confection created by Walt Disney via Mad King Ludwig. This castle had been conceived in the fourteenth century as a brute instrument of the power to tax, to resist resistance, and keep taxing. An impregnable shieldwall protected the *Bergfrid*, the monolithic medieval keep, but the most unassailable feature was that the schloss was up there, while they were down here.

Greta smacked her hand against the quay railing in frustration.

"It wouldn't have been easy but it would have been possible. You create the diversion, I stray from the tour, thirty seconds to get a device into the Jagdzimmer. It would have been *possible*!"

"Forget it. It was an insane idea to start with. I told you it was insane. Let's go home."

"We've still got the day to think about this," Greta said angrily. "Let's take a drive up anyway, see what the schloss looks like close up."

"What's the point?"

Greta looked away, resentfully, at the Niederwalddenkmal, half a kilometer north of the schloss. The massive bronze statue of Germania, victorious warrior Queen of Teutonic mythology, was another of Rudesheim's tourist draws. She looked across the Rhine, sword in hand, bearing the crown of the Hapsburgs and with the Imperial German eagle at her feet. Belligerent, xenophobic — statues like this had been shrines to the Nazis, as they were now for the DNV, Greta thought. It reminded her of Junia Dorner, which made her even angrier.

"I had a thought on the way out here," Otto was saying. "When we came through Wiesbaden, past the U.S. Base. You remember that Air Force guy I used to drink with? Bill Tomzak?"

"He was creepy. He used to talk about the war all the time."

"He was smart. Anyway, that word Uli used — *krokus* — I thought we could throw that at him. He was a Defense Intelligence clerk, a sergeant, probably made general by now. The guy knew a lot about a lot."

"Would he still be here? Most of the U.S. personnel's long gone: '*Auf wiedersehen* dear friends.'"

"It was just a thought. More productive than fucking sightseeing."

"I want to see that castle up close. Come on Otto, you've got the day off. Indulge me for half an hour. Are you going to drive or do I walk up the hill?"

They could see why a chairlift was necessary; the narrow castle road formed a series of tortuous hairpin bends. As they neared the top of the escarpment in Otto's old Mercedes, evergreen forest formed a dark, oppressive wall on either side. Greta couldn't help imagining this journey four hundred years ago, by ox cart, for an appointment with the inquisitor, knowing that the mere accusation of witchcraft was usually enough to carry the accused to the stake. But one didn't have to look nearly so far back in Germany's history, Greta thought, to find sanctioned genocide, the purveyance of mystery and death and purifying flames. And the DNV weren't history at all.

They had been on the road for fifteen minutes by the time they broke from the trees and the schloss appeared with dramatic suddenness, the massive east face of the shieldwall dispiritingly, brutally grey as it towered over the forest.

The approach road ended at the rounded entrance archway, half a kilometer away. An iron portcullis showed only the tips of its spiked teeth, permanently raised in favor of an electronic gate controlled from a glass booth.

Otto stopped the Mercedes a discreet distance from the gate. "Okay? Can we go now? We've been dreaming. Look at the security, and it would have been just the same on the tour. They'd have guards anywhere the tour route got near the private areas. Even if the chairlift had been running, they probably would have canceled tours with Junia coming tonight, not to mention Beck. Remember Baader Meinhoff?

What about Alfred Herrhausen for fuck's sake? They got him in a fucking armor-plated Mercedes in a three-car retinue of bodyguards." He raked the column shift into gear. "Had enough?"

"I want to hear that conversation in the Jagdzimmer."

"Forget it."

"We'll never get another chance. This is it."

He stuck a Gitane in his mouth, lit it, swore as he savaged the Mercedes's steering mechanism to turn the car around, a three-point procedure on the narrow road.

Greta exploded. "What the hell did you get me Schutz ID for if we're just going to quit?"

"It was a stupid idea, I shouldn't have listened to you. Frankfurt Schutz has no jurisdiction here."

"That idiot in the booth won't know. All we need is a pretext to get in for a few minutes."

"They would check."

She was desperate. "Catering. For the dinner. Flowers or something. We could get a van in Mainz."

"You're surely joking." Otto gunned the Mercedes back down the hill. Greta was turned back to the schloss, frantically seeking some solution in its blind walls when something along the top of the escarpment drifted into her peripheral vision, halfway between the castle and the statue of Germania.

"Otto stop."

"What for?"

"Stop the car!"

He braked irritably, then followed her gaze to watch a glass-enclosed, green-painted lozenge with a hard-hatted figure inside rise serenely, now with decreasing speed, towards a landing station at the extreme far end of the rampart.

The chairlift base lay at the end of Ober Strasse, the last fan-cobbled street before the vineyards began. The site occupied four residential lots. Judging by the houses either side, four handsome *Grunderzeit* villas had been razed for the project, no doubt commandeered with an irresistible offer from Erich Dorner. The single-story brick terminal was surrounded by a spacious parking lot, empty but for a panel truck from a company called CCG Electrical Control Systems, out of Mainz. The site was protected by a high chainlink and barbed wire fence bearing warnings of dangerous voltage and penalties for trespassing. A middle-aged security guard in a grey uniform was convinced by Greta's Schutz identification, impressed and excited by the rationale for her "spot check": an important visitor tonight, you couldn't be too careful when it came to security these days, right Alfred? He was in the right business, for sure. Those communist bastards, didn't they know it was over, didn't they ever give up? It was entrepreneurs like Fräulein Dorner made jobs for ordinary people.

She got a tour of the installation, took written notes as the CCG technicians explained how the chairlift worked. The double cable was strung between steel and concrete supports all the way from the base terminal to its twin on top of the castle's shieldwall. They carried two identical cars big enough for twenty passengers, one group going up while another returned, nursing awe and envy and embryonic nightmares from Junia Dorner's torture chamber.

Looking up at the schloss, Greta felt her anger rising like an unsheathed blade. Uli and Truong's death, the DNV funding, the products she peddled from Osnabruck, even this gruesome attraction on the schloss tour...how many ways could Junia Dorner, who already had everything in the world, profit from pain and death?

It was almost half an hour before she returned to Otto waiting in the Mercedes. She immediately picked up his cell phone.

"What happened?"

"Tell you in a second."

She dialed a number penciled in her note book. "Herr Brenken? This is Vektor Security head office in Koblenz. Supervisor Hintze has rearranged the roster to accommodate the repair work on the Schloss

Dorner chairlift. You're scheduled to go on duty at 6:00 p.m., relieving Alfred Ochsenknecht? It's been changed. You will please report at the terminal at 9:00 p.m. No, you'll be relieved at the regular time. No no, you'll be paid for the full shift." She grinned at Otto. "Absolutely. Enjoy the game."

She snapped the phone shut. "One happy security guard: he gets paid to watch Cologne versus Dusseldorf, we get four hours to play with the chairlift."

He lit a nervous Gitane. "What happened in there?"

"Remember Vektor? I used to moonlight for their Frankfurt office in the old days. Some of your guys still do it, right?"

"What the hell have you done?"

"Only one security guy in there, no one at the top terminal. He bought the spot check completely. I let him catch a glimpse of the Sig now and then while we were talking, for dramatic effect." Otto's gun, from his shoulder holster, the reason he wore a grubby polyester windbreaker, whatever the weather. "I said I'd be back for another check when he goes off shift. I'll see him to the door when Brenken doesn't show at six."

"What if he won't go? He may insist on transferring the shift in person."

"So then we'll have to rethink."

Otto frowned towards the base. "What if Brencken calls in to check?"

"And look a gift horse in the mouth? I don't think so, not in the middle of a game. Cologne–Dusseldorf's going to be close."

"What about after — he'll tell the guard that relieves him. Vector will find out."

"An administrative screwup. But won't matter, we'll be long gone by the time Brencken shows. Listen, there are two CCG guys working on the lift. Extremely helpful to the curious Lieutenant. Showed her exactly how it works. It isn't any different from a ski lift."

"How would you know?"

"I worked a Bavarian resort a couple of Christmases as a kid. That's what I did, I ran the lifts. Stop and go. That's it. The brake's automatic on this one, even simpler. That's where the trouble is, but they say they'll have it licked by mid-afternoon, then they're out of here. I wasn't too direct with the questions, but I got what we need. I know how to get the power on, then it's stop-go. You can get me up and back with your eyes closed."

"Jesus Greta..."

She grinned. "I haven't told you the best part yet. We were right: they have a dozen security guards up there when the tour's on, wherever a visitor could stray into a private area. Vektor has the whole contract. My friend Alfred's worked in the schloss many times. He knows it inside out. I asked him to sketch a possible scenario for me, a little 'proactive strategic planning' — he liked that — in the unlikely event that security was ever breached on the chairlift. In other words, how would an intruder most easily and quickly enter the castle from the rampart terminal." She grinned wider, flipped a page in her notebook. "It's hand-drawn but it's all here. Follow the dotted line. Everything depends on the garrison door, here at the northwest end, opposite the terminal. If that's unlocked then I'm in. All the way to the Jagdzimmer."

"Why should it be unlocked?"

"It's an outbuilding. It's only connected to the schloss via the dungeon. It's all on the tour."

"Why would anything be unlocked tonight, with Junia in residence? With Beck coming?"

"Look up there. Go on." Otto craned up above the terraced vineyards to where the schloss glowered over the village, a symbol of raw, incontestable power, only the very top of the *Bergfrid* visible above the rearing, massive ramparts.

"It was designed to be impregnable. The base of the chairlift is secure — they think — the main entrance is secure, we saw that. There's no other way in past those walls unless we're talking paratroops or an unimaginably high intelligence level, such as mine. Schloss Dorner is a closed system."

Otto ran a nicotine-bronzed finger along the pencil line. "The garrison to where? What's this, the dungeon?"

"Yep. I have to go down a level, under the garrison and through the dungeon to get to the archbishop's little staircase, right there. That's my way in. It'll take me into a bedroom right above the Great Hall. The Jagdzimmer's directly off the hall. Three minutes there, plant the device, three minutes back to the terminal."

He frowned at the drawing. "Hold on. The dungeon's here, but the entrance to the staircase is over here. What's this room?"

"The archbishop's staircase starts in the torture chamber. This sick twist enjoyed visiting privileges from his boudoir, which is where the stairs come out."

"You intend to go through the *torture chamber*?" He took out another Gitane to chain-light it.

"Don't. I feel rather sick already."

"I wonder why." Otto flipped the butt through the window, put the Gitane away. "There's a lot of risk. Junia or Beck's own security could come poking around anytime while you're up there. You could be seen by a servant, anybody."

"I'm trained. I did a week of hostage simulations last November. I can move quickly and discreetly. I'm fit."

"You want to take the Sig?"

"No."

"You can call Brenken back and disappoint him, you know."

"No. This may be our one and only chance to find a weapon to use against them."

"Your big stick?"

She smiled slightly. "Maybe all we need is one little flower."

"*Krokus*?" He made her look at him. "We can still turn the car around and drive back to Frankfurt. Tell yourself whatever you like Greta, but don't try to bullshit me; this is a horribly dangerous course of action with no guaranteed results. We don't even know for sure that Beck's going to be there. Christ, we only have Truong's word that this meeting is even taking place. I will gladly walk away from this any time you say."

She returned his gaze long enough to withdraw the blade's full length.

"Uli can't walk away, can he Otto?"

CHAPTER 16

Alfred Ochsenknecht's favorite niece was getting married at the weekend, on Mauseturm Island. The reception was taking place on a Rhine cruiser in midstream. Alfred had agreed to make a speech. He was glad to go home and practice on his wife. Otto had just spoken to Herr Brenken? He was on his way? Fine. It was cool, wasn't it, for September? Pray for good weather for Saturday.

The enclosed car moved with reassuring precision, carrying her swiftly and smoothly over the terminal's fenced boundary.

By the time Greta reached the first support, the terminal appeared below like a model. She heard the wind whisper around the car, the soft rumble as it passed over the supports, felt the sensual rush of vertigo, heart in her teeth, as the Rhine valley fell away.

Even now, adrenalized, she couldn't help but wonder at the beauty of the landscape below, Rudesheim like a toy village nestled in the valley beneath its terraces of laden vines, the shipping on the Rhine like charms pinned to a satin ribbon.

She resisted the temptation to radio Otto. There would be ample opportunity for that at the top. Let him concentrate on operating the car.

Halfway up she passed the descending empty car and now the castle's shieldwall loomed above her, visible at first through the glass roof panels, dropping below as the car climbed, up and over the shieldwall, continuing straight for the last ten meters before the loop, already slowing as the automatic brake kicked in.

It was only now that Greta understood the full scale of the schloss, its mass of blind stone. Apart from the windows in the relatively small, three-story *palas* below the tower, and arrow slits elsewhere, it offered few opportunities to take advantage of a magnificent view across the Rhine valley.

Opportunity enough to see the chairlift activity, she thought, but it wouldn't arouse suspicion: CCG had been testing the system all day, anyone looking out would see a CCG worker still doing that. They would see a hard hat and dark blue coveralls purchased along with Greta's leather tool belt from a work-wear store in Lorch earlier this afternoon. The sight of her talking on a two-way radio would seem perfectly normal. They would never imagine a Siemens microphone/transmitter in a case like a ring box in her right pants pocket.

The car was skimming the ground now, slowing to a crawl, almost at the loop. She could see that the rampart terminal was identical to the base but without the parking lot. A walkway joined the gravel path that formed an inner ring around the *palas*. The signed tourist route ran through an archway into the garrison courtyard just as her sketch had shown. There was no one in sight.

Now.

Greta got up from the bench seat and positioned herself by the door. She tested the release, even though she knew the door would remain automatically locked until the car had stopped. Just like an elevator.

Now!

"Stop!" she cried aloud, but the car was still in motion, rounding the loop and beginning its return, towards the battlements and the sheer drop beyond.

"Damn it, *damn you!*" She hauled on the inactive door release.

Five meters from the edge of the rampart now and the car was picking up speed. Greta slammed her fist down on the release.

The action could have had no effect on the brake; when the car stopped, it must have been at the whim of the still-faulty braking system.

It hung, swaying gently in the still, early evening air, approximately one meter from the edge of the rampart, on the valley side. Below it, the face of the shieldwall fell almost vertically to its base amongst the terraced vines far below.

She was stranded in mid-air.

Her radio crackled. "Got a problem Grets."

"You don't say."

"I don't know what it is."

"Find it. Solve it."

"I'm trying."

"Great."

"Give me five minutes. I need to concentrate."

Maybe he could reverse it. No, better not get fancy. Better to run her down to the base terminal and try again.

She gave him five minutes to the second.

"Otto?"

It was a few moments before he responded, a clatter as though he had dropped his radio. "I don't know what the fuck's going on here."

"Jesus."

"How far are you from the rampart?"

"Why for chrissake? Can't you get it going?"

"Just look!"

She went to the end of the slightly swaying car. It was large enough to accommodate twenty passengers — not in width since it was designed to pass close to its twin on the return cable, but it made up for that in length. The fact that the doorway looked out over a sheer drop did not mean that the whole cable-car was impossibly far over the edge of the battlement. One of the car's skylights doubled as an emergency exit, a removable panel; if she could exit from the roof, a manageable jump would land her on the parapet, assuming the braking problem was beyond Otto's skill to fix.

"There's a removable roof panel," she reported. "I think I'm near enough the rampart to make it. But you've still got to get me back."

"I'm working on it! I need some time. Just hang in there."

"I thought that was the problem."

It was a problem that grew intense, and finally unbearable, until Greta's fear began to lose all connection with the schloss — she was out of view anyway, except from the very top of the tower — because claustrophobia is overwhelmingly a terror of oneself. Forty-five minutes since the car stalled, and she had exhausted all distractions. She now dreaded Otto's voice, which she had heard go from frustration, to rage, to abject apology and back to rage, none of which had moved the car one millimeter.

"It's no good," he finally admitted.

"So I go."

"Maybe I could get hold of CCG."

"And explain it how? By then they'll be in dinner, I won't even be able to get into the Jagdzimmer. It isn't seven o'clock yet. If I can get into the schloss, bug the room, at least you'll be able to tape. As long as you don't screw up the DAT as well."

"Greta...this is not my fault."

"I know. Just keep working on it while I'm gone. We won't be able to talk once I'm inside. I'll be in contact as soon as I get back to the rampart."

"Grets?"

"Don't say anything else, Otto. I'll see you."

She stood on a seat to unlatch the roof panel and banged it out. Onto the seat-back until her head and shoulders were clear, far enough to haul herself out.

She inched her way, on all fours, up the incline of the car's roof. It was only slightly cambered, making it unnecessary to grab onto the greasy steel cable above her head. The width of the car spared her any temptation to look down until she reached its end, and then she forced herself to focus exclusively on the rampart.

Greta jumped.

For one freezing moment of terror it seemed as though she lacked the upward momentum to reach the edge of the thick stone wall. She landed in a half crouch, but though her Nikes came short, scrabbling on the weather-smoothed stones, both her hands were in place to claim purchase; both arms, strong from bench pressing sixty reps of fifty kilograms, easily levered her up and over the battlement.

Screw you Grentz.

She walked casually along the designated path to the garrison courtyard, almost strolled. If anyone was going to see her, she was a CCG worker. The automatic brake had failed. Her colleague would be picking her up outside the main gate. Did they check outgoing traffic? Would they call Vektor?

Slow it down. *Casual*!

She reached the archway to the walled courtyard, where she stopped to get her bearings. The courtyard was cobbled, the stables apparently converted to garages for castle vehicles and groundskeeping equipment. The garrison door was at the right of the courtyard, age-blackened oak inset with iron studs. There was no question of it being locked: it stood half open.

Greta had brought Otto's magnesium flashlight in her tool belt. The powerful beam revealed a featureless stone gallery beyond the door, approximately ten meters long, its wooden roof supported by half a dozen timber columns. A cold flagstone floor, bare, damp stone walls, windowless except for arrow slits. If this was where the garrison had been quartered, Greta dreaded to think what the dungeon below it was like. Her beam had already found the pointed stone archway in the far wall, near the big door connecting with the living quarters. Beyond the arch, stone steps led down into the darkness. A newly painted wooden sign affixed to the wall at the top of the steps read:

FOLTER KAMMER

TORTURE CHAMBER

Greta noticed a progressive change in air quality as she descended the narrow, wear-cupped steps. The staircase was much longer than she had imagined, and with every downward meter she felt the atmosphere cool and thicken, settling on her face and hands, imparting a deep cellar chill even through her clothing. Her flashlight caught the dark glitter of groundwater oozing into the stairwell, she heard steady dripping from a number of unseen locations. She noticed a smell, faint at first but increasing as she traveled down, of putrefaction, something disagreeable and undigested in the bowels of the schloss. It wasn't hard to think of it as the essence of misery, of terror and pain and hopelessness.

The thought of the witches, young women, girls. Children...

Greta felt a sudden infusion of resolve. She did not hesitate now, purely businesslike in her inspection once she reached the bottom of the staircase.

Lights had been installed in the tunnel-vaulted ceiling, a gang of switches by the steps, but Greta didn't need to turn them on. Her flashlight projected brilliantly through the absolute darkness, revealing that she was in a divide between the dungeon's two sections. To her left was a single long prison cell behind full-length iron bars, little different from a modern lockup except for the lack of bunks or sanitation, and the presence of manacles, three sets chained to the wall, of the same aged black iron as the bars. Straw on the floor, a touch of period atmosphere for the tourists, adding its own musk to the by-now almost suffocating weight of damp and slow decay.

Nothing inside the cell could be hidden from the guards, just as nothing outside, in the rest of the dungeon, was hidden from the prisoners, who could witness everything taking place beyond their cell, in the other half of the dungeon, a ghastly preview of their own fate.

There were no bars around the torture chamber. Presumably the victims were escorted over to their agonies under close guard and returned in no condition to attempt any kind of escape. She saw more ceiling lights, strategically placed to highlight the numerous instruments — in some cases large engines — of torment.

Greta tried not to let her beam linger as she cast about for the entrance to the secret passage. Yet the shapes rose darkly, insistently in the flickering play of light, taunting her with the small knowledge she had gained through natural childhood curiosity: the rack was the chamber's grand centerpiece, then the looming sarcophagus of the Iron Maiden with its close-fitting spiked door; the wheel, perhaps even more terrible in its simplicity, this example tilted on an adjustable pivot to give the executioner a better striking angle from which to smash the spread-eagled victim's joints. Devices lurking everywhere in her peripheral vision, with their levers and springs and hinges — the carpentry and craftsmanship of agony.

Another sign announced the secret passage, through a small opening on the far side of the chamber. There was no door.

The tunnel was so narrow that she had to angle her shoulders sideways to prevent them brushing the damp walls, and even at five feet four she had to duck her head.

It led straight for about fifteen meters before the steps began. Many more than she had taken from the guardhouse, the baron's bedroom was presumably on an upper level of the *palas*. Again Greta's anger energized her, a potent remedy for her aching leg muscles and rasping breath as she climbed the seemingly endless succession of steps. Again she noticed the quality of the air changing, still trapped and stale, but gradually shedding its heavy dampness, its penetrating chill.

The staircase ended with a narrow doorway, open to a tiny room. Greta gasped as her flashlight found a face, a stab of terror before she realized that it was her own reflection in one of dozens of small mirrors set into the walls and ceiling of the room, alternating checkerboard-style with painted wooden panels.

She leaned closer with the flashlight and saw that the panels bore

Renaissance depictions of religious subjects, or rather a single subject, Christ's torment and agony at Calvary, given copious and graphic interpretations.

Little more than a closet, what purpose had it served? An antechamber in which to prepare for the butchery below stairs? A place for the archbishop to do penance for his monstrous deeds or to exalt them? Perhaps both, with the mirrors and the morbid religious studies combining into some kind of auto-erotic experience to engorge his psychosis.

She felt a draft on her face, very slight, coming from one corner of the *studiola*, realized that the facing wall was actually a door, and slightly ajar.

Greta turned the flashlight off and slowly pushed against the wall, flinching at every tiny sound she made, until she put her head out into a spacious room, a bedchamber with a massive canopy bed, roped off as were other items of furniture. Another tour sign confirmed that this had indeed been the archbishop's room. Velvet ropes defined a path across the bedroom. Heavy curtains were drawn, the room in darkness except where light entered from a corridor through an open doorway on the far side.

Greta froze halfway into the room as footsteps approached in the corridor, darted back inside as a slight figure passed the doorway, of a blond teenager in a traditional black and white maid's uniform, leaning back to balance the stack of folded bedlinen in her arms. Greta didn't move until she heard the maid begin to descend a staircase near the door.

Greta crept from the closet, her Nikes squelching softly on the bare wooden boards. She reached the door and listened again. The maid had descended to the foot of the stairs where she was joined in conversation with another, older woman; the maid was scheduled to go off duty, meeting her boyfriend down in the town, but the older woman — housekeeper? — had tasks for her. Their voices faded, echoing into some other part of the castle.

Still Greta hesitated before leaving the room, every pore of her body open to every sound from the castle. From the floor above she could hear a faint piano, soon joined by an orchestra, a Mozart piano concerto. Junia or one of her guests? It would mean they hadn't started dinner yet.

She stepped out into the corridor, her pulse suddenly racing, excitement straining at the leash of caution as she realized that her map was accurate — she had come out right beside the grand central staircase, carved and red-carpeted, sweeping down to the Great Hall. The Jagdzimmer was at the far end of the hall, off a short passage.

She unzipped the right pocket of her windbreaker and gently closed her fingers around the Siemens transmitter, like a good luck charm. She spent five seconds in prayerful, terrified silence, then darted out and across the landing to the top of the stairs.

She froze, tiptoed backwards as another servant, an elderly man wearing traditional butler's tails, entered the hall. In white gloved hands he carried a silver tray with three plates of food in small pink portions, and a dish of lemons.

Smoked salmon.

They were in the Jagdzimmer already?

Greta's dismay rooted her to the spot, her fists clenched tight in miserable indecision, still like that when the manservant reappeared carrying his empty tray and a large woven basket across the hall, where he was met by the housekeeper.

"Is everything ready, Anton? I want to sound the gong."

"That idiot Ernst forgot to fill the log basket, the fire's nearly burned down."

"He's gone, it's his night off."

"I know that!" uttered the man. "I'll give him the rest of his life off if he doesn't pull his finger out."

"You'd better get going," said the woman. "Her majesty said dinner at 7:30, she meant 7:30."

"I don't know what they need a bloody fire for in September," Anton grumbled as they passed under the stairs. "We didn't light the fires for Herr Dorner until November. That American. They're soft..."

Their voices faded. Greta looked at her watch.

7:28.

Two minutes. And the Jagdzimmer was empty.

It was now or never.

Greta took the wide carpeted stairs two at a time, her hand skimming the massive polished rail.

Damn her Nikes, squelching again on the ancient flagstones as she sped across the vast hall, falling silent on islands of antique Oriental rugs. She passed watchful suits of armor and dark tapestries and bristling displays of weapons — fanned-out swords and pikes, halberds and battle-axes, a cold reminder of the risk she and Otto were taking.

The Jagdzimmer was exactly where the map said it would be, off a paneled corridor connecting the hall with the drawing room.

There was no question that she had the right room: not large, but every centimeter of wall space was taken up with trophy heads, a thicket of animal horns in sharp contrast to the dozens of soft black eyes that observed her entrance, come to life with reflected embers from the dying log fire. Heavy, full length curtains had been drawn, presumably to help warm the room. There was fur underfoot, fur throws on the eight chairs which were made of antlers. Hunting horns on the mantle, drinking horns on the table, horn-framed paintings of the chase, cutlery with horn handles, horn napkin rings, horn-mounted silver serving bowls...and everywhere the trophy heads bearing sad and gentle testimony to the excess.

The room's focus was a massive horn chandelier above the table, electrified, turned off now in favor of occasional lamps under vellum shades — soft lighting that maximized the play of firelight and shadow on the walls so that the room had the feeling of a hunting camp in the forest. Three elaborate places had been laid at the table, where the smoked salmon, simply presented with lemon and capers, awaited the diners.

Greta realized she could not reach any branch of the chandelier without standing on the table. She pulled out a chair, stepped gingerly onto its cushioned hide seat and then up onto the table, until the fixture twisted around her head like some fantastic head-dress, the needle points of several horns dangerously near her eyes. She raised the tiny transmitter in fingers grown suddenly slippery with anxiety, clumsy...

She dropped it, her forehead striking a horn point as she snapped her head to follow the tiny device, grinding her teeth against the pain as she crouched and picked it out of someone's portion of salmon.

She tried again, peeling the protective tape from the tiny adhesive strip, snaking her hand between the thrusting horns, applying the transmitter as near to the center of the chandelier as she could, where the surrounding antlers would hide it, wondering why she suddenly couldn't see properly out of her right eye, wiping it with the back of her hand, surprised to see the smear of blood.

Perhaps it was the distraction of the pain, or the intense concentration required to prepare and apply the transmitter — or perhaps Greta had merely underestimated her ability to monitor events in the hall from this distance; for whatever reason, she failed to hear the butler coming until he was in the immediate corridor, his arrival accompanied by the sound of a gong, insistently polite, from somewhere near the stairs.

Anton was directly outside the door to the Jagdzimmer when he accidentally tipped the log basket. No longer in his prime and unused to the task, he must have let the basket sag; he dropped a log, then two more rolled out. Greta heard three choked marimba notes as the dry timber struck the flagstones, then the butler's curses: "*Arschloch*! Lazy little shit! Just wait!"

Under the table. But there was no cloth. She would be seen.

Behind the door?

The curtains.

Greta vaulted down, the sound of her landing and her progress around the table mercifully absorbed by the fur rug. Her fingers searched desperately for the parting, she had time to dodge through but not enough to completely close the gap before Anton struggled in with the basket.

She held her breath as she watched him through the narrow gap, making his way to the hearth, his back turned now as he tended the fire.

Greta breathed. She turned her head as far as she could without moving her body in order to assess her immediate surroundings. There was enough room behind the curtain and the antique material fell thick and plentiful all around her. Heavy tapestry drapes at least four meters tall, up to the ceiling. But like most old fabric it smelled, musky, peppery...

Greta fought to maintain her self-control, calling up every atom of her will power to quell the need to sneeze.

When she saw that Anton was fully occupied with the fire, she twisted from the waist in order to look directly behind her: a double French door, the handles level with her waist. She risked moving her feet, turned enough that she could see how the doors were fastened: vertical bolts top and bottom, the top bolt extended to put the handle within reach.

Greta returned her attention to the room as the butler finished with the fire, drawing back when he turned to give the room a parting appraisal, her heart skipping a beat as he frowned sourly at the table, at the chair she had slightly displaced when she used it to climb onto the table. He straightened it. He bent a little closer to the surface of the table, his frown deepening as he swept a small area with his hand then inspected his palm. He emitted a perplexed grunt. He turned and went out.

Greta gripped the bottom bolt on the left-hand door and drew it easily. She looked up. Reached up.

The top bolt was approximately five centimeters beyond her fingertips.

She jumped, caught the knob, but it barely moved before her fingers slipped from the smooth brass.

It was too late to think about the bedchamber, retracing her steps through the dungeon. The dinner gong had sounded, they would be coming down now. This French door was her only way out. Just the one bolt, there was no lock, no keyhole by the handle. Just the bolt.

She jumped again, but this time there was no movement in the bolt.

Greta threw the curtain aside and crossed to the table in four brisk strides. She seized the nearest chair and hauled it — unexpectedly heavy — back to the curtains. With no time to find the drawstring, she stood on the chair with her head thrust through the parting like a puppeteer, and pulled down on the bolt with all her strength. It drew free with a sharp report.

Greta leapt down with a surge of exhilaration, the chair feeling marvelously light as she carried it back to the table and carefully straightened it, listening with something verging on satisfaction to the sound of voices from the Great Hall: Junia and Julius Beck and the American on their way to dinner.

She crept back to the curtains, parted them, and reached for the door handle, her fingers barely closing around it when she saw the Alsatian standing directly outside the door, his upturned mask a pane's thickness from Greta's hand, head cocked at a slight angle as he regarded her with a puzzled expression.

For several seconds Greta shuttled blurrily between disbelief and horror, until she saw the silhouette of a man coming across the lawn. He stopped and whistled to the big dog. He shouted something. The Alsatian barked once. The man left the lawn and began crossing the gravel path towards the French doors.

Greta had no choice but to step back through the curtains into the room. She listened, aghast, to the growing voices in the hall, an older man's voice standing out — Minister Beck? — almost at the corridor.

Greta flew to the other set of doors, thrust her head far enough through the curtains to allow an oblique view of the man as he stopped on the path. He shouted hoarsely at the Alsatian. He slapped his leg.

Beck's voice sounded very close now, in the corridor outside the Jagdzimmer, steps away — seconds away.

The Alsatian sidled back onto the path, still looking at the French doors where it had seen but not quite smelled her, confused perhaps by the scent of so much mummified game. The man started walking away. The Alsatian trotted after him.

Greta streaked back to the unbolted doors, and while there was no way she could have been fully concealed by the time Junia Dorner and her two male companions entered the room, neither could they have noticed the slight movement of the heavy curtains falling into place around her. There were no shocked utterances, the curtains were not torn aside. Beck merely responded to something Junia Dorner had said.

"I heard his speech. 'New European' indeed! It's priceless. Why can't he just admit it? He won't convince the voters for long. They're beginning to learn. They want a real German, a fat old German like me!"

"Did you see the statue?" Junia said. "Best time of day. Best view in the schloss from your room. Those New Europeans are a little afraid of her, I think. Sit down, both of you. Julius, you over there by the window."

Greta heard Beck sit heavily a few feet away from her curtain. The snap of a briefcase closing, from the floor by his chair, something rolling across the table. A horn napkin ring? Junia invited them to begin. The rattle of cutlery.

"My father was honored beside the Niederwalddenkmal in 1942, did you know that, Andrew?" Junia said. "He wasn't summoned to Berlin, Berlin came to *him*. Think of that. I was there, three months old, in my nurse's arms. My mother was on Hitler's left arm. She said he was always very courteous but he had halitosis."

"That's what being a vegetarian does for you," Beck said with his mouth full.

"Julius likes his meat."

"I like this fish. Why are we in darkness?"

"You want the chandelier on? The dimmer's by the door."

"I'll get it," said a strained American voice, moving across the room.

"My father stood on the Führer's right," Junia continued. "Then Robert Ley, Sep Deitrich. Himmler who brought an SS honor guard, three hundred standards. The National Socialist Motoring Corps turned out, just as they had done when Hitler laid the cornerstone at Dorner Frankfurt. There were two hundred guests of honor, dozens of reporters. Half of Hesse spread across the hillside. Imagine. They understood publicity, those people. My god, Julius, did they ever!"

"As do you, my dear."

"Just you wait. So many ideas!"

"But publicity is the last thing we need right now," the American said. "We have to make absolutely certain that Peiper's death never leads any inquiring mind to C.R.O.W.C.A.S.S. Kristian Peiper put out feelers with Hutchence. If he..."

"For God's sake shut up and enjoy this marvelous food," Beck rumbled good-naturedly. "We've run into a little weather, that's all. Please don't tell me you're going to get seasick." He chuckled through a mouthful. "Or should that be car sick?"

Stony silence.

"Why don't I pour the wine?" Beck said with a sigh. "And Mr. Vaughan, who is so American in his zeal for ignoring good cuisine, can pour out all the excuses why his renowned organization has given us such a fucking headache in Cleveland."

Greta heard the gurgle of wine being poured. She couldn't see Beck but she could picture him clearly from the recent barrage of media images — a burly man in his mid-sixties proud of his full head of hair, physically much bigger than the balding Chancellor who tried to avoid being photographed with his interior minister.

"Relish this, Andrew," he said. "This is Junia's late-harvest *Spätlese*. Thirteen percent in a Riesling! I drank a bottle the day I got married, two the day I got divorced! 'In the company of a young lady I drink neither Burgundy nor Muscatel, but an old vintage Rhine wine whose name I have forgotten, along with the name of the young lady... tum-te tum-te tum.' Well?"

Greta stood transfixed, listening as the delicate rattle of cutlery gave way to expectant silence.

"It was not anticipated that Peiper would return home before the end of the concert," Andrew Vaughan explained.

"Ah," Beck soothed acidly.

"What about the phone call?" Junia said irritably.

"A Canadian area code."

"Toronto. Shared by several million people."

"What's the significance?" Beck asked. Could he have sent the film there? Was he calling to warn them?

"It's going to take time to investigate that possibility."

Greta heard a sharp clatter of cutlery then Junia's voice, like jagged ice. "We don't *have* time. Don't either of you realize what's at stake here? Dorner represents one percent of this nation's entire gross national product! If I go down, you'll go with me, Julius. You'd better do some thinking too, Vaughan...your government has also guaranteed its loans to Dorner. If the Kondor dies because of this, Washington won't see a cent of them." Her plate scraped across the table. "I can't eat this. It's too hot in here."

Vaughan: "Shall I open a window?"

Greta felt the blood drain from her face. She listened to several seconds of roaring silence from the room beyond her curtain.

A chair was pushed back. A change in the direction of Junia's voice meant she was now on her feet, moving across the room. "It's vital we find out what Hansjorg Peiper did with the film. I don't care whether it went to Canada or the moon — we are *going* to find it."

She came around the table, her voice sounding closer to the curtain. Junia Dorner stopped. She grasped the drawstring and pulled opened the curtains.

She turned to the windows.

"You're tall, Andrew. The top bolt...No, sit down, it's open. It shouldn't be. Anton's getting forgetful in his old age."

She turned the handle on the right-hand door and pushed it wide open. The cool evening air poured into the stuffy room, gently stirring the heavy gathered drapes on either side. Junia remained standing directly in front of it, inhaling deeply. To Greta, frozen amidst the gathered tapestry less than a meter away, praying that her Nikes didn't squeak or her tool belt rattle, it was the sound of a predator breathing.

"The fire is backing up, Junia," Beck said matter-of-factly.

"It's pouring out smoke," Vaughan added shrilly. "Shut the window, you're making a backdraft." He started coughing. "I can't stay in here."

The window slammed shut. Vaughan sputtering, Beck chuckling — "talk about smoked salmon!" — all three of them making for the door where Junia bellowed for Anton, whose fault it was for using green logs. They would finish dinner in the drawingroom, it was warmer than the hall.

Greta felt her eyes begin to tear, the need to cough growing with every shallow breath, the need to be gone. Certain that the room was empty, she parted the curtains enough to see the table through the smoke, Beck's leather briefcase still on the floor beside his chair.

There was nothing useful for the microphone so far, and it would be picking up only silence or Anton's curses for the rest of the night. Greta was poised to reach for the briefcase when she heard voices then footsteps in the passageway. By the time Anton and the housekeeper entered the room to transfer the dinner things to a table in the drawingroom, Greta was on the path to the rampart terminal, fighting the urge not to break into a run through the gathering dusk, her fear of being scented by the Alsatian outweighed by anxiety about the cablecar. Was there another way out if it failed to work?

Halfway down the path, she looked left towards the castle's main entrance. She could see the gatekeeper in his booth by the great archway, beyond the courtyard which was now a parking lot. It was at least thirty meters across the lot, open ground all the way to the gate. The gatekeeper couldn't fail to notice her approach, would certainly see her pass the glass booth. Even if he accepted that she was with CCG, her explanation of brake failure during testing, questions would almost certainly be asked.

Her fear lifted when she rounded the terminal building. The car was in the loading bay.

She radioed Otto. "We're not going to get anything. I'll tell you when I'm down. Is the car working?"

"More or less."

"What the hell does that mean?"

"I've had it back and up a couple of times, the brake's got a mind of its own. The doors are somehow out of phase, you'll have to use the skylight again."

Greta used her toes and fingertips on the car's shallow window ledges and the drip sill. She dropped through the light.

"I'm in. Do it."

"Pray."

The car surged smoothly forward, rounded the loop and began its approach towards the edge of the shieldwall. Now it was clear, descending to the first support tower, Greta releasing her first breath since the loop when it slowed and then stopped, bouncing gently on its cable, five meters from the support.

"Tell me this isn't happening."

"It's overloading. The fucking circuit breaker keeps tripping."

"You've got to hurry."

"I'm hurrying."

"Someone's going to come. There's a perimeter guard with an Alsatian."

Agonizing silence.

"How long Otto?"

"*I don't know!*" he shouted into the radio.

"I'm getting out."

"You can't. I can see you from here. You're thirty meters above the ground, what are you talking about?"

Greta stepped up onto the seat, onto the seat back, levered herself out of the car.

"Greta?"

Five meters of cable to the support tower, which had climbing bars all the way down. Five meters wasn't so far. She'd aced the BKA assault course. She could go hand over hand with anyone.

On the police course it had been rope. This was steel cable. Thick.

Greasy. They had neglected to purchase gloves with her new work clothes.

"Talk to me for Christ's sake!"

"I'm going on the cable. I'm going for the tower."

"You must be crazy!"

"Don't start the car, I don't want to lose my hands."

Greta hesitated, glancing down towards the steeply terraced vineyards a hundred meters below. A momentary image of herself sprawled like a broken doll amongst the vines.

"Don't do it Greta, you'll never make it."

"Don't touch the controls. You hear me? Otto?"

"You're out of your mind."

"Whatever you do, don't start the car now."

She slid on her bottom down to the lowest edge of the roof. She stood and in one fluid motion reached up and grasped the cable, letting it slide through her hands as she angled forward, her feet still planted on the edge of the car.

She kicked away, using the cable's downward angle to aid her descent, fighting the compounding exhaustion in her hands and arms. Gripping the slick cable was harder each time, her fingers slipping ever more quickly from the slick woven steel. She was a desperate swimmer, arm over arm, ever faster to relieve her hands.

With a meter and a half to go, Greta became aware of her own body as a malicious force trying to tear her weakening fingers from the cable. She fought the perilous desire to look down.

One meter left to go.

Panting, but now each exhalation was tipped with a rhythmic whimper of panic. Kicking her legs only increased the unbearable pressure on her fingers but she was losing self-control.

Half a meter now, but the pain in her fingers and hands was becoming a dark eclipse, obscuring the light of her reason, to the point that she cared only that the pain would stop. She made no conscious decision to let go of the cable, her exhausted fingers made it for her.

No fear as she fell. Just an overwhelming sense of relief at the sweet

remission in her hands, then a sharp surprise as she hit, a blade of p
through her ankle, not even aware for the first few seconds that
cramped, blazing hands had snatched for purchase and found it.

Greta remained for nearly two minutes, sobbing with fear
exhaustion, hugging the thick steel trunk of the support tower,
cheek against the cold, wonderful steel. Then, stiffly, she bega
climb down.

CHAPTER 17

LIKE MANY GENTRIFIED BUILDINGS IN THE FLATS, TWO ROOMS HAD cashed in on its previous existence as a warehouse. Although the main floor restaurant offered a spectacular view of the Cuyahoga through sloped glass and cedar walls, the Deep Six wine bar in the cellar had retained the original tunnel-vaulting of grey river stone. The wine bar only made money for its owners at lunchtime, but it was an evening fixture for locals hiding from the tourists upstairs, often single businessmen like Kristian, on their reluctant way home from the office, who read the *Plain Dealer* financial section while they worked their way through an order of mussels and a half-liter of the daily special.

By 9:30 p.m. even these stragglers had made their reluctant way home and, as Kristian had anticipated, he and Jason had the cellar to themselves. Even the barman went upstairs after he had delivered a bottle of Chablis to a far corner table where Jason listened, considered, then displayed the usual Latinate elegance.

"Very well, why don't we assume the worst and obvious, scenario: let us say that Erich Dorner, on his deathbed, has given your father a film for safekeeping and that this film contains shocking material, possibly involving Dorner AG Frankfurt, shocking enough even to have precipitated your father's decline once he has viewed it. For reasons we don't know, he passes the film to a Canadian, possibly listed on your fax, possibly the recipient of several millions of Hansjorg's money over the years. Soon after that he suffers a breakdown while his hometown showers him with honors, returns home and is killed, possibly by someone attempting to retrieve this same film. We can't discount the possibility." A gentle pause. "In his last words to you, especially haunting in the light of tonight's discovery and your brief research, he asks you to forgive him."

Jay saw Kristian flinch and reached a hand across the table, placed it briefly on his arm. "I know it's in the back of your mind, Kit. I know what's preying on your mind and as your friend — as Hansjorg's friend — I will not allow you to countenance it. Your father was an honorable man from an enlightened, honorable family. That must be your paean, Kit; that and the absolute *certain* knowledge that whatever this film may or may not contain, Hansjorg Peiper did not join Dorner until 1945. Furthermore, he was thousands of miles away for almost the entire duration of the war, a prisoner of war in Siberia." The lawyer raised a stern ocean-breaker of an eyebrow. "May we proceed on that basis?"

Kristian nodded uncertainly. "Thank you, Jay."

"Very well. So Wendel Storey saw a Dorner 920 S at the spa. Is there a connection between this Ontario car and the CIBC account in Toronto? What does your instinct tell you?"

"That there's a connection."

"So does mine. In which case I'll need to give Blake a copy of your Canadian list, it may help loosen tongues up there at the bank. If it doesn't, we'll still have the list. How many names altogether?"

"Too many. We could concentrate on dealers in the greater Metropolitan Toronto area. That'd cut it by at least half. We could further isolate those 920 S customers who bank with the CIBC."

"Can you get that information?"

"It shouldn't be too hard. Even if there's no dealer record of payment for a given car, I mean if it's leased or financed through an external agency, luxury car owners almost invariably return to the dealership for service."

"Ah."

"You run a Jaguar, right? Would you take it to Joe's garage? No. You take it to a Jag dealer. It's a complex piece of machinery. Same with Dorner owners." Kristian took a drink, licked his lips. "And they pay for their oil changes and their front-end alignments either by check or credit card, of which every dealer's accounting department keeps records."

Jay was frowning. "A check would be easy to trace to a particular bank, but..."

"Credit cards too. I called Visa and Mastercard: whatever financial institution issues it, its identity is encoded in the first four digits of the card number."

"But your 920 S owner could bank at the CIBC and still use American Express. That wouldn't help you."

"American Express and Diner's Club are rare in Canada."

"But not unheard of."

"What's to lose? It'll take my secretary no more than an hour to call twelve Toronto dealers, see who settles their bills with CIBC-issued checks or credit cards. At least we could give them priority."

Jay's lack of comment was skepticism enough. Kristian slumped back in his chair, desperation in his voice. "It's a place to start, isn't it?"

The lawyer took a careful sip of wine, touched his napkin to his lips. His gaze became ironic. "Why go to all this trouble? Why not just hand it over to Nate Hutchence and his compatriots at the Agency as he likes to call it? In fact, why haven't you told him any of the things you've told me?"

Kristian was listening intensely.

"He's offering powerful influence and connections in the investigation of your father's death," Jason went on. "He has tried — twice you say — to apprise himself of any pertinent details you might possess. Why are you playing hard to get? Why not simply hand him the

list and the bank details and let his friends in the CIA have at it? Cou
of hours work for them, at the outside. Hmmn?"

Kristian felt this skin prickle.

"First," Jay said, "let's assume that the film in your father's sa
keeping contained evidence of wartime atrocities at Dorner. Hov
your company faring, as we speak?"

"Poorly."

"This new van though, this Kondor: it represents a ray of ho
yes?"

Kristian nodded. "A very bright one."

"But a last ray."

Kristian drew a breath to speak, then let it out and nodded rel
tantly.

"And the Kondor launch would be seriously jeopardized, woul
not, if Dorner's closet was suddenly thrown open to reveal a horrify
skeleton?"

"It's an image business," Kristian admitted. "We probably woul
survive."

"And who would suffer? Dorner employees of course, and y
shareholders. What about the lending institutions?"

"They're mostly covered."

"Aaah. And why is that?"

"The German government has signed massive loan guarantees
Dorner. So has the United States. You know this."

"Because your company is 40 percent American-owned. Guar
tees for how much?"

"Three point five billion."

"Enough of an investment to break into a man's house to prot
it? Enough to kill for, by accident or by design if necessary?" Jason l
ered his head slightly, pondering his Chablis while he turned the gl
"To tell you the truth, I never liked Nate Hutchence all that mu
Came from power and privilege, but I hear he's made friends in so
decidedly low places lately."

"What do you mean?"

Jason paused uncertainly. He scanned the empty room, moved his wineglass aside in order to lean in close over the table. "I know your father always tried to see around the man's politics, to keep their friendship intact. I think you've done the same?"

It hadn't been easy at times, especially lately: Hutchence had always been the Republican Party's most vocal supporter of military spending, but as a decorated hero of Korea and a lifetime National Guard officer, that had been understandable. But his increasingly unsympathetic line on inner city crime and his recent criticism of welfare spending had been far harder to accept, even from a loyal family friend.

"There are rumors," Jason continued quietly. "I shouldn't be discussing this, I certainly hadn't planned to."

"What?"

The lawyer gave a reluctant sigh, pressed even closer. "I have a client who has dealings with this senate subcommittee Nate Hutchence serves on. He might be further right than we thought. Apparently he's been using his influence to keep the heat off several of these armed militia groups. I'd be measuring myself for a libel suit if I said this on the record, but I hear he's been linked to some vicious people in the last year or two. White supremacists. Neo-Nazis with ties to similar groups in Europe." Jason appraised him for several seconds, accommodating his shocked reaction, then nodded gently.

"I know the sort of question this begs, Kit: what's the possible link between Hutchence and Junia Dorner? We've already discussed the economics tonight, but what about a political angle to this? Do we know where Junia Dorner stands politically?"

"The world's full of rumors, Jay."

"Such as?"

"I've heard one that suggests she's gearing up to support Beck if he runs for chancellor in the next German election. I don't believe it."

"Beck?"

"Federal interior minister. Makes Nate Hutchence look like a hippie. Been cultivating the nickname 'Iron Fist.' It'd be a horror show if he ever got the top job."

"With Junia's financial support?"

"But I don't listen to rumors, Jay."

"But what if it were true. Junia Dorner...I mean, this is your boss we're talking about. Your company."

Kristian shook his head. "You're wrong, Jay. Junia isn't my company. Those workers on the line out there in Oakwood, taking pay cuts to see us over the hump, they're my company. Perry Salkield with his prissy ways, eighty hours a week if I need him: he's the company I keep. Memories of my Dad, all the ways he helped his workers. Coming home for my bedtime story then driving back to the office at 9:00 p.m....that's always been Dorner for me. My Spyder, forty years old and still running great. The Kondor, my concept I hope you know. Decent transportation: reliable, safe, a reasonable price, built to last and beautiful if you have an eye for it. That's my company, Jay. Whatever Junia Dorner is or isn't, nothing in the world's going to change the things I've cherished all my working life, and my father before me."

Jason nodded slowly. "I commend you for all that, Kristian. Heartily. That kind of commitment is rare in our cynical age. You're steering by the stars — wonderful — but you may just be heading for a dilemma. This film and the ripples it may have already caused: we've agreed it could spell disaster for everything you would champion. What will you do if and when you're faced with a choice? What if you discover the truth and find it to be as unpleasant as we have surmised? How easy will it be for you to choose between that truth and your commitment to Dorner?"

Kristian's eyes blazed bright. "How can you even say that? We're talking about my father's death!"

"But as you just reminded me so eloquently, Dorner was his life." Jason swallowed the rest of his wine, looked over at the blackboard menu and made a small, disappointed noise.

"What?" Kristian demanded irritably.

"I had my eye on the sea bass but I've definitely lost my appetite." He looked sharply across the table. "If Hutchence has sinister motives and this fellow Vaughan is his creature, then we need to worry about this meeting at Oakwood. Seriously. They'll be relentless the moment they suspect you know something. But what am I saying? They'll have suspected as much ever since you first mentioned the word *CROW-CASS* to Hutchence."

"So what do I do? Play dumb?"

"I think that would be advisable. Tread water until we've got somewhere with this Canadian business. When are you meeting, tomorrow?"

"After Dad's memorial."

"If I were you, I'd take the time to bone up on your poker game."

CHAPTER 18

GRETA HAD MORE THAN FULFILLED THE SURVEILLANCE UPGRADE requirements, one of which had been to prove how small and how cheaply a discreet listening device could be built from off-the-shelf components. She had used two surface mount Seimens hearing aid elements, creating a spread spectrum wireless microphone with an upper frequency range of 954 MHz. The transmitter used a Mitsubishi codec chip from a cellular telephone with a noise canceling circuit, fine in almost any situation except the Jagdzimmer, where the circuit had been swamped.

"It sounds like the mike's inside a beehive," Otto said bitterly, dousing his Gitane in his coffee mug. "I can't hear a fucking word."

Anything they might have gleaned from the first fifteen minutes of tape was overwhelmed by the combined, complaining hum of a hundred rheostat-controlled bulbs in the chandelier. The blanket of noise had thinned slightly when Vaughan had turned up the dimmer at Beck's request, but not enough to render their conversation audible.

"It's digital tape," Greta said, choking with frustration. "Give me ten minutes in the BKA audio lab...ten minutes and I'd have them clear."

"I did the best I could," Otto said irritably, referring to the graphic equalizer he had borrowed last night from Schutzpolizei inventory after they got back from Rudesheim, which was little better than the EQ in a high-end home stereo system. She rolled the tape for the umpteenth time, chopping down the treble and midrange sliders, boosting the bass with the amplifier way past its threshold.

"What's the point?" Otto demanded. "You said there wasn't anything directly incriminating anyway."

Greta snatched up the headphones.

"Forget it!" Otto shouted at her. "We've been through this ten times!"

She listened again in vain hope, to the point where the recording lapsed into a sudden, by now familiar, phase of silence — the moment when Anton, presumably, had finished transferring the dinner to its new location and had switched off the antler chandelier in the Jagdzimmer. The moment coincided with Otto tearing out the headphone jack.

"Face it, Greta, we blew it. We took a gamble, it didn't pay off. We should count ourselves lucky we didn't get killed."

She didn't even bother to stop the tape. She dropped the headphones on the rug and went silently into the kitchen.

Otto was hard on her heels. "Good. Walk away. We've buried Ulrich. Get on with your life."

Greta's ears were ringing, her upper body plated with pain, her eyes and throat burning. She went to the bathroom and pressed a cool cloth to her face, held it there, grateful for the protective darkness. It was 8:00 a.m. Neither of them had slept last night after Rudesheim. Too much adrenaline, then too much coffee had overcharged her nervous system.

She went back to the kitchen and opened the fridge for the last bottle of Domspatz, the Bavarian brand Andreas had favored and which she still bought out of habit as an occasional, disinterested beer drinker. She got two glasses from the cupboard (never any need to ask Otto), filled them and slid one down the counter to him.

"The American, Vaughan, she wondered. "He talked about *krokus*. He said Kristian Peiper was putting out feelers with Hutchence. Who's Hutchence?"

"I don't honestly give a shit at this point." Otto slumped down in a chair at the table, raked his hands through his thin hair. He looked as bad as she felt. "Sounds to me like Kristian Peiper is involved with these people, with his father's death."

"No."

"Why no? You were investigating him in the BKA. Why was that? There must have been a reason. Bunch of Nazis, right? Capable of anything."

"Stop it."

"How the fuck do you know what he is? All you did was fetch and carry him for a couple of days."

"A week."

"They never even briefed you on the guy."

"He worshipped his father. You could see it."

"How sweet. What...you think a guy who's conspiring to off his old man is going to go round *advertising* it?"

Greta slammed her hand down onto the counter. "You have no idea what you're talking about!"

"Well, well...hit a nerve huh? Whooo. Sorry."

"Be quiet." Her voice was dangerously soft, but Otto wasn't intimidated.

"Fine. Good idea. A quiet life. Bust my quota of nice regular villains, take my kid to soccer games, collect my fucking pension. Maybe Junia Dorner's got a point, you know: maybe this film, wherever it is, whatever it is — maybe everyone should just let it lie."

She glared at him, grinding her teeth.

"I've got a cousin works for Dorner," he said, "ever tell you that? Electrician at the Koblenz plant, three kids at home. There's been a lot of layoffs already the last couple of years, you want to kick them when they're down? Some kind of righteous asshole..."

He stopped mid-sentence. Greta, raising her beer for the first sip, spilled the first inch down her shirt as a man's voice boomed from the livingroom.

Beck's voice.

"Where's the damned light switch?"

The din of the rheostat, its buzz subsiding as the dimmer was turned full up.

Beck again: *"Where did that old fool put it?"*

Vaughan: *"There, on the floor by the sideboard."*

Beck had come back to the Jagdzimmer.

For his briefcase, with Vaughan.

With the chandelier full up, there was no interference. Every syllable was clear.

"Does Hutchence have anything to go on?" Beck asked.

*"No. It's his opinion that Peiper is holding back. Something he isn't revealing. He knows about C.R.O.W.C.A.S.S., possibly even about the film, but he isn't saying **how** he knows."*

"So we must see him."

"I've already arranged it."

"You have a strategy?'

"It would be naive, at the very least, to ask for the truth. I'll tell Peiper a lie, gauge his reaction. If he knows I'm lying, he'll show it. That's as good as a confession."

"I know the technique, but it only defines the problem, it doesn't solve it."

"If Kristian Peiper proves uncooperative, it will be made clear to him that his cooperation is urgently required."

"How clear?"

"He'll be warned."

"Be careful. Junia sees him as a valuable asset."

"But not indispensable. I'm getting his phones monitored, it'll take…"

Their voices faded into the corridor outside the Jagdzimmer, beyond the microphone's range.

Greta stood frozen in the livingroom doorway as the player lapsed to silence. Thirty seconds of dialogue, framed by tape hiss. She had missed it, must have advanced over it every time, into the void that stretched to the end of the tape.

Greta rewound, played it again then again, until 8:45, when Otto had to return to Keplerstrasse.

"You've still got nothing that Dorner's lawyers couldn't bury with bullshit."

"But it proves Kristian isn't part of it. "

"I need the equalizer back."

"I need to know what's on this film."

"Good for you."

"You don't care why Uli died? If Kristian Peiper knows something...I could go to the States."

"Don't even think about it." Otto finished hauling wires out of the equalizer. "You heard Vaughan, they're onto Peiper like flies on shit. You want to kill us both, just call him up." He dragged his shabby windbreaker off the back of the chair, punched into the sleeves.

"Look at me, Otto!"

He tucked the equalizer under his arm and headed for the door. Greta moved to block him, her arms folded intractably across her chest.

"I've had enough, Greta. I don't want this any more. I've got a good job, a pregnant wife, plus I'm alive. I especially like that part."

Greta stood aside, stonefaced.

"There's a real world out there," he said. "In case you've forgotten." He opened the front door, walked out into the summer afternoon.

"You said you'd call Bill Tomzak last night."

He stopped, sunglasses on by the time he turned around. "You're obsessed, you know that? Like Uli. You want to end up like him?"

"Did you ask Bill Tomzak about *krokus*?"

"It doesn't matter now, does it. It's history."

"What did he say, Otto?"

"Nothing."

"Bullshit."

"No it's true. He said he'd meet us at the Gasthaus zur Sonne. I'm going to call him and cancel because I've changed my mind. I don't care anymore. There you are."

"Meet us when?"

"Greta..."

"*When?*"

"Lunchtime."

"You bastard."

"Fine. I won't call him. Go on your own. Twelve noon, you know where it is. Do whatever the fuck you want, just keep me out of it."

"You'll come."

"I wouldn't count on it."

"You'll come."

Ten years ago, when Otto used to drink with him, Bill Tomzak had been a Sergeant-Clerk at the U.S. Air Force base in Wiesbaden. He was university-educated, rare for a non-commissioned career soldier, comfortable with the secure routine of his clerical duties that left him ample time to read military history and listen to jazz.

Greta had liked him for his air of self-deprecation, another rare quality in the God-given United States Air Force. With the sky over West Germany dark with American military air traffic, with its streets and bars and bedrooms occupied for decades by swaggering steak-and-milk-fed *Amis* — with American forces personnel everywhere, it had been fine to meet a self-proclaimed American nowhere man. Now, however, as she watched him enter the Gasthaus zur Sonne at noon, stooping to clear its low beams, his face drawn long with premature age and disappointment, she could see that he never had gone anywhere.

"Sure I remember you," he said. "Schutzpolizei Officer Schoeller."

"Greta deserted us for the BKA," Otto said on his way to the bar.

"I quit a few weeks ago," she explained. "I'm going back to university, taking a teaching diploma." She made room for him on the bench beside her but he sat opposite, looking at her through his mask of weary amusement.

"I'm still clerking, save you asking." He shrugged his rounded shoulders. "Doesn't look like I'll be producing any students for you. Did try to get married once, though."

"No luck?"

"Are you kidding? Lucky as hell. I might have wasted years discovering what she really wanted was an officer who played golf. Major Craig. Said so on his golf bag. She gets to salute every time he makes a hole in one."

Greta smiled uncertainly, glad when Otto came back with the jug of *Apfelwein* and two grey and white crockery *Bembel*, the unadorned Hessen equivalent of Bavarian *Steins*. Greta was already drinking Riesling. She had never developed a taste for the flat, sour cider with which Frankfurters slake their thirst. Tomzak had no such reservations, began drinking it with steady enthusiasm, unaffected by the high alcohol level: his long face grew no more animated, his words still came out dry and ironic. Though assigned to the U.S. Defense Intelligence Agency with NATO, he had failed to rise above Master Sergeant-Clerk in the last ten years, and now he never would.

"I can understand why you called me. Sounds like you need a paper shuffler."

"We need a historian," Otto flattered.

"Historians teach in colleges and write books. I'm a paper shuffler. If you read as much history as me, you'd believe it."

"No way," Otto said. "You could teach military intelligence anywhere and you know it."

Tomzak refused to acknowledge the compliment, reached for the jug and topped up Otto's almost-full *Bembel* then refilled his own empty one. He accepted a Gitane and a light.

"It ain't the flower. Not *krokus*. It's an English acronym. *C.R.O.W.C.A.S.S.* — Central Registry of War Criminals and Security Suspects. It was run by the Allied High Command in Paris starting in

1945, the result of a tireless collection of witness testimony, close interrogation, rigorous prosecution. But you want to know if there's anything on Dorner in the registry?" He shrugged. "There isn't."

Greta felt the blood rising to her face. "You got us here to say that?"

"The absence means one of two things: either Dorner's wartime record is clean, or else it's been cleaned up. My guess would be the latter."

"Recently?"

"No. It would have to have been right after the war, in forty-five. Didn't we used to hear how humane Erich Dorner was, standing up to the SS over the treatment of his labor force? A regular Schindler? Sounds typical Paperclip to me."

He saw he had lost them, smiled. "Okay, you want the seminar, I'll give you your money's worth. It's simple enough. Nineteen forty-five, the European war's over, but it's still playing in the Pacific. Ike's got two headaches, the Japanese plus the Ruskies in Europe, impatient to start the cold war. Potential advantage for the U.S.: a small army of German scientists and technicians floating around over here, guys like von Braun, Strughold, Eitel, Debus...world's best, geniuses in their respective fields. The Americans know that if we don't get them someone else will: the British, the French, God forbid the Russians. Rocket propulsion, aerodynamics, optics, aviation medicine...a gold mine of talent."

He took a deep drink, watching them over the rim.

"In Dorner's case the talent was in mechanical engineering. A U.S. company, American Dynamic, had already scrambled to grab a 40 percent share in Dorner as soon as the final bell rang in the European theater. Dynamic was already heavily contracted by the U.S. Navy to develop beefed-up undercarriages for carrier aircraft in the Pacific. Dorner were specialists in that area. So let's say there *had* been atrocities at Dorner: this kid stinks, says Dynamic; someone give it a bath, wash behind its ears before we take it home. They didn't have to ask twice, there was already a beautiful system in place to do the scrubbing."

He helped himself from Otto's pack, accepted a light.

"It was called Operation Paperclip. Basically your standard Washington snowjob, the kind we're so damn good at. A combined cover-up by War and a coerced and pressured State Department; it involved rewriting the war records of the approximately five hundred scientists they deemed indispensable to national security. A little high altitude testing at Dachau, a little poison gas exposure at IG Farben, a few deep-freezing experiments, a mere twenty thousand slaves dying at the Nordhausen rocket facility — no problem. Paperclip just rewrote history to get U.S. visas for anyone the War Department wanted, even if they'd already been recommended for war crimes prosecution in Europe. A guy called Gruhn, office in the Munitions Building in Washington: his job was to keep Paperclip activities from civilian government departments, from the media, from the public. Try to see it in the context of 1945: avowed Nazis getting VIP treatment from the U.S. military while the world reels in horror from Auschwitz and Buchenwald. Paperclip carried horrendous flap potential."

He leaned towards Greta across the smooth, scarred table, his voice low and portentous. "And we're still doing it, right?"

Greta glanced sharply at Otto, then back to Tomzak who was grinning, his teeth yellow with neglect. "Otto didn't have to tell me. Hey, I'm the U.S. Defense Intelligence Agency, baby: your Bundesnachrichtendienst, your Bundesgrenzschutz...I can say all your big words and a lot of little ones: GSG9, BfV, BKA...I've shuffled around with all of them. I certainly got a whole lot of classified paperwork across my desk while your Wiesbaden office was investigating Dorner."

He watched her surprised reaction through a pall of cigarette smoke then leaned in again, the odor of his breath reaching her, sour with tobacco and *Apfelwein*.

"Funding the extreme right, correct? Deutsche Nazional Volkspartei? I wasn't surprised when the BKA paper dried up. How many employees does Dorner have worldwide?"

He took another cigarette from Otto's pack, leaned back against the lumpy wall and surveyed them with his dry, disappointed eyes.

"Please don't assume that I want to know why you're here. I've never liked getting involved in things." He lit the cigarette with unnecessarily cupped hands. "Emotionally underdeveloped, I guess. One of the symptoms is a childlike desire to stay alive."

He regarded them intensely through the smoke for several seconds. Finally he smiled his tired yellow smile.

"It's just possible that Paperclip missed some CROWCASS files on Dorner."

"Where?" Greta said.

"I was going to say G2, U.S. Army Intelligence here in Frankfurt, General Clay's outfit. But Clay was pro-industry all the way. CROW-CASS material, hell, even Nuremberg testimony if it ever got that far...he'd have handed it to Paperclip tied up with a red, white and blue ribbon. Shred one for me, boys!"

Showing off, Tomzak had grown animated; he drained his *Bembel*, reached for the jug, looked at Greta's glass. "Ready for the apple?"

"Where would they have missed Dorner files?"

He poured slowly to make her wait. "From September '45 through the summer of '47, before it ultimately became the CIA, American intelligence flourished briefly as the Strategic Services Unit. The SSU, under a Colonel Eddy. A brief metamorphosis — sort of like a maggot before it develops into a fly."

He paused for a reaction.

"A couple of years back I was assigned to retrieve some old SSU stats — nothing dramatic, just some ancient fuel expenditure accounts, comparative figures for a Division audit. I sent a corporal up to Headquarters in Berlin, supposed to be an overnighter, turned out he was there almost two days looking for this SSU shit. Know where he finally found it? At the receiving end of a makeshift pistol range under the Military Attaché's Office at the U.S. Embassy. They'd been using the files for a slug trap. We must have dug a dozen rounds of .45 out of that fuel budget, required a little creative arithmetic before we sent the figures up to Division. A few holes in our addition, you might say."

"What about the rest of the files," Greta asked. "Did you leave them there?"

"Think a career clerk could leave poor little orphan files in Berlin with no one to shuffle and stack them every night?"

"You have them?"

He smiled with mock regret. "I *had* them. All the SSU material came through the Wiesbaden base on the fifteenth of last month. We did a preliminary categorization before it got shipped to Suitland."

"Where?" Otto said.

"Military Intelligence Archive at Suitland, outside Washington DC. Sorry folks, you're two weeks late. It's gone home like everything else except the really worn-out old crap no one wants, like me."

"Did you see any reference to Dorner in the SSU files?" Greta said gently.

"Are you kidding? There were about two *tons* of paper. Of course if I'd known what to look for..."

"What happens when it gets to Suitland?" Greta asked, ignoring a warning look from Otto.

Tomzak shook his head. "It'll hang around in receiving for a couple of months, then it'll become declassified toilet paper. Lost forever. Suitland's probably the most disorganized document repository in the world, worse than ever since we started pulling out of Europe and the Philippines. They're buried alive up there, one big avalanche and it never stops snowing. If they're really fastidious they might throw something in one of the old footlockers they've got up there on the second floor, otherwise it'll get dumped on the paper mountain like everything else. A requisition for your SSU material...Christ, you could be waiting thirty years, assuming they don't shred it out of desperation in the meantime."

Greta stared at him, unblinking. "You know any of the clerical staff at this place?"

"Of course."

"Know any of them well?"

"Sure."

"Sure you do," she said evenly. "You're a Master Sergeant. You're the top clerical rank in the United States Air Force with how many...twenty years' service?"

Otto, silent until now, shifted impatiently in his seat. "Forget it, okay? He's told you what you wanted to know."

Greta ignored him. "You could pick up the phone right now, couldn't you Bill, tell one of your old buddies at Suitland to segregate the SSU material from Berlin before it goes on the mountain. You could do that, right?"

He looked vaguely amused. "If I could, if it *was* segregated, what then?"

"Then they look for Dorner references. War crimes, atrocities, whatever Paperclip might have missed. They fax them to you. Or me if you prefer."

"That would be treason, Fräulein Schoeller. I don't believe any of my friends want to get court-martialed for treason any more than I do."

Greta stared at him for a long moment then stood up. "Thanks for your time. It was nice to see you again. You coming Otto?"

"You think I'm being obstructive, don't you?"

"I would hope not."

He smiled. "Flexing my atrophied little muscle, right?"

Greta raised her eyebrows. "Self-knowledge is a rare attribute, Bill. It's a pity you didn't make officer."

"Shut the fuck up, Greta," Otto snapped.

But Tomzak was smiling very faintly. "Sit down."

"You have something helpful to say?"

He lowered his voice enough that she had to lean close to hear him against the background din. "I could get the material segregated."

"And?"

"I could get you clearance to see it. Nothing can come out, but I could arrange clearance for you to enter the archive."

"You mean I'd have to go to the United States?"

"That's what I'm saying."

"How soon can you call?"

"Soon as I get back to the base. Washington's six hours behind, if I call at 2:00 I'll get someone. Theoretically you could fly tonight, be at the archive bright and early tomorrow morning."

"Why theoretically?"

Otto stared at her. "Hold on just a minute here."

"To what? We don't *have* anything to hold onto. That's what all this is about."

CHAPTER 19

THE DORNER EMBLEM OF AN ARMORED GAUNTLET HAD ORIGINATED with Erich Dorner's purchase of the schloss at Rudesheim. Still the company symbol of strength and safety (though under review on the eve of the Kondor launch), the giant mural dominated the main conference room on the mezzanine level at Dorner America's Cleveland Headquarters. For today's event it had competition at the opposite end of the room, from a twenty-foot reproduction of Hansjorg Peiper's official company portrait.

The room was filled to capacity, a tumult of voices in several languages from knots of Dorner executives representing most of the twelve countries in which Dorner products were manufactured and sold.

Kristian had worked with many of them, in many parts of the world. It was because they knew him that his presence inflicted solemnity on every cheerful group, and while the condolences may have been heartfelt, there was a sense of relief when he moved on and they could go back to speculating on the sensational nature of Hansjorg Peiper's death.

The automotive press was out in force, but they ignored Kristian, stuck close to the German contingent, hungry for whatever tidbits Junia Dorner might throw them concerning the Kondor preview on Monday, at the Frankfurt Auto Show.

Hansjorg's portrait hung above a dais on which three chairs were arranged around a central microphone. Kristian took his place next to Junia while Bryce Tevlin gave the introductory address.

Tevlin had come to Dorner from the home appliance industry, was known in Cleveland as "Rinse 'n Hold" for his lack of decisiveness. A bean counter who bore no love of cars, he was nervous at the microphone, aware of the rumor that Junia was already shopping for his replacement. Tevlin's tribute to his dynamic predecessor was as dry and reduced as Hansjorg's ashes.

Kristian tried to make up for it in his own address, but Junia outdid him.

"This story is the truth and it happened on the autobahn on the way up to Kronberg, from our little house in Rudesheim."

Laughter.

"I was sixteen years old, sitting in the back of a 1958 606 sedan. Me in the back, Hansjorg driving, my father next to him in the front. We were on our way to a big important dinner at the Schlosshotel Kronberg, visiting heads of state, and it was pouring rain...raining so hard you could have rowed a boat along the autobahn.

"Why were we in a 606 that night? Not a very fancy car for such an important occasion, but there must have been one around at the schloss and Hansjorg was intrigued by it. You remember the first year of the 606? Good car, but it had this thing no one could figure out: it took three tries to start in wet weather. Not two, not four. Always three times. We used to call it the *drei* car which is quite funny when you say it in English!"

An appreciative ripple of laughter.

"Hansjorg was running Brazil then; they didn't make the 606 down there, but he'd heard about this starting problem, wanted to see for himself. It was already raining when we left Rudesheim. Sure enough, three tries. I remember Hansjorg turned off the engine, tried again. Three times! 'Come on,' my father said, 'we're going to be late.' So off we went, Hansjorg shaking his head, couldn't believe it.

"He was very quiet on the autobahn, we couldn't get a word out of him. He wouldn't talk to us. All of a sudden, before my father realized what was happening, Hansjorg pulled over and stopped the car. He turns the engine off. He starts it again. Third time she goes. He turns around. 'Anyone bring an umbrella?' No umbrella. He releases the hood, starts to open the door. By this time my father is going bananas...we're going to be late, it's going to be a national scandal, El Presidente and his beautiful young French wife and five hundred important people waiting for us at the Kronberg. My God!

"Hansjorg is deaf. He gets out, in his evening clothes. My father tries to pull him back but he's like a crazy man. Out into the torrential rain in white tie and tails. My father starts feeling very bad about it, starts to get out himself, decides he's not that crazy, settles for hooting the horn and banging on the windshield, while I'm laughing my head off in the back seat.

"Hansjorg was under the hood for I don't know how long. Finally he gets back in, soaked to the skin. 'Go ahead,' he says to my father, and he points at the ignition — it was still in the dash in those days. My father doesn't move. 'Do it!' he says. 'Start the car!'

"'Can I do it?' I said.

"'Sure Junia, you do it.'

"I did it. I reached over and turned the key."

Junia stopped, casting a misty gaze over the sea of silent, enthralled employees. She turned sideways to Kristian.

"First time," she said quietly, her voice thick with emotion. "First time," she repeated into the microphone. "It was the distributor. We changed the design. Every 606 after that started first time. Then it really was the dry car."

Junia held up a small, unadorned hand to quell the applause.

"How many of you remember me standing here talking to you in 1985? You Americans used to call yourselves yuppies back then, sitting there in your hornrims and your brand new Armani suspenders."

A warm current of laughter, drying the instant she resumed, as the audience realized she was no longer smiling.

"We said *Ssssssh...Detroit is asleep. We said Don't wake Detroit. We are going to strike while the monster sleeps.* Didn't we say that?"

Kristian remembered. He had been sitting in the front row that day, and Hansjorg had been on the dais beside Junia. She had used the same tone of voice as now — *sotto voce* — requiring an investment on the part of each listener.

"But what happened? Detroit woke up. Something we had never imagined when we looked at those ugly, overweight jalopies next to our sleek beauties." She allowed a long, uneasy silence. "The monster woke up, *reared* up, gnashed its teeth. Now it's even breathing a little fire, *nicht wahr*?"

Kristian shifted uncomfortably in his seat, along with most of the audience. She hardly needed to rub their noses in it: Ford's last quarter profits or the new Lean Team at Chrysler or the runaway success of GM's single sticker pricing policy. Everyone in the room, especially the Americans, was painfully aware of the solid, stylish new cars from the Big Three.

Junia smiled again, held up a calming hand. "I told you that story about Hansjorg Peiper for a reason. He was a man who did not know the meaning of defeat. A man whose nature demanded that he never give up. Who saw every adversity as a personal challenge. Has he taught us these qualities? I think so. Have we been daunted by hardship? I think not. We burned but we did not flinch from the fire. We ached but we did not rest. And at last, at long last, we have forged a magic sword. A product like no other before it, a wonder of design and engineering. A low maintenance engine, thermoplastic body panels, an aluminum frame and side airbags back and front. What's the name we have graven on our magic sword? What's the word that Detroit hates to hear?

What's the word on Dorner's glorious future in America?" Junia cupped her ear towards her audience.

The first attempt was self-conscious.

"I can't hear you!"

Still ragged the second time, but nearly everybody had joined in.

Junia snatched the microphone from its stand and strode to the edge of the dais. "That's not going to scare anyone. Say it like we mean it!"

"Kondor!"

"What?"

"Kondor!"

"Come on!"

"KONDOR!"

"Again!"

"KONDOR!
KONDOR!
KONDOR!"

"Stand up and say it!"

Junia's audience rose to its feet, chanting, the repetitions like air-burst explosions, a two-minute barrage ending with a long shock-wave of applause as she descended the stage, ignoring Tevlin as she drew Kristian towards the exit. With her entourage and the automotive press still some way behind them, Junia leaned close. "We're going to be launching the Kondor in the United States within the next eighteen months. When we do, I'm going to need someone in that office upstairs who loves cars, the way your father loved them. Not someone who sees the automobile as a domestic appliance. You understand what I'm saying, Kristian?"

She looked at him, searching his face. "Don't worry about this meeting."

"You've met Vaughan?"

"He has some disturbing things to say, there's no getting away from it. It involves us both, you and I, on a personal level." She glanced back towards the auditorium where two large young men in expensive suits

— Junia's bodyguards whatever their job description — tried to hold the reporters at bay. "I wish we had more time to talk. I'll have to deal with this. I'll see you up there."

Hansjorg Peiper's former office, always a home place for Kristian, had been transformed into a sterile reflection of Tevlin. A few obligatory prints of Dorner products had replaced Hansjorg's challenging modern oils, a couple of rubber plants stood in place of the Henry Moore and the quirky Art Nouveau umbrella stand, back at Canterbury Road now. Tevlin's paltry library huddled in one small corner of what had once been a bookcase overspilling with volumes on engineering and music and art, history and travel besides a wealth of industry-related material.

For some time Kristian stood immobilized beside the great window, gazing north towards the lake, his ears still roaring from the tumult in the conference room. A shudder passed through him, of anger at the way she had evoked his father's name in her manipulation of the crowd. A second shudder of fear as he thought back to his conversation with Jason Steele-Perkins last night in the Deep Six: should he have listened more closely to the rumors of Junia Dorner and Beck? She could offer much more than campaign funds. With such a gift for oratory, she would be a velvet glove for that Iron Fist.

Vaughan and Junia came in together, twenty minutes late. He was a tall, soft-looking man, clumsy in his movements, wearing heavily framed spectacles with high-index lenses that drew his temples together.

"Kristian. Okay if I call you that? Senator Hutchence said a lot of good things about you."

His hand was soft and damp. A big, friendly, awkward man, devoid of menace. "I'm sorry he couldn't be more enlightening on the phone. Fact is, even now we haven't had time to brief him properly."

They joined Kristian at the apex of the corner window where two pairs of Corbusier chairs faced each other, a last vestige of Hansjorg, purchased long before the eighties fad for them. Junia sat down, a signal for the men to follow suit.

"We're busy people so I'll get straight to the point," Vaughan began. He looked at Kristian. "We think we know who was in your father's house that night. We believe it was a contract agent in the pay of your competition. Someone hired by another automobile company, possibly a consortium. We're not positive yet which company or companies, although we're getting close. We think the Japanese are involved."

"He means they still don't know who is responsible for your father's death," Junia said impatiently.

"Fräulein Dorner, perhaps I might explain something," Vaughan said with the mildest trace of annoyance. "The Directorate for Business Intelligence is a relatively new organization. We're..."

"Why so modest?" Junia smiled coldly. "Tell Kristian who you are. You have United States senators broker your meetings, you say 'walk' and both the FBI and Cleveland homicide get right up and walk off the investigation. Obviously you're not the Better Business Bureau."

Vaughan shifted uncomfortably in his seat, nudged his glasses up the bridge of his nose. "You're right, the Directorate enjoys many of the capabilities of our parent agency. My point was going to be that our caseload is heavy. In case you're unaware of the statistics, the United States lost over one hundred billion dollars to trade-secret theft last year. Unchecked, that figure could grow another 50 percent in the next ten years. The Russian government has an entire department dedicated to targeting and stealing American industrial secrets, and that's child's play compared to what our so-called allies are doing. Japan, South Korea, France, Israel...it is a relentless assault." The mild, weak eyes settled on Kristian. "Even Canada. Which is why we're particularly interested in the fact that your father attempted to call a Toronto number, even after he was attacked."

Vaughan leaned forward, wriggling his features to reseat the heavy spectacles atop the slide of his nose. Kristian felt his scrutiny — Junia's too — like a guilty schoolboy. He felt his arms bound to the chair as if by ropes, felt his face coloring, betraying every thought. A voice impersonating Kristian, a disembodied ventriloquist's voice, said: "My father was five years retired. He kept no industrial secrets. He had no sensitive material, no access to new data."

Vaughan blinked mild eyes at Kristian through his thick lenses. "Yes he did, Mr. Peiper. Through his friendship with Dietrich Kamp." He looked at Junia. "You're developing an electric version of the Kondor, isn't that right?"

"*Jaaaa*," she said, long and warningly.

"Kamp is closely involved in that project, as he has been with the conventionally powered version, correct?" Again he looked at Kristian. "You are aware, of course that Dietrich Kamp and your father were close friends? I believe they shared a number of interests, music, philosophy, art."

Kristian had been proud of his father's unorthodox friend: in the late sixties Dr. Kamp had been the official guru of Europe's counterculture, LSD and free love and Oriental philosophy, which had been the subject of his doctorate. Now in his own late sixties, Kamp had once again risen to international celebrity (and enormous wealth and influence) as the head of Kamp Communications based in Dusseldorf, Europe's largest supplier of software and computer chips for home and industry. Without Kamp's central processing unit, any version of the Kondor would be grounded.

"As an automotive engineer, your father was keenly interested in the flywheel technology being explored for the concept van. Kamp had access to all the flywheel data, some of which he shared with your father. He was perfectly well aware that he should not have done so. As a result of his actions, highly secret material may have been lost at Canterbury Road."

Junia raised the thin blades of her eyebrows for Kristian. "I'm sorry. I know this isn't easy to hear. It was painful for me too."

"I should add that Kamp is now under investigation by the German government," Vaughan continued, "for suspected complicity in other technology transfers, some involving German national security." He looked forthrightly at Kristian. "There's an element of trust in me telling you this. It was the Directorate's opinion that such information not be given you at this time, but considering the tragic personal consequences of Kamp's actions, I convinced them that you had a right to know. That you could be trusted to keep this knowledge private. Kamp is currently unaware of his investigation. For now, that must not change. It is vital to the investigation that he not be approached."

Vaughan's glasses had slipped again. He used his middle finger to push back the heavy frames, discolored, Kristian noticed, by acids from his skin and hair.

"As Fräulein Dorner and I have already discussed, Dietrich Kamp maintained close ties with *her* father, too. It is our belief that a package containing the most sensitive Dorner material passed from Kamp to Hansjorg Peiper through Erich Dorner's hands sometime in early May, in Frankfurt. We think this was the package you described to Nathan Hutchence, that it was almost certainly this material that precipitated the break-in here in Cleveland." Vaughan looked closely at Kristian. "There is a possibility that Hansjorg Peiper placed it in safekeeping. We haven't yet been able to discover where. Obviously Canada is a possibility since he attempted to call Toronto that night."

No more than two or three seconds elapsed, but their silence groaned eternally. Kristian's fingers closed around the arm of his chair, slippery against the soft leather. He felt an icy tickle of perspiration down his ribcage. He felt wooden, his tongue enlarged like an idiot's, ludicrously unconvincing to a professional like Vaughan who must be reading every thought. He should have cancelled.

He made what felt like a stupendous effort to control his speech. "What was in the package?"

"Mechanical drawings."

Kristian felt himself drowning. The effort required to stand was that of breaking through a plate of ice, gasping for air. He walked to the window on legs he could no longer feel, pursued by their silence. Their reflection in the window, rendered spectral by the daylight, threatened him with watchful stillness.

They knew.

There was nothing to lose now, nothing to release except the choking anger, bubbling up like water in his lungs.

"Mr. Peiper? Is anything the matter?"

Still with his back to them, he squeezed his eyes shut, tried to see the wrecks on valleyside, tried to smell timothy and engine oil.

"Kristian? What is it?"

Where was his father's hand?

He opened his eyes and looked to Lake Erie, a purple-grey band northwest beyond the city core, far distant, but always totemic for him.

Across the water, almost within sight, was Canada.

Suddenly he stopped fighting, felt the fear flow back inside him to some lower, temporary reservoir. Anger alone fueled his actions, his body strong again as he turned to them, his eyes blazing clear at Junia Dorner as he walked willingly, carelessly, into their trap.

"That was a good story you told downstairs." Kristian's smile was ice. "But I'm like him more than you ever dreamed. I care about this company the same way he did...too much to see it abused. And I'm not a quitter either, Junia; once you've got my interest, I don't care how hard it rains, I'm like a dog at a bone. A dog on a rat."

CHAPTER 20

SUITLAND, MARYLAND.

Documentary evidence submitted to Allied Military Tribunal, Nuremberg, May 21 1945. RE: Dorner AG, Frankfurt-am-Main.

I.
Testimony submitted by: Lieut. Colonel William Demaris, Chief Medical Officer, 9th Battalion, United States Third Army.

On the morning of March 26th, the 9th Battalion, a forward unit of the U.S. Third Army to which I was attached, advanced into an industrial southwest sector of Frankfurt occupied by the Dorner Automobile Works. Known before and during the war as a manufactory of automobiles, it had been turned over to war production and as such had been the target of recent allied bombing which had reduced the plant to approximately one-tenth productivity. The factory was in ruins, barely operating.

The work force consisted almost entirely of slave labor — Russians, Poles, Jews, a few French nationals, even some German servicemen drafted from punishment battalions. Workers were housed in unheated quarters under atrocious conditions. According to workers' testimony, over 10,000 had been present at the Frankfurt plant during peak production, though we found 200 living persons and 327 corpses, the most recent victims lying where they had died, the rest in a mass grave behind the plant. In most cases, the causes of death were determined to be starvation, disease and exhaustion, though there were cases in which violent death had unquestionably occurred. (See attached for detailed pathology.)

Most of the work force had dispersed into the surrounding area following the hasty departure of their SS overseers. The state of those that remained was deplorable: their clothing was completely inadequate, almost all were without overcoats, many more were shoeless, their feet bound in rags. Sanitation was almost non-existent, the meager toilet facilities entirely contaminated with excretion. I noticed many cases of spotted fever, spread by lice which infected nine out of ten persons. Many were covered with open sores.

Preliminary psychological assessment revealed a general state of deep shock amongst the liberated prisoners, who had barely energy to comprehend the meaning of our arrival, as though they had lived in hopelessness so long that the prospect of freedom was, literally, beyond belief.

Those wretched souls who could offer testimony recited a litany of barbarism on the part of the SS. We received reports of random, arbitrary executions on a daily basis, as well as reprisals for acts of perceived mutiny or sabotage at a rate of five workers randomly selected and executed for each individual act. Collapsing from starvation and exhaustion, neglecting to install a single nut or bolt, the least assertion of independence...all these were defined by the SS as mutiny or sabotage. We were then shown the crane from which reprisal hangings were carried out before the assembled work force, and on which the corpses of the innocent victims were then left on display.

We had been on the factory site for over an hour before the president of the company, Erich Dorner, was apprehended along with several officers of the company, in administrative buildings removed approximately one-half mile from the factory. All of them claimed freedom from responsibility for the condition of the labor force. This, they protested, was the exclusive domain of the SS unit attached to the factory, which, as mentioned above, had fled during the night before our arrival. Dorner and the others were more than adequately dressed, in generally good health, and, though supplies of food were scarce throughout the region, they were not underfed.

II.
Written testimony submitted April 10th 1945 by Captain Theodore Bentley, United States Seventh Army, region of Frankfurt-am-Main, to: Central Registry of War Criminals and Security Suspects (CROWCASS), Allied High Command, Paris.

On the afternoon of March 28th, an SS unit of nineteen men was captured by the French First Army near Mainz and handed over to my unit for questioning.

The prisoners had been traveling on foot for two days and nights. They claimed to have become detached from a Waffen SS unit, the 12th SS Panzer Division which, according to reliable intelligence, now proven, was not present in the region at the time. Further, the poor character and physical makeup of the captured individuals made it clear that these were not elite fighting men.

Upon interrogation by my team, it was learned that the prisoners were not soldiers, but members of the SS Totenkopfverbaende (Death's Head Unit) assigned to guard duty at the Dorner Automobile Works in Frankfurt am Main. Although the prisoners have remained uncooperative, inquiries at the Dorner factory leave no doubt that they may be held to account not only for the inhuman condition of the surviving Dorner workers, but also for numerous deaths at the plant, both violent and as a result of neglect. (It should be noted that many of the surviving workers liberated by the 9th Battalion, U.S. Third Army two days ago, too weak to be evacuated, have already died, most from cholera and dysentery.)

A search of the prisoners by the French had already shown one of them to be carrying papers marked "Top Secret" for the attention of the Inspector of the Air Force and copied to SS Obergruppenführer Oswald Pohl at the office of the SS Reichsführer. The documents indicated the existence of other, filmic, material which should have accompanied them, although none was found, and a thorough search of the exact location in which the prisoners were apprehended produced no such film. It wasn't until the morning of March 29th, after a night of close interrogation, that one of the prisoners revealed that the film has remained at the plant, in the hands of the company president, Erich Dorner.

In response to my request for the film, I was informed by Third Army headquarters here in Frankfurt (where Herr Dorner is being held), that it has already been transferred to the Registry. At the same time however, documents examined by my own team, here enclosed, provide every indication of the nature of the film. I feel a strong obligation to warn prospective readers that, however shocking conditions may have been at the recently liberated factory, those crimes pale in comparison to what is described herein. These documents make a daunting study. One cannot imagine viewing the film. Indeed, the events so cold-bloodedly enacted and described in these pages, even in the light of ongoing discoveries at Bergen-Belsen and elsewhere, seem terrible beyond imagining. If the Registry will indulge me in a further opinion, I believe it is the very personal scale of this barbarism that makes it the more unbearable.

The odor of mildew from the neglected, half-century old documents had already brought her to the edge of vomiting.

Greta gently closed the file. Her hand remained for a few seconds, hovering over the paper docket but not quite touching it, as if to make certain it stayed shut. Slowly, holding it with the tips of her fingers, she returned the file to its shallow cardboard box.

She stood, leaning against the edge of the reading table. The archive seemed stifling. She took several deep breaths before undertaking the journey to Corporal Norrie's desk with the box.

"Y'all done that one? I still got your other box here." He looked at her with concern. "Hey, maybe you should sit a spell. Warm in here, get used to it after a while. You want a drink of water, somethin'?"

Norrie brought her water. She drank only a few sips, fearing she would vomit if she didn't get air.

He saw her to the door, attentive, kindly — any friend of Bill Tomzak's was a friend of his — mercifully lacking in curiosity, perhaps to be expected of a man with access to a million secrets. "Y'all have to sign out at the front desk and go all the way through clearance on your way back." He grinned. "This was a nightclub, I could just stamp your hand!"

"I would be grateful for you to please keep that material for me," Greta said in her classroom English. "I will return in thirty minutes."

Greta submitted herself, wordlessly, to a body-search by a female Marine, and left the archive. She took the elevator down, walked out past the Marine guard at the main entrance of the glass and concrete low-rise, like any fifties office building except for the stiff sentries and the surreal addition of a steel tank-trap on the underground parking ramp.

She walked, seeing only concrete and cars in their universal dreariness, assailed by the images conjured by the SSU files, of no more interest to the United States government than so much toilet paper. But Europe had been twice transformed since the U.S. Third Army marched into Frankfurt. It was all ancient history.

Even in the torture chamber at the schloss, there could be some absolution for those long-ago priests and executioners. Life itself was brutal then, for almost everyone, a litany of pain, disease, bereavement, ignorance and death from cradle to early grave. The agonies of the wheel and the stake were not anomalous in the medieval world.

But this?

The perpetrators of these horrors had been modern people. They had analgesics for their physical pain and psychoanalysis for their ter-rors. They had the lesson of a recent "war to end all wars." They cherished hopes and dreams for themselves and their children with every expectation of fulfillment. They measured their lifetime with wristwatches, an abundance of time. Erich Dorner and his SS crea-tures were not God's servants, neither a God of love nor of righteous anger, merely those of a diseased, sharp-faced orator with a mustache like a toothbrush.

Greta had left Frankfurt at 6:00 p.m. last night, gained six hours in time zones and spent the night at a Washington hotel. She had fore-gone breakfast in order to be at the archive early, wasn't hungry now but knew she should eat something. She bought an apple from a con-venience store stocked mostly with potato chips and pornography — gaping female genitalia and the snouts of guns — paying a wary Viet-namese through a scratched plastic window as thick as a slice of white bread. She stopped at an empty bus shelter to try to eat it, at the edge of what seemed a featureless grey wilderness. She did not see America's foreignness, none of the thousand details that had fascinated her on the bus from her Washington hotel early this morning. She could see only the second box from Berlin awaiting her on Corporal Norrie's counter.

She left the apple, untouched, on the bench in the shelter. Some-body would take it, hungry enough to risk poison or razor blades.

She went back to the archive at 12:25 p.m. and resubmitted her iden-tification. She'd had to risk traveling on her own passport, there had been no time for Otto to harvest false papers from the broad field of Frankfurt villainy that owed him favors. But Tomzak had smoothed the way, preclearing her as a journalist researching the history of state/industrial relations within the automobile sector for the business supplement of the *Frankfurter Allgemeine Zeitung*.

The duty officer checked her documentation and confirmed from his own records that she had been pre-cleared by the U.S. Defense Intelligence Agency in Wiesbaden. By 12:35 she was once again in the first floor East Section with a laminated pass clipped to her blouse, in the paper maelstrom that was Suitland's Declassified Repository.

Tomzak had been accurate in his description, except that the dented footlockers around the walls were no longer accessible given the mountains of files building around each one, their contents protected by the sheer weight of paper. This morning it had taken Corporal Norrie several minutes to clear a study table and chair for her — all other horizontal surfaces, including the floor of the archive, were covered with precarious stacks of files awaiting categorization. There was a high noise level, shouted instructions and jokes and complaints — as much racket and floating paper as a trading floor while clerks with armloads of material labored through narrow canyons to and from various dump sites, obeying the dictates of what was, by Norrie's own admission, a largely haphazard filing system.

"Nobody wants this old business. The classified section, now that's a smooth operation. Can't hardly see a single piece of paper in there, just a bunch of mainframes, big old reels goin' round all the time. Too weird."

Norrie had managed to keep the Dorner boxes safe for her, pushed them both across the counter. "Second one's older," he explained. "See that code?" A faded green X was stenciled on the lid. "Before the war, a green X meant the contents was secret, highest classification before we invented top secret, then ultra secret for signals intelligence. Means it's pre-war."

She took the material back to the table (it had already accumulated a shallow drift), sat down and stared at the second, unopened box.

Her fingers trembled as she reached for the lid. It would be in here, the reason Uli and Hansjorg Peiper had died, a secret powerful enough to destroy an industrial empire.

The box released an even heavier spoor of mildew than the first one, the brown file folders inside blighted with pasty grey spots. Fifteen folders, all the same size and colour, all bearing the secret X.

Greta began to frown, the lines deepening as she fingered the files, as it became clear that the contents of this box bore no relationship to the first one, to Demaris's and Bentley's written testimony.

She removed the top file which had seemed, at first, to be empty. Only when Greta spread it fully open on the table did she see the narrow, yellowed newspaper clipping that was molded to the folder's inside crease. She tried to remove it until it tore slightly. It was bonded to the damp folder with mold, but by carefully flattening both folder and cutting, she could at least read it.

It had been taken from the morning *Voelkischer Beobachter*, a leading Nazi daily, dated August 30th, 1939, four days before European war was declared. It carried a report of a civil airplane disaster involving an American airliner, a Pan Am "Clipper" out of Lisbon that had crashed into the sea following takeoff, with the loss of all on board. The passenger list had included fifteen American technicians heading home after a six-month furlough in Germany. The report described them as specialists in various fields of automobile design and manufacture who were returning to the big American automobile companies that loaned them to the fledgling Dorner company in Frankfurt. The account ended with a verbose, mildly barbed conceit to remind Greta that the *Beobachter*, like every other German paper at the time, existed chiefly in order to peddle National Socialist propaganda.

While our countrymen naturally regret the loss of life in this incident, it remains to be said that it would almost certainly not have occurred had these unfortunate passengers been traveling to the United States with Lufthansa, unrivaled in reliability and service, which had indeed just delivered them safely and punctually to their ill-fated connecting flight in Lisbon. Regrettably, Lufthansa trans-Atlantic service will not become an option for American passengers or any others until Germany's peerless National Airline has secured landing rights in New York.

Exactly fifteen other folders in the box, all brown, containing a single sheet of paper bearing the seal of the United States Embassy in

Berlin, Military Attaché's Office, dated July 5th, 1939, a few weeks before the outbreak of war. Greta lifted out the first sheet.

SUBJECT FOR SURVEILLANCE:
Name: Wilhelm Fuechter
Birthdate and location: March 2nd, 1899, Lansing, Michigan
Occupation: Metallurgist
Employer: General Motors Corporation, Detroit, Mich.
U.S. Address: c/o Herman and Clara Fuechter (parents),
*   608 Belvedere Street, Lansing, Mich.*
German address: c/o Dorner Motorenwerke AG, Frankfurt am Main
Temporary Work Visa: # 77D4006 Issued by the Reich Economic
*   Chamber, June 30th, 1939*
Visa expiry: December 30th, 1939

The sheet had been stamped in three places: *SURVEILLANCE TERMINATED*, with the date of September 10th, 1939. That was three and a half months before the visa expiry date, but only a few days after the Pan Am crash.

Now she grasped the connection: Wilhelm Fuechter had been one of those German-American specialists on the Pan Am flight from Lisbon. Fifteen American victims, fifteen case files here — it appeared they were all young or early middle-aged men of German-American extraction, all working for Dorner, all on exchange from U.S. automobile companies.

She flipped through the files: Otto Jaeger, Carl Kramer, Konrad Flen, Joseph Rauschning...metallurgists like Fuechter, chemists, engineers from several disciplines, a number of highly skilled tradesmen.

Greta began again, working through the box to confirm the pattern. Their visas had all been issued on or around June 30th, 1939, to expire six months later, around December 30th. All cases had been closed on the same date as Fuechter's, all files given the same stamp: *SURVEILLANCE TERMINATED*.

It wasn't difficult to speculate as to why they had been under observation: although the United States would not be drawn into the war until Pearl Harbor in '41, America's official — and economic — sympathy was with Britain and her allies. Given the deteriorating situation in Europe, the presence of all U.S. citizens in Germany must have been monitored, however casually, by the American authorities. The presence of these particular fifteen citizens, highly trained *German*-Americans working for a company already involved in war production, had obviously come to the attention of American intelligence. It had begun keeping tabs on the workers as soon as they arrived in Germany.

Which agency? The Strategic Services Unit Tomzak had described, the maggot before the fly? No, 1939 was before the SSU had come into being. The FBI? Yes, probably Hoover. Surveillance to start with, but as soon as hostilities in Europe began to look inevitable, he would have begun exerting pressure on the workers' parent companies in Detroit to call them back.

Of course. They were on that Pan Am flight because they had been recalled from Germany on the eve of war.

She sat back, disappointed but also relieved that this was not the expected box of horrors, because it brought her no nearer to the truth. What of these folders on the table in front of her? Was there any connection between them and the film Bentley had referred to?

Greta opened the last file, her disappointed glance so cursory that she almost missed the discrepancy.

Again a single sheet of official paper, but this time the seal did not belong to the U.S. Embassy in Berlin. It was from the Secretary of State for External Affairs in Ottawa, Canada. Below the official letterhead, in marked contrast to the elaborate heraldry of lions and unicorn and *fleurs-de-lis*, was a personal note in faded fountain pen ink.

November 15th 1939
Ted,
Hope this reaches you safely (i.e. no bloody U-boats in the Diplo-
matic Channel!) Many thanks for the dope on this fellow
Buelow-Schwante. Clever of you to peg him as a Canadian cit-
izen. Won't be able to do anything much about it other than
keeping an eye on the family in case your hunch is right — as
you can imagine, we've got our hands rather full at the moment.
Not to worry, temporary distraction — we'll have that little
paperhanger pasted to the wall by Christmas.
Cheers!
Arthur.

Greta counted the folders again: apart from the one containing the *Beobachter* clipping, all fourteen had contained case sheets except this one, probably because this case had been referred to the Canadian government in Ottawa. All previous cases involved Americans killed in the crash, but not this one. Buelow-Schwante, the fifteenth technician, the subject referred to in Ottawa's letter, was a Canadian citizen.

But what was this "hunch" that the letter had also referred to? And why would the Canadians need to watch Buelow-Schwante's family in Canada? Or was it misinformation, designed to be intercepted by the *Abwehr*, to confuse them?

And yet...

Canada had been mentioned in the Jagdzimmer. Hansjorg Peiper had called Canada the night he died. Toronto. Beck himself had wondered if Hansjorg Peiper sent the film to Toronto.

CHAPTER 21

S<small>HE TOOK A CAB BACK TO THE</small> W<small>ASHINGTON</small> S<small>ENATOR, AN OLDER,</small> undistinguished business hotel with no nice views of the White House or the Capitol, and called Bill Tomzak at his Wiesbaden apartment, as requested.

"No problems?"

"Access was easy. Thank you Bill. I really appreciate it."

"You don't sound happy."

"It wasn't happy reading."

"Uh oh. Not such a rosy picture at Dorner AG Frankfurt?"

"Not according to U.S. Army testimony."

"You found CROWCASS documents?"

"You were right, someone did a total whitewash on Dorner. The reports say..."

"No thank you. I don't need to know this. Not that it surprises me. Remember Friedrich Flick at Daimler-Benz, the good Direktor Flick?"

"I knew he was a fascist."

"Oh, avid. Convicted as a war criminal in '47 because of his treatment of slave labor, served a lousy three years. Then the Bonn government returned his confiscated property, including a 39 percent holding in the company."

"Which has prospered."

"Strength to strength. I'll bet you Simon Weisenthal takes the odd Mercedes taxi."

Greta hesitated a moment. "I need one more favor, Bill."

"Sorry. You wanted access at Suitland, you got it. I'm glad I could help."

"This isn't about Dorner. Maybe indirectly, but there was a second SSU box at the archive which didn't make sense." She briefly described the *Beobachter* clipping, the surveillance files, the letter from Canadian External Affairs about the fifteenth crash victim, Buelow-Schwante.

"Nineteen thirty-nine? It sounds unrelated. Should I ask why you're interested?"

"I'm not sure I could give you an answer. Let's just say there's a possible Canadian connection in this. Do you have any connections in Ottawa? They must have some kind of archive there, right?"

"Of course. The National Archive. You want RG25, Canadian Citizens Abroad, Germany."

"Showoff."

"We're NATO, Greta, we've had Canucks here forever, working hand in glove."

"So will you call?"

"Why not, it's not a big deal. Pre-war External Affairs material will have been declassified by now. Ottawa's way better organized than Washington. Less shit up there mind you, but they're naturally tidy people, like the Swiss. You ever been there?"

"No."

"Ought to go. You're pretty close to the border right now. Toronto's a nice town. Clean as a pin. Got a great ball team."

"Can you call Ottawa now?"

"Now?"

"It's only 3:00 p.m. there. Would you mind? See if there's anything under Buelow-Schwante, call me back? I'll refund the long distance."

"Wow." A slight pause. "Say, didn't your Dad used to rep for Henkell Trocken?"

"My God, how do you remember all this stuff?"

"Only salient facts, my dear. I want a case, vintage, extra-dry."

Greta had seen a lot of American movies on TV as a child, romantic comedies made years before she was born, Audrey Hepburn, Cary Grant, Doris Day and Rock Hudson. For a long time they had colored her idea of America, images of wealth and leisure, an apartment in some exciting American city, a softly lit penthouse with a panorama of city lights sparkling beyond its window-walls. It was not at all like Greta's view of Washington this late afternoon, which consisted of the inner courtyard of the Senator, a kind of dungeon for the kitchen trash, oozing greasy steam from the range vents, grey spattered with pigeon droppings, luminous in the gloaming.

And Rock Hudson had died of AIDS.

At 5:00 p.m., 11:00 p.m. in Frankfurt, by which time Greta had grown lonely and depressed, Otto found the first opportunity to call her. It helped to hear his constricted, pessimistic voice and to talk about her findings at Suitland, as she had been unable to do with Bill Tomzak.

"I thought those documents supporting the film were going to be in the second box. I'm guessing Paperclip got them along with the film. Maybe none of it ever got to CROWCASS."

"What about the second box," Otto said. "This Canadian thing?"

"Hansjorg Peiper tried to call Toronto the night he died. Maybe we've got something here."

"Come on. Fifteen people die in a plane crash in 1939, before the war, years before Paperclip. How could there be any connection with the film?"

"I talked to Bill Tomzak. He's making a couple of phone calls on it."

"It's not going to take us anywhere. Sounds like we're still at square one. We can't get any of that material out of the archive, even if we could use it. And listen — one word to the media and that stuff is gone before you can blink. The CIA don't need to say please to the U.S. military."

"They won't find it easily."

"Get real."

"I didn't give it all back to the desk. I didn't put Demaris's testimony back in the box when I handed it in."

"What are you talking about? You said they body-searched you."

"Absolutely. Marine Corporal Prescott. She and I became quite intimate."

"So how..."

"I didn't bring it out. I left it behind in the archive. Bill Tomzak was right, the unclassified section is a mess. Back wall, third locker from the left, front right corner, middle of the pile. No one saw me. It's a zoo up there."

"Jesus Greta."

"And Norrie didn't check. I gave him the boxes, he threw them straight into the refiling cart. Unless Vaughan's got ESP he's never going to find it, but it isn't enough. Nothing at Suitland brought us any closer to the film. We need that film, Otto. I need to talk to Kristian Peiper."

"No."

"If he knows something, we put together what we've got, maybe it's a lock and a key."

"They're watching him."

"Why were those surveillance files in the SSU vault, Otto? Why that letter from Ottawa?"

"Come home."

"They were talking about Canada in the Jagdzimmer. I've got a feeling about this Buelow-Schwante thing. I've crossed an ocean, Otto, I'm a couple of hundred miles away. There's got to be a safe way to do this."

Otto was shouting: "Right now, going to Suitland, you've got your head in the oven with the gas on. You want to *light it*?"

Greta let go a long, shuddering breath, carrying the energy and excitement with it.

Otto's voice softened: "I don't want to do this any more, Greta. I've got to think of Leona."

"I know," she murmured.

"We're going to call this kid Greta if it's a girl. We both agreed."

"That's nice."

"It's time to quit, Grets. We tried hard."

"Yeah. We tried."

"When's your flight?"

"8:30."

"Lufthansa security's brutal these days. You'd better be out there by seven." A beat. "Okay?"

She could feel her throat tightening, her heart beating there. She could see the car in her mind, a white Dorner 600 with a little bloody hole in the headrest. They could do that to Kristian Peiper, without a thought.

"Greta?"

"I'm here."

"I'll see you in a few hours. I'll be at the airport."

CHAPTER 22

KEN BODDINGTON UNSCREWED THE CAP FROM A MICKEY OF CUERVO
Gold tequila. He poured into a Styrofoam coffee cup, passed the flat
bottle to Phil Baylor who poured then passed to Marty Tesluk and on
to Kristian. Salt, lemon, Schlitz to chase it. He poured two inches,
drank it in one then emptied his beer bottle.

"Listen," Ken was saying. "I'm over in the Chassis Shop this
morning, in Dave Kravenger's office. Nine o'clock his phone rings.
'That's right,' Dave says, 'the usual: large ojay, four eggs sunnyside, six
rashers white toast strawberry jam. Make that marmalade, double
double on the coffee.'"

Kristian passed back to Ken who took a nip for the story.

"I'm thinkin *what*? Canteen don't take phone orders. I reckon the
deli, right, didn't think no more about it 'cept Dave ought to consider
his cholesterol a little bit. So we're talkin', couldn't have been more
than ten minutes, there's a knock on the door, in comes this guy with
a big Thermos bucket, starts unloading Dave's order. Six bucks even.
Nearest deli's twenty minutes away way out on Crandel, right? I mean

this guy only just put the friggin' phone down, what *is* this?" Ken pressed forward. "Listen to me, they got an underground kitchen down there in Chassis. I swear to God. Password, the whole deal, you'd never know in a million years. Dave says they've got three guys doin' fifty breakfasts a day while he covers on their jobs." His big shoulders rocked with laughter. "I thought I'd seen everything in this goddam place, I swear to god."

Phil went to the bar for another tray of beers. Unlike Kristian, who'd worked his college vacations on the line with these men, Phil was here out of appreciation for Hansjorg Peiper, for good drink and outstanding bullshit, and because he was Kristian's friend, not necessarily in that toasting order.

The tequila came around again and Kristian took another double, simple medicine to silence the questions for a few hours, a temporary and frail shelter from the maelstrom of anger and fear.

The wake was well underway, two hundred Dorner employees crammed into one end of the tunnel-like parts storage facility to pay tribute to Hansjorg Peiper, still "The Boss" as far as this crowd was concerned. Health and dental plans, pension schemes and company subsidized vacation packages — benefits adopted industry-wide for decades — had been Peiper innovations in Cleveland, and they weren't going to forget it. A cardboard facsimile of that time clock the Boss had banished was rigged up over the stage, where the tight country band — all workers — performed to a plunging dance floor.

Most of the partygoers were still in work clothes smelling of new car and sweat and ozone, familiar faces reminding Kristian how much he despised the white-collar snobbery of those who talked of the work force as grunts and rivetheads who did the bare minimum at an extortionate rate of pay in order to spend their leisure time at bingo or guzzling junk food in front of the tube. A very small percentage fit that profile, but it was a lot easier to think of Floyd Sissons playing pedal steel up on-stage, Kristian's first team leader, who spent his summers volunteering at a cancer camp, or Joanie Villiers on the edge of the dance floor with her second husband, a single mother when Kristian worked with her in lay-down assembly, who saved enough to buy five acres near Oberlin, and a white mare for her daughter. Or Ken Boddington across the table, the kind of line supervisor who'd catch a missing washer or hinge-pin and make the correction himself unless the problem became chronic, at which point he would deal with the worker personally, without any word to management. A decent man, intelligent and direct. An honest man.

Kristian's mood followed the loose, sentimental pattern of his thinking, and it swung. His hand tightened on the beer bottle, teeth clenched as the grinding anger came back.

"This is my goddam company," he muttered. "Right here."

Ken and Marty glanced at him, frowning. "Say what?"

Kristian stared back at them with the fierce conviction of several ounces of tequila. "What would you do for the plain truth? Right and fucking wrong. All these jobs, all these lives. I'm asking you, Ken, if it came down to the simple truth."

"Asking me what Kris? I'm not following you buddy."

They were distracted as Phil Baylor returned with fresh beers, two apiece, and talk turned, inevitably, to cars. Although too busy to make Frankfurt this year, Phil knew all about the show.

"They've got a whole section for special-order vehicles in Hall 3, rich boys' toys. I hear they've got a Hummer this year."

"So what?" Marty said. "Schwarzenegger's got half a dozen."

"*Hasta la vista*, baby."

"This ain't no one's rec vehicle. Custom-built for Saddam Hussein, except he never took delivery. Bulletproof windows, full-armor plating. Sucker's got close to three-hundred-pounds feet of torque at seventeen hundred rpm in spite of the weight."

"Sounds like you, Phil!"

"Sixty percent grade capability, four rads in case it gets a little warm in the desert there, Runflat tires for when the bad guys shoot 'em out."

Ken grinned. "I hear the radio sucks."

Laughter all around the table, decaying as Kristian got up, unsteadily, unsmiling.

"What's up buddy? Feelin' okay?"

"Just fine. Take a piss."

He made his way back through Parts Storage, its empty parts racks disappearing into the darkness beyond the exit. Tevlin's latest cost-cut had instigated on-demand parts delivery from outside suppliers. Typical Rinse 'n Hold, it wasn't a deep enough cut to make any difference, but had cost twenty warehousing jobs, and the new suppliers had so far been unable to guarantee so much as a wiper blade or a tail-light bulb reaching the line on time.

Storage had been dimmed for atmosphere, and the constellation of lights out on the factory floor hurt Kristian's eyes as he walked, shakily, past the door-frame line towards the washrooms. The line was up and running, a wispy, pale-skinned riveter with disproportionate biceps hauling an air gun from point to pre-drilled point around the frame, tethered by the anaconda power hose. Kristian should have been used to the racket — he'd done the same work for many summers — but the whipcrack of the rivet gun assaulted his ears this afternoon, hammering nerve-ends. A constant barrage of noise from above, too, the drag-chain conveyors that ran all the way from Stamping, feeding the line with hoods and trunks, fenders and doors, the raw, bundled modules swinging precariously from the chain, unfinished edges sharp enough to cut a worker to the bone from the slightest unprotected brush.

Shying from the sound, Kristian didn't register his page until the second announcement, by which time he was at the men's room. His ears roared as he swayed at the urinal, streaming onto a wad of chewing gum lodged in the basket — it looked like a little brain — wishing he could empty his head as easily as his bladder, trying to imagine how he was going to attend to business next week in Frankfurt; his Lufthansa flight was booked for tomorrow, Saturday, night.

He took his call in the door-frame supervisor's empty portable, where the plant operator transferred him to Molly at office reception.

"That woman called again, Mr. Peiper. Sophie Kempf. I told her you were out of the office. She left the same number, still wouldn't let me patch her through to your secretary and she wouldn't use your voice mail."

"Don't worry about it, Molly."

"She was insistent, Mr. Peiper."

Just as he'd done when she first called an hour ago, he told Molly to throw the number in her waste basket. "It's six o'clock. Shut that board down and come on over. There is one shitkicking little band happening here, and you are a dancing fool if I remember right."

Molly Thorpe was in her early sixties, had been the Dorner receptionist for as long as Kristian could remember. Everybody's mother, no different with Hansjorg, she had naturally planned on attending the party.

"I don't mean to interfere in your personal affairs, Mr. Peiper, but..."

"This is not personal, Molly, believe me."

"She sounded very anxious."

"You have a big heart, Molly, but in fact she is a deceiver. A mercenary and a liar, and I will not speak with her. Come dance."

Kristian replaced the receiver, stared at it, past the dark spots dancing in his vision.

Junia's work.

Junia Dorner was involved in what had happened at Canterbury Road. Vaughan and Hutchence too, just as he had discussed with Jason Steele-Perkins. After yesterday in Tevlin's office, he was certain of it. And they knew he knew they knew...

"Fuck it," he muttered, hauling himself out of the suddenly too comfortable chair, his brain overloaded. But he'd meant what he said, no idle threat: he was going to the end on this one. They must be sweating. Junia must be desperate to use Sophie Kempf again, she was usually more subtle than that.

Standing, Kristian dug into his pants pocket, pulled out a reduced version of the fax from Dorner Canada, the names of Toronto customers who had bought 920s. He blinked repeatedly to try and make the words settle into order.

Angus
Anlauf
Apicella
Assmann
Atkins
Baines
Buelow-Schwante
Byles
Cerniuk
Chan
Chambers
Claus

As he had estimated, there were still over a hundred names. He had called only a third of them so far, drawing hostility, curiosity, answering machines...wasted time. None that he had spoken to knew his father.

Swaying, he ran his finger down the list, leaving a long smudge of machine oil from the supervisor's handset.

Not now. He was losing it.

No more to drink. Home, something to eat, then he'd call a dozen more names. Not from home. A payphone. Safer now. But he wasn't afraid. Funny how much he wasn't afraid. No fear. Only loathing.

He went back to the party, danced happily with Molly, bought another round but excluded himself. The band was well into the bridge on "Someone to Watch Over Me," the way Willie Nelson had covered it, before Kristian realized what they were playing, and its significance.

He'd actually believed that she was sorry. The things she'd said outside the hotel. He'd tried to tell himself that she'd been truthful about that at least, about acting against her will. But here she was again, like Junia's hot, stinking breath down his neck. It was almost worth calling just to see. Almost curious enough to call the number just to see what she'd come up with this time. It was time to go anyway.

"Me too," Phil concurred, raising his giant bulk from the table where he made his farewells with Kristian. "Going to have some fun tomorrow," he said on the way to the exit. "Flying down to Cincinnati for the Indians game. I got box tickets. You want to come?"

"Frankfurt."

"That's right, you're going tomorrow. Minute you get back, I'm going to take you up. You won't believe this airplane, the difference is unbelievable."

"Some nerve, Phil, you talking about rich boys' toys." A month ago, Phil had traded his venerable Cessna Centurion for a brand new 206 hangared at Burke Lakefront.

"Talking of which," Phil said, "I parked next to your Spyder in the lot. I sure as hell hope you're not considering driving home."

"You?"

"Cab. Grab a bite?"

"Not hungry."

"Give it half an hour, it'll kick in. Drop you home anyway, it's on my way."

Kristian measured Phil's rolling, breathless gait down the traffic aisle, past the door-frame line where nothing at all had changed for the young riveter.

"These are good guys," Phil observed. "Ken and Marty back there, they're good company. I can see they thought the world of your Dad."

"He thought the world of them."

A brief silence before Phil said: "The cops got anything yet?"

He glanced sideways at Kristian for a reply, but Kristian only shook his head slightly.

"Why not?" Phil demanded. "They've had plenty of time. The fuck we payin' these dipshits for? That shit that went down in Frankfurt, that package old man Dorner gave your Dad...you reckon that had anything to do with what happened?"

Should he tell Phil? He wanted to so much.

"Listen," Phil went on. "Your Dad had an alarm system, right, which didn't go off. So whoever got inside the house knew the code. I mean, aren't the cops working from there?"

"They've checked all the people who knew the code, plus the security company."

"Listen, Ken was talking about that just now. He said the same outfit has the plant contract. Guardian, right? Was your Dad's system put in while he was still CEO?"

"I guess so."

Phil had also been drinking steadily, his small eyes tequila-brilliant. "So maybe the job was part of the main contract: video monitors, remote locks, guards...all that. Maybe someone here could get access to all the Dorner security codes, including your Dad's, claim it was company business."

"Ken likes to talk, Phil. Nice guy, but he likes the role, you know, like he has an intuition about every nut and bolt in this place, the shaman thing."

"I don't know. Maybe if the cops looked real close around here, maybe you'd find some little cocksucker with security clearance and an extra thousand or two couldn't look you straight in the eye, what I'm saying?" He caught Kristian's arm, drew him up. "Listen, somebody got that security code from..."

He never finished the sentence. It was the riveter who first raised his voice in a shrill scream of warning although the raw fender pressing was falling too fast to be avoidable.

The fact that it landed ahead of them, by a scant three yards, was due only to Baylor's zeal, the fact that he had physically apprehended Kristian in his enthusiasm for Ken Boddington's theory. The forty-pound steel module slammed into the concrete at an oblique angle and lunged sideways, its razor edge slicing through the floor's heavy rubber skin, carving it from the concrete in a trembling black curl.

Baylor threw up his short arms in a dumbstruck appeal to a gathering knot of workers awed by the close call.

"Thirty years," exclaimed a grey-haired woman in a baseball cap. "I ain't *never* seen that before!"

"Sue the bastards!" said a man.

"Psychological damages!"

"Hooooly *shit*!"

By now the door-frame supervisor had arrived. "You guys okay? How in hell'd that thing come off the drag? Was it the only piece?"

It was agreed that only one pressing had fallen, from a rackful still on its way down to the fender line.

"Stop the conveyor!" shouted the supervisor, and the word traveled back through the factory like the captain's orders on a ship. "Someone go get a manager," the supervisor told the crowd, and two men hurried away. He turned back to Kristian and Baylor. "You want to sit down, use my office. You want to see anyone from medical?"

Baylor, stunned but rudely sobered, shook his head.

"Mr. Peiper?"

Kristian wasn't listening. He was looking up, as he had done for one split second after the riveter screamed, wondering whether had he seen or merely imagined a hurrying figure high on a catwalk, amongst the labyrinth of steel platforms around the drag chain.

He looked down at the supervisor, said quietly and absently:

"Would you excuse me?" He began walking, stiffly at first, towards Parts Storage. "Wait for me Phil. I need to talk to you."

"Where you going?"

"Get a phone number."

CHAPTER 23

GRETA HAD HER FLIGHT BAG, WAS ON HER WAY OUT OF THE DOOR when the room phone rang.

"Okay," Bill Tomzak said. "It's gone up to two cases. You opened up a real interesting can of worms here, I only just got off the phone with Ottawa. Tighten your seatbelt."

Greta lowered herself onto the edge of the bed. "They had the same newspaper report in RG25: fifteen technicians working for Dorner, recalled to the United States in 1939 via a Pan Am Clipper out of Lisbon, which crashed into the sea shortly after takeoff. The Germans said engine failure; according to RG25's material, the U.S. Embassy was more of the opinion that the Clipper blew up three miles out over the sea."

"A bomb?"

"The Americans suspected it; fifteen top-level technocrats returning to U.S. companies like GM and Ford, all heavily contracted to the U.S. military, already pledged to aid Britain and her allies; they know an embarrassing amount about Reich war production, not to mention the technical secrets of one of its most important contributors."

"Dorner."

"If you were the German war office, would you want them to get home safely? But this gets even juicier: I had to go back to the base tonight, use DIA clearance before they'd fax me this shit."

"Three cases. A vineyard."

"Actually, this is one great story, the RG25 clerk got off on it just the same — we're sharing the movie rights."

"So tell me."

"You seen *Casablanca*? Lisbon was kind of the same deal in '39. Much intrigue. Anyway, the Americans apparently got a French intelligence report that two Gestapo agents had been observed at the airport terminal before the Clipper took off. Just after the Dorner party had checked in and were heading down the Pan Am jetty to board, the Gestapo were seen escorting a man out of the terminal to a privately chartered aircraft. One of the French agents got a photograph; the U.S. Embassy identified him as an engineer on loan to Dorner from the Packard Company in Detroit, Michigan."

"One of the fifteen," Greta whispered, intrigued. "The Canadian."

"Bingo! Richard Buelow-Schwante. The youngest and brightest of them all. A brilliant engineer. A prodigy, in fact. After the French report came in, Ottawa really beefed up their files on him: born in Kitchener, Ontario, working-class family, father worked as a meat packer. Richard went to work for the Packard automobile company in Detroit at fifteen. He must have been a whiz because Packard paid for his education — put him through the University of Michigan for engineering, graduated in two years. Still there?"

"Keep going, I'm listening."

"The American 'hunch' you read about? They figured he was alive, the only one of the original fifteen auto experts who wasn't at the bottom of the sea. They suspected he went on working for Dorner throughout the war, maybe quite happily, considering he'd volunteered to work in Nazi Germany in the first place. Remember he was of

German extraction, second generation, would have grown up speaking German." She heard the click of a lighter, Bill inhaled sharply. "That's as far as Ottawa goes."

"You mean that's it?"

"Kinda fun though."

"But what happened in the end?"

"There was no end. The war started, good old Canada jumped right in with Britain, Canadian External Affairs had slightly more pressing things to worry about than one truant automotive engineer. Case got buried. That gal tonight at RG25, she had bigger goose-bumps than me."

Greta smiled for the first time all day. "Sounds promising. She single?"

"As a matter of fact."

"I think we're back to one case, Bill. Better go. I've got a plane to catch."

CHAPTER 24

MOLLY THORPE CONFESSED THAT SHE HAD NOT DISCARDED THE number but had actually slipped it into Kristian's pocket on the dance floor. The pink paper square carried a long distance number with a Washington code — one he'd used many times for business reasons — then a three-digit suffix.

Thank you for calling the Washington Senator. If you know the room number of the guest you wish to speak to, please enter it now, or dial zero for reception.

He added the suffix — 458 — and waited.

Three rings. Four, five.

"No answer?"

They were sitting in Phil Baylor's 920 in the factory parking lot, Kristian in the passenger seat with the cell phone. It had taken exactly fifteen minutes to tell his friend what he knew and what he suspected, which had talked out some of the anger.

"This isn't like I thought. I don't feel this any more. Half an hour ago I was ready to kill someone. I don't feel anything."

"Hell, they tried to kill *you*. Nearly killed *me*."

"No I don't think so, Phil. If anything, it was a warning. They're saying they want this film and they're going to play hardball to get it."

Eight rings. Kristian dialed zero.

"*Senator Hotel, how may I help you?*"

"I'm trying to reach a guest in room 458."

"*The name?*"

"Sophie Kempf."

"*One minute please.*"

Kristian bit his lip, looked sideways at Phil. "I shouldn't be dragging you into this."

"You didn't. They did."

"I shouldn't have told you. I'm sorry."

"Don't sorry me, buddy. Some asshole just nearly dropped half a fucking automobile on my foot. I'm going to do whatever you need me to do."

The receptionist came back on. "*I'm sorry sir. There was a guest registered in room 458, but the name was Schoeller, not Kempf. I'm afraid you just missed her, she checked out a few minutes ago.*"

Kristian swore inwardly. "Did you deal with her personally?"

"*Yes sir.*"

"Petite, pretty...chin-length dark hair? German."

"*Yes, that would describe the person. I have a message here, she left it with her key, said she was expecting a call. If you'd care to give me your name...*"

"Kristian Peiper."

"*That's right sir, the message is for you. There's only one word here...well two, it's hyphenated. Booellow? Byooeelow? I'm sorry, I don't speak German.*"

"Spell it."

"*B U E L O W hyphen S C H W A N T E.*"

"That's it?"

"*There are two question marks after it.*"

"Two."

"*Yes sir.*"

"Thank you."

Frowning, he turned the handset off and gave it to Phil. "You got something to write with?"

"Move your arm." He rummaged in the armrest compartment, gave Kristian a ball-point and a parking violation. "What's going on? What happened?"

"She left a name."

"Whose name?"

It took writing it out to generate the first faint impulse of recognition. He had shown the Toronto list to Phil just a few minutes ago, it lay unfolded on the dash.

Kristian's hand was shaking as he lifted the paper, his eyes falling instantly to the place they had skimmed over a hundred times in the past few days, oblivious.

As with all the other names of Toronto Dorner owners, there was a first name, *Gertrude*, an address: *15 Crescent Rd., Toronto, Ontario.*

And a phone number.

He stared at the page with his mouth slightly open. "It's here. On the list. Why would she have this?"

"You mean..."

"Sophie Kempf. Schoeller. Whatever her goddam name is." He gazed blankly up at his friend. "Why, Phil? And why give it to me?"

Phil waited helplessly.

"A trick? But why? If this is where the film went...that's what Junia wants. If Dad passed the film here and they had this name, why tell me? Why wouldn't they just go get it?"

"So call the number. What have you got to lose?"

Kristian got an answering machine, a middle-aged woman's voice, gentle, educated, self-assured. A person one might like to know.

We can't get to the phone right now, but if you'd care to leave a message...

Who? After so many hours of pouring over the list of names,

waiting for one of them to call out to him, such an impasse was unbearable. So many possible answers, barely two hundred miles to the north.

Gertrude Buelow-Schwante's tape ran out and the line went dead. Kristian's hand tightened around the receiver.

"How far's Toronto, driving? Around four hours?"

"Wait a minute: you just finished telling me the CIA are on your case. All they have to do is follow you to Toronto. If your Dad's film is there, you're going to be leading them right to it. I mean, I don't know anything about spooks except the movies, but somehow I don't think your job training included countersurveillance."

"Why the hell are you smiling? This isn't serious enough for you?"

Phil's eyes glowed but it wasn't alcohol. They held clear and steady as he replied: "You need me."

"Why?"

"You need me to fly you in."

"No way, Phil. This isn't your problem. If that fender wasn't an accident, it means Vaughan's got people watching every move I make, maybe right now."

Phil wasn't hearing him. "I'm Can-passed."

"What the hell's that?"

"Canadian customs pass. Open border. A lot of border pilots have it."

"But I don't. I'll have to go through customs. That's too much attention."

"I radio in my pass number, say I'm flying alone. Toronto Island Airport, the check rate on Can-pass planes is between 10 and 20 percent. Less at night. It's a small risk."

Kristian shook his head. "But nothing's changed here, Phil: you have to file a flight plan don't you?"

"Sure."

"How long before we take off do you have to file?"

"An hour."

"Right. So they've got all the time in the world to get surveillance in place at the other end."

"If they see you board the plane. Surely to Christ we can get you on board without..."

"We can't risk it. If Dad really did give the film to this Buelow-Schwante person, I'd be handing it to Vaughan on a plate, and probably endangering her and you."

But Phil was brightening again.

"What?" demanded Kristian.

"So I don't file for Toronto. I file for Cincinnati. We get in the air, we pull a U-turn, just like the Colombian coffee ad."

"Wait a minute: the Canadians..."

"Have radar the minute we hit their air space. I've been flying twenty-five years Kris, you don't have to teach me. This new 206 handles like a dream, unless you're blind or mentally handicapped, you just can't fuck up. I can fly under six hundred feet. Shit, we did strafing runs in 'Nam under three, with people shooting back!"

"You hadn't been drinking."

"Are you kidding? I was wasted on Thai stick half the time. Anyway, do I look drunk to you?"

Kristian gnawed the inside of his cheek. "That's how low you need to fly?"

"Six hundred feet. It'll be dark in an hour. They'll never see us. We'd better not make it Toronto Island, it's too busy. We'll find a little field where they've all gone home. I've used Buttonville before."

"Give me the phone. I want to try her again."

Still the answering machine. Kristian's breath hissed from his nostrils. "Why go there if there's no one home?"

"Because she's there and you're here, buddy. Maybe she's just out at the show. Or she'll have neighbors who know where she is. You're doing this because you're going to Frankfurt tomorrow, for a week. They could beat you to it by then."

Kristian squeezed his eyes shut for five seconds. Then he nodded. "Take me by Canterbury Road. I want my passport."

CHAPTER 25

At under six hundred statute miles, on a cool, windless late summer night with no interference from Canadian Customs, the cab ride into downtown Toronto from Buttonville airport took half as long as the flight.

Kristian had insisted on going alone to Crescent Road, where the answering machine still played in a presumably empty house. He had cited the element of danger and his need to be alone if and when he met his father's liaison, but he suspected that Phil's protests were half-hearted, that he preferred to stay with his new airplane, having landed it illegally on a deserted foreign field. Phil had brought his cell phone; if he didn't hear from Kristian by midnight, two hours from the time they landed, he was to fly back alone.

Kristian had been to Toronto several times on business, often with his father, had always found it easy to compare with Cleveland: close in size, with a multicultural population, both commercial ports on a Great Lake, both cities with winning baseball teams. Rosedale, too, boasting gracious English-style houses on mature lots, put him in mind of Canterbury Road.

Number 15 Crescent Road was midrange Rosedale, accommodation for an au pair, perhaps, but not servants — a family home, not one of those many Rosedale mansions with a tennis court and a guest house. It was built above street level, reached by a dozen flagged steps up to the wooden porch. There was a double garage on the right side, dug out at basement level. For a 920 S?

Kristian paid the driver and climbed to the front door in the gathering dusk. The porch light was on, and what looked like a landing light on the second floor. He rang twice, then walked left to the end of the porch where a flagstone pathway led to the back. A weak patch of light spilled onto the end of the side lawn where a rusted child's swing-set stood at a tipsy angle. The house itself was mildly deteriorated: the brick needed re-pointing, a downspout had lost its extension, the wall stained where rainwater and snowmelt had leaked down to the footings. He had to mind his step where several flags had heaved over many hard Ontario winters.

The light shone from a glass paneled kitchen door through a dusty fly screen. He opened the screen and rapped on the window, which brought a marmalade tom with a head as round as a T-ball, up on its hind legs against the door.

Kristian knocked again, which increased the cat's demands but failed to produce anyone from the dark interior. He tried the door, startled to find it open.

The cat wove its way out through Kristian's legs, butting with its solid head, then followed him inside, into an attractive kitchen: professional quality copper pots hung from a frame above a wide central island, good chef's knives sheathed along one side of a scarred butcherblock; he saw a halogen range, three specialty ovens set into a brick column, a library of cookbooks shelved above the double refrigerator. The walls were decorated with a collection of woven baskets and hanging bunches of dried herbs alongside some assured framed drawings including several female nudes.

The exterior of the house had prepared Kristian for general negligence, but the kitchen revealed the touch of industrious and creative hands. A pile of unopened mail lay on the counter, addressed to Gertrude Buelow-Schwante. With the cat still twining through his legs, mewing, he opened the fridge. Except for condiments — half a dozen kinds of mustard — the shelves were bare.

The empty fridge, the mail, a cat hungry for attention: the owner was away. So why was the door unlocked? A neighbor looking after the cat, who had forgotten to lock up? Maybe they had just been here — the cat's bowl beside the door was full of kibble. Would they come back?

He tried to think what he would say. Gertrude Buelow-Schwante had been a friend of his late father; he'd never met her but happened to be in town and thought he'd drop by, found the door open. Any interest from the Toronto police and he'd lose everything. Then of course there was Phil's Cessna, which would be automatically confiscated if he was caught flying it in without observing protocol. He'd better be quick.

The big kitchen occupied one-third of the house behind a long central stair hall. A diningroom and then a study lay on one side of the hall, a spacious livingroom on the other. He started in the study.

A desk stood by the single window, on which a new IBM Aptiva was connected to a phone jack — there was the answering machine — the computer now dormant behind its screen-saver of drifting star-fields. Odd, he thought: on most new systems, ten or so minutes of downtime turned a screen-saver off. He nudged the mouse, which prompted Gertrude Buelow-Schwante's Windows 95 desktop, the light from the awakened screen showing the study walls lined with shelves containing hundreds of books: university textbooks covering a range of subjects too wide to have served a single student: chemistry, physics, mathematics, art history, English, French and German literature, philosophy and sociology...texts for all levels, from undergraduate to highly specialized study. A number of books on music — harmony, counterpoint, music history, biographies of composers and performers. It was these, along with bound copies of *The Strad* magazine, that prepared Kristian for the elegant tableau in the livingroom across the hall.

The porch light reached in far enough to show more bookshelves and a large collection of recorded music at the back of the long room, as well as an impressive stereo. He saw comfortable seating between a stone fireplace and a Bosendorfer grand piano. But it was the front third of the livingroom that held Kristian's attention, spurring his heartbeat. A cello leaned against a straight-backed, rush-bottomed chair, its sensual shape given a diminishing echo in a viola and two violins resting on three other, identical chairs. A bow, carefully slackened, accompanied each instrument. A music stand stood in front of each chair, parts for a Mozart piano quintet.

A family of instruments, poised in the darkness, they might have been playing themselves, magically, in the empty house.

Who lived here? What had they meant to his father, that he would communicate with them in secret, send them a small fortune, attempt to call them with his dying breath?

Kristian turned from the room, his heart and his imagination racing, hearing again, suddenly, his father's parting words in front of the Cleveland Orchestra the night he died. He stopped in the hall and looked up the staircase, holding his breath as the dim upstairs light revealed an arrangement of photographs around the half-landing. He went up.

There were several photographs of a handsome woman with a heart-shaped face, at various ages up to her late fifties by which time her long, thick hair was grey. With no other information except the voice from the answering machine, he knew somehow that this was Gertrude Buelow-Schwante. Other photographs followed the development of two upright, intelligent young women, unquestionably her daughters. Kristian's father was in four pictures, although one of them instantly captured Kristian's attention. In it, Hansjorg was almost a boy, standing beside a sad blond woman outside a little snow-covered house with a tin chimney and a white picket fence.

Leaving, thought Kristian. He hadn't articulated the feeling when he had first shaken this unexpected photograph from the envelope at his Old River Road apartment, but it seemed undeniable now: the mood was one of unhappy departure. Of loss.

He was still transfixed by the picture when he heard the cat. He hadn't noticed its absence, but it was mewing now, insistently, somewhere on the upper floor, scratching at a door.

Kristian swallowed, his throat suddenly dry, his pulse racing again. Could it be possible for someone to be asleep upstairs? Or was he too late, were Vaughan's people here already?

Kristian's heart was pounding, charged with sudden adrenaline as he crept up the last half-flight. If there was even the remotest chance that Gertrude Buelow-Schwante was here — a heavy sleeper? hard of hearing? — he had to know, had to see her.

Kristian tried to speak as he reached the door where the cat was still scratching, at the end of a short corridor.

But it was slightly ajar, so why was it resistant to the powerful tomcat, on its hind legs now, trying to push it open?

Why wouldn't it open?

He pushed, found no resistance, looked into the room with barely time to see the profile of an empty, made bed in the streetlight bleeding through drawn curtains. No awareness of the process that took away his legs and brought him to the carpet on his stomach, his right arm transformed from a useful limb to an instrument of blinding agony in the center of his back.

The white core of the pain was extinguished as his arm was freed. He rolled in terror, jerking away with a shout of alarm as his assailant came at him again, seeing a shadow picture now, of deep-set eyes, high cheek bones and chin-length hair.

CHAPTER 26

"My name is Greta Schoeller. Chauffeuring for Dorner was a cover. Until a few weeks ago I was a Lieutenant in the German Federal Police but I've acted alone in coming here. I know how and why your father died. I know about the film."

When she saw his implacable face, her attitude hardened. "I understand. I don't expect you to trust me. That's partly why I left you the message in Washington. If I was working for Junia Dorner's interest, why would I have shared that information with you?"

"To see where it took me."

"How *did* you get here?"

"No. You talk."

"Your activities are being monitored by the CIA. We're in immediate danger if they know you're here. I have to know how you traveled from Cleveland tonight. Quickly. We can't stay here."

"I'm listening Sophie. Or Greta or whatever your name is."

The light was off in the bedroom. Kristian stood by the door, holding his shoulder, Greta by the window where she could watch the street through the parted curtains. She told him as quickly as she could: the BKA investigation that had led to Ulrich's discovery of the film, his death and then Truong's, about Otto and Rudesheim and Suitland, Maryland.

"When I left you that message in Washington, I couldn't risk telling you more because I had no idea how closely you were being monitored. I knew you were coming to Frankfurt sometime for the show; I thought I'd catch up with you there, hoped the name might trigger something in the meantime. I hoped it would be a token, a sign that you can trust me. I wasn't planning on coming here."

Kristian stared at her, unmoved. "Why did you? You found a name in a sixty-year-old file, and you knew my father called Canada that night: I don't believe that was enough to make you change flights."

"There was more to the name. It's too long a story."

"Tell me."

With one eye nervously on the street, she told him what Bill Tomzak had unearthed about Richard Buelow-Schwante. "It was the added incentive I needed, although the impulse didn't hit me till I was at the airport, ready to board my scheduled flight back to Frankfurt. I had an hour to wait, I called directory assistance for Toronto, learned there was one listing for Buelow-Schwante. The only one in Canada. There was a Toronto flight immediately available, two hours duration, two hundred dollars. I'd already flown an ocean, I couldn't pass up the chance."

"Didn't you call the number?"

"Of course."

"And got an answering machine."

"So did you, right? It didn't deter you." She moved in from the window. "How's your shoulder?"

"Hurts."

She crossed the room towards him but he backed into the doorway. "I'm sorry."

"I've heard you say that before."

"Please Kristian...I swear I didn't know why you were being

investigated in Frankfurt, and I didn't care. Every instinct told me you were honorable. Decent."

"But you lied to me anyway."

"I thought you'd never notice the exchange. At that point I knew nothing about the DNV funding, but I was certain whatever they were looking for, they wouldn't find it on your computer." She took another step. This time he didn't draw away. "That week together. I've thought about you so much. We were good company. I know you felt it too."

He could see her face clearly in the glow of the landing light. She was looking unwaveringly at him, her violet eyes wide and clear, soft shadows accentuating her cheek bones, the delicate line of her jaw. Whatever his mind was telling him, his body knew nothing of it, reawakened to the powerful attraction he had felt from the first moment he met her, inflamed by the knowledge that it was a shared desire.

He looked away, turned from the room. "If there's any clue here we have to find it and get out of here. We'll talk somewhere else."

"I already found it."

He spun round.

"Downstairs," she said. "I think I finally found what we've both been looking for."

She led him down to the study. "If you're wondering why the back door was open, I picked the lock...it's really criminal what they teach you in the BKA. I also violated Gertrude Buelow-Schwante's personal computer." She sat down at the Aptiva's keyboard, the tomcat jumped into her lap. "She got an e-mail from Germany last Monday."

Greta opened the Windows desktop, clicked the e-mail icon, on into the mailbox. The communication was in English, from Kamp Communications in Dusseldorf. Kristian read over her shoulder:

> *Gertrude:*
> *After much soul searching I have decided that no just purpose*
> *will be served by making our aim the destruction of the Dorner*
> *organization although, having now finished analyzing — also*

digitizing — the film, I believe it is well within our power to do so. Without question we could sabotage the Kondor launch and that, given Dorner's current vulnerability, would itself probably spell the beginning of the end for the company. I hope I do not have to stress that it is not my professional involvement in the Kondor project that discourages me from taking such a path: by waiting until after the Auto Show to begin negotiations, we will avoid acting under the eyes of the world's press, and only those who deserve it will be punished, not the thousands of innocent people who depend on the Dorner organization for their livelihood. As for yourself, have no fear: from the moment you board my plane in Toronto, you will be under my protection. Go peacefully.

Dieter.

Greta closed the fax and returned to the organizer. She looked up. "So we know where the film is. And Gertrude Buelow-Schwante. I assume you know who Dietrich Kamp is?"

It was a moment before Kristian could respond, his voice almost a whisper: "He and my father were friends."

She looked surprised, impressed. "Close friends?"

"Your tape from Rudesheim, when you heard Vaughan planning to deceive me...he tried to tell me my father was killed because he had industrial secrets, data given to him by Dietrich Kamp. I knew it was a lie."

"Kamp would be a powerful ally," Greta said. "What's his interest in the Kondor?"

Kristian's thoughts were racing. It took him a moment to rein them in. "Kamp licensed the central processing unit. His chip runs the Kondor's on-board computer."

"That's important?"

"Life or death to the launch. The CPU controls acceleration, ventilation, heating, the lights. If Kamp withdrew the license, we'd be back at square one: research and development, cost and timing, everything."

"Can't you use someone else's chip?"

"We'd have to completely reverse-engineer the car to avoid infringing on his rights. A total nightmare. Kamp pulls out, the Kondor's dead. Simple as that."

"You think he's planning to use that as a lever against Junia Dorner? Imagine...something that small. Junia then Beck..."

"Then Vaughan and Hutchence. I wonder who else, how high it goes. But it sounds like he won't need to pull the chip if he has the film."

"Obviously the film is key. The U.S. testimony I found at Suitland, it'd be damaging, sure — Junia certainly wouldn't want that to get out, but she could always defend her father, blame it all on the SS. I saw nothing in the report to implicate him directly. She might even try to get mileage out it, how Erich Dorner stood up to the SS. We've heard that before. But for some reason the potential in this film terrifies her. They're all scared to death of it."

She closed the e-mail, highlighted the entry in the mailbox.

"What are you doing?"

"Deleting it. Same reason I hid that material at the archive. If anyone follows our trail..."

Kristian looked nervously out of the study door, towards the back door, then back to the desk where Greta was writing. "What are you doing?"

"Getting Kamp's e-mail address, just in case. But I'm going to get Otto to use police access to trace them."

"And say what?"

"We'll have to work it out. We've got a lot to discuss. I want to know how *you* got here."

"I'll tell you all of it."

"You're saying you trust me?"

Kristian made no conscious decision to reach for her as she rose from the chair, but suddenly she was in his arms. He had intended the embrace as a bond of solidarity, but then they parted slightly and he looked at her face, her skin lucent, softly shadowed beneath her cheek bones, the finest lines at the corners of her deep blue-violet eyes. They found each other's lips, tender for a moment before their mouths opened, suddenly ravenous with desire, a single groan rising from their throats, all control, all sense of situation and predicament beginning to slip away when Gertrude Buelow-Schwante's telephone rang.

The Aptiva's communications center took the call as Kristian and Greta clung to one another. Its external speakers monitored Gertrude's greeting and then the message.

Kristian released Greta, his heated blood running cold at the tone of Phil Baylor's voice.

"I don't know if you're there Kris. Oh man, I'm screwed. I'm round the back of the terminal, there's RCMP out on the field. Two cars. They're all over the Cessna. I guess we didn't make it past the radar. I don't know what you're going to do."

Kristian recovered from his shock and lunged for the handset. "Phil!"

"Jesus, man, I really blew it. I should have known it was a dumb idea, I must've been on fucking tequila time."

"Is it just Mounties? Can you tell?"

"I dunno. There's two marked cars, that's all. I'll never get back through the border. I might as well go out there."

"Tell them what?"

"I won't mention you. Maybe we weren't followed to the airport in Cleveland. There's a chance no one saw you board. Vaughan...whoever it is you've got after you...you've still got a chance no one'll connect you with this."

"Meanwhile it's your ass and your plane. I can't let you..."

"Forget it. Cut and run. Just do what you gotta do, buddy. I'll think of something."

"Phil..."

He broke the connection.

Kristian stared at her helplessly. "I just lost my ride." He told her quickly who Phil was and what had happened.

"So you knew Vaughan was surveilling you. Unless they followed you, do they have any way of knowing you came here tonight?"

"No, I don't think they know Gertrude Buelow-Schwante exists."

"I still want to know how you found out. Tell me you have a passport."

He nodded vaguely.

"We'll walk for a cab. I don't want to use this phone. First pay-phone I'll need to call Otto, get him to find Dietrich Kamp. I wonder if this woman's got a private number or an address for him here." She took the chair again and began searching the desktop, reacting with efficiency to the intimacy of a moment ago. "We need him, Kristian. Kamp's where the film is, Kamp's where we find Gertrude Buelow-Schwante. I'm already booked to Frankfurt on a 6:00 a.m. flight. It wasn't full, you can get on it. Assuming Vaughan isn't onto you, we'll be less conspicuous on a commercial flight, but we should travel separately. No one's looking for me. If you're apprehended, you'll need me free to get to Kamp." She found nothing on the desk, went back into the computer for Gertrude's electronic address book, thinking aloud. "The question is, are we smart to return to Germany? Canada's supposed to be a country with a conscience." She looked round at him. "Is there any involvement with Dorner in Canada?"

For a moment he didn't respond, his mind still busy with the ramifications of Phil Baylor's call. Greta swiveled the chair fully around, reached up for his hand. "Come on, don't disappear on me. We're going to be fine here, we're doing fine."

He nodded uncertainly.

"What about Dorner Canada?"

"A small marketing network, a few dealers."

"No Canadian loan guarantees."

"No."

She considered, then shook her head. "That still doesn't translate into security. This goes too high. I've spent long enough in the BKA to know what Beck and Vaughan's resources mean. Right now, I'd feel better being on the same continent as Dietrich Kamp. He has a substantial power base even without the Kondor chip or this film. You me,

Otto, Gertrude Buelow-Schwante, your friend who flew you here... Dietrich Kamp just may be powerful enough for us all to stand behind when this thing blows."

Greta found nothing for Kamp in Gertrude's computer files. Kristian followed her into the kitchen, her hand on the door when she turned and looked into his eyes. "Your father...my friend Ulrich...whatever the secret they died to protect, I think we're almost there, Kristian."

"There's more than one secret." His attention shifted to the wall where a framed travel poster hung beside the door. It had been issued by the German National Tourist Office, featured a picturesque town northeast of Frankfurt called Steinau an der Strasse, on the "Fairy Tale Road." He had noticed it on the way in, but hadn't registered the town's name. It showed the half-timbered *Amtshaus* where the brothers Grimm spent their childhood, with a double cameo of Jakob and Wilhelm.

Kristian's voice was low and husky. "My father's family had a house there."

Greta drew close to him and took his arm. "You told me that in Frankfurt," she said softly. "A holiday house."

"There are photographs of him upstairs, Greta. Pictures I've never seen, going back years. He sent money here, a lot of money. He never told me."

"Come," she whispered. "We have to go. We'll talk on the way to the airport." She exerted the slightest pressure on his arm, but for a moment he stood rooted, staring at the poster.

"He tried to call here the night he died. After he had turned away from me, his own son." He looked sideways at her, tears in his eyes as he searched her face. "Who are these people, Greta? Who was my father?"

They had five hours, most of it spent in a hotel lounge on the airport strip. By flight time they had exchanged every detail of the perilous journeys that had brought them to this point, which Greta relayed to Otto Volk at Keplerstrasse before they boarded. He would trace Dietrich

Kamp, either he or one of Kamp's people would be waiting to meet their Lufthansa flight in Frankfurt. As an extra precaution, for Greta's sake, Kristian was to remain separate from both her and Otto. He was to rent a car and stay on the B-43 for Offenbach. Otto would follow him discreetly. By the time he had reached the roundabout at Offenbach, they would know if he was being tailed.

Greta was reasonably confident they were unobserved as they entered Toronto's Pearson International Airport at 5:00 a.m., but they checked in separately, sat at either end of the departure lounge and in separate sections of the half-empty plane.

The constant threat of interception, the worry of Phil, the terrifying uncertainty of the next twelve hours and the churning questions only Gertrude Buelow-Schwante could answer...in spite of this Kristian's exhausted body enticed him towards sleep with images and sensations of Sophie Kempf, so unexpectedly restored to him as Greta Schoeller.

They had embraced at the hotel bar, lovingly. He could feel her imprint, the phantom of her shape in his arms fitting perfectly against him as he drifted towards sleep, the wonderful flex of muscle in the small of her back. Her hair like fine dark silk, with the scent of strawberries.

He let exhaustion claim him as the Boeing 767 breasted the Atlantic off Newfoundland, allowed his desire to disperse as he rocked gently on the cusp of sleep, tumbling...

For Greta the overwhelming temptation was to find excuses to pass his seat while he slept, but she could make the journey to the toilet only so often without drawing attention to herself.

Yet he was with her when she closed her eyes. She was still filled with wonder at his tenderness, the way he had taken her hand when they parted in the airport cab, drawing it up so that her knuckles lay against his cheek. Even now she could feel the delicious contrast, the rasp of his beard and his soft breath feathering her wrist, her slight smile even now rimmed with cool silver from the impression of his mouth.

An ache arose in her. She had been lonely for a long time, starved of affection and sexual pleasure since Andreas left.

She liked this man, she told herself, the only way her reasonable nature could deflect the suspicion that she loved him. He was intelligent, sensitive. He had a luster of decency and honesty, qualities she had sensed from the moment she met him in Frankfurt. Already she missed him with an intensity that went beyond physical desire, out of all proportion to the amount she had known him, which anxiety only deepened. She wanted time with him, a lot of time.

But how much did they have?

CHAPTER 27

LIKE MOST HONEST PEOPLE, KRISTIAN HAD ONLY EVER IMAGINED THE state of mind of a smuggler approaching customs; the thought of coming up to the line with a quantity of drugs or a firearm, the anticipation of a sudden hand on one's shoulder....

He didn't have to imagine this evening. Even when he was through customs and security, passport stamped, even as he proceeded out of the security zone and during the fifteen minutes it took him to complete the rental contract for a Dorner 800, he was still gripped by terror.

As arranged, he called Otto's car from the rental office, fingers trembling on the buttons, the receiver slippery in his grip. Otto's rank, Hauptkommissar, had prepared Kristian for spit and polish, but the phone impression was far from that. Otto's voice sounded strained and weak and he had a bad smoker's cough — several times during their brief conversation he had to lean away from the phone to exercise it.

"What's happening?" Kristian demanded. "Greta with you?"

"Right here."

"Where's Kamp?"

"There's good news and bad news. Good news is, I'd say you're clear. The airport's policed by a division of the Schutzpolizei, I think I would have caught it if there was a welcoming committee. Maybe you weren't tailed to Toronto, maybe your buddy with the plane took the whole rap."

Kristian made a mental promise to buy Phil Baylor a new Cessna if the RCMP had confiscated it. "What's the bad news, Otto?"

"I haven't been able to reach Kamp yet. He's out of the country until tomorrow, some New Age retreat in Wales of all places. Apparently he does this regularly, none of his people can get to him there. Greta and I already talked about using Interpol, she agrees it's going to draw a lot of attention, a bunch of questions we don't want to answer yet. We don't have that long to wait — he's supposed to be back tomorrow midday."

"*What?*"

"This guy marches to a different drummer, you knew that."

Kristian had to admit that the Welsh retreat sounded typical Kamp; he had made headlines recently with his *cyberschlussel* theory, that human beings had the capability to launch themselves into "free cyber-space" utilizing the body's own electrical circuitry. "I understand he's due back midday tomorrow," Otto continued. "Some Dorner event at the showground?"

Junia's preview party for the Kondor, in the ballroom of the Hotel Maritim. Kristian was also scheduled to attend it.

"What about Gertrude Buelow-Schwante?"

"Apparently she's with him."

"This is insane."

"I know. It's bad timing."

"Let me talk to Greta."

"Let's get you out of the airport right now. What are you driving?"

"Dark green Dorner four-door."

"Brand loyalty?"

"Last car they had."

"Lucky. Plate number?"

He gave Otto the license number of the 800, a luxury sports sedan not sold in North America.

"Okay," Otto said. "We'll tail you a couple of cars behind till Offenbach, make sure you don't have company. Go over the traffic island, make a left then first right on Bettinastrasse. Pull over as soon as you turn in."

At last he heard Greta's voice. "Hi."

"Hi. You okay?"

"Someone to watch over you."

"I'll remember."

"I'm here, Kristian."

"Greta?"

A heartbeat before Otto broke the spell. "Don't drive me into the ground in that 800. I'm in my own car, she's getting on."

Kristian sat for a moment after he hung up, still amazed by what he had almost said, thoughts of Greta distracting him from the worm of disquiet that had begun to nibble at him...something Otto had said, just out of reach...all of it overlaid by renewed fear of interception as he located the car, wondering why they had told him it was the last available rental: there seemed to be several cars in the rental company's lot. Reserved, or maybe they belonged to staff.

He drove with utmost caution out of the terminal and onto the B-43 south of Frankfurt. It had been a seven-hour flight and they had lost six more in the time change, 7:45 p.m. by the time Kristian had circumvented the traffic island at Offenbach and pulled over onto the side of Bettinastrasse.

He had been aware of the Mercedes only since the roundabout. It drew up behind him now and all three of them got out. Not even the smoker's cough had prepared Kristian for Otto's appearance: doughy features under a scrubby beard, a beer gut, smudged, heavy-lidded eyes. He was wearing a new white cast on his left hand and wrist.

"You're okay," he said, tossing aside a cigarette. "Looked like you had a Golf GTI with you for a while, had me worried till he turned off at Sachsenhausen."

"What happened to your hand?"

Greta answered for him: "Dive and fire on the range yesterday."

"Fucking careless," Otto said.

"Broken?"

"Some little bone with a long name. Completely fucks up your grip if they don't set it right. So what do you want to do? You've got some time to kill before we can expect to hear from Kamp."

"What about you?"

"On duty tonight. Busted hand, busted neck, what do they care? Pedophile case, I was telling Greta: Turkish immigrants, city's crawling with them. I swear, man...that's how they keep their women virgins for the wedding night, bugger little boys."

He looked from Kristian to Greta, beside him, saw their discomfort, shook his head. "Yeah okay, I've been missing a bunch of sleep. She was a cop, she's heard it all."

"Seen it all." She looked at Kristian. "At least I have now."

A truck went by, its airwash buffeting them, Otto's cast knocking against the Mercedes's hood as he steadied himself, wincing with pain.

"You go back," Greta told him. "We'll be okay."

"Make sure you keep in touch. Kamp's people know I'm waiting, there's always a chance he'll call in sooner. What are your immediate plans?"

Kristian looked at Greta. "I've been thinking about Steinau."

"Steinau an der Strasse?"

"My father's family had a weekend place there," he explained to Otto. "There was a Steinau poster in Gertrude Buelow-Schwante's kitchen." To Greta. "It's still pretty early. I'd like to ask around, see if anyone remembers them. I've never checked it out before."

"Then what?" Otto said. "It's only half an hour to Steinau on the autobahn."

"Then I don't know."

"Just remember you had a scheduled flight from Cleveland. People are going to start wondering why you're not on it. Beck's people,

Vaughan's people. A place like Steinau, off the beaten track...not a bad idea. Be super careful on the road: speeding, a tail-light bulb, you don't want to get pulled over for anything."

There had been no expression of intimacy in front of Otto, but Greta drew closer now, reached for Kristian's hand. "Do you want to go alone?"

Kristian gently shook his head.

"Are you sure?" she said. "They're your ghosts."

He looked at her steadily, heedless of Otto's presence. "I want to be with you."

"You're taking a risk being together," Otto warned her. "There's no attention on you."

"I know that."

He shrugged sagging shoulders. "Whatever you say." He turned, slapped the roof of his car with his good hand. "You guys watch that speed now. I'm going to let you both go with a warning this time." He stopped, cocked his head towards the Dorner rental. "Got a cell phone in there?"

"Yes."

"Give me the number. If you can't reach me at the station, I'll call you. Come to think of it, let's do that, I'm going to be in and out. Midnight, okay? Be in the car at midnight, I don't care what else you're doing."

He had the number, getting into his Mercedes when Greta called back to thank him. He paused for a second, his small, smudged eyes heavy-lidded, said something Kristian didn't catch.

"What did he say?"

"I don't know."

Kristian watched in the Dorner's rearview mirror until the Mercedes's tail lights were two red periods in the gathering darkness. "What's he like as a cop?"

"You mean is he honest?"

"I'm sorry, I wasn't..."

"Where it matters, yes he is. Absolutely. I know he comes across as a bigot but it's just talk. He's a good man. He's in some pain, more than he lets on."

"What's dive and fire?"

"What you see in the movies, crazy cops throwing themselves on the ground blazing away at bad guys. They have to put range time in every month, all ranks." She reached across the transmission tunnel and took his hand. "Hey. Look at me. We're doing okay. We've made it this far."

But not even Greta's nearness could silence the tiny voice from some remote corner of his mind. It nagged too distantly for him to hear the nature of its complaint, anyway obscured by fragmented, swarming notions thrown up by the events of the last twenty-four hours but still there as they left Frankfurt and joined Autobahn 66 for Steinau an der Strasse.

CHAPTER 28

THE BROTHERS GRIMM ARE CELEBRATED ALONG A TOURIST ROUTE that runs over half the length of Germany, from the Frankfurt suburb of Hanau almost to the North Sea. All along the Fairy Tale Road, charming towns boast of their ties with Jakob and Wilhelm: Fuldatal where you might meet "Hans in Luck," Sababurg with its Sleeping Beauty castle, Hameln where the Pied Piper plays daily and visitors are cautioned to take children firmly by the hand.

Yet in terms of the Grimm's biography, the first fifty kilometers of the Fairy Tale Road are the most significant: Hanau, where the brothers were born, Gelnhausen, Wachtersbach, then Steinau where history tells us they spent an idyllic youth. These are the towns that surrounded them in childhood, half-timbered houses on cobbled streets spreading up the gentle, forested hills of Hessen's *Mittel Gebirg*, shepherded around market squares, church spires and the courtyards of Renaissance palaces.

Steinau was typical: a main street called Bruder-Grimm-Strasse, the palace tower and the three-tiered spire of the Reinhardskirche floating above gabled orange roofs. Kristian imagined the Peiper family arriving here from the city, a much longer journey then in their boxy Wanderer. But they would have been happy wanderers, Hansjorg and his three sisters in the back seat, trading verses of songs, singing harmony...always music. He imagined the children's growing excitement as they neared their holiday house, passing the fountain in the cobbled town square from which the Frog Prince forever retrieves the ball for an ungrateful bronze princess, turning now onto Ziegelgasse, the "Tiles Lane."

Kristian parked next to a stone trough into which water poured from the mouths of a two-headed gargoyle, its features weathered smooth by five centuries. The trough held Greta's attention, a moment before she saw where Kristian was looking. "That one?"

It was almost a period caricature, the golden stone foundation supporting three stories of half-timbering at the high gable end, startling black on white, the old beams criss-crossing as delicately and ornately as stitchwork on a dirndl.

The front door was at the top of a flight of stone steps, one half-story above the cobbled street and flanked by shuttered windows. The knocker on the oak door reverberated inside the house but brought no response. Kristian rapped again, waited. It was full dark by now, but there was light in the house; through the front window they could make out a big open-plan room with large abstracts against lumpy whitewashed walls, bookshelves, an earthenware bowl of fruit inches away on the deep window ledge, a dehydrated orange and two leopard-spotted bananas.

"Looks like they haven't been here for a while," Greta said. "Who are they?"

"As far as I remember, he's a lawyer in Frankfurt. I think she owns a gallery in the city."

They walked a little way up Ziegelgasse where an open archway accessed the walled back garden. The back porch light showed a pathway of stepping-stones meandering towards a woodshed, warm red brick and aged beams, piled to the roof with a winter's supply of logs. Espaliered fruit trees grew up against the old brick, dwarf pines stood along the path amongst unusual earthenware pots and several abstract stone sculptures, patina'd by the weather. Everything about the house and garden connoted good taste, regardless of money spent. The Peipers would have approved.

"Help you?"

An unsmiling middle-aged woman was standing behind them on the opposite sidewalk beside the open front door of a much smaller house.

"We're looking for the owners," Kristian said. "Do you know if they're in town?"

Her round face was puckered with suspicion. "No."

"We saw the light," Greta added apologetically, "thought they might be home."

"It isn't their home. That's in Frankfurt."

"I wanted to meet them," Kristian explained. "My grandparents used to own this house, years ago. I was hoping to find someone who might know about my family. I live in the United States."

The woman paused to brush back a strand of grey-blond hair. "That your car? They got a car like that. Spent half a million marks fixing the house, never here."

"Thanks anyway."

She waited until their backs were turned. "It used to be the Lutheran parsonage. You want to find out anything you'd better go see the minister."

"Where does he live?"

"Up Neuss. I suppose you want directions."

They decided to walk through the winding streets on the edge of the town, where the ancient town wall still defined the core of the town, where frame houses had stood since before the Renaissance, several under reconstruction with the original reed and mud filler revealed in their walls. Europe always made Kristian feel his American-ness, new-minted.

Greta took his arm up Bellinger Tor, a narrow hill road rising southeast above the town. From here they could feel the wind on their faces, damp with the promise of rain, from the north where darkness cloaked the Vogelsberg hills. The street lights had ended, both of them peering through the darkness to find Alte Strasse.

"I hope she hasn't led us astray."

"I can understand the resentment," Kristian said. "City slickers buying up the good real estate, show up once a month. I wonder if they felt like that about Dad's family."

They found Alte Strasse halfway up the hill. By contrast to the houses in the lower town, the minister's bungalow looked blandly new. It was the last house before the street petered out into a track. A dappled work horse dozed in a fenced paddock beside the house, a white goose folded between its forelegs.

"They look like a fairy tale," Greta said. She stopped him at the minister's gate, put her arms around his neck and drew him to her. "When all this is over?"

The Neuss family had just finished supper, the small house full of the aroma of roast meat, reminding Kristian that he was starving, too keyed up to eat on the plane.

Bearded and heavyset, Neuss could have been a farmer except, perhaps, for his wide, slightly wonderstruck blue eyes. "It won't take a moment to show you the parish register," he said. "Come in, it's in my study. I was stealing a few minutes for tomorrow's sermon." They passed an open door, several young children and a smiling woman making costumes around the dining table, painting, sewing, gluing.

"A hive of industry," said Neuss. "It's the Grimms' birthday. We have our big parade tonight, at the witching hour." He waggled scary fingers through the doorway, received with giggles by the children. "They love it, they get to stay up stinking late."

"I wondered why there were so many people in town," Greta said.

He smiled as he held the study door open for them. "Actually neither of them were born today, but instead of celebrating twice, we do them both at once. I think the tourist office is afraid of wearing the poor old brothers out. I think Hanau does two birthdays, but they *were* born there."

The parson's study was a small, meticulously neat room at the back of the house. There was an open bible on the desk and a blank notepad, awaiting inspiration. He reached up and lifted down a heavy, cloth-bound book from the top of a cupboard, holding it easily in one hand while he cleared a place on the desk. He opened the register and sat to it.

"The name is Pfeifer?"

"Peiper."

"Of course. You're American, I can hear that. You're visiting Germany?"

"On business in Frankfurt."

The parson turned big pages crammed with careful handwriting in faded ink. His watery smile gradually dissolved into a delicate frown. "You say your father's family owned the parsonage on Ziegelgasse during the war?"

"Until 1943. They bought it around 1930."

He turned back. On the left side of each double page were the records of birth, baptism and death for each parishioner, with the parish accounts on the facing pages, expenses associated with the Lutheran church buildings. Kristian had noticed that the earliest entries dated from the mid-nineteenth century, the ink growing darker, the writing less florid, as the dates progressed. "Of course there are several earlier volumes of the registry," the parson said, "but they're in the *Rathaus*, in the archive. My family and I are relatively new in Steinau, but I thought...it's back here." He stopped, pointed at an entry for 1902. "You see there? The parsonage was sold to the Schein family that year, the first time in over three hundred years it fell into private hands. I believe my predecessors thought the house too old and dilapidated to be inhabitable."

Greta smiled over his shoulder. "And now only millionaire lawyers can afford it!"

Neuss looked up at her, his mild disapprobation touched with humor. "Herr Mutter has done a great deal of work to the structure. Whether or not he spends time in the house, he's saved it for the town."

"When was it sold to my family?" Kristian asked, aware that they were keeping Neuss from his sermon.

The minister's slight frown returned. "That's my problem, I don't believe it was." He turned the pages rapidly now, stopping several times to point out the name Schein. "There, 1920. There again, 1931. You see? The ownership keeps changing but it stays within the family. See? Always Schein. Great grandfather to grandfather to father to son. Ah, here, 1953, it goes to a woman, Monika Steuber, but Frau Steuber's maiden name is Schein. She's in my congregation, quite a character. Her daughter Martha runs the puppet theater." He turned to the last page that contained writing, in incongruous blue ball-point. "My immediate predecessor, I wish he'd used a proper pen. But you see...1988...Monika Steuber sold it to Herr Mutter after it had been in her family for eighty-six years. I'm sure the Mutters made Monika an offer she couldn't refuse."

Greta quietly linked her arm through Kristian's. She had to guide him back as Neuss stood to replace the register on top of the cupboard. When the parson turned, he saw, as Greta had already done, the look of grave concern on Kristian's face. "I'm sorry," Neuss said softly. "I don't know what to tell you. As you can see, there's no mention of Peiper. Are you sure you have the right house? The catholic church maintains..."

"No." Kristian shook his head emphatically. "That's the house. All my life, I heard about it: the house on Ziegelgasse. I've been here before to see it."

"Your father actually lived there?"

"It was their holiday home, they lived in Frankfurt like the Mutters. The whole family except my father was killed in the bombing."

The parson nodded sympathetically. "You know what I would do? Go down to the *Marionettentheater* and catch Martha Steuber after the show." He gave Kristian a kindly smile. "Martha's lived here all her life, she knows everything there is to know about Steinau; especially the parsonage since it was in her family for so long. If *your* family was ever here, she will know."

The night air had grown heavier by the time they got back to the town square off Bruder-Grimm-Strasse, the rain not far off. Kristian was grateful to Greta for not making conversation, keeping pace with him in his anxiety to reach the square.

The *Kumpen*, the town square, was charged with energy and excitement for the occasion. Banners hung from both the town hall and the Katharinenkirche, proclaiming the brothers' "birthday" with the same double cameo they had seen on the poster in Rosedale. An oompah band played in a tented stage facing the square. Ranks of tour buses in the municipal lot, packs of children chasing across the cobbles in excited anticipation of the parade, splashing each other from the fountain, exhorted by frazzled parents.

The puppet theater faced onto the square opposite the white-washed town hall, the *Rathaus*, in the same storybook style as the parsonage though larger and constructed entirely of stone. The marquee announced a double bill to mark the celebration: *The Bremen Musicians* and *Red Riding Hood*. There had been performances all day, the last one starting at 7:00 p.m., only ten minutes to go before it let out. They spent the time watching a clown perform on a unicycle, a simpleton in a too-small black suit and a bowler hat, nothing to do with Grimm but brilliantly inept as he wobbled and lurched within a circle of spectators, making desperate dashes on his out-of-control cycle, almost toppling into the audience before plunging away in a new direction, angled forward in terror.

He was funny. Kristian might have laughed aloud had he not seen himself under the bowler hat.

They found Martha Steuber in the ticket booth. She was in her mid-forties, plump, pale-complexioned, at first too busy to talk as she attended the souvenir counter, selling fairy tales and puppet kits. They inspected the foyer until she was finished, the marionettes hanging from hooks around the walls, the human figures disturbingly lifelike, full of repressed energy. It was as though they resented their strings, unable to respond to the recorded music that filled the foyer, toy instruments played with frenetic skill.

"Somebody made a mistake," he said to Greta. "Neuss doesn't know. You heard him, he said he was new in town. There's another register, or someone forget to make the entry."

Greta took his hand but he resisted her, wooden himself, with anxiety. Martha wrapped the last purchase, poured herself a cup of coffee from a Thermos behind the counter and came around to them, smiling through the steam.

"Now...how can I help you?"

"The parson, Herr Neuss, gave me your name," Kristian began quickly. "I'm inquiring about some former residents of Steinau. My name's Kristian Peiper. I'm American but my father's family lived in Frankfurt. Until the middle of the war they had a place here, on Ziegelgasse..."

"The parsonage," Martha said.

Kristian's expression suggested a dim lamp being turned full up. "You know of them?"

"Of course. The Peipers used to come here all through the 1930s. The parents were teachers?"

He grew tense with excitement. "My grandmother was a university professor at Mainz. My grandfather was the chief curator at the Stadelsches Kunstinstitut in Frankfurt."

Greta frowned slightly at the woman. "But you're too young to have known them."

"My mother used to talk about them. They had children, a boy and three daughters. Weren't they musical?"

Kristian threw his arm around Greta and hugged her close.

"Kristian was worried," Greta explained. "There was no record of his family in the parish register."

Kristian hurried on: "I knew they owned the house from about 1930 until '43. The registrar must have overlooked them because it shows unbroken ownership by your family."

"That's right," Martha said. "But the register is correct. The Peipers never did own the parsonage. They rented it from my grandfather."

"Rented?"

"Yes, for about thirteen years — as you say, from '30 until sometime in the war. My mother was a contemporary of the Peiper girls, I think she was always a little in awe of them because they were so clever, and lovely as well." Her face clouded. "Such a tragedy, what happened. That beautiful family. Such a tragic end."

A long-haired teenage boy appeared through the curtain separating the foyer from the auditorium, dragging a mop. "I could use some help, Mum. It's so gross."

"My son Heinz. You know those pictures Nana has of the Peipers?" she said to the boy. "This is Kristian Peiper. He's from America."

"Cool."

"One of our audience had a slight accident."

"Puked all over..."

"Thank you, Heinz." She turned to Kristian. "I'm sorry you keep getting passed around, but really you'd do much better talking to my mother. She's been in Alsfeld all day, visiting. Should be staying over but she insisted on coming back for the parade. It comes right by our front door. Some of the older residents don't like all the fuss."

"I think we met one."

"Not Mum. She should be back by eleven-thirty. She's rather unorthodox isn't she, Heinz?"

"She's crazy."

"He adores her. Can you stay that long? She'd love to meet you. Of course, if you're staying here tonight and you'd rather come in the morning..."

"We're not sure," Greta said.

"I'd like very much to talk to her tonight, if it's okay," Kristian said.

"Fine, everyone stays up late in Steinau tonight. We live on Schloss Strasse behind the palace, on the corner where it turns south, number twenty-three. Come and watch the parade with us."

"So you never lived at the parsonage?"

"Never, it was always rented out. You talk to Mother. Her long-term memory's very good."

"I really appreciate your help," Kristian said. "You said she has photographs?"

"Tons of them," Heinz assured him.

"Eleven-thirty then," Martha said. "Number twenty-three." She and the boy disappeared into the auditorium. Kristian and Greta were at the exit when Martha popped her head back through the curtain. "You say *your* name is Peiper?"

"That's right."

"They were your *father's* family?"

"Yes. Hansjorg Peiper. Dad was the son. Your mother's friends were his older sisters."

Martha Steuber's pleasant face clouded. "That's odd. I didn't think any of them survived the war." She shrugged, brightening. "I guess your father must have, because here you are, right? You should come back and see the show sometime." She hesitated. "You've got a couple of hours to kill, you have something to do?"

Kristian looked at Greta. "Eat?"

"Took the word out of my mouth."

Martha laughed. "And now you're even hungrier! There's a good place right here on Bruder-Grimm-Strasse. There'll be a run on tables but I'll give them a phone call. I send them enough business."

They thanked her warmly and went out into the square. "I hope they take Visa," Kristian said. "I didn't get marks at the airport." He felt in the empty breast pocket of his jacket. "I must have left my wallet in the car. It's just round the corner, I'll run and get it. You'd better go make sure of our table."

"You don't have to go, I've got money."

"Ah, but I've got an expense account."

Her hair danced as she shook her head, caressing the delicate line of her jaw, framing her smile in a way he had come to adore. "Expense accounts are for business." She kissed him. "This..." She kissed him again..."is pleasure."

"Yes I will accept that. But I should go get it anyway. The town's probably crawling with opportunists tonight, we don't want to take any chances. No cops."

She pouted: "Not even ex-cops?"

He held her, his arms tight around her, oblivious to the crowds of people around them. "This is like a sweet dream, Greta. In the middle of a long night. I don't want to wake up."

"We don't have to. Not for a few hours."

They had reparked on Stadtborngasse, a block north off Bruder-Grimm, one lucky spot between bumper to bumper tourist cars. He unlocked the car, and as he reached into the armrest compartment for his wallet, his foot struck the mirror adjust on the driver's door.

A standard luxury in the 800, the feature was designed to work in tandem with the three-position memory in the seat, providing three memory sets for the mirrors. The only flaw — Dorner was addressing it next model-year — was the exposed design of the switch; he'd read in the company newsletter that too many 800 drivers were complaining of inadvertently setting it off, usually with their elbows, a small but unacceptable annoyance in an eighty-thousand mark car. Kristian retrieved his wallet, touched the button again before closing the door, resetting it to position one, the way he had set it up at the airport.

Martha Steuber was right, the restaurant in the half-timbered inn was filled to capacity, even the lobby was packed with frustrated parents and hungry children. Kristian felt a pang of guilt almost equal to that of hunger as he shouldered his way through the crowd and scanned the tables. It seemed to be a family business, a darkly attractive woman with a touch of gypsy about her, waiting on tables, a young girl with black curls and a ring in her nostril, obviously the daughter, speaking perfect French as she took orders from a family of six at a window table. There was no sign of Greta in the diningroom. Had he missed her in the crowded entrance?

Once again he pressed through the throng. He called her name. He positioned himself outside the women's washroom, wondering if she was waiting in a lineup inside. After five minutes he asked a woman to inquire for him, but Greta wasn't there.

Kristian began to worry, was about to re-enter the diningroom when he saw the black-haired daughter searching through the crowd. She gestured when she saw him, rattled something in the air. "I'm sorry, we're so busy. Your wife described you very well, but there are so many people tonight. She said to give you this." She gave him a key on an oval wooden fob on which "Room 9" was hand-painted in a border of flowers. She noticed his surprise. "Your wife's name is Greta, right? I'm not giving her key to a total stranger?"

He smiled, trying to overcome the sudden spike of adrenaline. "No, I'm not a stranger."

"But you're not married, are you?" The girl eyed him sternly. "Are you in love?" Knowing beyond her years, he thought, to be expected in an innkeeper's daughter. Keen-eyed, but so was Kristian.

"That's a good question," he told her, turning to the stairs. "A wonderful question. The best question anyone's asked me all day."

A warm room at the top of the inn, three floors away from the noise. She was standing by the window. Enough streetlight shone between the drawn curtains to reveal that she had taken off her shoes and socks but was still wearing her bluejeans and her white cotton shirt. A bottle of red wine and two glasses glimmered on the bedside table.

"They're getting our dinner." She whispered.

"What are we having?" he whispered back.

"Tortiere."

"When?"

"When we ring."

For a minute neither of them moved. They gazed at each other, the moment falling softly, magically around them.

"Close the door."

He did so.

Her feet made no sound as she came to him. She took his jacket by the lapels and lifted it off, laid it on top of her own on the chair. She pulled his shirt from his waistband. Her cool, smooth hands slipped underneath, around his sides and over his chest, hesitating for a second as she brushed his nipples with the edges of her thumbs, stiffening them. Kristian leaned back against the door, sliding down until his face was level with Greta's, to kiss her.

Tender, teasing kisses at first, covering each other's faces with them. Their breathing came faster, murmurs of pleasure became groans of desire as they opened their mouths to each other like hungry birds.

They broke apart for air, smiling into each other's eyes, sparkling with happiness. "We deserve this," Kristian whispered.

"We deserve each other," she said. "Undo my shirt."

With trembling hands he addressed the tiny buttons on the lace-trimmed front. Then he drew the shirt aside, slowly, in wonder, letting the lace catch on the dark, tilted points of her small breasts. The sigh came from deep inside him as he knelt with his arms around her waist and laid his cheek against her belly.

"Greta…"

Her hands in his hair, guiding him up, urging his kisses over her breasts, caressing his face with her nipples, his eyelids, eyebrows, nostrils, the roughness of his stubble which brought a little cry from her throat.

He undid the brass button then the zipper of her bluejeans, and eased them down her legs, her hands on his shoulders as she stepped out. Kristian stood while she did the same for him.

"No," she whispered as he began to lower his underwear. "I want to do that, but not yet."

They went slowly to the bed, holding hands but at arm's length so that they could look at each other, Kristian marveling at the shape of her, the lovely tones and proportions of her elfin body. She smiled her own approval, with sudden mischief as she pushed him down and tumbled after him onto the duvet, their laughter immediately turning to sighs.

Kristian touched her reverently. Her toes, her feet, her pretty legs, along the silken inner thighs to the damp pout between them. He knelt and kissed the spring of soft hair beneath the white cotton, running the back of his finger along the crease where the damp material conformed to her, kissing then gently nipping the tender ellipses that formed her, his tongue at last discovering the bud of her clitoris beneath the material.

She groaned and hooked her panties off and kicked them away then drew him up the bed, her mouth and her legs opening wide to him. "Strawberries," he whispered. "It's not your shampoo. I can taste fresh strawberries."

Greta stopped his hand a second time when he addressed his own underwear. "Me," she said, and slipped from his arms. She knelt as he had done, feathering the aching bulge in his underpants, teasing it until he bucked involuntarily under her touch, pressing down with her free hand on his chest to restrain him as her fingers found the Y-front opening.

Greta murmured with pleasure as she sprung him free, lowering her head so that her hair brushed his belly and thighs, planting tiny kisses from the base to the tip of his erection, seeking the tiny spout with the point of her tongue.

When she took him fully into her mouth, Kristian gently lifted her head away and sat up, suddenly distraught.

"I don't want to come yet. I'm too close."

She smiled tenderly and folded her arms around him. "Do anything you want."

"But I don't want to."

"No?" She let him go and smiled luxuriously. "I do."

She pulled off his underpants then slipped back into his embrace and kissed him, lovingly. She lay over him to kiss him, with his penis nuzzled between her buttocks. She squirmed under him, took just the tip inside her for a teasing moment, then let it go and rubbed herself slick along its hard length. She lay beside him on her back, nestling her head in the crook of his left arm while she guided his right hand back to her sex.

He kissed her mouth, kissed her breasts, teased and tormented her nipples while he masturbated her.

"There. Oh Kristian. Oh my god..."

He gathered slickness from the soft furrow, his fingers loving the tiny, stiffened bud until he could no longer resist the ultimate intimacy and put his mouth to her, lips to her lips, kissing her sweetness, drinking her, never stopping for more than a second the concentrated flutter of his tongue-tip, both his hands free to explore the rest of her body, to assist the work of his tongue until she cried out for him to be inside her.

Kristian gave himself to her, dispersing the focus of sensation, making the whole of his body alive to hers, dispelling his anxiety, giving himself to Greta without reservation until her climax began to shudder through her, her mouth open in a silent scream, her arms locked around his neck, her feet locked in the small of his back so that she was suspended from him, a part of him.

She fell back onto the bed, lay for a moment smiling dreamily. She opened her violet eyes to him. "Your turn." Slowly she drew her knees up until they brushed the hair under his arms and whispered "Fuck me Kristian.."

He did it slowly at first, amazed and proud as he caressed her with his cock, feeling the pulse of her still-ebbing climax, the snug fit of her swollen sex, gazing into her dreamy eyes as caresses became long strokes. Swifter strokes. Powerful strokes that made her loins stir again.

"Greta..."

Unafraid now to connect with the epicenter, he moved faster, driving it, his cock growing from his core.

"Oh darling Greta..."

The root of him, his soul, the beginning and end of him, Kristian's whole body and being fused with unbearable, incontainable joy.

They sat up in bed to eat and drink most of the bottle of underestimated German red.

"You were so relieved at the puppet theater," she said. "Ever since you saw that poster in Rosedale, it was a priority for you to come here, wasn't it? What did you expect to find? What were you afraid to find here?"

"I don't know. Everything I've learned in the last few days... Dorner's been my life, even before I started working there. Erich Dorner was my hero, Junia too. One hundred percent positive image all my life, then in the space of three days I'm faced with...atrocities? Lies? *Murder*? Then I find out my father had this connection in Canada, with a woman I didn't even know existed. What am I supposed to do with all this? It's like a storm that won't end."

"But your family *was* here in Steinau. That's a certainty. You have roots. You need good, deep roots in a storm."

"But Dorner won't weather it. I feel it. Whatever the truth out there...I thought up to now that I'd have to make a choice between the truth and my company. I don't think there's any choice now. It's all going to blow apart."

"Don't say that till we hear from Kamp. It sounds like he's got a way to settle the score without ruining Dorner. He'll help us. That's what I feel."

He reached up for her hand, pressing it to his cheek as he looked gratefully into her eyes. He put her fingers in his mouth and gently bit them.

"Still hungry?"

He stirred against her.

"Wait. Talk to me. Tell me about him. Your father. You were so close, I could see that. Was he around a lot when you were a kid?"

Kristian settled happily enough against the pillows. "He had to travel, he didn't relish it. But he made up for it. He used to make a special trip home from the office for my bedtime story, even if he had to go back afterwards. Grimm in German." Kristian smiled. "He used to keep important business waiting for that. What about you? Your father."

"He was in the wine business. Sounds classy doesn't it?"

"It wasn't?"

"He was a sales rep for Henkell Trocken, you might say he used to bring his work home. We never got a bedtime story. He used to stay at some bar till he thought we were asleep, out of the way. I used to keep awake till I heard his key snick in the lock. Sometimes it took him a whole minute to find the keyhole. I got to think of that as normal. Even the shouting and the slaps out of nowhere. Kids like things to be normal."

"What about your mother?" he asked softly.

"She was even more of a victim than we were. She never stood up to him."

"I'm sorry."

"It's okay. A psychiatrist would say that's why I became a cop. Control, routine? Nice green uniform? Predictable, at least it was to start with, in the Schutzpolizei. We had this great little station on Keplerstrasse, in a converted villa. Wasn't like work at all."

"With Ulrich and Otto?"

"Yeah. Uli and I went through university and the Schutz academy together."

"So you met Otto at Keplerstrasse?"

"Yeah. Just ten of us there. It was like the family I always dreamed of. Secure, protected. A 9 mm on my hip, not that I ever had to use it. Lots of traffic duty, stop-go when I said, lots of predictable paperwork. Name, address, time of incident...fill in the blanks. Total control. I used to enjoy rousting drunks."

"At least you can see it."

Greta stared at the tent of her feet.

"And you quit the BKA for teaching. More control?"

She smiled. "I've asked myself that. I don't think so. I hope not. I did a stint with the outreach unit my last year in the Schutz, working with the street kids around the Hauptbahnhof. Made me realize cops can never be more than damage control, dealing with the symptoms instead of the disease. School empties, jail fills up. For every asshole pimp or dope pusher there's one impressionable school kid. I sound bleeding-heart but it's true."

They sat in silence for a while, sipping their wine, the inarticulate pleasure of being together.

"Did you and your wife think about having children?"

"We tried for five years. Endured all the tests. Melanie couldn't accept the fact that she was infertile. She refused to look at alternatives."

"Adoption?"

"I wanted very much to adopt a child, but that would have meant failure for Mel."

"That's why you broke up?

"I had an affair." He watched her fingers fall still around the stem of her glass. "I didn't know the person very well. I certainly didn't love her, but it wasn't a simple itch."

"Did you tell your wife?"

"The affair lasted three months. The woman I was seeing became pregnant."

"God. Did she have it?"

"Not interested. She had an abortion at two months. Injustice huh?"

"Your wife knew?"

"I told her. I had this fantasy Mel and I could raise the child."

"People have done it."

"It couldn't have happened for us. It took Melanie a long time to confront the fact that I was capable. I still don't think she completely believes I was the father." He smiled tightly. "Not that she isn't prepared to conduct divorce proceedings on those grounds."

"Do you still love her?"

Kristian rolled his head to look at her. "No."

"Does she love you?"

"I think she used to hate me, but even that's gone. She's got someone else in the wings. I'm not supposed to know and I won't go after them in the divorce unless Mel gets excessive. Really he's perfect for her." Kristian smiled faintly. "He's a gynecologist."

But when Greta turned to him, her eyes were brimming with

tears. He took both their glasses and set them aside, then enfolded her in his arms.

"Whatever happens, Greta...however this ends, I want us to be together."

CHAPTER 29

Schloss Strasse ran parallel with the valley a little way above the town. Lying outside the huddled confines of the old town wall, the houses here were bigger, on generous lots. Number 23 was no exception, a wide, three-story chalet-style house from the 1920's, surrounded by immaculate box hedges in an acre of treed garden, with a spectacular overview of the old town center and its story-book palace.

"No wonder they rented out the parsonage," Kristian said as they approached the front door and rang. Martha Steuber opened it.

"Mom isn't very well," she said quietly. "She came back from Alsfeld feeling dizzy. She's lying down. We're waiting for the doctor."

Kristian's concern barely masked his disappointment. "I'm sorry. I hope she's all right."

"I'm not particularly worried. She's had angina for years, but she refuses to slow down. I'm sorry you had to come all the way up here. Are you in Frankfurt for long?"

"Again we're not sure," Greta said.

"Perhaps you could phone tomorrow. I'm sure she'll be better by then."

A voice called from somewhere inside the house: "Martha? Who is it? Is it the American?"

Martha Steuber made an apologetic face. "I'm sorry, I'd better go to her. Try tomorrow."

The door closed softly. Greta took his arm down the path towards the low iron gate out to the street. "Don't worry, you'll be talking to her." She lifted the latch and the gate squeaked open. She put her arm around his waist as they stepped onto the road. "I know you're disappointed."

"Disappointed? After thinking about that family all my life, feeling so close to them...to talk to someone other than my father who actually knew them..." He gave an agonized glance over the neat hedge, back towards the house. "Wouldn't that be great timing if the old girl popped her clogs tonight."

She bumped him with her hip.

"I can just see it: I'll be the guy who dies of thirst one sand dune from the oasis."

They walked on, almost at the end of the hedgerow when they heard Martha Steuber call from the house. "Herr Peiper?"

Kristian ran back to the gate, saw her standing on the porch. She waved them back to the house. "It's no good, I've never been able to argue with her. She insists on seeing you. But only for fifteen minutes."

The chalet theme continued inside, with light pine floors and furniture and a hand-carved banister rail to the second floor. "Come on up, both of you. The royal bedchamber's a bit dark, Mum's due for a double cataract operation, she's supposed to rest her eyes." Martha lowered her voice as they neared the top of the stairs. "Her vision's very poor. She's left the operation much too late. She's just so stubborn. Fifteen minutes, then I'll have to haul you away or she'll never stop."

They could hear rock music by the time they reached the landing, vintage *Cream* from the floor above. Martha called up a set of narrow attic stairs: "Heinz!" *Strange Brew* swelled as a door opened at the top and they saw the teenager from the theater.

"Nana has visitors," Martha told him. "Could you please turn it down?"

"I just did and she told me to turn it back up."

"I like Eric Clapton!" came the grandmother's voice from her darkened bedroom. "Except when he was a junkie."

The music stopped. Heinz came down the stairs and accompanied them to the bedroom door. "She's got pretty decent taste in music."

"But I'm a woman of action," said his grandmother. "I could beat the pants off this boy at ping-pong till he was thirteen."

"And Sega," Heinz added proudly.

"Still could if it wasn't for my eyesight. This operation had better work — I intend to have virtual sex with Julio Iglesias before I kick off. As long as he doesn't try to sing. So who have we got here? Come on, come on...I can't see any of you way over there."

Kristian and Greta came to the bed where Monika Steuber was sitting propped against her pillows. They shook her thin, warm hand while Martha drew up two chairs for the visitors.

"How does my room smell?" Monika said. "Old lady? Pee and talcum powder? How ghastly!"

"No," Kristian laughed. "It smells nice. Like..."

"Herbs," said Greta.

"My potions," the old woman chuckled. "They would have burned me at the stake in Steinau once upon a time. Looks like I'm going to miss the parade, though. Get the shoe box Heinz, and mind my frilly underwear."

"Don't listen to her," laughed Martha. The boy rolled his eyes and went to a built-in closet by the door, reached up onto the top shelf.

A shoe box, where people keep photographs the world over. Kristian felt his pulse quicken as Heinz delivered it to the bed where the old woman folded her hands over the lid.

"Shall I turn on the lamp?" Martha said.

"Not yet. We've a little talking to do."

"Only a little," cautioned her daughter.

"I used to water the plants at the parsonage when the Peipers were in the city," Monika said. "For pocket money. Our house, but I never thought of it like that. I wouldn't go in it after they were killed. I wouldn't speak to the new tenants, I couldn't bear to go near the house. My father got angry about it, I think he even spanked me once, but I didn't care."

Even with the lamp off, Greta could see the look of rapt attention on Kristian's face.

"A little Saxon jeweler and his wife, the new people, a personal friend of Theodor Fritsch, the Frankfurt Gauleiter. Another vampire gorged on Jewish blood and confiscated Jewish business. Aaaaacchh...it still makes me want to scream. Of course your family were just exactly the kind of people that drove a pathological midget like Fritsch into a frenzy of envy: pure-as-gold Aryans but deeply intelligent, decent to the core."

Without losing its power, the old woman's voice now took on an almost dreamlike quality, a calm lyricism that asked not to be broken, even by her daughter.

"I was young before the war, but I remember it so well. To a child in a country town who never saw the beatings and the broken glass...they seemed like magical days in Germany, before the nightmare began for all of us. It's always summer in my memory, and there, always, I see the Peiper children. Older than me, tall and blond with their beautiful, serious faces. That boy was always in a clean white shirt with the sleeves rolled up, a sleeveless sweater. The girls always had the freshest cotton dresses...

"They used to ride everywhere on their bicycles, the whole family off on picnics at the *Schafsteg*, under the trees. You should have seen those Peiper girls in their bathing suits...long, beautiful limbs, straight backs. Dignified. All four children, like young eagles. I confess, I was intimidated though they never put on airs. They were beautifully mannered. No, it was more than that: they were kind, you see. Always trying to put everyone around them at ease." She suddenly snorted. "For god's sake, they were just superior human beings, that's all."

"They loved music," Kristian whispered, in transport.

"Oh yes, yes. Always brought their instruments, even the cello strapped to the roof of that old box of a car. Quartets...Silka with the cello, Barbara on viola, Hansjorg and Johanna played violins although they could all play any of the strings. Once they had to leave their instruments when they went home to Frankfurt, I can't remember why, maybe their car broke down or something. When I went to water their plants that time, I'll never forget seeing the instruments...it felt as though those young Peipers were right there in the room with me, the girls especially, those marvelous curves."

A noise escaped Kristian, in his throat, of recognition. Greta found his hand on the coverlet.

"That they should have been killed like that, a direct hit on the house! One bomb! That family of all families!"

Martha Steuber gave her mother, then Greta, a look of concern. Greta saw her glance at her watch.

"Mum..."

"And then Hansjorg at Stalingrad! Really, when you think of it, it's enough to make you stop believing in a god. Was he even twenty? Perhaps, just. But they've always preferred to slaughter them at that age, haven't they." She reached towards Heinz, patted his hand, kept it.

"Frau Steuber," Kristian said as gently as he could. "I'm not quite sure what you're saying."

"What's difficult about it? I lost all of them. I worshipped them. They were everything I aspired to."

"Lost him? You mean when he was taken prisoner."

"What? I mean when he was killed. They awarded him the iron cross with oak leaves. Posthumously."

"But Frau Steuber, Hansjorg Peiper wasn't killed. He was taken prisoner, he spent the war in Siberia in a POW camp. He came back in 1945. He became an engineer at the Dorner automobile works in Frankfurt."

"Who told you that?"

"My father!"

Martha Steuber was standing, massaging her wristwatch in concern. "That's what I tried to tell you, Mum. Kristian Peiper..."

"Tried to tell me what?" the old lady demanded irritably. "You said he was a relative of the Peipers."

"No Mum, Kristian is Hansjorg Peiper's son."

"Nonsense. You're a young man." She struggled to sit higher in the bed. "How old are you? I can't see you properly, damn it!"

"I'm thirty-six."

She snorted. "Then it's quite impossible for you to be Hansjorg Peiper's son. Of course you may very well have a father with that name, but he is not the Hansjorg Peiper I knew. Hansjorg was listed as missing in action at Stalingrad. He never came back. Do you think if he'd survived I wouldn't know about it? He would have come back here to see us. Of course he would. We would have been the first people in Germany he contacted. We would have *known*!"

"Frau Steuber..." Kristian struggled to his feet, spoke quickly, painfully aware of Martha Steuber's signals to terminate the interview. "My father had three sisters, Silka, Johanna and Barbara. His parents were academics, in Frankfurt. He spent his summers and weekends here in Steinau at the parsonage. He played the violin all his life. My father was the Hansjorg Peiper you knew as a child." Kristian said. "He died three weeks ago. I..."

The doorbell rang on the main floor. "That'll be Doktor Kriedman," said Martha with relief. "Heinz, would you please run down and let him in."

Now Greta looked at her watch. "It's ten to midnight, Kristian. Otto's going to call the car. We've got to go."

"Something's got mixed up somewhere here," the old lady said. "One of us is terribly misled. I'm sorry it has caused you such discomfort. You must come back and see me tomorrow, young man. We'll compare notes, try our best to sort this out."

"Don't make promises until you've heard what the doctor says," cautioned her daughter.

Heinz reappeared, out of breath from the stairs. "What's the problem here? You've got the photographs right there. In that box. You've shown me tons of times. Just show him the pictures of his dad, Nana. See if it's the right guy."

His grandmother spread her hands. "You see?" She lifted the lid of the box. "Young people! They're going to take over the world one day, mark my words. Turn on the lamp, Martha. Quickly!" She thrust the open box towards Kristian. "You look at them, I can't see anymore."

But Heinz was already reaching over Kristian's shoulder into the box, his quick fingers burrowing through the prints, dealing them onto the bed.

Kristian sank down again in his bedside chair, picked up the first print, then the second, while Heinz went on flipping and flipping them out.

"Here's another," Heinz said. "Here's another." Close to his eccentric grandmother, he was clearly proud of his intimacy with her collection. "Here's Hansjorg on his bike, should've had a mountain bike up the *Schafsteg*. This was Johanna's birthday. Fourteenth, right Nana? Dorky hat. Here's another...

"...here's another."

His mother had to put her hand on his shoulder to get his attention, to make him stop.

Greta was saying Kristian's name, but only at the furthest reach of his consciousness.

She didn't have to emphasize the urgency of getting back to Stadtborngasse. She had to run to keep up with him although he clearly wasn't thinking about Otto. His breathing came hard and ragged through clenched teeth as something grew inside him, dark, spinning, destructive.

"Talk to me Kristian."

His voice came hard and bitter. "You don't have to wonder now. You don't have to ask what I was afraid to find here."

"Okay, there's a mix-up. You heard what she said, go back and sort it out."

"I heard what she *didn't* say. Siberia? Did you hear Siberia, Greta? How about Frankfurt, building Dorner out of the rubble, twenty cars a week on acorn coffee and potatoes? Rio de Janeiro? Huh Greta? How about Cleveland. Did you hear one fucking *word* about Cleveland?"

Martha had given them a shortcut through the palace; crossing the courtyard, Kristian's voice echoed harshly off the high stone walls, startling the holidaymakers making for the town square where the birthday parade was about to start.

"Monika Steuber's no fool," he said. "She's in command of her faculties. Did you hear what she said? *Posthumous* iron cross, with fucking *oak* leaves!"

"Kristian!"

Greta lunged for him as he stepped blindly off the curb. The police car wasn't going fast but had to slam on its brakes to avoid him, skidding on the cobbles on Bruder-Grimm-Strasse, its driver glaring angrily. Greta fought a moment of panic, forcing the crooked smile of apology that tried to say he was no more drunk than half the people on the streets tonight.

Kristian noticed little of this. With Greta locked onto his arm, he almost dragged her onwards, across the street towards the entrance to Stadtsborngasse, pushing rudely against the tide of merrymakers. The town center had come alive since they left the inn, the sidewalks thick with tourists and townspeople wearing character masks and costumes from Grimm: Red Riding Hoods and Rapunzels, witches with poisoned apples and giants on stilts festooned with beanstalks.

Kristian registered none of it. "That boy in the photograph was nothing like my father. I've got pictures of him at that age. My father was thinner. His head was bigger. It was *nothing like him!*"

They reached the Dorner on the passenger side, where Kristian hauled the key from his pocket. Greta tried to take it from him but he snatched it away. He tried twice to insert it in the lock but his hand was shaking too violently. He raised his fist and slammed it onto the roof of the car.

"He *LIED* to me!"

People looked. Across the street, a father and mother glanced over in distaste and shepherded their children away.

Greta's voice was steady with controlled anger: "Stop it! You don't know any of this for certain. You're going to meet Gertrude Buelow-Schwante tomorrow. She may be on the phone in two minutes, then you'll learn the truth. Stop indulging yourself!"

The unfamiliar sound of her anger brought him up. He blinked at her, the passion drained from his voice, it sounded small and scared. "This afternoon I began to think there was light at the end of this tunnel. But it's always another train."

She put her arms around him from behind.

"It's not who he wasn't," Kristian said. "What terrifies me is who he was. *Where* he was. When."

She held him tighter.

"Ever since you told me what the Americans found at Dorner, I've had this one, single, granite certainty to hold on to: that Dad was far away from Frankfurt, a POW in Russia until the end of the war. But now...I don't know that any more. I don't know who he was." He turned to her. "I don't know who I am."

Inside the car, the cellular phone began to chirrup.

"Give me the key," she said unhurriedly.

She turned it in the lock, threw open the door and snatched the built-in cellular from its console cradle.

"Greta?"

"I'm here Otto. You're right on time. Did you hear from Kamp?"

"You bet I did."

She snapped a look at Kristian but he was walking woodenly around to the driver's side. "What happened Otto?"

"You've got to come back to town. Right now. Don't wait for anything. Come right to the station. Don't take the autobahn, though. Take Forty as far as you can."

"Why? The autobahn's so much faster. Forty's like a country road."

"I can't explain now. Just get going. I'll be here waiting. This is incredible, Grets. This is very fucking exciting. Hurry."

She replaced the handset, looked at Kristian now sitting behind the wheel, frowning. "Did you get that? He's heard from Kamp. Things are happening. You'd better let me drive." He looked merely puzzled. "Kristian?"

"Someone's been in the car."

"What are you talking about?"

He moved his head stiffly, looked up at the rearview mirror which reflected the middle of the back seat. The driver wing mirror showed him the door panel.

All three mirrors had moved.

"When I came back to get my wallet, I hit the memory switch for the mirrors. There on the door. It's a design flaw. It's easy to nudge it. I re-adjusted them. Now they've been moved again. Someone got in the car, knocked the button the same way I did."

"Maybe kids, messing with..."

"The inside mirror's moved too. They're all in another memory setting. Someone hit the switch."

"Is anything missing?"

Kristian shook his head. "It wasn't a break-in. The 800 has the most advanced anti-theft system on the market: unless you use the key to get in, I don't care how skilled, the alarm's going to go off. Someone had a key."

They stared at each other for a frozen moment. Greta had heard the change in his voice, that it carried a new, quiet confidence because the car, at least, was something he knew with certainty.

"Kristian?"

"What?"

"We're going to get out. Now. Right now."

"Leave the car?"

"Yes."

"What about Frankfurt?"

"I don't know. Get out."

Kristian opened his door. "Are we being watched?"

"Just do what I say. Lock the car. Make a show of it. Smile at me. Take my hand. We don't run."

They walked back to Bruder-Grimm-Strasse and joined the dense throng of people. "Make for the town square," Greta shouted above the din. "The more people the better."

An overweight Pied Piper came down Bruder-Grimm leading a gaggle of town children in tights and pointed shoes. Kristian looked behind them again, a pointless exercise given the immensity of the crowd. Close beside Greta, he still had to shout.

"What did they do to the car? A bomb?"

"Maybe. Maybe a tracking device. They'd have intercepted the call for sure."

"Why didn't you see them on the way to Offenbach?"

"Maybe they found out later we were here."

"How? How would they know which car?"

They reached the town square. A thousand spectators were massed around the fountain, the brass band playing at full volume on stage between the *Rathaus* and the Katharinenkirche.

It was impossible to know whether they had been followed or whether, by the time they emerged on the east side of the square, the dense crowd had filtered any pursuit. Kristian let Greta lead him, keeping close to the *Rathaus* wall until they were behind the stage amongst the parked service vehicles, an obstacle course of snaking cables for the lighting and sound equipment.

They stopped behind a truck advertising the tent and awning company that had provided the stage. They waited, watching the backstage area, empty except for one stagehand, an achondroplastic dwarf with a heavy extension cord coiled over his shoulder and a cigarette wagging in his mouth, skipping over the cables on his way to the stage, disappearing around it at the same moment that Kristian and Greta saw the man.

Tall, wearing a shirt and tie under a black windbreaker, he entered the backstage area the way Kristian and Greta had come, along the front wall of the *Rathaus*. He was walking slowly, tensed, alert to every corner of the area.

"Could he be security for the show?" Kristian whispered in her ear.

"No. He's SG."

He felt her hand on his arm, pulling him towards the rear of the tent truck, out of the man's view as he passed in front of it ten meters away. Now they could see the walkway between the *Rathaus* and the Katharinenkirche leading out of the square onto Viehhof, where a short right turn would bring them back to Schloss Strasse behind the old town center. But the walkway was open ground. If they tried to cross it now, he would see them.

The rear doors of the tent truck were open, the box stacked with folded canvas, aluminum poles and coils of rope. A place to hide, except that a scatter of heavy steel guy-spikes covered the tail — it would be next to impossible to climb up without disturbing them. He would hear it.

They went around to the truck's passenger side, keeping it between themselves and the man as he crossed behind the stage. Greta put a restraining hand against Kristian's chest, motioned him to stay put as she crept towards the front of the truck, crouching to stay below the hood. Kristian saw her stop, peer cautiously out, then ease herself around the front of the vehicle.

He waited, cursing the noise from the stage that drowned all other sound. He could still see the puppet theater across the square, where the Steubers had already changed the marquee to announce Rumpel-stiltskin for the Sunday matinee, the story of an exploited girl forced to spin gold and play guessing games to save her firstborn child.

He remembered the stories perfectly.

His father read them aloud almost every night when he was a little boy. The unexpurgated versions. In German. Particularly resonant because his family had owned a holiday house in Steinau an der Strasse.

Fairy tales.

And now Kristian had to play guessing games. Was it Hansjorg? No?

Was it Peiper?

Kristian ground his teeth, and in letting the pall of misery close around him, lost his immediate sense of danger. Facing the front of the truck, he didn't see the man materialize behind him at the back of the box. He couldn't hear the man, whose movements were professionally soundless, although Kristian might have felt his presence had he been fully alert. As it was, he remained unaware until the man spoke.

"Don't turn around."

Kristian moved involuntarily.

"Keep still!"

A split second's glance, but enough to see the gun in the man's right hand.

"If you move again, Herr Peiper, at all, I will shoot you behind your right knee. The same result if you fail to tell me where Greta Schoeller is. Where?"

He heard the man coming closer, stopping approximately two meters away.

"This is your last chance. A silencer doesn't affect muzzle velocity and I guarantee, with this weapon, you'll lose your lower leg. Where is Greta Schoeller? She was with you when you crossed the square."

Kristian heard him rack the automatic, then the man's sudden sharp cry. Kristian swung round, just in time to watch him sit heavily on the cobbles. Kristian saw him lunge for the gun that had fallen from his hand, saw a flash of silver from under the truck, heard a distinct crack as the steel tent-spike connected with his wrist. The man gasped and rolled away as the spike flashed a second time, leaving the gun on the cobbles.

In a second Kristian was on it, fitting his hand to the unfamiliar shape, amazed by its size and weight as he raised and pointed it at the man who was up again now, his right hand limp at his side, his eyes perfectly expressionless as he came steadily on, holding out his left hand.

"You don't need to die. Give it to me."

"Shoot him!" Greta cried as she struggled from under the truck.

The man shook his head and kept coming. "We know everything: Toronto, Buelow-Schwante, Kamp, the film. You'll only make things worse for everybody. Be careful please, that weapon has a rather light trigger action."

"*Christ, shoot him Kristian!*"

Kristian had not touched any kind of gun in his adult life. He did not mean to set it off, astonished by the results of an inexperienced index finger on the hair trigger. The silenced Glock bucked hard. The pistol's action and the jag of pain in his wrist distracted him for a split-second, denying him a full appreciation of the immediate result, the man in the windbreaker flying back and down like film on high-speed reverse.

Greta was on her feet now, springing towards him with the guy-spike raised, but there was no need to strike again. He lay on his back with his eyes and mouth wide open, his body trembling as he stared in disbelief at the ruin of his right hand. Hanging from a wrist already broken by Greta's blow, the hand showed a three-inch stigmata where flesh and bone had been blasted away.

Kristian had no sense of how long he stood, staring in disbelief at what had been achieved with one tiny mistake, at the blood already meandering between the cobbles. He showed mute compliance as Greta took the gun and pulled him towards the man. He followed her instructions to raise him to his feet and support him to the side door of the Katharinenkirche. He smelled of cigarettes.

She stopped them at the open rear of the truck, keeping the muzzle of the gun pressed to the agent's spine as she snatched up a roll of wide electrical tape from amongst the equipment littering the tail, stopped them again while she tried the church door — it was open — and listened.

The door led into the vestry. It was empty, like the rest of the church. The choir gowns hung in neat rows, crimson as the blood dripping steadily from the agent's hand.

"Kneel down on the floor," Greta told the man.

His face, though ghostly white, and the language of his powerful body, was defiant. He had recovered from the initial shock of his wound. He thrust Kristian aside, stood in the vestry staring at Greta. His eyes never left her.

She responded with a calm that frightened Kristian: "Your hand tells me hollow-point. You enjoy sex?" Her hand went to the slider.

He knelt, his face still expressionless, stone killer.

"Are you here alone?"

"No."

Greta looked at him closely, then smiled. "You're lying. Pity they only train us to *ask* the questions. What's your name?"

He remained silent, staring at her. He had stopped trembling. His limp hand lay at his side, soaking through his pants.

"Greta, he's bleeding a lot."

"Get his ID." She kept the gun pointed at the agent's head as Kristian reached into the breast pocket of his windbreaker and removed his wallet. Greta took it, the Glock absolutely steady as she flipped it open.

"*Sicherungsgruppe*. Thyssen. Captain?" She raised her eyebrows. "They sent a captain? I'm flattered, Thyssen. How high does this thing go? To Beck, or higher?"

The man remained still as a carving, facing front. Around Kristian's age, his cheeks were stretched on wide wings of bone. He had short, red-blond hair. He looked Slavic.

"All right, we'll do it like this," Greta said. "I'll begin counting to five. If I reach five without an answer, you're going to take another hollow point. Then I'm going to count again. You people killed my friend. You came here to kill me. I'm so angry, Thyssen. I have very little time and nothing to lose. One. Two."

Kristian was shocked by the sound of her voice, from some chill and barren place he had never imagined in her.

"Three. Four."

Thyssen, too, must have sensed real danger. "It's contained. It's Beck's show."

The man's face — his whole body spasmed as Greta pulled back the Glock's slider.

"That's the truth."

"Anyone else at Cabinet level?"

"I don't think so."

"What about in the United States?" Kristian said. "Does it go further than Hutchence?"

Thyssen never took his eyes off Greta. "I don't know. I swear."

"What's going to happen to Dietrich Kamp?"

He fell silent.

"Tape his mouth," Greta told Kristian." He hesitated. "Do it! I don't want him screaming."

"Greta..."

"Now!" Her eyes blazed at Kristian. "I already counted to four. Didn't you hear me? *Tape him*!"

"Executive action," Thyssen croaked.

"Against Kamp and Gertrude Buelow-Schwante?"

"Yes."

"How?"

Thyssen shook his head. "I don't know yet."

"When?"

" After tomorrow. After the Kondor preview."

A kind of smile flickered across Greta's mouth. "Sure. Junia's too good at public relations to mess that up. Some kind of accident, like Ulrich?" The Glock floated darkly in the air between them. "Like Ulrich Mayer, Thyssen?"

Thyssen watched her, afraid.

Greta controlled herself. "How did you find out about Kamp and Buelow-Schwante? How did you know we were in Steinau today?"

A sound from inside the church, the main door booming shut, unhurried footsteps echoing along the stone aisle towards the vestry.

Kristian didn't need prompting: he had already pulled off a foot of tape, slapped it over Thyssen's mouth as Greta jammed the Glock's muzzle under his chin.

The footsteps fell silent, still at a distance from the vestry. A second boom from the main door. Distant, echoing voices.

"Tape his hands behind his back. Tightly."

Greta waited until Kristian had made half a dozen passes with the roll, then grabbed it and handed Kristian the gun. He watched, fascinated, while she worked, her small hands a confident blur as she improved on his work.

Again she directed Kristian to help bring him to his feet, then went ahead through a connecting door and an adjoining room to where another, narrow, door revealed a built-in closet, its floor piled with tattered, discarded hymn books.

She taped Thyssen's ankles, forced him to the floor before taping them to his wrists, then with Kristian's help, pushed him into the closet.

"The blood," Kristian whispered as they re-entered the vestry. "There are smears all over the floor."

Fifteen seconds with choir gowns, bundled then stuffed under the gown rack. Kristian was shaking violently, needed every ounce of concentration to make his legs work, to stay with her as she ran alongside the Katharinenkirche towards Viehhof.

"Stadtborn," Greta hissed when they reached the street. "We've got to get out of here before he's found or the SG start to worry."

"But we can't take the Dorner."

"We're not going to."

They didn't enter Stadtborngasse from Bruder-Grimm. They circled around and came in from Neugasse, just in case Thyssen had a partner after all, still watching the Dorner. Greta considered it unlikely: in relieving him of his BMW keyring, Greta had found no radio.

Stadtborngasse contained five BMWs. Greta ignored the two 3-series compacts and an old 635 Csi, which left two midsized sedans. Thyssen's car was a late model black M5 with low-profile high-performance tires and a corkscrew antenna.

Like Thyssen, the car's interior smelled of cigarette tobacco. He must have been smoking while he watched the Dorner parked three cars ahead, had abandoned a cigarette in his haste to pursue them — it had burned to a broken grey tube in the ashtray. A pack of Winstons lay on the transmission tunnel. Beside it was a brightly colored plastic remote controller in the shape of a gun, plastered with lightning decals and fake dials and the meaningless words "Indy GT." A toy, made in China, intended to control a model car. Greta very carefully lifted it from the tunnel.

"There's a device in your 800. Probably to disrupt the brakes or steering, easier to explain than blowing us sky high. Easier to do the paperwork. Seems they always have to have a little paperwork."

She reached behind, laid the controller gently in the rear passenger footwell, then started the car and maneuvered out into the street. The BMW was race-tuned but she drove it sedately, inconspicuously southwest on Bruder-Grimm towards the junction with Bundesstrasse 40 for Frankfurt.

"Buckle up, all we need now is to get stopped for a seatbelt violation."

She saw out of the corner of her eye, the stiff, mechanical way he obeyed her, how his eyes remained fixed on the cigarette packet behind the gear lever.

"Don't worry, he won't bleed to death from a hand wound. He's trained to survive. Worry about us."

She looked sideways again and saw the distant, bloodless expression.

"Kristian?"

"What?"

"Don't disappear on me now."

"Okay."

"Are you cold?" She turned the heater up and put the fan on full. "Christ it stinks in here." Greta powered down her window and angrily snatched up the Winstons, to throw them out. A soft pack, domestic, with the U.S. Customs and Excise seal across the top, like the pack she had seen that night in the Hauptmeister's waste bin at the Fechenheim auto pound. But Greta noticed something else: Thyssen had pulled off the cellophane wrapper in order to write on the pack.

She came to a stop sign, braked before reading the scrawled felt tip: *800 dk green F:MX 451*

Kristian's Frankfurt-registered rental car, model, color and plate number. Below, Thyssen had jotted a Frankfurt telephone number.

Germans are considerate road users. The driver behind Greta merely flashed his headlights when the BMW failed to clear the intersection, then swung around it.

Greta, normally the best of drivers, was unaware of him, so vivid was the image evoked by the telephone number as soon as she realized whose it was.

Actually her own work number for five years. One she had answered dozens of times a day when she wasn't on traffic duty. The telephone number of a cream-painted house with sandstone details behind a wrought-iron fence on a tranquil, tree-lined street: a gracious address, a decidedly upper-middle-class family residence before it was acquired by the Schutzpolizei and became Polizeirevier Keplerstrasse.

Lucky Greta, that her first posting should have been so agreeable. So close to the Palmengarten, for quiet bag lunches when she could get off duty.

No.

She crushed the packet until it leaked tobacco onto her lap.

No.

"Greta?"

She stared down at the spilled grains of tobacco. "They've got surveillance on Otto," she said quietly. "That's how they got to us. Thyssen wrote Otto's station number here, along with the description of your car."

She looked at him, frowned deeply, resentfully, when she saw the expression on his face. "What? *What?*"

"I never told Otto what model car they gave me."

Greta made a small, irritable, interrogative noise in her throat.

"Tonight on the phone. At the airport, at the rental office. He knew it was an 800, but all I'd said was a dark green four-door sedan."

"You're not being clear."

"He said don't drive that 800 too fast. Complaining about his Mercedes. But I hadn't told him the model number. I remember thinking I should do that because there are half a dozen four-door models."

"You're mistaken."

"They said it was the last available rental, but there were other cars on their lot. They were making sure I got this one."

"*You're mistaken!*"

She threw the BMW in gear, pressing Kristian back against the seats as she accelerated hard, southwest towards Salmunster and Autobahn 66 for Frankfurt.

"Where are you going?"

There was very little time left, but Greta needed to know only one thing now, the only important thing.

Ulrich, Hansjorg Peiper, Kamp, the film...none of it mattered any more except knowing this, before their time ran out.

CHAPTER 30

THEY DITCHED THE BMW IN HANAU AND TOOK A VW JETTA, USING A technique Greta had once taught motorists to combat.

They waited thirty minutes under the linden trees on Holzhausen, a block west of Otto's building. At 1:00 a.m., most people were in bed, although the jumping play of television sets still enlivened several windows. They had a clear view of his building. Light from Otto's apartment and at one window below.

The front door was open. Cooking smells from the ground floor apartment, the sounds of muted conversation and the clatter of washing up. Greta went up first with Thyssen's Glock in her hand.

Otto's apartment was unlocked but empty. She saw the framed Japanese calligraphy which meant "House of Light," which was how Greta had always viewed this place. Leona's scrupulous lace curtains, her crucifix above the made bed. She always went to mass with her mother and sisters on Sunday mornings, sometimes stayed over the night before.

"Smell the cigarette smoke?" Greta said. "Leona hasn't let him smoke indoors since she got pregnant. He's been here since she left."

They found three cigarette butts ground out in an ashtray on the kitchen table. A bottle of scotch lay on its side on the counter, pieces of a tumbler scattered on the hard tile floor below, whiskey licking up a cupboard door above the broken glass.

Sudden movement from the hallway below. An interior door shutting. A long — suspicious? — silence, then steps through to the rear of the building. The back door opening then shutting.

The kitchen window overlooked a small backyard, little more than a turning space for the two-car garage. The downstairs tenant — a new neighbor this year, middle-aged, she couldn't remember the man's name — crossed towards the right-hand garage door carrying a lunch pail. She recognized his city transit worker's uniform, vaguely remembered Otto telling her he was a bus driver, obviously on the graveyard run tonight. At one point the man glanced up at the second floor, but Greta anticipated and darted back.

Enough light spilled from the ground floor to show him stooping to unlock his door. He paused with it half raised, then lowered it and approached the door on Otto's side. He seemed to be listening, his head angled sideways. Now he reached down for the handle, lifted it then suddenly dropped it, staggering back, dropping his lunch pail as he clapped his hand to his face.

It took Greta fifteen seconds to get down the stairs and out of the back door, sprinting across the yard ahead of Kristian.

By now the neighbor had already managed to switch off the ignition and was trying to lift Otto's limp body out of the Mercedes. With Greta taking his feet and the two men supporting his torso, they carried him out of the reeking garage and laid him down on the gravel.

"I'll go call an ambulance," the man said.

Greta caught his arm. "It's all right, he's coming round. Fresh air's what he needs right now." Otto was rosy from the carbon monoxide, breathing shallowly, but already beginning to stir. He couldn't have been exposed for long, must have sat in the car, deliberating.

"Are you sure?" worried the neighbor. "He needs first aid at least. Look, I'm a bus driver, I've trained in it."

"Lieutenant Schoeller. I know what I'm doing. I'm in Hauptkommissar Volk's detachment. And you are?"

The busman was outranked. "Gutman. Gunther Gutman. Yes, I've seen you here before. You were upstairs?"

"I assure you he doesn't need hyperveric treatment, Herr Gutman. Not with this level of exposure."

The man watched her check inside Otto's mouth and loosen his collar. "Do you think..." he stammered. "I mean...was he trying to harm himself?"

"My friend and I will wait with him until his wife gets home. Don't worry. We'll look after him. It may have been an accident." She lowered her voice. "May I ask for your discretion?"

The man nodded, all ears, flattered by her confidence.

"The fact is he's been drinking rather a lot lately. You can smell it?"

The man nodded. "Even when we were pulling him out of the car."

"It's a very lucky thing for Hauptkommissar Volk that he has you for a neighbor. Gutman, right?"

By the time Otto had uttered his first small groans, Gutman seemed convinced that, having saved the Hauptkommissar's life, his presence was no longer required. He had to get to the depot. As a matter of fact he was already a few minutes over schedule.

He had backed his car out and driven away by the time Otto's eyes cracked open. He raised his head and looked glassily at them.

He sat up and vomited scotch.

They took him back up to the second floor. They had stripped him, sponged him off, put him in his bathrobe and helped him to his bed before he spoke his first lifeless words to them.

"Why are you helping me? Why didn't you leave me?"

He was still drunk, deathly pale now that he had lost the poison's bloom.

"What did they do to you?" Greta said quietly. "Did they break your hand? Did you sell me for a broken hand, Otto?"

His head rolled back, the first dim spark of interest in his eyes. "What happened in Steinau?"

"We met a friend of yours."

"Did you kill him?"

"Tell me what I need to know, Otto. What happened? When did you turn?"

"You can kill me. Why don't you?"

"Talk to me."

He looked at her with a sickly, resentful smile. "Thyssen and Streeck took me Friday, after I called you in Washington."

"Who is Streeck?"

"Thyssen's superior. He's an SG major. Beck runs everything through Streeck."

"Go on."

"They had one of Junia Dorner's implements from the schloss. A metal glove. You turn a key and it shrinks. Intricate as a clock. I would need several operations. Thyssen told me that before he started winding. I hope you killed him."

Greta exchanged a look with Kristian; there was poetic justice in Thyssen's ruined right hand.

"He broke my hand before they asked me anything. They even had a doctor there to treat me. Langsdorff." A faint, dead smile played on Otto's cracked lips. "Ring a bell?"

His head rolled back to the window, to the spotless lace curtains.

"Did they threaten Leona?"

"Don't you want to know how they got us?"

"They threatened her, didn't they."

"Streeck's got a mole inside Bill Tomzak's organization. That request for Suitland clearance, your name came up. Poor Bill folded in a second. I always thought we'd be okay at the base. I thought it would be Truong that pulled us down. That's why I was so careful."

He looked back and held her gaze, willing her to read his silence as only Greta could. The muscles in her abdomen tightened, her whole body stiffening now, braced for the blow. Otto nodded his head with a barely perceptible motion and then he turned his head away again.

"It was only a matter of time before Beck got to Truong. The SG take care of their own. Uli already found that out."

"When?" Greta whispered.

"The night I talked to him at the leather bar. I saw him home when he got wasted. But then he knew. He struggled when he smelled the chloroform. Knew his poisons."

His head lolled back. "I didn't tell them anything while they did my hand, Grets. I would have died for you. You believe that?"

Greta was barely breathing.

"But then Fräulein Dorner called. She was somewhere in her jet. They put the phone to my ear. She was friendly. Friendly advice. Said she hoped I would be reasonable. She said there was no one in Germany, no one in the world to help me. She began to describe some of the other instruments in her collection. Imagine, she said. Imagine a pregnant woman in the Iron Maiden. I reckon you saw it at the schloss." The lifeless eyes rolled to Kristian. "It's an iron cabinet, shape of a woman. Heavy door, long spikes inside. When they close it…"

His face was drained of blood, his eyes empty as though, on one essential level, his attempt in the garage had been successful. His hopelessness seemed even to have overcome the effects of the whiskey.

"Whatever you think you need me for, it's going to kill my wife and unborn child. Just shoot me, Grets. I deserve it, not Leona. I killed Truong. I betrayed you. Not my kid."

Greta lowered herself onto the edge of the bed. "No one else is going to die, Otto. Junia lied to you: this conspiracy — Junia, Beck, Vaughan, Hutchence — I think it's contained there, higher levels of government are not implicated. These people are not above the law, I'm certain of it. Terminating the Dorner investigation, killing Uli and Kristian's father in Cleveland — they were limited operations run on Beck's power and Junia's checkbook. We need a line of communication to Berlin and Washington, and we've got one."

"Dietrich Kamp?" Otto snorted with contempt. "You *don't* have Kamp, they do. And they're going to kill him, as soon as the balloons have gone up over the Kondor, soon as they've busted his hands or doped him to find out where the film is. Then they'll get rid of him and this woman, Buelow-Schwante." He saw the question in Greta's eye. "No, I don't know what the film is."

"You never called Kamp," Kristian said. "He was never in Wales."

"Never in Wales."

"You never tried to contact him or Gertrude Buelow-Schwante."

"I know where Kamp's going to be tomorrow midday: with Junia Dorner at the Messe, and Streeck watching every move he makes."

"In the ballroom at the Maritim Hotel," Kristian said to Greta. "In the Congress Center. The Kondor cocktail party. Junia's demonstrating the van for industry insiders. She's going to drive it down the Via Mobile. A marching band, flags..."

"You were supposed to be there?"

"Maybe I'll still make it, slip in somehow. We have to warn Kamp."

"We can't stay here," Greta said. "They'll be looking for Thyssen by now. We're going to have to find some cover or we won't last the night."

Otto had slumped back, but now he raised himself onto his elbows, looked from one to the other in disbelief. "You enjoying this? If you're so sure this is about a few rotten apples, what the fuck do you need Kamp for? Go to the media, Greta. Huh? *Stern, The New York Times*, five hundred fucking satellite channels? Take your pick."

"No!"

The force of Kristian's utterance surprised Otto and Greta. He stood at the end of the bed gripping the foot-board, his voice thick with emotion.

"I don't expect you to understand this, but Dorner was my father's life and it's been mine, the only one I ever knew. Whatever Erich Dorner did in the war, whatever his daughter stands for now, whatever this film contains...that isn't what my company means to me, or the thousands of other people who give their lives to it every day. Generously. Splendidly.

Because they need to *eat*. We'll go to the media if we have to, but not till we've had one shot at trying to do this Kamp's way: Junia, Beck, Vaughan...we back them into the corner without destroying Dorner."

Otto struggled to sit up, his smile a mockery. "Quite a speech. How are you going to *do* all this? Wherever Kamp is, there'll be SG writing it down every time he blinks."

"Wherever he is? You said yourself, we know where he'll be tomorrow."

"But how do you think you're going to get into the Messe? Security will be out of this *world*. With Junia Dorner and Kamp in the showground, they'll have *Sicherungsgruppe* on all ten gates. As soon as Streeck doesn't hear from Thyssen, which is right about now, you won't get within a hundred meters of any entrance to the Messe before they'll have backup swarming you."

"No," Greta said. "They won't see us coming. They'll see a Schutzpolizei Hauptkommissar in a marked Schutz Opel. They'll see you, Otto."

CHAPTER 31

THE FRANKFURT MESSE IS A CITY WITHIN THE CITY. FROM PHILIPP-Reis-Strasse on the western perimeter to Friedrich-Ebert-Anlage at the easterly extreme, from the great marshaling yards of the Hauptgüterbahnhof in the south to the multi-laned traffic main artery of Theodor-Heuss-Allee along its northern border, the Messe represents half a million square meters of show and tell, the biggest and most centrally located metropolitan fairground in the world.

Ten vast exhibition halls are connected by glass-enclosed walkways elevated from a network of pedestrian and vehicle routes, relieved by parking for a hundred thousand cars. The "city" has its own hotels, restaurants, shops and entertainment centers, its own central square in the Agora, its own skyscrapers represented by the landmark, pencil-shaped Messeturm and the Torhaus, the symbolic gateway connecting the east and west halves of the fair and the entire site with the rest of the world: via the Torhaus terminal, the fairground is directly linked with Europe's busiest airport and train station.

The Frankfurt Messe is a forum for the most profound thinking and the most frivolous gadgetry, hosting exhibitions that inspire or merely beguile, reflecting humankind's soaring achievements and vulgar excesses. The pilgrims who separately flock to its most publicized fixtures, the Book Fair and the Auto Show, would admit that their events offer both extremes and everything in between.

Long before the Auto Show is officially open, the event is underway for industry insiders, in lavish temporary camps. Corporate flirtations begun at the Kronberg continue over schnapps at Mercedes Benz's famous rosewood bar, or beside the sake barrel at Mazda, to the pulse of *gagaku* drums; business fever fueled by Bavarian beer and *Weisswurst*, the white sausage served, according to the ancient tradition of ensuring its freshness, only until noon at Audi.

Dorner, at home in Frankfurt, always boasts the largest and most luxurious ice breaker at the show, this year in the ballroom of the new Hotel Maritim, where Emil Meert's liveried footmen were far outdoing Lufthansa's Party Division catering the other companies.

The Hotel Maritim is located at the east end, forming a triangle with the Messeturm and the Festhalle, where the Kondor would be previewed tomorrow by the world's automotive press. The east end was where the action was, why Greta had chosen Gate 10 off Philipp-Reis-Strasse, the most remote entrance at the far west end of the showground.

Greta had called Regine last night, for a place to go to ground. As vice-principal, she had keys to her inner city school, still out for the summer vacation but always empty at the weekend, with a staff parking lot tucked away behind the main building, backing onto the railway tracks. The police had given up on the vandalism, Regine said. They were letting the school go to hell, no more spot checks at night. Greta had to tell her only a little: that her brother's death had not been what it seemed, that they were helping Uli find some justice. With the promise of full explanation, she had handed over a key without further questions.

Major Streeck had been in touch with Otto as soon as Thyssen was discovered in Steinau, but he would not betray her a second time; Greta had convinced him that the conspiracy was limited, that Kamp represented protection for Leona. Greta tried to sustain herself through the long night by believing that, even in killing Truong, Otto Volk had been acting in large part for her. Sustaining, too, in a strange way, to imagine the pain he had endured for her before they inflicted the one unbearable agony that had turned him.

Now, at 11:30 a.m. on Sunday morning, she sat in Otto's Mercedes (still reeking of exhaust), on a narrow residential street called Funck-strasse, a few meters in from Philipp-Reis. From here she could watch Gate 10 less than half a block to the south, through Otto's binoculars. The guard — the SG agent substituting for the usual rentacop — looked alert but relaxed in a glass booth beside the barrier.

To the right of the gate, the great concentric pattern that forms Parking Lot 11 stood empty, same thing the other side in Lot 12.

Behind the booth the Via Mobile beckoned; as the Messe's long main thoroughfare, bisecting the fairground from east to west, it ran all the way to the Main Gate onto Ludwig-Erhard-Anlage, passing directly by the Hotel Maritim.

She held her breath as the marked Opel Vektra slowed towards the gate, prayed that Otto's appearance wouldn't panic the guard. Otto's pain, and whatever the little white pills he constantly shook from a plastic film container to control it, the whiskey and exhaust fumes and his shameful, sleepless nights — these had all conspired to give him a gaunt, grey, doomed appearance. Like Adolf Hitler, she thought, the ghost-führer patting the cheeks of his boy soldiers in a ruined Berlin.

The Opel drew up at the booth. Otto used his good left hand to pass his identification through the window. The guard handed it back, then picked up his telephone and dialed.

An endless minute passed, then two more. But that was to be expected, Greta told herself: it would take time for Streeck to be summoned to a phone, for Hauptkommissar Volk's message to be relayed to him and probably from him to Junia Dorner, amidst five hundred guests in the Maritim's ballroom: Volk had heard from Greta Schoeller and Kristian Peiper at 11:05 a.m. Unaware of his betrayal, they had called from a specific location in Hanau where they had long ago abandoned Thyssen's car. They were asking for Volk's help. Volk himself was at Gate 10, requesting to see Streeck for further instructions.

Streeck would admit him, surely. He would want to verify it first hand. To plan the next move.

Surely.

The guard put down the phone, spoke a few words to Otto, then raised the barrier.

Greta breathed again as she checked her watch. 11:34 a.m. Kristian had exactly twenty-six minutes in which to call her to say he was inside the Maritim. With the SG's focus on Hanau, just maybe he would have a chance to reach Kamp.

Twenty-five.

It should have been me, she thought. Not SG, but trained. Kristian on the other hand, even in a Schutzpolizei uniform borrowed from Keplerstrasse, was still a marketing executive. But Kamp knew him, had known him all his life through Hansjorg. There would be no time for mistrust and explanations this morning. Kamp had to be instantly convinced that Junia was onto him. Whatever his strategy, it had to be implemented immediately.

Twenty-four minutes.

If she didn't hear positively from Kristian at the end of that time, she would call the first ten national and international newspapers and television channels on her list.

CHAPTER 32

Whoever maintained the Keplerstrasse vehicle pool needed to look at the Opel; it leaked exhaust fumes into the trunk, giving Kristian a nauseating sense of what Otto had faced last night.

He pitched forward in the dark compartment as the angle of the car changed, which meant they were on the down-ramp into the parking garage beneath the Maritim Hotel.

The Opel featured a rear seat pass-through for skis, through which Kristian had heard the gate guard relay Streeck's instructions to Otto: parking level U1, southeast corner, row M which was the kitchen staff's parking area, take the elevator to the main floor where he would be met and escorted to Streeck.

"It's good this way," Otto called through to Kristian as the car leveled out. "Wait till I've gone then come in the same entrance. You'll be behind the main lobby, in the kitchen area. Once you're inside the hotel, they'll take your security clearance for granted. They won't question you in Schutz uniform. You've got my ID?"

"Yes."

"Use it only if you're stopped. Flash it, keep your thumb over the photo. I'll keep Streeck busy."

"They'll have already checked out Hanau."

"You got scared, you split. Just keep your shades on and get to Kamp. Okay don't talk now, we're getting near the bay."

Otto parked and turned off the engine. "It looks clear. I'm going to pop the trunk now. Get out fast."

Kristian heard the release, saw a crack of light below the trunk lid. "Okay go!"

Kristian pushed up the lid and scrambled out onto the oil-stained concrete.

"Stay over there, behind that camper. Wait two minutes before you come into the hotel, give me and Streeck time to find each other."

Kristian ran to a white VW camper parked at the corner of the lot, beside the hotel door. He slid into the space between the van and the wall, out of sight but with a view through the camper's tinted side windows. He could see Otto shutting the trunk lid, walking from the Opel to the steel fire door, ten meters from it when the door burst open.

A big man, crewcut hair, brown leather jacket and running shoes, three other men behind him.

"Major Streeck..." Otto's voice was high with surprise and fear. "I was just coming up. I thought I was supposed..."

Through the tinted glass, it was a violent shadow play, the dialogue amplified by the low, cavernous space.

"Hanau? *Hanau* Volk?"

Streeck punctuated the words by shoving Otto back towards the Opel until he slammed against the side.

"*Hanau?*"

He punched Otto in the face.

"*Hanau?*"

In the face again. One of the other SG caught him as he sagged, flattened him against the Opel.

"They called you at 11:05 from *where?*"

Another sickening blow.

"Did they have something to tell you this morning that they forgot to say last night at your apartment? When was that? Around 1:00 a.m.? How's the hand?"

They held him while Streeck used the butt of his pistol against Otto's cast.

"Gutman. You understand, you fat prick? Gunther Gutman, your polite downstairs neighbor. Best thing we ever learned from the Gestapo, Volk. You need to keep an eye on someone, let the Gutmans do it for you. A little man with a uniform, a bus driver bursting his buttons. He'll make route supervisor yet. But you know all about betrayal. Hmmn? Don't you, you pathetic sack of shit."

Another blow with the pistol. Otto screamed.

"Where are they, Volk? Someone in here? That would be fun. Anyone at home?" He rapped on the trunk. "Hello in there?" He held out his hand. "Give me the key."

One of the SG rifled Otto's pockets and unlocked the trunk.

"Pity. Put his hand there."

Streeck slammed the trunk. Otto roared in agony.

"*Where?*"

Kristian began to salivate, swallowing bile, looking towards the hotel door as it opened and a young man in a chef's uniform came out, stopping in his tracks when he saw the tableau around the Opel.

"Police business!" Streeck flashed his badge. "Bundeskriminalamt, move on."

"I have to get my van."

"Get it. Quickly!"

Kristian ducked down, rooted with helpless terror as the chef came towards the VW. The man unlocked the driver's door, got in, started the engine.

Kristian glanced wildly behind him. The corner slot, against the wall. Nowhere to go, and the SG were watching the van, waiting for it to leave.

Kristian did the only thing he could, moving backwards with the vehicle as it reversed out of the spot, crouched below the window line. There was another door ten meters along the wall, maybe nothing more than a maintenance room but there was no other option. If he could get close enough before the VW swung away and exposed him...it was that or be cornered.

The chef braked, shifted into forward gear, hauled the wheel left, hesitating for a last look at the federal cops and their bad guy.

"Move it!" Streeck yelled at the chef.

Kristian was running as the van began its turnaround, almost at the door when he heard shouts and glanced back.

Streeck was the only one with his weapon raised, steadying on Kristian when Otto's broken cast smashed down on his arm. Streeck recovered instantly, might still have hit Kristian in the doorway with a good fast shot had he not chosen to turn, in rage, on Otto.

Kristian heard the shot and guessed, had to force his mind to think ahead.

A stairwell.

No way of locking the door behind him.

They would have radio contact. The hotel would be swarming with SG.

Not a hope.

Kristian swooned with despair even as he climbed. He had bought himself a temporary reprieve, nothing more. He'd die here. He'd never see Greta again or find Gertrude Buelow-Schwante, never find out who his father had been.

But the stairwell didn't access the hotel. Serving more than one floor (Kristian could hear the door below smashing open as he fled up the fourth course), it came out in a glass-covered walkway on the building's south face, over the Via Mobile, now lined with Dorner flags for Junia's inaugural concourse run in the Kondor.

The walkway was part of a network interconnecting every one of the Messe's buildings. To Kristian's right, the *Rollschuhe*, the moving sidewalk, slid east towards the Torhaus, wide open for hundreds of meters. Ahead of him, a much shorter walkway ran south between the Festhalle and the Forum.

He sprinted south, not looking back until he reached a T-junction and heard Streeck's guttural shout. Kristian ran to his right, towards the extreme east end of Halle 3, smashing through a white steel door as Streeck cleared the junction and the first shot cracked past Kristian's head.

He spun round and crashed the door shut, gambling his last precious seconds as he looked frantically for the locking mechanism on the panic-bar.

An Allen key hung from a chain at the end of the bar.

He knew tools he'd been good with tools he was at home with tools he could...

The key went in.

He could hear Streeck screaming orders beyond the door. A body crashed against it, a shout of frustration when the door wouldn't move.

A bullet ripped through the door's double steel skin less than fifty centimeters from Kristian's shoulder. Three more as he ran from the locked door, down a short access tunnel.

He was not yet in the main exhibition space, but still in a behind-the-scenes area reserved for appearance personnel attached to the show, the car jockeys and the body polishers. An array of car keys was displayed alphabetically with plastic name tabs, representing all the exhibits in Halle 3: AC, Allard, Alvis, Auto Union...

For the first time it dawned on Kristian where he was: the exhibition hall that Phil Baylor had been discussing at the factory in Cleveland on Friday night (it seemed a lifetime ago), the venue for rare classics and special-order vehicles.

Bristol, Cord, Delahaye. Some of the hooks were empty, which meant that not all the exhibits had been delivered yet. He could hear voices and activity out in the hall, the prep crews working Sunday overtime to get the cars ready for the general public on Monday morning.

"You'd better hurry up, siphon the rest of the gas out of that

Hummer," the nearest crewman was saying. "Should never have gone in the lift like that. Supervisor finds out, our ass'll be hanging on the wall."

"The tow broke down," replied his mate. "That bastard thing's armor-plated, I'm not breaking my balls pushing three thousand kilograms. There's only a couple of liters in it anyway."

"Do it Kurt," said a third man tersely. "Break your balls, break anything but the fire regs."

Kristian went back to the key display, his eyes searching frantically along the rows.

Elva, Ferrari, Glas, Hummer...

Hummer.

There was an exhibition plan on the wall next to the keys, to assist the crews. The Hummer was on the basement level, one below.

AM General Corporation Hummer, from Southbend, Indiana.

... bulletproof windows, full armor plating...fucker's got close to three-hundred-pounds feet of torque at seventeen hundred rpm...60 percent grade capability...Runflat tires for when the bad guys shoot 'em out from under you.

Kristian snatched the key, pocketed it, and walked out across the floor, trying not to hurry, smiling as he passed Kurt on his way to an empty peg.

The service elevator was ten meters away on the right, at the edge of the second-floor exhibition area. Kristian jabbed the call button and waited, praying that the lift would arrive before Streeck did, and that it would be empty.

He attracted no attention from the busy crews: anyone in the Messe tonight had passed perimeter security and could therefore be assumed to have legitimate business here. Kristian could see out across the floor, the clusters of hot white halogen lights reflecting on a wide sea of brilliantly polished chrome and paint work. Two lovely rounded Lancia sports saloons from the mid-fifties, a group of equally sensuous Astons from the same desirable period and later.

007.

The hall was empty now except for the crews, but Kristian knew from all his years of shows how it would look on Monday, the public moving through this glittering sea in shoals, drawn by a seductive, siren call from each display.

Cars.

It was a world he had loved and censured with a helpless, visceral passion all his life.

His fist closed around the Hummer's ignition key, its small teeth biting deep into his palm as the elevator door slid open.

It was empty. He got in and stabbed CLOSE.

"Come on come on...*damn you come on!*" Many times bigger even than a normal freight elevator, the car-lift's door took an eternity to descend from its overhead sleeve.

Kristian could hear Kurt complaining, wondering who left the Hummer's key in the ignition. Then a sudden hoarse shout from out on the floor, and he saw Streeck in front of the Lancia display.

Kristian hurled himself towards the rear of the elevator, certain that he had been seen, but knowing also that Streeck wouldn't be able to cover the fifty meters to the elevator in time to call up the door.

It closed.

The elevator shuddered then settled into a smooth, silent descent. Kristian could hear the deep drumming of his heart, the hoarse chant of his breathing. His eyes stung from the sweat pouring down his forehead.

Unless there was a floor indicator outside the elevator, unusual with a freight, they wouldn't know its destination. The elevator had doors front and back, and they wouldn't have anticipated him using it. Could they get into place in time? Wouldn't they concentrate on securing the main floor exits and ignore the basement since there was no direct exit from that level?

But there were stairs. Wide terrazzo stairs beside an escalator, leading up to plate-glass double doors, in turn leading out to the Agora.

...60 percent grade capability, 40 percent side slope. It'll climb a wall.

Just maybe.

The powerful elevator alighted with a bump. The impact of a bullet felt like that if it didn't kill you instantly, so he'd heard...just a bump.

He braced himself as the door traveled up. But it revealed no phalanx of legs, no gun muzzles, no immediate end to life.

Or hope. Because now Kristian could see the hulking, ugly agent of his hope in the far corner of what appeared to be an unattended basement.

He sprinted for the Hummer, his shoes smacking on the rubber-skinned concrete. As he dodged between rare and priceless automobiles, nearing his objective, Kristian understood that although the main aisles and the stairs were wide enough to accommodate the Hummer, the huge vehicle had no clear way out of its corner.

At close to six thousand pounds around a low-geared V8, the fact that the Hummer was blocked in by several other exhibits presented a not insurmountable problem. Rather, it was the particular nature of the obstructions — one in particular directly in the Hummer's path — that caused Kristian a regret bordering on dismay. But it evaporated twenty meters from the armored car, when he looked back and saw uniformed running men on the stairs and the escalator, many more than had pursued him from the Festhalle, although Streeck was still out front.

Several of the uniforms raised weapons the instant they sighted him, but this time Streeck threw up a restraining hand. He could see no way of escape for Kristian, only that the basement level of Halle 3 was packed with the most valuable automobiles on the face of the planet.

Kristian crouched low, darting from one bespoke classic to another on his way to the Hummer: from a Duesenberg SSJ roadster built for Clark Gable, to a 1938 Alfa Romeo 8C2900 special-order coupe, rarest of the rare pre-war Alfa's, in dove grey; from an ultra-scarce blown Pegaso Z102 to a 1957 Ferrari Superamerica, custom made for the Aga Khan in the final year of his life.

Kristian had reached the last dream car, directly in front of the

Hummer, when they spotted him again and began to close in. Even now he lingered for a second to leave one final, apologetic caress on the flared rear fender of the most startling, most famous — and arguably most valuable — piece of automotive sculpture in history.

Then he was at the Hummer and its key was in the lock and Streeck knew instantly that the rules had changed. His was the first shot, whining off the armor plating just below the roof line before Kristian had quite closed the door.

He crossed his fingers and turned the key, and the V8 engine roared to life.

God bless you Kurt.

For a moment Kristian sat, frozen in the glove leather seat, staring in disoriented panic at the unfamiliar instruments and controls of what was essentially a customized combat vehicle. Controls for all-wheel-drive, geared hubs, its four radiators — even harder to get his bearings with pistol rounds smacking the cabin around him, the bulletproof windshield pocked in several places by the time he found the brake-release and made sense of the gears.

The Hummer lurched forward, and Kristian's confidence returned, a feeling of marvelous security as it gathered momentum, his earlier regret now surmounted by an unexpected sense of exhilaration as he closed the last few meters between the Hummer's blunt, caged snout and the Bugatti's liquid coachwork.

Pure Art Deco, the 1936 Bugatti Atlantique Electron Coupe was, and is, available only to the astronomically wealthy. Produced in minute numbers, it is the car that brings a momentary hush to any conversation between serious collectors. The Type 55 may be very slightly rarer, but the Atlantique is the true designer dream, an elliptical, wind-cheating, breathtaking exercise in aerodynamics from the Age Of Speed.

With Kristian's foot flat on the floor, the Hummer was going no more than forty kilometers an hour when it hit the Bugatti broadside. But it was three times as heavy, battle-clad, and collapsed the Atlantique's front fender and pretty engine cowling like tinfoil. As the

Hummer's prow found the Bugatti's block, it flicked the whole car aside like a lever, driving it into the Ferrari's delicate front end like a striker to a bell.

Something had overtaken Kristian, as though the almost constant flow of adrenaline over the last seventy-two hours had finally disrupted his personality, pushing him over the edge. He was grinning at his frustrated and horrified attackers as he sideswiped the Pegaso then plowed the little Alfa Romeo aside then bored on towards the last obstacle before the main aisle and his route to the staircase, full, at last, of a wild and perverse satisfaction.

At five thousand pounds, the huge Duesenberg was nearly a match for the Hummer. With his lips curled back over his teeth, Kristian braked, backed up over strewn wreckage from the Alfa, checked his seatbelt, and with a deranged cry floored the Hummer again.

He had expected to need three or four attempts to displace Gable's big car, but the Hummer wanted to climb. On the second run, its giant, knobbed front tires found purchase on the Duesenberg's hand-built coachwork — up onto the massive running board, up and over the long hood with its famous quadruple exposed pipes, all of it now collapsing under the Hummer's weight. Kristian's seatbelt cut into him as the Hummer's front end tilted down over the Duesenberg's far side, the back wheels slamming down after it, into second, then third gear for the first time as Kristian accelerated away from his thirty-second, multimillion-dollar rampage.

He saw uniformed men scattering as he took the aisle's first hard corner too fast, the back end drifting wide, corrected abruptly and expensively by the substantial front bumper of a Hispano-Suiza H6C.

Now Kristian was a few seconds from the foot of the staircase and he balked, wondering whether to use his momentum or whether to brake and throw the Hummer into its lowest gear to climb the stairs.

The two men halfway down the escalator decided him: latecomers to the shooting gallery, with the first full automatic weapons Kristian had seen, both agents commenced firing at the Hummer's divided windshield as it screamed towards the staircase. The bulletproof shield had been manufactured by P.P.G. in Pittsburgh, a two-inch glass-and-Lexan sandwich eminently capable of withstanding prolonged small arms fire, but the pocked outer sheet was taking so many rounds that it was becoming hard to see through. Kristian needed to leave quickly.

He mounted the staircase at 70 kmh in third gear and at a forty-five degree angle, the front end bucking so high that for a terrifying second he though the vehicle would flip. But the front slammed down again, and again he had four-wheel drive.

The Hummer was halfway up the six-meter flight when it began to lose momentum, then purchase on the slippery steel-capped risers, and now the machine-gunners on the escalator concentrated on the tires.

It was a mistake. As the air shuddered from the Goodyear Runflats, the resulting mass of soft rubber around each rim gave Kristian back the traction he had begun to lose. He threw the shift into very low and with the tachometer screaming over the red line, pushed the armored car up and over the top step.

Kristian was roaring to beat the engine as the Hummer raced across the main floor foyer, uniformed guards fleeing in terror as Kristian closed on the plate-glass double doors overlooking the Agora. By now his vision through the riddled windshield and side windows was too limited for him to fully enjoy the sensation of exploding through the glass doors, which the Hummer's speed and weight achieved without the slightest hesitation.

A dozen wide, shallow steps down to the floodlit Agora, and now Kristian leaned close to the windshield, peering with fierce concentration through one small patch of clear glass. Shredding what was left of the Hummer's tires, he fought to keep the vehicle on a straight, accelerating course as he crossed the open ground, between the bulky campers and assorted recreational vehicles exhibited on either side.

He flashed past the central obelisk towards the exit onto the Via Mobile. Every instinct told him to brake for the intersection, but he didn't have time to be judicious: he had seen the motorhome.

Another American oddity here, the Winnebago eight-sleeper blundered across the Agora far in excess of the speed for which it had been designed, braking now at a precise right angle from Kristian as the SG driver tried to block the only open exit.

Kristian shifted down again, praying that the Hummer's engine wouldn't seize — or run out of gas — as he built an instant 10,000 rpm, the right side actually brushing the Winnebago's radiator as he squeaked through the exit at 120 kilometers per hour.

Now Kristian had less than thirty meters in which to brake for the hard left-hand turn onto Via Mobile for Gate 10.

It wasn't enough.

The Hummer's speed, though substantially reduced, was still over 80 kmh going into the turn, its momentum, at six thousand pounds, simply too much to rein in. Kristian's concentration was now so completely on negotiating the turn with four flat tires, his vision so limited by the peppered windshield, that he had no inkling of the second approaching vehicle until it was broadside, directly in his path.

He saw it only for a second, but his educated eye registered the already classic profile of a Dorner Kondor immediately before the impact.

CHAPTER 33

Dietrich Kamp's Frankfurt house was a slender, three-story secret of mellow brown brick, set back from a treed square. Though elegant, it was inconspicuous in a row of similar buildings, a stylish assortment of offices and shops, restaurants and commercial galleries overlooking the square.

Greta got out of bed and went to the window, rubbing sleep from her eyes. She looked across to where a bookstore was opening, the clerk using a long wooden pole to fold down gold and black striped awnings. Customers came and went at a specialty bakery, a thin young man dressed a mannequin in the window of a couturier.

Life was going on. The thought depressed and angered her somehow, the way it had done the night Ulrich died. Frivolous life. Callous and blind. Life must go on? They would be saying the same thing after doomsday.

In front of the house, a cop in bluejeans carrying two Styrofoam cups got into a dark grey Mercedes sedan and shut the door, which made no sound.

There was no traffic noise. An unearthly silence surrounded the house, in a visual world with no sound track. Some special kind of glazing and insulation, she guessed. A computer somewhere in the house, filtering ambient sound? A cave of technical wonders, the townhouse suited Kamp better than traditional luxury although he already owned real estate all over the world, so Gertrude had said.

Greta blinked rapidly and took a deep breath — hard to shed the heavy mantle of sleep, induced by the sedative Kamp's personal physician had administered this morning. She had refused it at first, unwilling to make herself vulnerable, even to the kindness of strangers, but after two days and nights without it, she had been in critical need of sleep.

Eventually Gertrude's certain genuineness, along with the wonderful quiet of Kamp's house, had reassured her. She had slept heavily for twelve hours, had awakened thinking she had emptied her bladder in Kamp's guest bed. But it was sweat, from a dream of running up a down escalator with her father waiting for her at the top, his skin shining like metal. Made of metal.

She trudged to the ensuite bathroom, reconnecting the loose strands of Sunday night as she stood under a warm shower, turning the temperature control by slow degrees until it was almost cold.

She had called the media from Funckstrasse; they had found chaos inside the Messe, with the Kondor's wreckage as its gruesome centerpiece. Not a production model, the van had been a prototype, a show model not intended for on-road use, the much-touted wraparound airbags lacking a triggering mechanism. Driving at the head of the parade with the Messe's Geschäftsführer, Peter Soutin, in the passenger seat, both Junia Dorner and Soutin had been killed instantly. The accident, and the chain of events leading to it had drawn every news camera and microphone in the country, and then the world. First the arrest, in America, of a U.S. senator and a senior officer of the CIA, and then, at 6:00 p.m. Sunday, the suicide of Germany's *Minister des Innern*. The frenzied media had already unearthed shocking facts concerning both his planned future and his past.

Beck, it was revealed, had been through the *Ordensburgen*, the Order Castles which had represented the zenith of the Hitler Youth pyramid. Only for fanatical National Socialist boys destined to become the Nazi elite, the castles meant six years of merciless discipline and total immersion in Nazi ideology, with special emphasis on "racial sciences." Like the Order of Teutonic Knights on which their organization and ideals were modeled, the *Ordensburgen* were devoted to the principle of absolute obedience, in this case to Hitler. It was said that an Order Boy could never be denazified, could never go back.

Greta got out of the shower, dried, then dressed herself in the casual, perfectly fitting cotton clothes that had appeared at the end of her bed. She let herself out of the bedroom, crossed a landing to the nearest door, another upstairs front room, 1960s looking, white on white, natural fibers. Nordic restraint except for the triptych above the fireplace, the only painting in the room, shattering its cool serenity: it looked like a genuine Bosch, a northern Renaissance nightmare on three hinged panels. But to Greta, the most disturbing feature of the room was the computer terminal, hooked up to a large diameter monitor.

The film had been digitized. Gertrude had the disk. She had withheld it last night, insisting that Greta sleep first.

"He doesn't use this place very often. He doesn't like Frankfurt much."

Greta turned to the door as Gertrude Buelow-Schwante came into the room. "I heard you getting up." She gave Greta a look of motherly appraisal. "How are you feeling?"

Greta shrugged slightly. "You've heard from the hospital? How is he? Can we talk to him?"

A young sixty, although her hair was proudly grey, in a loose bun threatening to unravel. Her face was heart-shaped, clear-complexioned. In and around her eyes, the light and lines of a good sense of good humor.

"He's awake and alert, in some pain of course. They're assessing him as quite severely depressed. But he's extremely lucky; he'd have been killed instantly in an ordinary car."

"When can I see him?"

"I'm waiting for Dieter to call. You have to remember that Kristian's under arrest — not that he's going anywhere with two broken legs. It's only Dieter's influence that's kept you out of custody, but your movements are restricted. There's a GSG9 car on the street outside."

"I saw it. I'm under house arrest?"

"Essentially. But they're treating Kristian's case more seriously, of course; two lives were lost as a result of his actions, not to mention several million dollars worth of unique automobiles. Media madness has infected the whole world since you went to bed this morning, not even Dieter could prevent it after what happened."

She saw Greta glance at the monitor, put a gentle hand on her arm. "Let's take advantage of Dietrich's quiet house and his influence, and keep the world out for a while longer. You must eat."

"I want to see the film."

Gertrude drew her firmly towards the door. "Take my advice: eat first. You may not be able to afterwards."

Kamp's housekeeper produced a meal of legumes, fruit, nuts and juice; Kamp, as Greta already knew from his media profile, was a strict vegetarian who disdained alcohol.

"Where is he right now?" she asked between mouthfuls.

Gertrude glanced up at the wall clock. It was nearly 10:00 a.m. on Monday morning. "At the Justice Ministry or the U.S. Embassy. Things are complicated. The German government still doesn't have the complete picture. The Americans have Vaughan and Hutchence, but Beck controlled matters very tightly over here. With Junia gone and Beck's suicide, it's difficult for them to gather the facts. But ask me anything."

"Hansjorg Peiper knew he was in danger, didn't he? That's why he sent you the film."

"He knew the *film* was in danger. He was already under pressure to surrender it. Threats. But he wasn't concerned for himself, though of course he was terrified that Kristian would find out. He had filled Kristian's life with Dorner, he couldn't bear the thought of his beloved son discovering the truth."

Greta considered her fork, put it down carefully on the plate. "Which was much more than the film."

"He couldn't let Kristian know of *my* existence, which of course would have revealed Hansjorg's own identity."

"Did he tell you to contact Dietrich Kamp?"

"Not specifically. He always saw Dieter as a potential ally, but at that point there was no need for anyone else to be involved. He hadn't decided what to do with the film, only that it could not go back to Junia and be destroyed. Unlike Erich Dorner, who merely saw the film as a weapon to restrain his daughter...old Dorner thought Junia was ruining the company, by the way, which is why he summoned Hansjorg to Frankfurt, why he gave him the film in the first place. But Hansjorg Peiper was a moral man: once he had seen the film, nothing was ever the same for him. His conscience alone dictated his actions, but his legs had been cut from under him. Passing the film on to me for safe-keeping was the only thing he could think of to do. From what Kristian has told you, it sounds as though he had come to a decision the night he was killed. I think perhaps he would have confessed everything to Kristian at Canterbury Road that night." Gertrude sat back and folded her hands in her lap. "Kristian must be told who his father was, as soon as we're permitted to see him. I want him to hear it from me, not the television. It's become public knowledge since this morning. So has the contents of the film." She smiled slightly. "Ironic that after all you went through to gather the pieces of this puzzle, you may be the last two people in the western hemisphere to learn the truth."

Greta pushed her plate aside, half finished. "I'm ready."

"I doubt it. There are two files loaded into that terminal upstairs; the SS documentation is separate from the film and I strongly suggest you read it first, then decide whether or not you want to go on."

CHAPTER 34

W<small>RITTEN</small> <small>TESTIMONY SUBMITTED</small> A<small>PRIL</small> 10<small>TH</small> 1945 <small>BY</small> C<small>APTAIN</small> Theodore Bentley, United States Seventh Army, region of Frankfurt-am-Main, to: Central Registry of War Criminals and Security Suspects (CROWCASS), Allied High Command, Paris.

Greta read again the preamble she had seen at Suitland, from a report that had never reached its destination in Paris.

Like the film, the associated documents found on the SS guards fleeing the Dorner factory had been intercepted by Paperclip. Except for Erich Dorner's copies, possibly kept secret from any Americans, Paperclip had seen to it that both the film and its supporting paperwork had been destroyed. Another piece of history that had never happened.

Captain Bentley continued:

As anyone who has read the attached documentary evidence will attest, recent conditions at the liberated factory, however shocking, pale by comparison to what is described herein. I feel it my duty to warn any prospective reader that the enclosed documents make a daunting study. Indeed, the events so cold-bloodedly enacted and described in these pages, even in the light of ongoing discoveries at Bergen-Belsen and elsewhere, seem terrible beyond imagining. If the Registry will indulge me in a further opinion, I believe it is the more personal scale of this barbarism that makes it the more unbearable.

The documents, destined for the Inspector of the Air Force and the Reichsführer's office, provide irrefutable evidence that:

1) Heinous crimes against humanity were committed at the Dorner factory during the period February to August 1942.

2) They occurred under the absolute authority and supervision of the Luftwaffe Chief of Staff, the Chief Inspector of the Air Force Medical Corps, and the Reich Central Security Office.

3) They were committed with the direct cooperation of Dr. Erich Dorner, president of the Dorner Company, Frankfurt Main, and several members of his design staff.

Facsimile of documentary and photographic evidence submitted April 10th 1945 by: Captain Theodore Bentley, United States Seventh Army, region of Frankfurt-am-Main, to: Central Registry of War Criminals and Security Suspects, Allied High Command, Paris.

Exhibit:
Memo from: Dr. Ferdinand Rasch, Chief Engineer, Dorner AG, April 9th 1942.
The third test was conducted today at 10:30 a.m. utilizing the cockpit shell from a Junkers JU-87 dive-bomber mounted on the Dorner standardized 1204 chassis powered by a modified 8 cyl. engine of 5 liters displacement developing 120 hp. (The relatively large displacement is necessary in order for the test vehicle to attain sufficient speed over a limited approach.)

The adjustable crash wall was again used to simulate the diagonal angle of approach and impact of the aircraft with the ground. The wall was adjusted to 70 degrees, less than that of the two previous tests. Again the steel/concrete surface was padded with rubber under canvas to approximate the level of absorption or "give" encountered in high-speed impact with the ground. Padding may be removed in future tests to simulate impact with frozen terrain. Water-impact density will also be considered.

Test 3 was conducted using two Russian males, 23 and 25 years of age, in generally good condition, their size and weight falling within the guidelines prescribed by the Luftwaffe, as requested. The only departure being that the younger subject required distance spectacles, of no consequence since the spectacles were removed prior to the test to eliminate the risk of injury from them. (NB: The author has requested SS Obergruppenführer Pohl that a pool of subjects be created within the plant, to be made available for future tests, to which special rations and medical attention be made available in order that health standards be maintained within the pool.)

The TPs (test persons) were restrained in the pilot's seat and the gunner's seat aft of the cockpit. Both TPs were restrained with canvas torso belts anchored directly to the fuselage at four points using high tensile steel rings. Film cameras monitoring the test above and beside the crash wall have confirmed that both TPs were belted at the moment of impact.

Speed at impact of the test vehicle was recorded at 70 kmh, not, it must be understood, to approximate the landing speed of a JU-87, but rather to simulate the momentum experienced by aircrew in a partially controlled crash-landing situation. In future tests, various combinations of crash wall angle and test vehicle speed will be investigated.

Once again, the equipment may be considered to have failed the test, since both TPs sustained severe injuries as a result of the test, immediately fatal in the case of the "pilot" (subject No.1) while the "gunner" (subject No.2) died one hour and seven minutes later. In both cases, autopsy was performed immediately following death.

Detailed autopsy results, as supplied by SS Colonel Dr. Martin Roepke, attending physician, are attached. However, from a strictly engineering viewpoint, the cause of injury was clear and twofold:

a) the continued failure of the anchoring system rather than the belts themselves, which did not fail at impact.

b) the rigid construction of the primary control column which, in the case of subject No.1, was responsible for massive chest injuries.

Once again, the author strongly recommends the use of stronger anchors for the torso-restraints, while design work continues on the unique "collapsible" control column, a prototype of which will be ready for testing in approximately two weeks. In the case of Subject No.2, the author feels that little could have been done to reduce injury in the cramped gunner's cockpit (beyond the abovementioned modifications to the restraint anchors) without impractical and expensive revisions to the JU-87's overall design. It is some compensation, perhaps, that in terms of training and availability, air gunners are more expendable than pilots.

Further, after lengthy discussions with the Deutsche Arbeitsfront (funding having now been made available by the DAF), the author is happy to report that various models of Dorner automobiles modified with torso-restraints will soon be available for crash-testing. Again, the concept of a collapsible steering column is being explored for both military and civilian application, along with the interesting concepts of "engine deflection" and "impact absorption zones" in frontal collision situations.
Heil Hitler!

There was another memo from Rasch dated one month later. Another JU-87 with the new control column. Absence of chest injuries. The pilot broke his neck.

Another test three weeks after that. No gunner this time. The pilot was again Russian. Another broken neck. Work to be done investigating the possibility of head restraints.

One week later, another test using a restraining "cap" in a JU-87 cockpit shell. The pilot survived the impact with a broken collarbone and a mild concussion. For the first time in testing to that point, SS Colonel Dr. Roepke was required to administer a lethal injection following the subject's medical examination.

Another memo from Rasch dated June 13th, 1942. Six automobile tests had been conducted, described with the same clinical finesse that characterized all his reports. The supply of "TPs," Rasch noted, was no longer restricted by the Luftwaffe's physical requirements:

The occupants of the test vehicles must be seen to represent, as closely as possible, the average German family.

Greta blinked several times.

Her eyes saw the word but did not register it. Her fingers were suddenly paralyzed over the keyboard, unable to scroll the page.

She started the paragraph again, not believing.

The occupants of the test vehicles must be seen to represent, as closely as possible, the average German family. Four seatbelts have been provided in the test vehicle. Two in the front, two for the back seats, fully adjustable in order to accommodate immature test subjects.

For the first time since she had opened the file, Greta remembered Gertrude standing behind her, as a hand came to rest gently on her shoulder. Her own fingers remained suspended over the keys, trembling in the air, not quite touching them.

She turned slowly in the chair. Someone else's voice said: "Children. They used children."

Gertrude said nothing.

Greta stood, holding onto the edge of the terminal, testing her legs' ability to support her. She walked with a stiff, convalescent gait towards the window, out of sight of the words on the screen.

"Can I get you something?" Gertrude Buelow-Schwante said softly.

The silence was disturbed only by the faint, neutral rush of the computer's cooling fan.

"Do you wish to see the film?"

It was a full minute before Greta was able to reply. "They filmed the tests?"

"Yes."

"All of them?"

"Yes."

"The children?"

"Yes."

Greta gently shook her head. "No. I don't want to see it."

Gertrude came nearer, relieved.

"Now do you understand why Junia Dorner was obsessed with retrieving this material? And why she had to be so careful in revealing its existence to Kristian? The U.S. Army report you read at Suitland, the state of the factory when the Americans arrived — she wasn't so worried about that: no one in the world understood public opinion like Junia Dorner; she knew the world was already desensitized to what the first document described: Auschwitz, Hiroshima, Pol Pot, Rwanda, the Balkans…when the numbers reach a certain point, the crime becomes too big for the public imagination. Besides, there was nothing there to directly implicate her father in anything but neglect of his work force. He was afraid of the SS, right? Everybody was afraid of the SS. The SS did it. But *this*? And there is a brief second of footage when Erich Dorner appears in the film, overseeing the tests from an observation balcony, next to Heinrich Himmler. They're in conversation, with courteous smiles."

Gertrude reached behind her for the computer chair Greta had vacated, sat down.

"Captain Bentley was right, it's the human scale of this that makes it unbearable, and of course Junia realized that. A brilliant marketeer, she could see the headlines: *Human Crash Test Dummies at Dorner*. Imagine it, in the age of tabloid television — film footage of those children. She knew what an instant, accessible horror it was, even for the jaded nineties, just as she had an unerring instinct for effective advertising. The whole world would relate to it, in outrage. She was justifiably terrified. She knew the Dorner company would have been..." She stopped, sighed. "Dorner *will* be history after this, I'm afraid."

Greta found her voice, a painful rasp in her throat. "Kristian knows?"

"I don't know if he has radio or television."

Gertrude came to the window, put her arm around Greta's shoulder. They both looked down into the square at the grey Mercedes in front of the house, turning together as a phone rang in the room behind them.

CHAPTER 35

Late Sunday afternoon, Kristian was transferred from the Messe's medical center to the Saint Elisabeth Hospital northwest of the Palmengarten.

He was guarded around the clock by GSG9, the tactical arm of the Federal Police. They did not attempt to control admission at street level, but movement in and out of Kristian's wing was tightly monitored. In spite of it, Sunday night saw two reporters make it as far as his door before being repulsed by the room guards.

These incidents were Kristian's only distraction from his pain. The ceiling-mounted television above his bed, when he finally gave in to it, deepened the pain almost beyond his ability to bear it.

He was sinking in a dead lake. There was nothing on the other side, nothing to strike out for. No jeweled palaces, no hot sand beaches with trade winds stirring the palms. Those, too, were childhood's lies.

No mountain passes, no bandits. The truck couldn't go, how could it go? It was a wreck.

Kristian was sorry when the nurse came in and turned the television off, out of concern. Sorry when she adjusted his blood-pressure cuff and put Demerol in his intravenous — at least the physical pain in his legs was indifferent, and the Demerol could have no affect where it really mattered.

"They've returned some of your things," the nurse chattered brightly. "Your watch and wallet are here. What's this? It's from a violin isn't it? See? I knew that! Where's the rest of it?"

"Keep it."

"I'll put it right here by the bed with your watch." She felt his forehead with the backs of her fingers. "Your visitors will be here soon."

He would have to learn the pain's indifference. It was the only possible strategy. He reached to the bedside table, slowly, fighting the pain of his broken ribs like a swift river current, until the violin bridge was in his hand.

Dead wood.

He would start learning now not to feel.

Greta came in first. She closed the door and stood with her back against it, trying to look into his eyes. Distressed at her failure, she hid behind a nurse's smile as she took in the details of his confinement, the laceration on his face, his encased legs raised above the mattress by wires.

At first she didn't know what to say. She sounded like the nurse. "All strung up! We should get Martha Steuber in here, you could be the Pied Piper. You led them quite a dance over at the Messe."

"'Reckless driving causing death.'"

"Who says so?"

"The State Prosecutor for Hesse."

"Don't worry. As soon as they learn the facts. Dietrich Kamp is making sure they do."

"I'm not worried."

She sat on the edge of the bed and carefully took his hand.

"Don't feel guilty, Kristian. Don't forget how close she came to killing us."

"I knew Peter Soutin. He had three children."

He knew everything. Greta was certain of it. There was the television above his bed.

"Otto died for nothing."

"No, Kristian. He died to make whole everything he had broken."

She raised his hand and kissed it, then glanced towards the door. "Gertrude's here. Are you ready to see her?"

He didn't reply.

"When did you learn about the film?"

He turned away from her, lay perfectly still, staring at the window.

"You know who your father was, don't you?"

No movement.

"Kristian, you have to believe me: the answer is no. Your father didn't know. I couldn't bring myself to watch the film but I've read all the documentation. Your father is never mentioned in the evidence."

"Really."

"Believe Gertrude then. Hear her out. Your father shared everything with her. Let her tell you."

Greta was gone for five minutes before she came back with Gertrude Buelow-Schwante. She was beautiful — articulate and intelligent and sensitive, just as he had guessed from her phone message. Kristian saw this with absolute objectivity. He felt no more connection to her in person than he had to her answering machine.

She made no cheerful preamble: "They're only giving us fifteen minutes, Kristian, and there's so much to say. I understand you already know what is documented in the film your father sent me, and that he was already there, at Dorner, in 1942."

Kristian watched her, saying nothing.

"If you're thinking he knew about the crash testing, he did not. I'm certain he knew nothing about it until Erich Dorner gave him the film in Frankfurt."

"You mean you're hoping."

Gertrude drew up the visitor chair and sat. Greta went around to the other side of the bed and settled on the edge. Boxing him in.

"He was working exclusively on engine design during 1942," Gertrude continued. "Not structural development. The tests were carried out in strictest secrecy. He didn't suspect anything like that was going on. I realize that still leaves the terrible conditions at the factory, the disease, the starvation rations — you can rest assured Hansjorg tried his best to intercede with Erich Dorner on the workers' behalf."

"He told you that?"

"I believed him, Kristian. I looked into Hansjorg Peiper's heart many times in the years after he made himself known to me. I would have seen it if he'd been hiding that part of the truth, the most important part. How could he lie about that, after he had found the courage to reveal so much truth?"

She saw the first small spark of energy in his eyes, leaned towards him. "I know how it must hurt you, that he never revealed himself to you. But he was so ashamed of the falsehood. He loved you so much, more even than you realize. You were his very soul, Kristian."

She gave the television a look of disgust.

"Will you hear the truth from me for fifteen minutes?"

She took his silence as agreement. She produced a sheet of paper from her skirt pocket, unfolded it, then placed it in his hand. "Something Dieter did for me, it might make things easier. A point of departure, at least."

A reproduction of a black and white snapshot of a sad looking, fair-haired woman and a teenage boy outside a small house with a white picket fence. The same photograph Kristian had found in the box from Canterbury Road and again on the stairs in Toronto, although the image had been transformed: the resolution here was crystalline, sharp in every detail.

"Dieter enhanced it digitally," Gertrude explained. "See the car beside the house? It was a blur on the original, now you can read the license plate."

He looked up from the picture. Gertrude was smiling with gentle encouragement.

"Canadian. Ontario. And I was blond before it turned grey. Like her. My mother." The print quivered in his fingers, even though he already knew the bare facts from the television.

"This is my mother and father," Gertrude said. "I'm your half-sister. And our father's real name was..."

"Richard Buelow-Schwante."

Gertrude drew closer, encouraged by his participation. "When did you first suspect it? Before Steinau?"

"At your house. When Greta told me about the plane crash...it became a possibility."

"Shall I tell you who he was? A small-town boy from Kitchener, just west of Toronto. A German settlement, used to be called Berlin before the First World War. That's the Buelow-Schwante's house in the photograph. Five children. The mother died when Richard was thirteen. Father was a meat packer in spite of his aristocratic name, barely literate, yet here was Richard, gifted, almost a prodigy, languishing in the local school. One of his teachers took an interest, began tutoring him privately when he was fifteen."

She looked tenderly at the photograph on the bed.

"Annamarie Hoffman. She was also German-Canadian, in her early twenties, herself an oddity given the slender qualifications of most grade school teachers at the time — Annamarie had a mathematics degree. She tutored Richard for a year. He spent every available second at her apartment. Is it so hard to believe what happened? They were already intimate in their intellect, a motherless, misunderstood boy and his nurturing, lonely teacher, both of them isolated by their talent and their interests in a dreary provincial town."

Gertrude smiled softly from Kristian to Greta. "Is it so hard to understand them becoming lovers one afternoon? One slip."

"But she became pregnant," Greta said. "With you."

"Yes, and the truth came out. Richard's father horsewhipped it out of him."

Greta covered Kristian's hand.

"Annamarie lost her job and disappeared. Richard — our father — had no idea where she had gone. It was many years before he found out she'd been packed off to a home for unwed mothers in Montreal. She died there, giving birth to me with inadequate medical attention. She had spent the last weeks of her confinement having her name legally changed to Buelow-Schwante, a keepsake for me...perhaps she saw it as a beacon to guide Richard to his child one day."

Greta snatched a tissue from the box beside the bed, gave it to Gertrude. She dabbed her eyes and nose, recovering her equilibrium.

"He knew nothing of what had happened. His father threw him out of the house. Richard found his way to Detroit, just across the border, got a job at Packard. The rest you know in detail: he shone there, they paid for him to go to university for engineering, he went to Frankfurt on furlough in 1939. You know that he was too valuable to Dorner to be allowed to perish on that Pan Am Clipper, and you know how Erich Dorner maintained the fiction that he *had* died with the others."

Greta was frowning. "What was Erich Dorner's leverage with the Gestapo? Did they owe him a favor?"

"He was friends with Theodor Fritsch, the Frankfurt Gauleiter. Fritsch had dabbled in race car driving before the war, nowhere near good enough to make the Dorner team but he'd never given up hope. Erich Dorner needed a German identity for his kidnapped Canadian engineer, Fritsch knew the Peiper family of Frankfurt and Steinau an der Strasse. An extraordinary case: first the bomb, then Hansjorg missing in action at Stalingrad...Fritsch saw an opportunity to toady up to Erich Dorner, so he exploited the situation. Richard Buelow-Schwante — our father — got Hansjorg Peiper's identification. Of course they didn't actually use it until after the war, with the story that Richard, now Hansjorg, had materialized from a Russian POW camp."

Kristian spoke at last. "He'd been at Dorner since 1939. Why didn't they try to get identification sooner?"

"Up to 1943, Erich Dorner hadn't been particularly worried. But things had changed by '43: the war wasn't going well, America was in it by then, they'd had Stalingrad, El Alamein — Dorner could see that defeat for Germany was only a matter of time. Smart businessman, he began planning for his company's post-war future, in which he must reserve a place for his most brilliant young engineer. But he knew that might not happen unless Richard Buelow-Schwante got a watertight identity — a strong risk that the Canadians would track him down and imprison him for treason if they discovered who he was: a Canadian citizen working for the enemy, designing war materials? No one was anticipating Paperclip at that point. Even in 1945, when Paperclip was rescuing Erich Dorner from the War Crimes Commission, he convinced Richard Buelow-Schwante — now Hansjorg Peiper — to retain his alias. Paperclip was, after all, a covert *American* operation, and his star engineer was Canadian. Much easier to stay with the status quo, let sleeping dogs lie."

"At the bottom of the Atlantic ocean," Greta said.

"I know this all begs the question: was he happy to be there all this time, a cog in Hitler's war machine? I'm afraid the answer is yes, but to be fair, we first have to understand his relationship with Erich Dorner. Herr Doktor Dorner was the parent figure he had always needed — approving, nurturing, a brilliant example of everything Richard aspired to. And while he may have been appalled by conditions at the factory, he believed Erich Dorner when he claimed that his hands were tied, that the SS were responsible."

"He knew who Hansjorg Peiper was. He knew at the time what happened to the family. Didn't he?"

But it wasn't a question. Kristian's voice was small and dry, but its intensity filled the room

Gertrude reclined in the chair, appraising him. "Yes. They faked those snapshots of him in the Wehrmacht, staged them using vehicles from the factory, supposedly taken on the Russian front. Yes he knew. He never tried to defend himself on that. He confessed to me that he had slipped on an extraordinary, courageous life like a suit of purloined clothes: Hansjorg Peiper, missing at Stalingrad, back from Siberia to help Erich Dorner make an automotive miracle — not even Junia Dorner ever learned the truth of his real identity. None of the wider Peiper family ever suspected, nor did former friends like the Steubers in Steinau. They went on living with the truth: that the real Hansjorg Peiper was dead in Russia."

She sat up again, looked boldly at Kristian, her voice growing slightly louder, her syllables more distinct. "He was very young. Young and naive enough to believe that the Pan Am flight really had crashed with engine failure. It was a few years before he fully understood who the Peipers had been. But when he finally did, the knowledge transformed him."

Gertrude reached for Kristian's cold, unresisting hand.

"He told me the change really began when *you* were born. If he was going to go on living a borrowed life, he had to do so in a way that would honor Hansjorg Peiper's memory. The Peipers had been intensely cultured people, so our father set about cultivating himself, making music in particular a central part of his life, using his increasing personal wealth to bring it to others less fortunate...those orchestras and schools he endowed, the scholarships he created...he strove to give *back* some of what Hitler's war had taken, which he had contributed to by working for Hitler's cause. Our father's generosity, his humanity as an employer...he wanted that to make up for the terrible crimes he felt he had abetted."

"How did he find you?"

Gertrude let go of his hand, exchanged a worried glance with Greta; there was a carelessness to his voice, and in the way he had almost arbitrarily changed the conversation's course. As though the question had arisen from the mildest curiosity, although his eyes never left Gertrude's face.

"He found me easily enough, Kristian. He was a man with ample resources, after all. He started off looking for Annamarie Hoffman, traced her to Montreal, learned of her name change, found me very much as she had intended him to. There I was, adopted, married and divorced with two young daughters. I'd reverted to my maiden name, Buelow-Schwante. That made it easier for him. I was overwhelmed at first, suspicious of his motives, especially uncomfortable with his insistence that I remain a secret from you and your mother, his Cleveland family. But eventually…"

"He supported you financially."

She did not falter. "I resisted at first. But eventually it was a combination of real need and realizing that he had no ulterior motives. I began to see what his help would mean to my girls — the security, the opportunities." She straightened, a shade of anger in her pride. "They both have graduate degrees, both happily married, one's a teacher in British Columbia, my youngest is a vet. She also plays the viola. Principal in her community orchestra. They were his grandchildren after all. And yes…maybe we were the Peipers. Or the family of one of those Americans on the Clipper. Maybe he was still atoning."

Kristian looked away, towards the window. His breath shuddered in his battered chest.

Greta touched his cheek with an anxious hand. "Kristian?"

Gertrude looked at her watch and stood. "I've tired you out. The rest can wait until tomorrow." She looked at Greta, a signal to leave.

"Go ahead," Greta said. "I'll be out in a minute."

Gertrude Buelow-Schwante turned for a moment at the door, opened her mouth to speak but had no more words.

Greta reached out, cupped his chin, gently turned his face towards her.

"I love you, Kristian. Whatever happens, I'll be here."

She placed her hand on the bed as she made to stand, felt the small, hard object under the covers and lifted them back.

"What's this?"

It was the bridge from a three-quarter size violin.

"I don't want it," he said. "Take it. Take it away."

CHAPTER 36

SHE TOOK IT UP A NARROW FLIGHT OF STAIRS ON LORAIN AVENUE. The repairman's name was William Foy. He liked the violin. It had personality, he said, more than usual in a three-quarter size. A small sound but sweet. Pure. People always talked about Italian violins, but the Germans knew what they were doing.

Their red wine was also underestimated, Greta suggested.

Her English was very good.

It had improved, she told him, after six months in the United States.

William Foy was middle-aged, bearded and balding with a plait halfway down his back. He had a boy's blue eyes. They didn't need the old bridge, he'd already put a better one on. He smiled and said that bringing any kind of bridge to Cleveland was like coals to Newcastle, but perhaps she hadn't heard the expression yet. A poor joke anyway.

Frankfurt, too, was full of bridges. Over the Main.

Did she miss her country?

Not often.

She got out her wallet and he told her that it was being taken care of by a Mrs. Ingrid Schumacher. He turned the violin over, holding it delicately in his fingertips. See? Only an expert would ever know that the neck had been broken.

Did he play?

A little.

William Foy put the violin to his shoulder, his fingers resting for a moment on the fingerboard as he composed himself.

Then he awakened the small, sweet voice.

The End